AWAITING MADAME

LIFE INSIDE THE HOUSE
OF ONE ÜBER-CLASS FAMILY

A NOVEL

DAN WELTNER

Available from Amazon.com, CreateSpace.com, and other retail outlets.
Also available on Kindle and other devices.

Cover Design: Jayson Salomon
Portrait Photography: Beth Dixson
Cover Photography: iStock

To Jayson: the epitome of unwavering patience and unconditional love.

1

November 1, 2001

Clearing customs in Marrakech sucks. There are no lines, no signs, and no supervision — just a mob of impatient travelers jostling for first dibs. And each time newly arriving passengers rush in, the pack tightens and the scene swells. Somehow, during the most recent influx, I got caught in the middle.

Sandwiched in place, I try not to panic — even though things are getting worse. A tense stillness has now replaced all the pushing and a dull rumble of protest is rising from those trapped around me. Hell. This can't be good. Come to think of it, this place reminds me of the rowdy cattle-call auditions I dread attending. These folks are acting like a bunch of cutthroat dancers — minus the union monitor and the leggy showgirls — desperate to book the job. I'm screwed. Past experience reminds me that this situation rarely pays off.

By some miracle the crowd maintains equilibrium. But if I tried to stage this exact scenario, the choreography would never work; even the slightest variable could lead to collapse. And since each of us plays such a precarious role, we'd never survive to see opening night. I don't think any theater producer in their right mind would assume such a risk.

Weird. Up until now, I've never imagined being trampled to death or considered that a stunning mosaic floor of colorful Moroccan tiles might be the last thing I'd ever see. So I wonder, is this what crosses the mind seconds before a stampede?

Forty-five minutes later, lucky to be alive, I walk toward baggage claim with my retro Pam Am carry-on bag slung across one shoulder. I can't believe I made it out of there in one piece. No doubt, the sense memory of that holding pen will prevent me from ever going to another open call. But then again—I laugh to myself—it will also inspire a fantastic near-death monologue the next time I need to impress a director.

After a glance at the empty luggage carrousel, I search for customer service. And once inside the small fluorescent-lit office, I begin to explain how I'd already checked my bag for Paris yesterday, before being re-ticketed to Marrakech, since Madame—my employer—decided to relocate at the last minute. But midway through my rambling explanation, an English-speaking attendant interrupts, uninterested in Madame's itinerary. He hands me a claim check and tells me that my suitcase should arrive before midnight tonight. Although I'm not convinced, I take the ticket and leave. Within a few feet of the baggage office, I exit security and enter the clamorous pickup area. I pause. Another intricately tiled corridor.

I soon start up the aisle of drivers—reading placards—looking for anything marked: *Matthew*, *Matt* or *Mr. Whyteman*. But nothing catches my eye. Well, nothing except the fact that I don't blend in. All these drivers are men with dark hair, dark eyes, and light-brown skin. Most are dressed in conservative Muslim attire. And then there's me—the prepped-out, corn-fed WASP—with a vacant stare on his face.

My heart beats out of my chest. Ashamed to admit, I'm envisioning photos of terrorists I've seen in tabloids. How stupid. I'm profiling these men, even though I understand that Morocco had nothing to do with September eleventh. What's wrong with me? I live in the melting pot of New York, so this environment shouldn't seem like a novelty. But for some reason it does. This place feels different. Maybe because there's no mix here. It's just me. I'm the odd man out. Damn. I wish I wasn't wearing this dumb matchy-matchy Banana Republic outfit. On the other hand, what

I have on doesn't matter. Seriously. I could be tattooed, pierced, sporting a goatee, and costumed like a biker dude, and I'd still be typecast as the all-American guy next door.

Preparing to shift gears, I stop and affirm that I will not become someone who believes followers of Islam are evil. I force a deep breath in, hold it, then slowly exhale and start walking again. But my heart keeps racing anyway. And as I observe more visitors uniting with drivers and watch a large tour group depart with their guide, my mouth goes sour. Could I be the only person traveling solo?

In the midst of my third pass, I notice someone new up ahead. He's wearing a dark suit, carrying a blank sign, and making a beeline toward me. As he nears, his big droopy eyes remind me of a St. Bernard dog; his tanned, caramel complexion is imprinted with pockmarks. Do I trust this guy because he's clean-shaven and appears businesslike? Breathe. Stop stereotyping.

A few strides later, the man stops in the center of the aisle and flips the card to read in my direction. Relief. There it is: *Monsieur Mathieu*. I hurry closer and point to his sign. "Hi—that's me," I insist, fascinated by his overgrown eyebrows.

"Bonjour, Mathieu," the man says, and gives a subtle nod. "Mon nom est Bahir."

"Ah…bonjour, Bahir." I smile as we shake hands, thinking my high-school-level French doesn't sound too bad. "Nice to meet you."

"Je suis le chauffeur de Madame." Bahir motions toward the exit and takes off.

"Oh, très bien!" Should I have said *très bon*?

Bahir ups his walking tempo and spews off something so fast I can't tell what he's saying.

Oops. He must think I actually speak French. "Uh, oui, oui," I stammer, still trying to sound cool. I keep pace with Bahir and compose my most useful French phrase. "Excuser-moi, Bahir. Je ne parle pas français."

"Oh, pardon, Mathieu."

I glance at him. "Parlez-vous anglais?"

"Non, Mathieu. Je suis désolé."

I understand he is apologizing for not knowing English, but why should he? I'm the one with inferior language skills. "No, no, Bahir...je suis désolé."

He nods. "Merci, Mathieu."

Once we step outside the terminal, the Moroccan sky expands like Montana on acid. Its piercing blue color is juxtaposed by the pinkish tint of the red clay buildings. The sun is blaring and the heat is scorching—*a nice dry heat*, as grandma used to say. While we head toward the parking lot, I roll up my shirtsleeves and begin to relax. Much better than November in New York.

Bahir leads us to a minivan, opens the passenger-side door, and gestures for me to jump in. And by the time I buckle up we're on our way. After turning on the stereo and lowering the car windows, he shouts over an Arabic-funk song and uses lots of overt gestures to indicate that the air-conditioning is only for Madame.

"That's fine," I answer, thrilled to no longer be cooped up in airplanes. "Feels great!"

As we drive out of the parking area, I accept that small talk with Bahir is limited, so I sit back, chill out to his awesome music and decide to take in Marrakech. Right away, I become intrigued with a series of huge billboards, lining the roadway—each one showcasing a giant close-up photograph of the handsome King of Morocco. I figure George W. could never get away with this in the States, since the pores on his nose would look horrible at this scale. And when we turn onto the main road, I'm surprised by all the commotion. Pedestrians are everywhere and the highway is a free-for-all. I suppose folks are out running errands. They must be marketing, maybe heading to or from work. But who knows. Motorbikes transport families of four and compact taxis are loaded with six passengers each, driver makes seven. Women stroll along gravel sidewalks, some in long flowing garments, others not. Tattered donkeys pull unstable wooden carts, camels graze near a gas station. And the congestion is unbelievable. No joke. The pollution and traffic in this town makes rush hour in Manhattan look like Doodleville, Indiana. And even though I assume Bahir is a safe driver, right now I'm not so sure. At the moment, we are swimming upstream against oncoming cars like we're playing a game of chicken. But Bahir doesn't scare. He just barges ahead—unfazed.

Exhaust fumes sear my eyes and burn in my lungs, as I remind myself that I've made the right decision to come over here. Really. How hard could this gig be—to spend a year overseas, serving as the personal fitness trainer to an octogenarian heiress?

My daydream vanishes when Bahir swerves to avoid a pothole and damn near wipes out a street vendor. Crap. I glance in the side-view mirror to check on the guy in the road but can't see anything except a rusty-pink cloud of dust. I look at Bahir, ready to convince him we should turn around, but he's oblivious so I keep quiet.

Bahir soon veers onto another highway, this one heading away from town. And within a couple of minutes, the traffic eases, and the desert landscape becomes decidedly barren. He amps up the radio, accelerates full throttle and double-clicks the power locks. The instant I hear that clicking sound, I'm hit in the gut with a surge of adrenaline. Shit. What the fuck was I thinking? Did I just accept a ride from an absolute stranger in a foreign land on blind faith? I must be crazy. What if Bahir turns out to be some terrorist spy on a mission to kidnap a dude named Mathieu?

I look over at Bahir. He's not much bigger than me. If we get into a fight, I could take him—if I had to. I look outside at the dense layer of smog dozing along the horizon. But the problem is, the only fights I've ever done have been performed in acting class. Damn. I glance back to Bahir. Does stage combat even work in real life?

About a half hour later, Bahir makes an unexpected turn off the highway, stops the car and shuts off the radio. Here, tucked between two giant palm trees, is a gigantic red clay archway with an enormous wooden door—punctuated with oversized brass buttons and trimmed with carved markings. A bronze plaque on my side of the archway reads: *Paradis*. My eye wants to add an *e* to the end—but if it was once there, it has long since weathered away. I watch the huge door split open, exposing the entrance of a lavish estate. Towering trees canopy a pink-pebbled driveway and the yard is full of lush tropical greenery, vibrant flowers, and perfectly-placed bushes.

Okay. So if Bahir drops me off at someplace other than the home of Madame, I could end up being murdered in the most beautiful garden landscape I've ever seen. But let's face it, this cocktail story beats the one about getting crushed in customs.

When I turn back to Bahir, an elderly man steps out of a small stone gatehouse off to the left of the archway. This dark-skinned bearded man has on a beige full-length hooded robe with long sleeves and he looks old enough to be Bahir's grandfather. As the attendant pauses at the side of the car, places one hand on his heart, and bows his head down, we coast in. Bahir greets the man in Arabic and I give a little wave in his direction—I wish I knew the real name for his traditional-looking garment.

The next thing I know, two German shepherd dogs lunge at the car, barking their heads off. I press the button to close my window and Bahir laughs. And when the dogs snag at the end of their leashes and let out howls of anguish, I realize I've overreacted. Diagnosis: sleep deprivation.

I watch the gate close behind us and everything becomes quiet—including the dogs. This is unreal. I think the chichi word is *splendiferous*—whatever that means. And as Bahir continues driving us along the gravel lane, I put my window back down and lean out a little to take it all in. A fragrant combination of herbs and flowers takes hold as we coast past a vineyard. Then, a fiercely tart breeze rushes in as an orchard of miniature citrus trees comes into view. I try to make up some creative paint-chip names for the various shades of yellow, orange, and green—but I can't think fast enough.

The first turn reveals rows of palm trees in every shape and size. The next curve gives way to a dramatic border of oversized aloe plants. We wind past more fruit trees and an olive grove. After that, it's banana trees, herb gardens, and more flower gardens. And when the overwhelming smell of roses fills the car, I close my eyes a moment. I could shit a brick. Either I'm going to live like a king for the next year or get chopped to bits and buried under those bushes. Snap. Either way, this job is bound to be one hell of an adventure.

I open my eyes and look left. We're now driving alongside a huge lawn area—large enough to house a stadium. And up ahead on the right, I see a tall, skinny, white guy with slicked salt-and-pepper hair sauntering toward the driveway. He's got on a dark suit, similar to Bahir's, and he's coming out from behind the trees. From the side view, this man's posture is perfectly erect—except for his head that juts forward like an anteater sniffing for insects. He's got big flat shoulders and his broad forehead casts a dramatic shadow over his beak-like nose, while his recessed chin seems to be in search of his neck. The house must be hidden up there near him.

Bahir slows down and points at the man. "Je vous donne à Alistair."

"Oh. Okay. Thanks, Bahir," I say as he stops the car. "Merci! See ya later. I mean…à demain."

"Inshallah, Mathieu." Bahir places his hand on his heart. "Inshallah."

Note to self: find out what *inshallah* means.

By the time I grab my carry-on bag and reach for the door handle, Alistair has opened the door for me. I look up at his sallow face and start to step out. "Bonjour, Alistair. Mon nom est Mathieu."

"Hello, Matthew!" He sounds like a gruff British Airways employee. "I'm Alistair—the butler."

Thank God, he speaks English. "Oh, hi. How are you?" I stand up and he slams the door behind me.

Awaiting Madame

"I'm fine." Alistair groans while Bahir drives away. "But you, sir, are late for lunch." He pivots on the spot and speeds toward a narrow path leading into the trees. "Follow me to the kitchen."

Walking behind him, I notice how his slicked hair is trimmed above his white collared shirt. His elongated hands dangle from his navy suit jacket and his spindly frame allows the cuffs of his gray pinstriped pants to swing atop his shiny black patent leather shoes. Alistair reminds me of Lurch from *The Addams Family*—not the actor who played Lurch, but the actual man who inspired the character we now know as Lurch. He's a trip.

Once we arrive, Alistair pulls the screen door open and motions for me to step inside. "Mathieu has arrived!" he shouts into an empty pantry area. "Announcing, Mathieu!" he yells even louder.

I exhale and walk in.

Is anybody home?

As soon as I clear the threshold, Alistair releases the door behind me. And by the time the screen door bangs, he is gone. Wait a minute, was that it? Did he just show up to walk me fifty feet from the driveway to the kitchen, only to announce my arrival? Come on. That's kinda silly.

Before I know it, I'm no longer alone. Several servants appear from around the corner in front of me, walking single file in my direction. The men are dressed in the same navy/gray ensemble as Alistair and Bahir, and the women are wearing matching blue and white striped maids' uniforms.

Whoa. They're still coming.

After the procession comes to a halt, the dozen or so workers crowd around and greet me in Arabic, French, Italian, and German. Overwhelmed by the attention, I wonder how long they have been waiting. Have I inconvenienced them?

But as they continue to bombard me with names—all of which I immediately confuse and promptly forget—I fixate on a tall, sturdy, pale-faced woman who is standing alone at the back of the group. She looks about sixty, sixty-five, with her stack of wiry, silver-gray hair piled up on her head. And unlike the rest of the women, she is dressed in a black polyester dress—three-quarter sleeve—accented with a clean white apron, white cuffs, and a pointy white collar. She has to be the alpha maid.

As she walks toward me, her eyes become squinty and unapologetic—like she's listening to a not-so-talented child practice the violin. "Welcome, Matthew," she says, with a strong German accent, and reaches both arms in my direction. "I am Barbara. We have heard such wonderful things."

"Great to meet you." I receive her callused hands. "All good, I hope." Duh. That made sense. She just said: *vundebar dings*.

Barbara disconnects from my grip, grabs me by one wrist and turns me to face the group. "Quietly, please!" Everyone listens up. "Matthew comes to us from New York City." She sounds like she's standing at the pulpit. "He is a professional singer/dancer… fresh from the bright lights of Broadway." She gives my wrist a mighty squeeze. "We are most fortunate to have him here amongst us."

While the staff gives an understated round of applause, I realize Barbara must have done some online research about me. Jeez. I'm glad she didn't mention my bum knee. The last thing I want, is to start off the year looking like a weakling.

Barbara dismisses the workers. "Thank you, everyone," she says and lets go of my wrist. "Partial siesta today—then back to your stations." And before the staff can clear out, Barbara leads me around the corner—from where the workers emerged. She informs me that she has served as lady-in-waiting over the past thirty years, and adds that *she* is the only one in the house with around-the-clock access to Madame's privy chamber.

I act impressed. It's all so *Elizabethan*.

Next, she hurries us forward into the kitchen, offers lunch, and tells me to sit down at the long rustic wood table.

So I do. I can tell she means business.

Without delay, she presents a multicolored ceramic bowl full of couscous and grilled vegetables in brown sauce. "Take a moment to nourish." She places a basket of unleavened bread on the table, a few inches shy of arms reach. "Staff lunch is finished; however, it is not a problem—for today. When you are done," she pauses to pour me a glass of white wine, "Alistair will accompany you to your living quarters, across the way."

As I chow down, I try not to appear exhausted and starved. But I am. And the meal is delicious.

"Matthew, you have big shoes to fill around here." She sharpens the look in her eye. "There is no doubt about it, everyone loved Kevin, the previous trainer. He served Madame and Monsieur for more than a decade."

"Oh, yeah. I know, me and Kevin both—"

"But I must warn you," she interrupts, "it was quite a shame how we watched that athletic boy turn flabby over the years. I need not remind you that most Americans are lazy and do tend to pick up weight easily. Therefore, if I were you," she smiles and looks down at my dish, "I would be careful not to overdo it."

On that note, I stop mopping my plate with the tasty warm bread and conceal chewing my last big bite. Bug off lady, I think to myself. If Kevin did this job for ten years, I can do it for one. Weirdo.

After a second glass of wine and a tangy mandarin orange for dessert, my head is spinning as Barbara clears the table. "Alistair will meet you outside." She turns her back and heads toward the sink. "Go rest. I will phone your room later, in time for tea."

"Sounds good." I start to leave, sensing she needs to get back to work. "Thanks for lunch." I turn the corner leading into the pantry and see Alistair waiting behind the screen door.

He pulls the door open. "To your room, squire!" he calls out, totally overplaying his dialect.

I step outside. "After you, sir." I mimic his intonation but he doesn't notice.

"Very well then," Alistair answers from a few yards ahead of me.

As we wind our way along the garden path, I somehow manage to catch every cobweb and snapping branch that Alistair skillfully avoids. And I soon realize that this walk is going to be much more complicated than the one from the car to the kitchen — so I should be paying attention to where we are going, but I'm too tipsy to care.

Roughly five minutes later, we arrive at the isolated staff housing area. Alistair nods toward my room and mumbles something under his breath. Then, like a shaman approaching a temple, he jingles the keys and unlocks the door.

The moment the door opens, a burst of stale thick air pummels me. Alistair steps inside, flips on the lights, and there, mounted on the wall before us, is a life-size portrait of a naked woman. I swallow. I step in and scan the room, only to find that every wall is chock-full of paintings of naked women, large and small. That is, the painting themselves are large and small, while the female subjects are mostly Lane Bryant/Rosie O'Donnell/Hillary Clinton — in an ill-fitted campaign suit — size. The artwork is striking. However, seeing this number of female nudes hung together seems sick. I can't breathe. I turn toward Alistair to ask if he can remove some of the art, but he's gone, already heading back toward the house.

So what's his deal anyway? Is he *my* butler? Will Alistair materialize every time I need to go somewhere? And what's up with this room? Did my dad call ahead and give strict orders to have me locked up in such a butch place? Have I been shipped off to one of those scared-straight compounds as seen on *Dateline, 20/20, 60 Minutes*? Will I become the first man to perish from torture-by-camel-toe?

Before long, I decide if I don't calm down and take a nap, I'm going to pass out. So without thinking, I toss my carry-on bag to the nearest chair, undress in two moves, and slip under the sheets of the narrow twin bed — underwear on.

Crap. That nap was pointless. I'm not even sure I slept. I had one restless dream after the next, suffering through a jet-lagged chronicle of my lifelong struggle with cats. As in *cat*, the mammal, not *Cats*, the Broadway musical—although I'll never get over my botched audition for that gig either.

Today's dream started out in the late '70s, with my two childhood cats roaming our yard in the farmlands of southern Indiana. These two tabbies wore black studded collars and strutted the fields like rock stars. I dreamed about how they would disappear for days on end and eventually come home covered in burrs, begging to be groomed.

In the next section, I was in college, hanging out with a friend and her two Siamese cats. Her cats moaned constantly and put their horny asses in my face—my friend thought it was sweet. She and I used to get together at her place for make out sessions, because she liked the safety of being in love with a gay guy, and I liked practicing my kissing technique. I figured that someday, when I'd finally get to kiss a guy, it would be a really good first kiss. One night, while drinking some beers in her living room, I developed huge hives and got bright red scratches on my neck and face. The scratches were my fault, not the cats. My friend panicked at the thought of us not being able to hang out at her house anymore. But in the end, it all worked out, we just started meeting on campus instead, in the basement of a science building.

After that, things shifted to a few years later in New York, when I knew this hippie girl who was way into holistic remedies—the type who uses organic sea sponges every month instead of store-bought tampons. She believed that my cat allergy could be cured, by consuming large quantities of papaya enzymes. So I tried. Under her supervision, I started taking megadoses of these chewable pills from the health food store. They reminded me of Flintstones vitamins—without Wilma and Betty. My friend would invite me over to her East Village apartment to hold her longhair Persian. And in my dream, I even agreed to join her at a cult meeting twice a week. The goal of the meeting was to heal my past-life grievances; to help me get in touch with what went wrong in my ancient psyche that may have led to this disastrous present-day condition—known as adult-onset feline allergy syndrome. Three months of pill popping passed. My palms turned orange and I was beginning to attract fruit flies. I was still scratching, sneezing, itching and cursing every time I left her apartment.

In the final episode of the dream, I was sitting on her hemp beanbag chair and caressing her kitty, when I looked up at her and abruptly said: so I'm allergic to pussy, what's the big mystery? She didn't answer. She just grabbed her cat and told me to get out. While I was heading down the tenement stairs and she was yelling at me about not coming to the chai social on Friday, I woke up. Exhausted.

I'm still tucked into bed when my phone rings.

Like a three-toed sloth, I roll over to answer.

It's Barbara.

"Matthew," she feigns surprise, "certainly you are not still asleep?"

"Oh, no, of course not!" I perk up, suddenly responsible for defending every lazy American.

"Come then, it is teatime. I will meet you in the kitchen."

I happily accept her offer and start getting dressed—only to realize that I haven't got a clue about how to get back to the kitchen. Should I call Alistair?

"René is Madame's dearest companion and her closest confidant," Barbara mentions as she pours our tea. "He is to be handled with kid gloves. He has been with Madame, well, since forever and he is responsible to coordinate her every visitor. He knows how to run defense for Madame and considers himself her nearest of kin." She slides a cup across the table in my direction and then opens a cookie tin full of treats. "He and Madame are the only ones in the house at the moment...of course, that will change from time to time."

As Barbara continues, I grab for a cookie and tally the staff I've seen so far. Right now, Alistair and three other men are in the pantry polishing silver; two women are here in the kitchen prepping vegetables. During my walk over, I got lost long enough to count three women in the laundry house, three administrative types working in the office near the garage, two older men snipping flowers in the stone flower hut, and two housekeepers mopping the white ceramic entranceway. Then, thanks to the guy adjusting poolside umbrellas at the guesthouse, I made it back to the kitchen after passing about twelve gardeners who were stooped at various spots around the yard. Damn. Including Barbara and me, this means there are at least thirty staff members on site.

"René will enhance any conversation with a bit of comic relief, social commentary or a lesser-known fact," Barbara continues, as I remember to include the elderly front gate security man and the two German shepherd dogs to my list. "Matthew," she snaps, perhaps noticing my lack of attention, "you will begin early each morning with René—before Madame awakens. He will train daily. And developing a solid bond with René will help ensure job security. So please, Matthew," she confides while I reach for another spicy cookie, "do your best to inspire him…if you would like to remain here in the house with us."

"All right then. I'll do my best." I smile, hoping I don't sound like I'm mocking her. But I am.

"After you finish with him," she starts again. "You will be on call for the remainder of the day and night…whether it be for Madame's personal workout, or to train her houseguests. And, Matthew," she reclaims my attention. "Please do not exit the compound walls unescorted. Madame has no interest in providing ransom for a foolish American."

"Oh, okay…makes sense," I say, now anxious about losing my freedom. "Hey, is Olivia around?" I ask, trying to remember if I included her in my staff count.

"Olivia?" Barbara repeats with a cool edge in her voice.

"Yeah. Madame's personal secretary…her assistant, the

woman who hired me," I stop blathering, finally realizing I'm being redundant.

"Why do you ask?" Barbara stands and clears the dishes.

"Well, Olivia was so great with my contract—figured I'd thank her."

"Fair enough." Barbara answers from over near the sink.

"Nonetheless, she is not on site…I cannot say when she might return."

"No biggie, I'll just shoot her an email."

"That would be fine, Matthew. You are free to use the staff computer here in the kitchen. However, the Internet signal tends to come and go."

"No prob. I'll just get online whenever."

Barbara returns to the table, closes the cookie tin, and stalls with her hand still glued to the lid. "Matthew, may I ask," she begins, with a somber look on her face, "how are things in New York, after the events of eleven September…do you mind saying so?"

"Uh, no, I…I don't mind." My stomach twists into a knot. "There's not a lot to say. It's…it's just been really quiet these past two months. You know…quiet for New York."

Barbara drags the container across the table. The irksome metal-on-rough-wood sound would make any foley artist smile. We are suspended in a bizarre slow-motion moment until she lifts the canister up to her chest. "I dream of the Big Apple," she pauses, "such an exciting place, such activity and life."

"Yeah, well, normally it is," I answer, reliving the horrendous smell of the chemical fires that burned for days. "It's usually much more hectic. I think that's why the calm feels so eerie."

"Were you near the buildings when it happened?" She shifts forward as if planning to sit down again.

"Close enough." I picture the rolling cloud of smoke engulfing lower Manhattan. "I was at my apartment in Brook—"

"Oh, Barbara!" A man's voice flamboyantly beckons from around the corner. "Has our dear Mathieu arrived?"

I grin. This guy's affect would stick out anywhere, even in a Noël Coward production.

"In here, René, finishing tea!" Barbara shouts toward the pantry then looks at me. "We will have to continue with this later," she whispers in the split second before René glides into view.

I look at him and crack a big smile.

The barrel-chested René stands no taller than five five, and must be mid to late sixties. He's wearing a khaki-on-khaki safari outfit, with a brimmed canvas hat, wide woven belt, and a four-pocket shirt with epaulets. His hiking pants—tucked into shin-high lace-up boots—are contrasted with a pumpkin-colored neckerchief. "Ah...Mathieu," he floats toward the table. "Welcome to Paradis!"

"Thanks." I stand and get a closer look at the vermilion hue of his freckly, sun-damaged skin. "Thanks so much."

"Here is my portfolio, you will find it to be self-explanatory." René hands me a thick leather-bound file and scans my body from head to toe. "Ah, dirty-blond," he mentions under his breath, "nice lean swimmer's build, how serendipitous."

In search of diversion, I look toward the sink; only to find that Barbara and the two kitchen helpers have vanished. So here I stand with René in an awkward moment of silence—trying not to glance down to see if my fly is open.

"Come along, Mathieu," he says, as if sharing a secret. "If we go now, we will have plenty of space to roam and scratch while Madame remains above stairs."

Before I can so much as smile again, he bolts out of the kitchen and into the pantry. He moves forward with one arm swaying to-and-fro and the other hand nesting limply upon his prop canteen that is suspended across his torso by a pea-green silk sash.

In a flash, we exit the service area and into an open-air living room that looks out onto a breezeway. White archways line the space and frame a jungly courtyard. Everything is grand in scale, yet still inviting; very livable.

"Madame herself is responsible for the creation of the textiles throughout the house," René calls out, while weaving a serpentine pattern through the exterior archways. "Not to mention, her meticulous input with the garden landscape design."

I do my best to appear casual, to listen without gawking, to observe without staring, and to agree without gasping. But this place is beyond. It would make a great cover story for *Life of Leisure* magazine. Thank God, I'm holding onto René's portfolio, otherwise I wouldn't have a clue about how to occupy my hands.

"Look around, Mathieu." He points to the pictures on the wall. "You see these, this entire array of wildlife etchings, the whole lot once belonged to Queen Isabella—and now they are here with us."

"Oh, how lovely," I say—as if *lovely* is part of my everyday vocabulary.

René prances us through the first two levels of the house—like he's chaperoning a group of elementary school children—and describes the décor as if it all belongs to him. He implies that it was his inspiration that brought Madame to the final placement of the bolsters on each of the seventeen sofas and he accepts full credit for the arrangement of everything, including the lily pads in the frog pond. And by the time we step out onto the stately second-story terrace, I grasp the scope of the entire grounds. Breathtaking.

"Bienvenue dans mon jardin d'hiver!" René declares with a gesture large enough to obscure the panoramic view.

Shoot. I can't remember if that means *winter garden* or *river garden*? "Merci!" I match his level of excitement.

René stares beyond the balcony wall and informs me that the olive trees were shipped from Sicily and supplemental palm trees were harvested in Fez. He then explains that each bird, fish, reptile, and insect has been carefully orchestrated to ensure a fully operational ecosystem.

"How stunning," I add, unsure about what adjectives might do this place justice.

"Look at the abundance of trellised walkways." René gestures as if tracing the outline of a crossword puzzle. "Observe the aesthetically pleasing pattern. Most charming, yes?"

"Awesome."

"And there…you see, Mathieu," his eyes laser in on the garden gazebo, "that is where—weather permitting—you and I shall join Madame for your welcome lunch tomorrow." His cell phone rings. "At precisely twelve thirty." He answers the phone and turns his back to me.

I focus out over the grounds and try not to listen, but I can't help overhearing that he's pissed off about something. And while René works himself into a fast-forward French-speaking frenzy, I wonder if I should leave and give him some privacy, but I'm not even sure I could find my way downstairs on my own.

René continues his telephone rant and rushes back inside the house; so I follow. He yells his way through the second floor and soon charges down the front staircase. I'm running to keep up, and careful to assure safe distance so I don't interfere.

When we arrive downstairs near his bedroom—off the interior courtyard—he enters his room and shuts the door in my face. Mystified by his lack of closure, I chill for a moment next to the rubber tree plant outside his door. And when I glance over at the garden gazebo, I recall what René said right before he freaked out on the phone. Cool.

I've been invited to have lunch with Madame tomorrow.

"Matthew," Barbara's voice echoes behind me. "If René is finished with you…you must return to your room."

By the time I turn around, I see Barbara enter the house; no time for chitchat.

So I go.

I start walking—unsure where I'm going.

Then, after a few wrong turns, I manage to find the kitchen, and from there I'm able to track the one familiar route back to my room. Whew. I unlock my door and step inside. Do homing pigeons cope with this level of anxiety on a daily basis?

Within minutes of plopping down on my bed, my phone rings.

"Are you up and about?" Alistair asks, as I leaf through René's portfolio. "Might we take a moment to talk about the telephone?"

"You mean, talk on the phone?" I correct his word choice.

"No, talk about the phone," he repeats.

"Uh, sure," I say—still unclear about what he means.

"Very well then." He hangs up.

A short while later, I'm lost in René's complicated medical history, when Alistair knocks. "I am here to explain the phone." he proclaims, before I can even get to the door. And the moment he enters, he pauses to blatantly ingest the artwork; he rubs his hands together, practically drooling. Then, as if being reanimated by smelling salts, he snaps to attention and drops both arms down by his side. "Matthew, I am here to explain…the telephone." He gestures toward the nightstand with a Frankenstein-arm. "Over there is a landline."

I look at the phone to illustrate that I understand his lesson thus far.

"If the phone should ring," he warns, "pick it up, say Allô, and identify yourself. In the event that you do not answer by the termination of the third ring, the international switchboard will take a message on your behalf."

I nod. So far so good.

"For each unanswered call, you earn one demarcation. It is up to you, Matthew, to contact the switchboard for your daily messages…and remember…all demerits will remain on file as an indication of your incompetence."

The phone rings and scares me to death.

Alistair lets out a challenging grin.

Stunned by the coincidence that someone might be calling while he is explaining all this, I rush to the nightstand and grab up the receiver—mid-second ring. "Allô, Matt." I hear a recording of a female operator: *Ceci est un test…seulement un test.*

With a vague smile behind his otherwise hollow eyes, Alistair returns to slobbering over the paintings. "Not a bad dry run." He steps closer to one of the smallest works of art.

This is some crazy bullshit. "Thanks." I hang up.

He looks at me. "Be forewarned, Matthew, each demarcation will lower your daily income by thirty-three percent, which means you will be docked an entire day's pay for every third call you miss."

"Really?" I laugh, assuming he's pulling my leg. But if it is a joke, he doesn't let on.

"Remember," he gives a stern look, "within the myriad of phone extensions...you are responsible for only this one. Suppose you can manage?"

I nod.

"Now as for these, here...you see? The cord leading to the shower, this call button beside your bed, that switch next to the toilette, the toggle over there by the armoire, and that tasseled antique throw-pillow—no, not there—THERE!" he shouts, as if trying to dislodge the confused look from my face. "All of these," he quickens, "the tassel, the toggle, the switch, the button, and the cord...are ne touchez pas." He pauses, licks his lips, and inspects another painting. "Never," he smiles without showing his teeth, "to be touched...by you."

Got it, fucker. "Cool."

His face turns as bland as Wonder Bread. "So, Matthew, are we now clear about the telephone?"

"Yep." I look at the large assortment of tasseled throw pillows on my unmade bed. "Everything's clear."

"Speaking of everything, has Barbara outlined access to the hypo-allergenic linen closet or the location of the organic cleaning supplies?" He turns to leave.

"No, not yet."

"Classic." He pauses to peer at a few more paintings. "Apparently, that woman is incapable of doing anything right these days. But in any case, she will get to it...most likely when she explains drinking water, biscuit rations, fresh fruit allowance, and the broom closet." He looks at me. "Pay particular attention to the broom closet...she will issue a pop quiz at that point during orientation." Alistair clasps his hands and nudges an elbow toward another painting. "That one's quite nice." A cruel scowl haunts his face as he shifts toward the door. "Wouldn't you agree?"

My eyes widen. I have no idea what to say about my lack of interest in a hairless cherub. "Thanks for warning me about Barbara's little test."

"Hell hath no fury like a woman scorned," he says, and picks up my baggage receipt from off the nightstand. "I will deliver your luggage as soon as it clears customs." He steps outside and starts away.

What the fuck was that random quote supposed to mean? "Thanks, man...and thanks for talking to me about the telephone." I shout, but he doesn't look back.

Earlier, during tea with Barbara—before we talked about René, and my duties—she shared some dirt on Alistair. She told me that Alistair has served in the house for more than twenty years. "We have staff seniority," she said, and gave me a devilish look. "But I trump him by almost a decade." Barbara explained that Alistair was initially hired as a footman and soon escalated to valet—working exclusively for Monsieur. "It is nearly two years now, since Monsieur passed away, yet Madame has decided to keep Alistair around." She glared. "To no avail." After that, she explained that Alistair has five kids with three different women, and confessed that his entire wage goes toward supporting those children. He sends weekly checks to each household, visits them on the occasional holiday—but otherwise, he doesn't have much of a life outside of his job. Does *she*, I wondered?

As I watch Alistair continue down the garden pathway, I feel sorry for him. But maybe I'm feeling sorry for myself. Sorry, because it's confirmed: he's not my butler after all.

Later—tickled for answering by the end of the first ring—

Barbara calls to invite me to dinner. I hop out of bed, rush to the kitchen, and join a lively gathering of twelve European staffers who are dining family-style. I suppose the local workers have gone home to eat. But I don't know.

We sample an offering of whole roasted fish, assorted grilled meats and veggies, a few pastas, and some creamy risotto with sautéed mushrooms; an ample quantity of wine pours freely and baskets of that yummy Moroccan bread get refilled without anyone asking. And for tonight only, because *Matthew's arrival* is a special occasion, Barbara permits us to sample lots of other tasty side dishes—presented in silver—that have been recycled from Madame's table. We attack the leftovers like vultures and no one seems to care where the food has been. Then, after taking seconds and thirds of everything, a few staff members reset the table for dessert. Before long, we plunge into a huge wooden platter of cheeses and a bountiful assortment of fresh fruit. The buoyant atmosphere reminds me of performing the *Food Glorious Food* number, in a shoestring staging of *Oliver!* But the cost of this meal alone would surpass that show's gruel budget by a long shot.

From what I can grasp—based on intermittent translations of German, French, and Italian—staff chat is about the daily goings on. Sensationalistic. Who overheard Madame dictating the letter to her grandson? Who picked up specific details regarding René's telephone argument? Who learned that Madame has postponed the arrival of her most-trusted gal pal?

It's fascinating to observe the interaction of these people who eat, sleep, and work together, twenty-four hours a day. But, as I wondered earlier about Barbara and Alistair, does anyone on staff get to have a life outside the house? Must be tough.

As I continue to interpret gestures and piece together snippets, I become intrigued with those staffers who choose to dine in silence. Everyone seems to know what to say to get a laugh and what subjects to avoid. But for a few, it seems better to say nothing in front of this shrewd gossip-hungry crowd.

Once the eating slows, Barbara stands up, prepared to

make a few closing remarks. And for the first time all evening, the kitchen grows quiet. I sit forward in anticipation, as Barbara slowly unfolds a white linen napkin to reveal a singular, longish, dark brown strand of hair.

"This fine specimen," she preaches, "was discovered today in the guest bathroom off the foyer." She pauses to present the evidence, swaying her hand from one end of the table to the other. "Yet no guest came calling this afternoon," she bellows. "Let he amongst us, responsible for inappropriate shedding, please stand up."

I chuckle.

But no one else finds her funny.

So I grab my wine glass, compose a serious look, and sit back in my seat. I can't believe this is for real.

Ending the pregnant pause, Barbara refolds the napkin, tucks it into her uniform pocket, and sternly exits the room.

Dumbfounded, the rest of us then tidy up the kitchen and splinter off to our rooms—without further conversation. And although Alistair is one staffer who had little to say during dinner tonight, he did give me a knowing look when Barbara concluded her speech. I briefly made eye contact with him before I squelched my laugh, but I knew enough to be discreet. I already know I don't want to get on Barbara's bad side, because that could make my one-year assignment seem endless.

It's a few minutes past midnight, end of day one, when I hear a gentle knock at my door.

"Your belongings have arrived," Alistair states.

"Thanks," I call out as his footsteps fade away.

As soon as I open the door, I'm so relieved to see my stuff, I just drag the suitcase inside and hop back into bed without unpacking a thing.

2

At twelve fifteen the next day, my phone rings. And even before I answer, I know it must be Barbara, calling to confirm the twelve thirty lunch appointment with Madame. "Come, Matthew," she says with added stress on my name, "meet me in the kitchen. I will show you to table."

"On my way," I hang up and speed out.

When I arrive at the entrance to the pantry, Barbara opens the screen door and hurries me inside. And after a quick scan of my tame J.Crew forty-percent-off ensemble, she approves. "The moment Madame comes down, you and René will join her." We exit the pantry and pass through the first conversation area of the open-air living room. "Follow his lead, Matthew…never initiate directly with Madame."

"Okay," I barely get out as Barbara guides me toward the center archway. I see a round table for three has been set up outside in the gazebo. Pre-show jitters. Everything is white on white—the linens, the china, the flowers, the seat covers, the chiffon drapes. I glance back to Barbara. "Anything else I should know?"

"Do not become accustomed to dining with Madame." She marches away toward the kitchen. "Kevin was at table only once in ten years, just like you, Matthew, the day after he arrived."

As Barbara's voice trails off, I look to the gazebo again and notice Alistair making some last-minute adjustments. Hair slicked, he's wearing stark white gloves and looks totally dapper as he glides clockwise around the table, using a foldable wooden ruler to calibrate each place setting. In one pass, I watch him measure from seat back to table ledge. Then on another round, he gauges the distance from six o'clock on the charger plate to nine o'clock on the water glass. Next, it's twelve o'clock on the wine glass to the apex of the snapdragon centerpiece. Alistair works with the concentration of a mad scientist, tinkering away in his lab, his movements graceful and fluid. He is surprisingly upbeat out here on the playing field today—much more so than the somber downtrodden butler I dealt with yesterday.

Transfixed by Alistair's attention to detail, I hold steady near the grand archway, anticipating my cue. And although I don't usually suffer stage fright, waiting here makes me anxious about meeting Madame. I interlace my fingers and crack my knuckles. What could we possibly have in common? My only association with super-rich ladies comes from the stuff I've seen on TV, like Linda Evans as Krystle Carrington on *Dynasty*.

"Mathieu! Mathieu!" René flies out of his bedroom and leaps onto the lawn. "I am here!"

I conceal a laugh as he bounds across the courtyard—he looks hilarious. Today's safari outfit is every bit as coordinated as yesterday; this one leans more army green and less khaki—a touch of camouflage, no hat, his combover of grayish-strawberry-blond hair exposed. I step forward and wave, but refuse to yell back to him. It doesn't seem smart to be hollering like I'm lost in an Indiana cornfield right now.

"Why, there you are," René pants, while batting his eyes toward the sky and patting one hand atop his chest—indicating his rapid heartbeat. "The thought had crossed my mind that you might overlook our little lunch date."

"How could I forget?" I chuckle as he arrives. "I've got nothing else to remember."

He plows ahead without considering my response. "Now, here is the plan." René sounds like he's organizing a military campaign. "I will meet Madame solo, around the corner at the elevator, position one." He points down the breezeway. "Greetings, small talk, did you sleep well, etcetera and so on. Soon after which, we shall proceed from the elevator, toward table...you will be stationed here, en route—position numéro deux." René uses both arms to secure me in place, at the very spot where I'm already standing. "As Madame approaches, hold your mark, Mathieu, no eye contact until she acknowledges your presence. Then, after interpreting her body language, I will handle the introduction."

"But how'll I know when to say hi, if I'm not looking at her?"

"She is coming!" René rushes off. "We shall ad lib the rest!"

Seconds later, the elevator door rattles open. "Francesca!" René shouts, as if yelling *curtain up*. "Splendid day indeed."

"Sublime." Madame responds in a tenderhearted voice.

"Shall we proceed to table?" René speaks loud enough to include me, but I don't hear an answer from Madame—only footsteps echoing on marble and an occasional bird chirp. "Francesca, Mathieu has arrived from America and will be joining us today."

Then, by the time I hear *day*, Madame comes into view, arm-in-arm with René. She's radiant. And even though her walking is slow and unsteady, she carries herself like a majestic goddess. Her white hair is cut short to accentuate her high cheekbones. Her thin frame and long limbs give her a regal appearance, while her fresh Ivory-soap complexion shames the overly made up cast of *Dynasty*. She's amazing. She's got on a super thin, V-necked sweater in the palest shade of yellow I've ever seen. White blouse. Practical flats. And her ecru linen pants appear casual yet refined. Did I just pull out *ecru*?

Strange. She's not wearing a single accessory. What did I expect? A tiara for lunch?

As they continue toward me, I imagine how happy my high school French teacher would be—to hear me say *Bonjour, Madame*, to this glamorous lady in such an elegant setting. I'd better look away.

They pause at my post.

"Francesca," René calms himself. "I present, Monsieur Mathieu Whyteman."

I look up at Madame and dive into her translucent green eyes. Phenomenal.

"Hello, Matthew. Welcome to Morocco."

"Pleased to meet you, Madame." I bow my head out of respect and try not to initiate an unasked-for handshake. "Thanks for having me," I add, reminded of Audrey Hepburn in *My Fair Lady* when she is presented to the upper crust: *how kind of you to let me come*.

"The pleasure is all mine, Matthew." Madame angles toward the table and looks at René. "Shall we?"

The three of us move along the sidewalk toward the gazebo—Alistair stands at attention near the table—and my nervousness dissipates. But, the moment I look down at the dizzying array of silverware at each place setting, it engulfs me again. Outside in. Just eat from the outside moving in.

Only a few steps later, I wish I'd paid more attention to my mom's obsession with *Miss Manners*. Every morning at breakfast, I'd zone out over cereal while mom would read aloud from the newspaper, Judith Martin's tidbits of social advice. But something tells me that this issue—how to survive lunch with a zillionaire in Morocco—never came up in one of those columns.

As soon as we step inside the gazebo, René exhales—his mission complete. "Francesca, here. Mathieu, there." He motions to our seats with the exuberance of a court jester bowing before the queen. "Merci, monsieur," René adds, as Alistair cautiously steadies Madame into her seat.

I wait for Madame and René to begin to sit. Then I sit down as Alistair places Madame's napkin in her lap and walks away. Us guys are left to fend for ourselves. And the moment I place my napkin on my lap and observe the perfect symmetry of Alistair's table, I chill out. Everything is so balanced, it's hard to tell whether they're hosting me or I'm hosting them. Comfy.

Madame turns to me. "How was your flight yesterday?"

"Oh, it was fine. No problem," I lie.

"And your accommodations here in the house?" she asks sincerely.

"Just great." I glance toward the backyard, imagining how fun—but so wrong—a trampoline would be. "Everything's beautiful." I look back at Madame.

Alistair arrives table side, now holding two bottles of wine. "Pardon, Madame. House white or house rosé?"

"White will be fine." She nods at her glass. "Merci."

He pours.

While Alistair swings around Madame to serve René, Madame looks at me again. "I hope you do not mind being housed in the side yard."

"No, no. I don't mind." I clasp my hands in my lap, realizing René has chosen the rosé. Am I supposed to side with Madame and pick white? "It's great over there."

"And the walk, to and from...do you find it troublesome?"

"No, no, not at all."

As I replay my stupid, uptight, stammering responses— no, no, it's great, no, no, not at all—Alistair leans forward and presents the bottles. I look at the labels—*Paradis*—designed with an illustration of Madame's elaborate garden, including this very gazebo. And the line drawing looks like the view from the second-story terrace—without René and his ranting phone call. Oh, I get it. So when Alistair offered house wine, he meant it. "I'm fine." I pause. I don't want Madame to think I'm a lush. "No wine for me...thanks anyway."

"Lemonade," Alistair suggests with an American pang.

"That'd be good."

Madame looks at me. "It is good, Matthew. A fine choice," she says and dismisses Alistair to his side-station.

René shifts in his seat as if squelching a thought. "The lemons are picked fresh daily, from the trees near the front gate." He shakes his head euphorically. "Delicious."

And before I can blink twice, Alistair has removed my wine glass and presented the lemonade. "Thanks, Alistair," I half-whisper.

Madame and René lift their glasses to toast, so I grab mine.

Madame glances at René then turns toward me. "To our year together!"

We sip. My stomach drops. What the hell am I doing? I don't belong here. I should be in New York. I'm supposed to be performing!

René turns to Madame. "Mathieu knows our Kevin."

"Is that so?" Madame sets down her glass.

I look at René then Madame. "Well, sort of…I mean, we both go to the same physical therapist."

René sits up even straighter. "Mathieu comes highly recommended."

"I am certain he does." Madame pauses as Alistair arrives at her side once more.

"First course." Alistair lowers a silver tray with three tiny appetizers. "Canapé of caviar with crème fraîche."

The bulbous, bluish/black fish eggs are perched on a dollop of white cream on top of a thin communion-type wafer—no run-of-the-mill saltine. And each appetizer is presented on an individual dish. I watch Madame lift her tiny portion from the serving tray. Apparently it's self-serve.

Alistair gallops around to René and then me. "Bon appétit!" He returns to his side-station.

"Bon appétit!" Madame and René respond in unison.

Madame swallows her appetizer in one bite, while René stares at his. "A charming amuse bouche!" He slurps it in.

Following suit, I pop mine. And the second it hits my tongue I realize I don't like it. I try to play it off. I construct my face to appear relaxed and reach for my drink to help gag it down. Bad choice. Now the cream is curdling in my throat as the lemonade rushes down. Gross.

"Francesca, Mathieu is a dancer."

It sounds like René is reminding her of a previous conversation.

Madame looks at me. "The ballet?"

I take another swig of lemonade. "No. I wasn't really cut out for that. I'm more into musical theater. But I've studied ballet." I shut up and put down my glass. Breathe. She didn't ask for the whole damn résumé.

René fluffs his napkin and reaches for his wine. "The Great White Way."

"What is Broadway?" Madame poses her question as if they are playing *Jeopardy!* "So you sing as well, Matthew?"

"Kind of." I blurt. "Let's put it this way…I'm a decent dancer who knows how to act, choreograph, and carry a tune. Oh, and I can dance captain, when push comes to shove."

Madame smiles as if she gets my sense of humor. "How wonderful."

René sips his wine. "Whether it be ballet or Broadway, a dancer's life is short-lived and full of sacrifice."

Madame tilts her head and gives me an inquisitive look. "Might you agree, Matthew? A life of sacrifice?"

I cringe at the thought of disagreeing with René. "Yeah. It's pretty tough. But I love it."

"Matthew," Madame rests her hands on her lap as if she's got all day to listen, "how does one summon the determination?"

"Oh, I don't know, for me it comes naturally." I glance at René, then back to Madame. "I mean, I always liked dancing around the living room when I was a kid. I guess it just stuck."

"Those like Mathieu," René gives into a fervid smile, "are to the manner born."

Alistair sweeps in and removes our miniature appetizer plate, leaving the charger plate behind.

Madame's face takes on a glow as she reaches for her wine glass. "Oh, how I envy a dancer's dedication…to possess such relentless passion."

She envies me? Ha. I bet she'd change her mind if she spent even one night in my fifth-floor-walk-up, shoebox apartment, disturbed by the noise of recycling trucks first thing in the morning. "Oh, thanks."

René turns to Madame. "Francesca, we must get down to business."

"Must we?" Madame sips her wine and looks at me, letting me know she is teasing René.

As Alistair circles the table again, placing an empty bowl on top of each charger, I notice another waiter has arrived on the scene. The new guy is holding a large white ceramic terrine and has positioned himself away from the table in Madame's blind spot. And since I don't see a barbecue out here, I assume he is the runner to and from the kitchen. But if this guy is supposed to be Madame's taster, he is one bite too late.

René leans toward Madame. "We have avoided our exercise long enough." He looks at me. "Mathieu is here to transform our lives for the better."

Madame puts her glass down. "I suppose you are right."

René smirks, as if he just convinced a vegetarian to eat bacon. "Indeed I am!"

I look at Madame. "Hey, maybe we could do something later today?" I hesitate and look at René.

Shit. I just initiated with Madame.

Fuck.

Backtrack. "I mean…if you guys want to."

Alistair rolls his eyes and heads over to accept the terrine.

Madame zeroes in on me with those riveting green eyes. "Not today," she answers gently. "Perhaps tomorrow would be best."

"Tomorrow works." I play off my response with a smile and pray for Alistair to hurry back to the table.

Sustained silence.

Why can't René throw me a bone?

More silence.

After what seems like eternity, Alistair finally steps up to Madame. "Second course, soupe de légumes." He leans down, allowing her to reach the long-handled ladle.

"Tomorrow sounds terrific," René says to Madame. But she's too concentrated on serving herself to respond.

I watch Madame take her scoop and flash to Linda Blair in *The Exorcist*, puking pea soup on the priest. Cancel that. Back to Linda Evans.

"Merci, Alistair." Madame lets go of the ladle, after taking barely enough soup to coat the bottom of her bowl.

Alistair crosses to René, who takes the exact same quantity as Madame, and soon it's my turn. But after my third ladle full, Alistair yanks the tureen away and transfers the dish to the second waiter. They both appear confident that Madame won't be asking for more. I wonder if I'm going to starve. And as the second waiter heads toward the house, Madame takes her first tiny bite. We begin.

René skims away from his chest, drags the spoon to the rim of his bowl and blots. He swallows. "Tepid," he says, chin down, "as soup ought to be served."

I taste mine.

Basic.

Could use some salt.

"So, we shall start tomorrow." Madame returns to our conversation. "René, you may go first." She looks at me with a mischievous glint. "And if he endures, then I am willing to give it a go—"

I cut her off with a laugh. "Sounds like a plan," I say, now considering whether or not the importance of lukewarm soup was ever mentioned in *Miss Manners*.

Soup happens fast. The moment Madame finishes, René finishes. So I stop too. Now I know I'm going to starve.

Alistair swoops in to remove our bowls—once more leaving that charger plate behind—then glides over to meet the co-waiter who's just returned from the kitchen. This time, the waiter has a large silver tray with three enormous eggs, each one balanced on its own porcelain stand.

What the heck?

Alistair returns to the table, and balances the tray between Madame and René. "Third course. One-minute ostrich egg."

They reach for their eggs at the same time, but Madame's fingers touch one nanosecond before René's. Then, as they lift their dishes, they each acknowledge Alistair before he crosses to me.

I take the remaining serving. "Thanks, Alistair." I glance out to the yard again. Could there be a free-range ostrich wandering the grounds?

"Enjoy," Alistair calls out and returns to his post.

"Astounding." René bubbles as if he's just excavated a dinosaur egg.

"Tremendous." Madame picks up a butter knife and uses it to steady her egg.

I watch in horror, as she begins to chip away at the shell with her teaspoon—skillfully cracking around the upper curve. Okay. Major speed bump. I have no idea how to do this.

Still observing Madame, I pick up the same utensils and attempt to imitate her technique. But this chiseling act isn't as easy as she makes it look. The moment I begin, my shell transforms into a mound of jagged splinters; hers looks like she has access to a scalpel.

"Matthew," Madame pauses to lift the crown of her egg off to the side—exposing a pool of runny yolk, "how is your family doing in the wake of eleven September?" She looks genuinely concerned.

In a jolt, my helpless egg bears the brunt of a much-too-forceful whack. My face goes red. I watch yolk cascade down the shell, drip off the pedestal, and stream onto my charger plate. Please let it stop before soaking the tablecloth.

I gather enough composure to answer. "Oh, um, everyone's okay."

I suddenly fume. How idiotic. Everyone is *not* okay.

René glances at my messy plate and motions for Alistair. "Send in the soldiers!"

Madame looks at me, as if René is disrupting a sacred moment. "Well, we were all deeply saddened, Matthew...and most concerned."

I peek down at my egg and my stomach bottoms out at the thought of having to relive this 9/11 conversation for the rest of my life. I look up at Madame once more; I'm not sure what to say. "Thanks for asking."

Alistair arrives with two white whicker baskets of toasted breadsticks. "Et voilà, the soldiers...for dipping," he tags on—no doubt for my benefit. He tucks the breadbaskets on either side of the centerpiece and walks away.

Whew. Glad he pulled focus again. I reach for some bread.

As we dab toast sticks into our runny eggs, René steers the conversation away from the topic of 9/11, and gets into a story about the health benefits of raw food. But he soon transitions to safety concerns. "Remember, Francesca...years ago...how ill our dear lady Catherine became?"

Madame looks at René as if recalling a happy moment from her youth. "Indeed she did."

René reaches for his wine. "Tainted Caesar. Guaranteed to jump-start one's weight-loss regimen."

While the two of them continue dipping and reminiscing, I can't think of an unusual food-poisoning story, so I just hang back and listen; fascinated by the way René and Madame relate to each other, as if trapped in a bygone era. It's wild. Both the vocabulary and the cadence of their conversation reminds me of all that boring stuff we were forced to study in theater class—Chekhov, Ibsen, Shaw. I can't believe these characters could still exist in real life, but I guess they do. And I don't get *why* there is so much silverware on this table, if our meal is about spoons and finger food? Strange. Maybe the knives and forks are just hanging around like extras in a movie, to help things look legit.

"Might you agree, Mathieu?" René asks, ready to teach me a lesson.

"Oh, I'm sorry, I missed that last part."

Madame turns to me with a calm expression. "Do you agree, to forgo salad and proceed with dessert?"

"Sure!" I smile. "Soup counted as veggies, right?"

Madame beams. "Then it is settled. On with dessert."

Alistair arrives at her side. "As you wish, Madame." He motions to the second waiter and they start clearing the table. Half-eaten eggs get snatched and excess silverware swiped. Dessertspoons are moved into place and new charger plates appear—an inch or so smaller than our first set. The other waiter helps expedite this transition, but he is careful to remain invisible to Madame.

At last, Alistair steps forward with the highly anticipated dessert—a tray of chocolate mousse in old-fashioned champagne glasses. This time, he positions himself between Madame and me. "Coupe de chocolate." He lowers the tray almost onto the table.

Madame shifts away. "Matthew shall choose first."

Alistair edges the tray to my side. I stare at the delicate swirls of cream atop the three camera-ready dishes. This could be another test—like when the phone rang yesterday during my telephone tutorial. "After you, Madame." I look into her gorgeous eyes and tilt my head as if removing a top hat. "I insist."

Madame reaches for her cup. "Merci, monsieur."

I reach next. "De rien, Madame."

"So you have some French, Matthew?" Madame pauses, as Alistair crosses to serve René.

"Just a little." I laugh. "But, sorry to say, my French teacher grew up in Nashville."

"Tennessee," René chimes in and takes his cup from Alistair's tray. "Home of the Grand Ole Opry."

Madame lifts a modest spoonful of airy mousse from her dish. "And this is somehow unfortunate?"

René looks at me. "Only if one prefers to sound French,"

he says, sounding southern enough to be sitting on the backlot of *Gone With The Wind*.

Madame laughs and looks at René. "I do love my Scarlett O'Hara." She takes her first bite.

I smile and dig into my chocolate.

Blackout.

This is the best thing I've ever tasted.

"René," Madame pauses to reach for her water glass, "do you recollect how much chocolate you squirreled away last year in anticipation of Y2K?"

"Just shy of two years ago already, Francesca, if that is imaginable." René smiles. "And I prepared merely enough chocolate to override the shock of worldwide computer failure."

Madame takes a drink of water and looks at me. "Matthew, we had an entire storage room full in France," she begins, letting me in on a joke, "more chocolate than two people might possibly consume in a lifetime." Madame puts down her glass and becomes serious. "Ironically, we spent the first days of the new millennium in Mykonos." She looks at René. "No chocolate whatsoever."

René leans forward. "Everything worked out for the best," he consoles.

Alistair steps in to top off Madame's water. She looks at me again. "So, Matthew, how long have you been in New York?"

Whoa. Talk about a non sequitur.

I pause. "Coming up on seven years now."

René flicks a gnat from his mousse. "The seven year itch, eh…time for a change? Do tell."

"Yeah, something like that, I guess." Hell. Maybe he heard about my knee injury from Kevin and he knows I had to take a break. "I'm just really happy to be here." Hum. That came out a little flat.

Madame glances at René and reprimands his nosiness without saying a word. She then looks at me. "Well, regardless of circumstance, Matthew," she pauses, and scoots her chair away from the table, clearly ready to leave, "we are honored to have you." She begins to stand.

René pops to attention beside her, and Alistair moves in from behind.

I get up slowly, trying not to emphasize the fact that she's having trouble getting out of her seat.

Madame barely makes it up on her own. "Thank you for joining us, Matthew." She smiles and takes René by the arm. "I look forward to our first session tomorrow."

"Me too." I nod and hold my spot. "Thanks for lunch."

While René escorts Madame toward the house, Alistair and I wait silently at the table. I wonder what happened in Mykonos? What ever it was, Madame doesn't want to talk about it—like me, when it comes to the topic of my knee injury. I have no plans to tell Madame that I only agreed to come here because I've been kicked off stage. I know she wouldn't be thrilled with the idea of hiring *sloppy seconds*.

With Madame out of sight, Alistair hurridly busses the table. "Smashing, Matthew," he mumbles, without looking at me. "Excluding that dodgy egg."

"I know. That was embarrassing."

Alistair laughs to himself and points toward the backyard. "Head off to your room that way." He walks to his side-station. "In the event Madame decides to sit a spell in the living room."

"Okay." I walk away. "See you at dinner."

Fast-forward—almost twenty-four hours later—and I'm once again walking over to meet Barbara in the kitchen; I have on my navy blue Nike trainer outfit.

"Matthew, there is no time to discuss the morning workout with René, but congratulations are in order." She motions me in through the screen door. "He was most pleased." She sighs and hurries off around the corner. "Now...show me what you have planned for Madame."

Come on. Barbara needs to evaluate Madame's workout?

"Sure, I'll take you through it." I follow her into the kitchen. And while the chef and the sous-chef are prepping for lunch, we pull two chairs away from the staff table and sit down facing each other. I begin to instruct Barbara as if she's Madame. "Sit up straight," I say. "Keep your shoulders back, take a deep breath in...now slowly exhale." I try to keep a straight face as Barbara pretends she can't understand my instructions. She's lost in a parody of a confused old lady, slouched down in her seat. And even though she looks hilarious, I keep going. "Once more, inhale two, three, four...exhale two, three, four, five. Good...now this time, make your exhale slightly longer than the inhale." Man. Her lung capacity is unbelievable.

Seemingly satisfied after two deep breaths, Barbara drops her silly impression, claps her hands together, and jumps up from her seat. "Very good." She shoves her chair up under the table. "Now, get upstairs and go to work." I stand and she laughs at me. "Did you actually believe I was serious?"

I fake laugh as she returns my chair to the table. "Of course not." Hell. I'm anxious enough about going upstairs for the first time, so I don't need her games right now. "No, really...that was a riot."

"Come, Matthew!" She damn near calls me like a dog and darts off toward the pantry. "Enough stalling."

As Barbara leads us into the foyer, I ramble about how excited I am to work with Madame. But Barbara doesn't care. And after we get into the elevator, I can see that she is concerned with more important issues—much more important. The lighting in here deepens her frown lines, big time. "Matthew, do not push her today. You do not want to start off on the wrong foot—" Mid-sentence, the elevator door opens on the third floor and we step out into a small entranceway. "Slow and steady will win the race."

Thanks for the vote of confidence. "Got it," I whisper.

We arrive at the entrance to Madame's spacious chamber. I coach myself into a deep breath. It's awesome. The simplicity of design is mesmerizing; I can't stop staring. The space is full of mostly white Moroccan décor and accented with a few pieces of blown glass—antique Italian? The centerpiece of the room is a white four-poster bed that sits atop an off-white woven rug. And in the center of the bed is a pile of fluffy lapdogs in varying shades of taupe. Then, before I have time to take in any more details, the little dogs go wild and announce our arrival. Barbara guides me through the bedroom, avoiding the nippy pack. She soon heads toward an exterior door that leads onto a terrace. I walk close behind her, praying not to step on a paw—so far so good.

Once we step outside, I see Madame from behind. She is in all white today, and sitting on a padded rattan chair, shaded by a trellised archway of flowering vines. Her hair is coifed exactly like yesterday. But her shoulders appear even thinner; my memory fattened her up a little. Suddenly anxious, I realize that the empty seat facing her will soon be mine—no table between us today.

We continue forward, and I turn my attention to the surroundings, in hopes of calming my nerves—an old audition strategy that rarely works. Madame's terrace is longer than it is wide, sheltered by flowers, and lined with French doors on the left side; the right side looks over to the garden. The view up here is much more intimate than the second story terrace. I love it. So secluded.

Barbara arrives at the workout area. "Pardon, Madame," she says, playing the role of a soft-spoken chambermaid. "I have Matthew here to join you."

"Merci, Babar."

I grin at Barbara, from behind Madame, assuming her pet name is inspired by the French elephant book, *Histoire de Babar.*

She returns my look as if to say *shut up.*

I step forward, now confident that I've got some dirt on Barbara. Sweet.

"Hello, Matthew." Madame motions to my seat. "How nice to see you again."

"Thanks...you too."

As I sit down, Barbara corrals the dogs toward the bedroom door, shushing the pack repeatedly. Strange. It's been three days already and I had no idea those feisty little creatures were up here. Maybe they never leave the third floor?

Madame shifts in her seat and turns her head in need. "Babar." Madame calls politely. "Babar?"

I scan Madame's expensive-looking white tracksuit and her sleek white leather sneakers. She's impeccable. And all this white just makes her green eyes appear even more astonishing.

Barbara steps onto to the terrace. "Oui, Madame, je suis ici."

"Babar...might you fetch my sunglasses?" Madame makes her request in an unassuming tone, speaking in English as if explaining the situation to me.

"But of course, Madame." Barbara turns away with a sense of urgency. "Immédiatement."

Madame then looks at me, ready to begin.

I wonder if I should do a brief intake or just get started. "Do you want to wait for the glasses?"

"No, no...we shall begin."

"Uh, okay, good," I hesitate, "so, uncross your ankles and place both feet on the floor in parallel—like you would if you were skiing," I say, remembering that René mentioned Madame's passion for cross-country this morning during our workout.

Once Madame mimics my position, I begin the *Barbara breathing series*. And after a couple deep breaths, we progress into a few shoulder rolls. But when I see how stiff Madame actually is, I reevaluate my entire class plan. What was I thinking? She can't do squat thrusts.

While Madame and I continue with flowing arm movements and a simple series of seated stretches, I observe the flurry of activity behind her. Barbara and two housemaids dart back and forth in the bedroom looking for the sunglasses; the lapdogs bounce around, barking like mad.

"How did you enjoy working with René this morning?" Madame asks, oblivious to the anxious search.

"It was great," I say, distracted by two more housekeepers

who are canvassing the office area to my right.

"Do you happen to see Barbara with my glasses?"

"Not yet. Shall I go check?" *Shall*, yikes! This place is already rubbing off on me.

"No, no. I am sure she will return. The glasses are there in plain sight…on the bedside table."

Before I'm forced into more padded conversation, Barbara steps outside with a silver tray—sunglasses on top. "Pardon, Madame, vos lunettes." Barbara presents the tray while the pack of lapdogs heel at her feet.

We pause from the workout. "Ah, merci, Babar…parfait."

As Madame takes her glasses and puts them on, I notice an additional maid standing behind Barbara, carrying yet another silver tray; there are two more maids framed in the bedroom doorway, hands folded in front of their aprons. In a flash, I feel like Little Orphan Annie in the home of Daddy Warbucks, with all the attendants standing by. I smile and hear Andrea McArdle belt: *I think I'm gonna like it here!*

Madame adjusts her glasses and two of the dogs yap with excitement and jump up onto my lap. Then, before I know it, another dog jumps up on Madame's lap. "Ah, ha, Matthew, what a pleasant surprise," Madame cheers. "The Pomeranians like you—Antoinette and Celeste are sometimes aloof; however, they appear drawn to you. Look, Babar."

Barbara steps aside, with tray held high, and maintains a penetrating stare in my direction. She is either jealous of my connection with these dogs, or pissed that I know about her pet name. But maybe she's just on guard in case she has to rush in and administer CPR.

Madame looks down at the doe-eyed pooch in her lap. "This little one is my youngest. Her name is Charlotta…mon petit King Charles Spaniel."

"Hello, Charlotta." I lean forward and look into the dog's oversized eyes, thrilled to find a bond with Madame. "What a sweety."

Barbara swaps trays with the second maid and steps forward again. "Pardon, Madame, vos médicament."

"Merci, Babar." Madame lifts a tiny pill from atop a small porcelain dish and reaches for a glass of water, also on the tray. Once Madame is finished, she returns the glass to the tray and Barbara exits the terrace—taking the three remaining dogs and the additional maids inside with her.

As the bedroom door closes, I hear a lyric song coming from a loud speaker in the distance.

"Ah, do you recognize the chant, Matthew?" Madame strokes Charlotta. "The call to prayer. Is it not mellifluous?"

Melliflu-what? I nod. Can't she *dumb it down* a little? "Yeah. It's awesome."

"The glorious sound of our devout muezzin." Madame pauses to listen as if she's never heard it before. "Five times a day, he climbs high into the minaret and sings out to the faithful followers below."

I pet the dogs and take in the chant. I've already heard this music several times since I got here but didn't really give it much thought.

"I cannot imagine I will ever tire of his distinct voice or the melodic tune." She peers over her sunglasses. "That is enough for today." Her gracious expression pierces me. "Do you prefer, Matthew?"

I stroke Antionette and Celeste, unsure about ending the workout so soon—we've hardly done anything. Or maybe she wants to know if I want to be called *Matthew* versus *Mathieu*.

"Sure...let's pick up here next time."

"Very well, we shall meet again. Tomorrow at eleven."

"Sounds good."

Madame shifts forward in her seat, and Charlotta jumps down from her lap. "And remember, Matthew, if there is anything you need, Barbara and Alistair are both here to serve you." She stands with ease—completely unassisted today. "Please do not hesitate to request of their service."

By the time she's up, I'm up. And my two dogs are down. I hope to appear respectful by standing, yet empathetic toward the yapping Pomeranians I've just pitched onto the porch. Luckily, Madame doesn't seem to think dumping the dogs is a big deal.

"Merci, Matthew…merci beaucoup."

"Merci, Madame."

"Beautiful French sound, Matthew." She motions the dogs toward her bedroom and turns to leave; the Arabic chant continues in the background. "Not too Southern for my taste. Not at all."

Within a few steps, Barbara comes outside to assist her. Whew. I wasn't sure if I was supposed to escort Madame back inside or not.

As I watch them leave, I consider that with any American princess, I'd expect to see some designer logos stitched to her outfit or the word *JUICY* embroidered across the ass of her fancy sweatpants. But with Madame there is nothing—just an air of pure class.

The moment the call to prayer finishes, Barbara charges out onto the terrace. "You are still here?"

"Yeah," I answer sarcastically. "I don't know how to get back to the elevator without going through her room." I smirk. "Figured I'd chill out here 'til she goes down to lunch."

"Cut the bull, Matthew." Barbara leads us away from the bedroom, out from beneath the trellised area. "The service stairs are over there." She points left. Another expansive terrace.

When we pause at the corner of the house, I shield my eyes from the blaring sun and locate a door on the far side. Barbara is being ridiculous. I wouldn't have discovered that on my own. "Oh, okay. Thanks."

She gives me a little shove. "Never again pass by way of the front elevator. Always the back staircase for you."

Then, as Barbara turns to leave, I start across the rooftop garden and replay what Madame just said. Sure. Barbara and Alistair are here to serve me—like that'll ever happen.

3

Life on the estate is rolling along and the cogs of the house churn with utmost precision. The staff works seven days a week, so there is no difference between workweek and weekend. Happy to say, I've hit my stride. But I also have to admit that the initial excitement of joining the ranks has faded, especially now that a sense of routine has taken over. I mark off each day on a calendar, although sometimes I get confused about whether I've already marked it or not. I think we're up to day twelve.

Every morning, soon after coffee, I train René. Then, I go back to my room, do some mundane rehab exercises and wait for the ten forty-five phone call, in which Barbara instructs me to meet Madame promptly at eleven on the upstairs terrace.

After I finish the brief stretch-and-pet class with Madame and the dogs, I have about an hour for a yoga workout before lunch.

In the afternoon, my job becomes one of mastering how to live like the idle rich. Siesta. It's kind of strange sleeping in the middle of the day. But after a huge meal, and a couple glasses of wine, I manage.

I awaken in time for afternoon tea and rush to the kitchen, for a complement of treats that are clearly intended to fatten the trainer's belly. And even though I have tried to rationalize my sugar addiction by explaining that *carbohydrate loading* was once a proven athletic regime, my excuse gets lost in translation.

Once teatime is finished, the staff heads off to their stations. But without any houseguests to train, I have nothing else to do—and everyone knows it. So I do my best to stay out of the way until dinner.

Hiding in my room, I am very much aware of how hard Madame's staff works. They are busting their butts, while I'm twiddling thumbs between workouts. Every day, the indoor and outdoor living spaces are cleaned on a strict timetable. Floors are mopped, dry basins are polished, spotless serving dishes are given the once over, and already-clean cabinets are dusted again. Bedding gets changed, laundered, and ironed—including the sheets on unused beds—and not one pillow goes even two hours without being fluffed and freshened. The gardeners tend to the yard in sections, apparently moving with the light. They weed, dig, and plant—pinch where necessary—as if they have to get everything done in one day.

Although some tasks happen daily, others occur in rotation—not unlike the show schedule during summer stock. The Saturday/Tuesday chores during my first week, became Thursday/Sunday of the second week. And the cast around here behaves much the same way we actors do during a three-month run in the middle of nowhere: vying for attention, gossiping backstage, and looking to get laid.

Due to isolation, and the monotony of their schedule, the staff lives a life consumed by the comings and goings of prominent guests. As witnessed at dinner the first night—and every meal since—the servants thrive upon hearsay. Peering through peepholes and listening behind doors, retelling Madame's table conversation, it's all part of the chores.

In the pantry, the chrome-plated appliances are strategically angled in such a way as to reflect distant activity. While sweeping the floor, a housekeeper can travel from toaster to coffee grinder to hot water pot, and have an omniscient view of the first floor breakfast nook, salon, and formal dining area. To see into the great room requires moving closer to the silver tea service—but rest assured, every area throughout the house is visible from at least one distant vantage point. What might happen next? What intrigue might be exposed in the drawing room today, under the watchful eye of an antique silver spoon?

One of my favorite things to observe is how stories get passed around the table at mealtime. Whether it happened yesterday or years ago, if it gets a laugh, it gets repeated. For example, if two workers are having a giggle in Arabic, someone will translate it into French, and someone else will take it from French into English. If it originates in German, it often gets translated into Italian, then French, then back to Arabic, and so on. It's a riot to anticipate hearing the next laugh and witness which language delivers the better version. By the time I hear the third or forth generation, I wonder if the story I'm getting even remotely resembles the original.

I've heard a lot of outrageous dinnertime stories, such as the one about the housemaid who got fired for not knowing the difference between a teaspoon and a demitasse. And several about Monsieur's nurse, a woman whose tits were so big she had trouble seeing over them to take his pulse. But the one significant story that has yet to be discussed around the kitchen table is the history of Barbara and Alistair. This story gets passed around in the wings, never openly, and is hailed as one of the best-kept house secrets—ever. And of course, everyone on staff knows about it and wants to make sure that the new guy knows too.

Multiple versions have been shared with me by various workers, while hiding behind stairwells and tucked into storage closets. And even though I can't tell which interpretation is true, I've pieced together one version I like best.

Typical evening, about ten years ago, Barbara would wait until midnight before inviting Alistair into her room. They rattle around in the uncomfortable and much-too-small twin bed of her modest staff quarters. Then, with no time for foreplay or post-coital affection, the two finish within a few minutes and Alistair leaves—his shirt miss-buttoned and tie tossed to one side.

One atypical evening—also back when—shortly after Alistair walked out of Barbara's room, her call-buzzer sounded. "Oh, no...Madame is calling," Barbara thought. She found it odd that the call-buzzer sounded in steady repetition—*enk, enk, enk*—but she proceeded upstairs anyway. Much to her dismay, once Barbara entered Madame's chamber, she discovered Alistair—on Madame's bed—fucking one of the gardeners. The gardener was on all fours with his face shoved into a pillow. And the pillow was inadvertently pressing Madame's bedside call-button—*enk, enk, enk*.

Both the gardener and Alistair realized that Barbara had interrupted. Yet, with hardly a glance in her direction, the two men chose to continue. Barbara was disgusted by what she was seeing, so—after observing for a moment—she stormed back downstairs to her room. In a bitter rage, she phoned Alistair's third wife—to whom he was still legally married. During that frantic phone call, she told the wife *everything*, yet failed to mention that she—Barbara—had also been a link in Alistair's adulterous chain.

So, as the story goes, Alistair officially divorced his third wife later that same year. And, to this day, he blames their failed marriage on that late-night phone call from Barbara.

Due to the fact that Alistair hated Barbara's dishonest handling of the situation—and Barbara hated Alistair's unfaithful behavior—the ex-lovers have since learned to cope with one another, strictly as co-workers.

Nowadays, in hopes of avoiding each other, Alistair and Barbara have mastered well-adapted maneuvers throughout different service corridors. They have formed alliances within the staff, and found ways to manipulate one another without ever speaking or making eye contact. When forced into the same room—at staff mealtime for instance—he tends to converse in French and English, while she will hold court in German and Italian. Alistair might reenact a story about Madame dribbling her soup during lunch. Then Barbara will take over with a pantomime of how

René gaily rearranged the flowers in the foyer. The whole act is like watching two washed-up comedians compete for laughs in front of the UN General Assembly.

But since everyone around here knows that Alistair and Barbara each have the authority to get us fired for *failure to comply*, we laugh along and appear amused. And it is fairly amusing— but maybe not truly funny for those workers who are genuinely trapped in this place. I think I'm the lucky one; my days in this house are numbered.

4

Snag. I haven't seen Madame in a week. She hasn't been feeling up to working out, so now all I've got is training René—and that has turned into a nightmare.

His daily workout consists of a power walk throughout the grounds, followed by some light stretching in his room. And although this sounds simple enough, it's not. During our thirty-minute walk, René is endlessly talkative. He stares forward toward the path and rambles on, without leaving any space between words for reaction, comment or contemplation. Our walking pattern is precisely repeated day after day, as are his incessant stories and fragmented thoughts that crop up at specific garden landmarks. For him, each time is the first time. But for me, six-weeks-worth of René reruns is more than I can take.

Upon exiting his room, René will inevitably pause near the birdbath, look up to the early morning sky, and make a comment about how the chill in the air will soon give way to the heat of the afternoon. Then, we launch into The Walk.

René goes with the bounce and curiosity of an Arabian colt and, as always, he dons his white-on-white summer training ensemble. A floppy white safari hat and white plastic sunglasses with thick circular frames accessorize his oversized white linen blouse. The cut of the blouse creates a billowing train as he moves briskly forward through the foliage. His thigh-tight white cotton stretch pants feature elasticized cuffs that snug his ankle-high white sneakers. He refers to his workout attire as a *timeless* look. He reminds me, that it reminds him, of his heyday visiting Key West, Florida, long before the Euro-boys defiled Miami Beach.

We're walking—he's talking.

A giant terracotta pot full of edible flowers stimulates his top-ten list of wilderness survival tips. This is followed by a row of flowering datura bushes, which brings up a story about poisonous tea, gypsy politics, and how Viagra once gave him a bloody nose. Darting past the tool shed triggers global warming, standardized school testing, and a complete bibliography of his favorite philosopher, Noam Chomsky. Bonsai gourds and miniature roses germinate memories of his boy lover who ran off with the circus. And the circus story is immediately followed with one about some elite athlete, who once made a pass at him in a public restroom. At the reflecting pool, he mentions his not-so-recent bout with skin cancer and the apparent sun damage suffered by the gardeners. He then recites Von Luschan's chromatic scale of skin color, and uses this method to classify the staff as we approach the rippling water sculpture.

His stories go on and on, and the landmarks never change. And The Walk is timed so perfectly, that every day as we pass alongside the great lawn, the automatic sprinkler system turns on and a flock of feeding guinea fowl lifts into flight. At this point, René looks skyward to ponder the tragic Lindbergh kidnapping case, and shares a few more tales about his former lovers.

As we continue ahead, he mentions how incredibly handsome Kevin—his other trainer—was. He tells me about how remarkable life used to be, when Kevin was on staff for Madame and Monsieur.

But today, after having religiously repeated our walking/ storytelling pattern every day for the past forty-one days—here on day forty-two, almost at the *Kevin* spot—he tangents into a brand new tale. He suddenly details a list of dos and don'ts when it comes to being around Madame in public.

Maybe he knows we're going somewhere?

"Now, most importantly, Mathieu, when walking with Madame, one in your position of service does not stand directly beside her. Always remain two paces aback, lest one might appear aggressive. And when moving en masse within the retinue, your place as trainer is at the rear of the group—never, under any circumstance ahead of a houseguest. Of course, I have the option of moving forward or back as I please!" René shouts, lets out a hearty laugh, and skips along the path ahead of me.

But within three seconds of joyfulness, he trips and falls down—CLONK! René has gone face down, flat out on the pink-pebbled walkway. The moment I register his fall, the automated sprinklers kick on and the flock of guinea fowl takes flight. And for the first time ever, René is silent.

The vibrating patter of the sprinkler system grows louder as I rush forward to help him. I see blood running from his chin onto his white blouse; blood draining from both hands; and yet more blood dripping from his right knee. For a brief instant, I'm flooded with the painful memory of my knee injury, but soon redirect to René. He needs me. Besides, my ligaments didn't bleed like this. This is awful. I glance toward the main house; we're at least two football fields away—no cell phone, and no first aid kit.

Then, by the time I look back at René, blood is everywhere. The once pink pebbles beneath him are tinging red, and his sprightly demeanor has gone missing. I assume his blood-thinning medication is making this situation much more complicated than it needs to be. But we need to act fast. Strange. I'm not sure if I'm more stunned by the quantity of blood he is generating or by his quiet response to this traumatic moment.

René looks up at me through his bug-eyed sunglasses. "Kevin...what shall we do, it is not that bad is it?"

Crap. He thinks I'm Kevin. "Let's go back to the house," I begin calmly, even though his face has turned whiter than his hat. "We'll ask Barbara to disinfect the wounds."

"Wounds...with an *s*?" René pauses and looks forward along the path, as if planning to continue his regular route.

I nod *yes* and offer to help him up, but he ignores my gesture and pulls out a small packet of tissues, stowed inside his sock. Dab. Dab. Dab. "Let's go back," I say, as he trashes his final tissue. "We should head to the house to get more supplies." I take him by the arm and help him up to his feet. He can hardly stand— let alone walk two hundred yards.

"I prefer our normal routine," he insists. But after a few awkward steps, René stops—he can barely bear weight. "Oh, Kevin, perhaps you are right. It now looks as though I am bleeding here, there, and everywhere." He speaks with a sweet sense of musicality.

I take a beat. Did he just give me credit for the idea to go back to the house—or was that because he thinks I'm Kevin?

René looks at me, totally out of sorts. "We shall end our walk here, Kevin...are you willing?"

I agree, offer an arm for support, and off we go—straight across the great lawn, pausing from time to time, to allow the sprinkler jets to redirect.

As I watch the blood from his hands run onto my forearm I feel sick inside. I'm nervous, thinking about the stories of his promiscuous past. I hate him for bleeding all over me, and I regret being used as his human crutch. I think I should be concerned for him, and I am—at least I think I am.

Back in his room—damp from the mist of the sprinklers—we stand before the full-length mirror in his white marble bathroom, looking like a pair of blood-sport enthusiasts. René's breath smells like wet metal and his stringy hair sticks to his forehead as I remove his still white safari hat. "Barbara's on her way," I reassure.

When Barbara arrives—her doctor's bag in hand—the two of us undress him. Alcohol, gauze, and cotton balls go flying as she tends to René. She douses the wounds with a thick coating of antiseptic powder. Then it's more powder, more gauze, and still more bleeding. I'm careful with each touch; any opening I have could lead to a blood-borne illness. But I know my anxiety isn't going to change what is actually happening. He's already bled all over me.

"Tell me, Barbara," René says, sounding disappointed, "why on earth would there be no intravenous injection of tissue extract available in this house?"

"René," Barbara placates, "we are presently in Morocco, not on the continent."

He goes quiet again, satisfied with her response.

I have no idea what these two are talking about.

After observing a few more minutes of Barbara's doctoring, I make eye contact with René. "Should I ask Alistair to bring you anything?"

René winces and asks for a glass of warm milk. "And, Kevin," he squirms, "would you please send in a few of the chef's tasty homemade Moroccan cookies?"

"Sure." I walk toward the bathroom phone. Now doesn't feel like the right time to correct him about *Kevin*. Barbara looks at me and shakes her head, indicating I should use the phone in the bedroom, *not* the bathroom. So I leave to make the call.

After phoning Alistair with René's request, I use an few alcohol wipes to clean the receiver. If this guy drops dead, I don't want my fingerprints anywhere.

When I walk back into the bathroom, I find Barbara nursing and cleaning at the same time. She's unbelievable—such speed, flexibility, and athletic agility. She's got one eye on René's slowing wounds, as she wipes the floor, polishes the fixtures, and shines the mirror. "Not to worry, it will all come clean," Barbara reassures him, as she adjusts the water temperature in the bathtub where she's rinsing his training outfit. "There we go," she says, and pats René as if she's just diapered a baby. "All better now."

With his bleeding under control, and his cookies and warm milk on the nightstand, René dismisses Barbara. He asks if I'll stay in the room with him. "Would you mind, Kevin, just for a moment...could you?"

"Sure. I'll stay," I answer, wishing I could work my name

into the conversation. "If Madame needs me, Barbara'll know where I'm at." Bloodstained and all.

As René crawls into bed, I take a seat on the large inflatable exercise ball we normally use for our workout. He stares straight ahead—subdued—and takes a sip of milk. "AH! As if I had not nearly bled to death already!" He waves his hand in front of his face. "Now the kitchen has plans to obliterate my taste buds!"

René slams the glass down on the nightstand and reaches for the plate of cookies. He gobbles one down in pursuit of the hot milk, and then holds the plate under his chin like a reflector panel.

After a few minutes of nothingness, René mentions that both his parents passed away early on. He tells me that his mother suffered from dementia and she was completely *gaga* by the age of fifty. "Momma was gone before I turned twenty," he says, in a slow, subtle manner. "I hardly recall daddy."

It seems that the tedious René I know has taken a sabbatical—at least for the time being. He has dropped his veneer, and he looks like a miniature man, lying here in his huge bed.

Within a few sentences, René confesses that his parents left behind a trust fund for him; enough money to last ten years—give or take a few. "Not by any means a lavish sum." He warms his hands around the glass. "Merely enough to maintain basics for a short while."

René soon admits to going against his better judgment, and mentions gambling his entire inheritance on a plan to make even more money. "I would sooner live large for a few months," he says, with the twang of Julia Roberts in *Steel Magnolias*, "rather than sustain a mediocre existence, leading nowhere."

I sit tight on the exercise ball—resisting the temptation to bounce—as René transitions into a story about setting out in search of a wealthy sponsor. He explains how he traveled throughout Austria many years ago, in hopes of finding the right match. "To locate a woman in need of companionship," he declares, his mouth visibly dry. "I knew she was out there somewhere."

Much to his surprise, he soon learned that the inner circle of old-money folks was a tightly knit group and many didn't welcome him, the newcomer. Even though he had purchased the proper attire—shoes being key—and bought his way into private clubs, his plan was taking more time and money than expected. He socialized with everyone he could and told tales of how his time spent in Switzerland had grown passé—both Davos and St. Moritz. He inflated the story of his lineage—something about how his great-grandfather's design technology was integral in the construction of the Flatiron Building in New York City. And although his ancestral story was not true, he thought it sounded prestigious. He also thought it was obscure enough to not be readily questioned by his new friends. "The joys of a pre-Google life, Kevin… you are much too young to understand."

One evening, while attending the theatre, René zoomed in on Madame who was in the lobby during intermission. He had an usher in stitches, and caught Madame's eye in the distance. René was well aware of who Madame was and knew of her approximate net worth. So—after walking over to introduce himself—he casually mentioned that he was joining a small private group for cross-country skiing. He invited Madame to come skiing twice a week for the remainder of the season. "Would you care to come along as my guest?" he asked. Madame agreed.

Their relationship gestated over the next nine weeks and during that initial span, René had learned how to make Madame smile. He plied her with appropriate wit and garnished it with minute dashes of sarcasm. She'd laugh. She liked the way he could simultaneously include and/or deflect others with a mere glance or turn of his head. His body language and social craft was something Madame herself did not possess.

He was invited to many of her functions and soon became known as *the life of the party*. With Madame's husband often away on business, René—though fifteen years her junior—could stand in for Monsieur and keep pulse with the pompous art dealers, the foreign dignitaries, and the endless lineup of mealtime intruders.

Alas, what started out as a simple scheme for René, soon evolved into a way of life. And based solely on his ability to make her smile, Madame has provided for René for over forty years now.

The moment he finishes his story about seeking Madame, René falls asleep—leaving an assortment of cookie crumbs stockpiled in his white chest hairs. I sneak away from his bedside, and pray to exit unnoticed. But when I open the door, I find Barbara down on her hands and knees—right at my feet—busily sweeping the sidewalk with a whiskbroom. Strange. This is a gardener's job, not hers.

"René can be such a baby," she whispers. "He took a small tumble. That is all."

I latch the door behind me. "I think he's okay now."

Barbara stands up and holds out her dustpan like I'm the dead-leaf inspector. "Madame is still not feeling well." She walks off toward the side entrance of the house. "She will not exercise today."

I follow. "Do you think it's anything major? I mean, it's been a full week now."

"No." Barbara deposits her dustpan and broom inside the utility room, and looks at me. "She will pull through, Matthew. She always does."

"I hope so. I'm starting to get worried about her."

"Trust me, there is nothing we can do. She becomes this way from time to time." Barbara checks the sky as if estimating today's barometric pressure. "Why don't we take a walk?"

"Sure. Where to?" I ask, accepting the fact that I can't force Madame to work out.

"Have you seen the giant cactus?" She walks away from the house.

"Nope, don't think so." I wonder if she's teasing me.

"All right, then...we must." She picks up some speed. "We absolutely must!"

"Sounds cool," I add. "But why haven't I already seen it?

You know, on my walks with René?"

"Because René is terrified of large succulents." Barbara chuckles. "Madame installed the cacti because she is fascinated by the tenacity of any life form that thrives in drought conditions. And this section of the garden is her place to escape whenever she seeks privacy."

We eventually slow down and enter the secluded cactus pass. "Neat. I love those flowering ones," I mention, realizing how this variety of dangerous-looking plants makes an ominous setting for an otherwise casual stroll.

"Matthew, please excuse René's mistake," Barbara comes to a halt and looks at me. "When he referred to you as Kevin."

I try not to appear insulted, but I was. "Oh, no prob."

Barbara steps off the path to snatch a long cactus spine from a plant that is almost as tall as she.

"He must've gotten confused 'cause of all the blood," I say, as Barbara uses her thorn as a toothpick.

She starts walking again. "René was most enamored with Kevin. You must view his transposition is a compliment."

As we move deeper into the pass, the climate becomes so arid it's difficult to breathe. I think it's even too hot to break a sweat. I pause to catch my breath.

Barbara stops and looks at me. "It was most unfortunate how our Kevin departed the house without maximizing the benefit of his retirement package."

"What's that?"

"It is not in your contract?" She removes the thorn from her mouth, incensed by her own question.

"No, I don't think so."

"Well, it should be." She points the tiny dagger in my direction as if I might become her voodoo doll. "The retirement clause states that any employee who serves for fifteen consecutive years is automatically vested in the plan. Our impatient Kevin left at the start of his eleventh year."

"Oh. I guess I never considered lasting that long."

Barbara walks on. "Or do you mean to say, you never imagined *Madame* lasting that long?"

"No. I didn't really think about it. Swear. I figured I'd come over, rehab my knee and then get back to performing."

"Your knee?" She pauses and looks down at my legs as if hoping to discover a prosthetic.

"It's gonna be fine." I balance on one foot to prove my point. "But the director didn't think I could get through eight shows a week, so he took me off stage during previews."

"Such terrible news." Barbara tosses the thorn aside and continues along the path. "What is this, *previews*?"

"Oh, it just means I missed opening night." My heart sinks as I catch up to her.

Barbara looks as me, ready to play therapist.

I decide to change the subject. "So go on…tell me more about this retirement thing."

She shakes her head as if I'm a lost cause. "Well, as I said, there is eligibility after fifteen years…and then, of course, when the time arrives…there is the final will and testament."

"Do all you guys get named in the will?"

"Of course. Any household employee who has dedicated a lifetime of service—like myself—will receive something in the end."

"That's awesome."

Barbara squeaks out a devious grin. "For instance, when Madame's brother passed away, his manservant collected enough to never work again…for a man who spent merely fifteen years."

"Really?"

"However, the day Madame is no longer with us," Barbara hesitates, now wearing an uncharacteristic look of despair, "I will be forced into retirement."

"So you can't imagine working for another family?"

She shakes her head *no*. "I will happily accept any amount Madame shall bequeath…and slip away—perhaps to an island in the sun."

The image of Barbara on the beach in black polyester tickles me rotten, but I don't let on. "What about getting in with an even bigger family...you know, use your connections." I'm reminded of my own career struggle for a fleeting instant. "Couldn't that happen?"

"It is impossible for me, Matthew. No one would be willing take a chance on this old gray goose." She smiles and nods ahead toward the exit. "Besides, there would be no prestige or honor in another household. Not after working for Madame. No one else could compare."

As we emerge—unscathed—from the giant cactus pass, Barbara's pager rings and startles us both. "I must return to Madame," she apologizes, already hurrying toward the house. "But I thank you for this stolen moment."

"See ya soon." I pause and watch Barbara leave, realizing that she and the rest of the staff are playing a waiting game. Everyone around here is basically keeping things in order, until the time comes to collect their retirement and/or inheritance checks. And it sounds like I've arrived in this house a little too late to take advantage of that deal. Shit.

I step forward and locate another of René's garden landmarks in the distance—water feature number seven. And recalling a shortcut to my room, I head toward the nearest trellised walkway. I glance down at my shirt and consider chucking it. It's ruined. There's no reason to keep it, except for posterity. But how could I dispose of it without anyone finding out? I can just see Barbara enlisting the staff to humiliate me, as she unfolds my dry, bloodstained t-shirt over the dinner table. Hell. I'll stash it in the bottom of my suitcase.

Once I step onto the shaded path and start toward my room, I scope out the backyard, and once again marvel at the splendor of this environment. Everything here is so vivid: the colors, the smells, the sights, and the sounds—not to mention these people, and their stories. Madame's world is full of heightened theatrical elements. I suppose I'm seeing it through fresh eyes, since I've never been totally alone in the backyard before. Where are all the gardeners?

The moment I round the bend, the great lawn comes into view, and a sudden spurt of excitement hits me. Fuck. I should write a show about this place! I could go back to New York and put these freaks on stage. Seriously. My own one-man show. A show in which I portray each and every one of these kooks. It would be a riot. This absurd world could be the hot-ticket event of next season.

A spontaneous *petit jeté* sends me forward.

The show is basically writing itself. Really. All I would have to do is reenact it: the characters, the comic situations, and the awkward feeling of being trapped in a place where I don't fit in. This will be my comeback.

I let out another small leap.

If my knee heals completely, René will have a few song and dance numbers; if it turns out just so-so, I'll simplify. I could do a sparse reading—one man/one music stand. Or I could go vaudeville; traipse around the stage with a moldy prop suitcase—plastered with faded travel stickers—and prattle on about my year overseas. Nostalgia sells.

I scan the lawn once more, and envision doing a few cartwheels, but quickly remind myself that that's not proper etiquette around here. So I stick to the path. I increase my walking tempo, straighten my back, tighten my ass, and cross my arms around my waist as if concealing a stomachache. And within seconds, my Barbara imitation comes out. I can hardly breathe, but I've got her nailed. "Vundebar dings."

A beat later, René's flamboyant sashay takes over my stride, and his vivacious swing takes control of my hips. "Mathieu," I say as I skip along the path, "good heavens, Mathieu, I would never confuse you and Kevin...preposterous." I bat my eyelashes and burst into laughter. I've got him to a T!

And faster than a strike of lightening, my spine straightens, my head juts forward, and my tempo slows a bit. I become

Alistair. The moment I achieve his alignment, his distinctive English accent flies out of my mouth. "Come off it, Matthew, you can't enact us on stage...you'd be sued for libel."

I break character and pause to catch my breath.

Ever since I arrived, I knew I'd been inwardly mocking these folks. But God, it feels good to finally let it out!

When I get back to my room, I race inside, grab the notebook I'd planned to use as my travel journal, and start scribbling ideas for the show. The Walk with René comes first because it's fresh. And as I recall the specifics, my hand can't keep up with my mind.

After The Walk, I stand up and experiment with each major character in a way I might have done for my physical acting class in college. But now it's on my terms. Physical Acting 101: a dancer's approach—embody the character's walk, add a gesture or physical tick, and allow the voice to emerge based on the physicality. And so what if I don't sound like they do in real life, no one will ever know the true story anyway.

Revved at the thought of portraying René, Barbara, Alistair, and the often-silent Bahir, I hit a roadblock. Madame. She poses the biggest challenge. How can I do justice to such an effortless woman? Her sense of ease is the very quality that makes her so tough to grasp. Fact is, Madame is so unpretentious, I bet Meryl Streep would even be stumped by her. She's going to take a lot of work.

I place my journal on the nightstand, toss my t-shirt into the garbage, and head toward the bathroom. Screw it. I'll have wardrobe distress another shirt when the time comes.

I turn on the shower and strip down.

I've got to find a nugget of truth in order to play Madame from the heart. Otherwise, she'll come off like another boring rich lady. She's more than that.

After I step into the shower, I close my eyes and allow the hot water to wash away the craziness of this morning.

So what *does* trigger authenticity?

5

Three days have passed since René took his fall and he's lost his confidence for doing The Walk. He's not calling me for exercise; neither is Madame. Word from the third floor has it, that Madame is still sick and she will spend a few nights in the hospital for observation. The estate is tingling with anticipation—not because Madame isn't doing well, but excited by the possibility of having an evening off. So when Barbara calls me to explain that she, Madame, and René will all be *out of casa* for the next forty-eight hours—therefore, I am free to do as I please—I conceal my excitement. And as soon as I hang up with Barbara, Alistair rings to invite me to join him for a boys' night out. I spontaneously accept, not sure where I'd go on my own anyway.

Come late afternoon, the household chores are finished and Madame is officially away. I meet Alistair by the rear gate, where we hop on his scooter and speed out through the service entrance. It's super hot and dusty, and Alistair's scooter isn't the most comfortable ride, but I don't care. I'm just glad to be free.

Within a half-mile from the compound walls, the two-lane country road narrows to one; we slow down a little and pass through a cluster of small clay houses—single room dwellings all smothered together. Turns out, there are a lot more people living in this shantytown than first meets the eye. It's hard to imagine. I can't even tell how some of these buildings could still be standing. Are they all actually inhabited?

The road widens and Alistair zooms onward. I'm overwhelmed by the hardship these villagers must endure, yet stunned to see smiles on the faces of the barefooted children playing on a mound of dirt nearby. Talk about contrast. I doubt Madame ever travels this back route. Of course she is aware that severe poverty exists—but witnessing this situation within a stone's throw of her property-line is shocking. This must be tough for her. Damn. If I had Madame's money, would I feel compelled to fix this situation. How much would it take to even make a dent?

When Alistair merges onto the main highway, I cough out a mouthful of dust. He speeds forward and yells over the noisy bike—something unintelligible about where we're headed.

"Sounds great!" I shout, as he changes lanes without so much as a glance.

The closer we get to town, the more intense the traffic becomes. We are swerving around like a carnival ride, much the same way Bahir drove home from the airport. Crazy. But this time, we have no protection: no doors, no windshield, no seat belts, and no helmets. It dawns on me that our behavior is stupid, but I love it. I can't remember the last time I felt so fucking *alive*!

About a half hour later, we arrive in Marrakech: faces dirty, hair mussed, and butts numb. Alistair parks the bike in the middle of a long row of other bikes that all look the same. After the parking attendant makes a chalk mark on the seat of the bike, we're off for our night on the town.

Standing curbside, it looks as though we'll never find a safe way to cross this six-lane street. Why can't we walk a few blocks up to the traffic light—wouldn't that be easier?

"That is the place to be...the heart of old Marrakech." Alistair points toward a huge crowd of people on the other side. "The famous central market," he says and gestures to the street sign, "Jemaa el Fna."

By the time I glance up to the sign, Alistair has broken into a jay-run across the street. I take a deep breath and dive after him, into a sea of honking cars, trucks, and mopeds. I figure if I survived clearing customs, I can escape this too.

Somehow, we make it to the other side, where Alistair plunges into the crowd, never once checking to see if I'm with him. I follow his tall frame and keep a keen eye on the back of his white shirt collar as he winds his way into the square. It appears that the locals have come here to sell their goods, perform random acts of entertainment, and pick the pockets of those tourists who look worthy of being picked. I can't get enough of this rambunctious mess.

First off, we see an old man weaving fortunes for anticipating followers who've gathered in a circle around him. Then, we pass a stall offering freshly squeezed orange juice, followed by a few booths piled high with mounds of ground spices. The intense colors of the spices are captivating. But the potent combination of cayenne pepper, chili powder, ground cumin, ginger, cinnamon, nutmeg, and turmeric makes me sneeze. Next, we hurry past a few stands selling sweet stuff—candied fruits and exotic nuts—but I still smell spice.

In the adjacent area, an herbalist sits cross-legged on the ground, selling dried bits of every imaginable plant, herb or seed. Some people are asking him for teas, others want his items au natural. And close to the herbalist, a troupe of Arab break-dancers upstages a struggling magician. Then, behind the dancers' area, an elderly medicine man sells potions and chants for those who wish to be healed. Hum. I wonder if this medicine man and the herbalist we passed earlier are in cahoots? I think they'd make a good team.

Around the next turn, the snake charmer and the monkey handler pose wild animals for a prime photo opportunity. The workers assure onlookers that no one will be harmed, as long as some coins are tossed into their tin can. And next to the animals, vendors with no official post have scattered blankets on the ground—offering everything from gumdrops to Drano.

Later, we see a guy making money off rows of dirty, unopened Coke bottles that are laid out on the ground in grid formation. The idea of his game is to hook a bottle by using a stick with fishing line and a wooden ring tied to the end. Many folks line up and pay to play, ignoring the fact that the dusty soda prize looks unappetizing.

I continue following Alistair, as he moves behind the crowded piazza, into a narrow alleyway full of little shops.

"Welcome to the souk, Matthew!" he yells, and pauses for me to catch up. "This area is quite extensive, so it's best we stick together in here." Alistair starts along the uneven roadway. "Even natives have been known to get lost in this labyrinth." He laughs. "Which means we don't stand a chance."

"It's awesome! Thanks for bringing me here. I've never seen anything like it."

"Throughout the Arab world," Alistair begins, reminding me of my least-favorite history teacher, "these bazaars are commonplace." He smiles. "But this one is quite special."

As we stroll the narrow passageways and wander without purpose, we find traditional local handicrafts in a kaleidoscope of colors. There are beautiful inlaid wooden boxes, decorative hanging lanterns, and tons of hand-woven rugs. Alongside some unidentified food items, we see lots of baked goods—some fresh, others not so fresh—and stacks of designer scarves, handbags, and shoes—probably knock-offs.

"Ramadan has officially ended," he shouts over the hum of the crowd, "so tonight is more turbulent than usual."

"It's unbelievable." I slow down, hoping he will too. "So what's Ramadan?" I hurry ahead again.

"Come on, Matthew, you know...the high holy days for the Muslims...but I don't believe they refer to it as *high* or *holy*."

"Oops. I didn't know about it. When did it start?"

"One month ago."

"For real?"

"Didn't you notice how sluggish the gardeners have been? They've been fasting during the daylight hours for the past month."

"Actually, no—I just thought they were overworked."

He stops. "They're ready to drop from not eating during the day, and wiped out from celebrating after dark."

"Sounds like a vicious cycle."

"*Vicious*, I'm not so sure, but they do like to play it up."

"Well, it must be challenging, don't you think?"

"So, they should quit their religion if they don't like it!" He turns to walk away.

The instant Alistair steps forward, a rogue mule, pulling a rickety wooden cart, appears out of nowhere. I grab his arm and hold him in place as the cart passes, only inches to spare. I look him in the eyes. "Maybe that was a warning from God?" I nod toward the back of the cart.

"Whose God," Alistair smirks and pulls away from my grip, "yours, mine, or theirs?" He marches on.

A desert chill rushes in, as the shops in the souk begin to close. More carts and scooters flee the alleyways; mangy dogs and feral cats meander the streets in search of scraps. Some couples walk hand in hand, oblivious to the stench of urine, dog shit, and rotting garbage. And as the crowd continues to thin, Alistair and I agree it'll be safer to head back to where we started.

Once we get back to the main square, I notice a bunch of outdoor eateries off to one side. Row after row of picnic tables are jam-packed with hungry customers and a thick cloud of smoke rises up from the grilled lamb, chicken, and beef. It's hellacious commotion in smell-o-rama—*audacious*, when compared to our sterile life inside the house.

Standing here at the heart of Marrakech, I get a sense of the strength and spirit of these people, and this city. I'm flooded with the sensation of a warm embrace under the chilly evening sky—or maybe that warm embrace is just someone's hand reaching into my back pocket?

Moments later, ready to leave the square, we see Bahir walking up ahead of us. Alistair tells me Bahir is with his wife Hessa—and their two small children. We rush forward to say hello. And after Alistair exchanges a few words of Arabic with the family the whole group turns toward me. With socially adept flair, Alistair introduces me to Bahir's family as if I'm an honored guest.

I receive them, as if they're attending at a post-show meet-and-greet. "Bonjour, Bahir…Hessa."

Alistair converses in French with Bahir and Hessa, while I make animated smiley faces with the kids. The little boy must be about seven and the girl around nine or ten. They are adorable. And Bahir's wife is strikingly beautiful—her dark eyes radiate between the loose pleats of her silk head wrap as she allows Bahir to do the talking.

When Alistair offers to treat everyone to pizza and ice cream at a nearby restaurant, the children bounce up and down with excitement, begging their parents to accept. And without much discussion, Alistair and Bahir lead us away from the noisy crowd, onto a quiet tree-lined street. The kids grab my hands and swing my arms back and forth as we follow behind them.

I look back to confirm that Hessa is okay at the rear.

She nods.

I think she's happy to have a moment to herself.

A few blocks later, the children and I nearly hyperventilate as we repeatedly practice counting from one to ten in French, at breakneck speed—first counting forward, then backward. Our annoying singsong rhythm and little walking dance gets some unwanted attention. But we refuse to stop—we're having a blast.

By the time we arrive at the restaurant, the kids and I are still caught up in silliness, and the jovial mood continues through dinner. Conversation about favorite school subjects, sports, icky homework, and what board games are the most fun, makes dinner seem ordinary. Up until now, I'd only seen Bahir as a driver and never considered his life outside the house. I knew he went somewhere at night, since he wasn't eating dinner at Madame's, but that's as far as my thoughts went.

Outside the restaurant, the children each give me a big hug goodbye. We've become friends. And as I watch Bahir's clan walk away, I consider the millions of Muslim families around the world who are just like Hessa and Bahir—loving parents, putting their children through school, and working to provide a comfortable upbringing. I then wonder how many of these families have suffered or become casualties of war due to American involvement.

I glance toward Alistair, ready to initiate a conversation about American politics—and my shame associated with the actions of the United States military—when I become distracted, by a dusting of Parmesan cheese on his upper lip. "Thanks for dinner," I blurt. "That was fun."

"Bahir is a good man," he says with a sigh.

And the way he watches them leave makes me think that Bahir could have been the gardener Alistair was banging when Barbara interrupted. But I can't tell.

I don't think I'll ask him right now.

"Care for a drink?" Alistair interrupts my thought.

"Sure." I flick my index finger under the tip of my nose thinking he might take the hint to dust his upper lip. He doesn't.

After walking a few blocks, we enter an upscale bar full of middle-aged, pasty-white businessmen in suits. In addition to the businessmen, one-third of the clientele is comprised of the most beautiful Moroccan women in the known universe. These women are smoking hot, and the men are about as sexually appealing as the Quaker Oats guy. Weird combination.

In the corner of the bar, on a platform beneath a thatched-roof, a three-piece band is performing *Margaritaville*. The lead singer stumbles on a few of the Jimmy Buffett lyrics, but he has enough pizzazz to keep this gang jamming, and no one seems to care. The intoxicated businessmen sing and sway with glasses held high, while the exquisite women pose at various spots throughout the room. Some of the women tote cocktail trays while others slither solo—tracking their prey. Alistair and I make our way to the bar and find a place to stand next to the fully occupied bar stools.

Drinks now in hand and nowhere to turn, Alistair and I are subconsciously bouncing to the beat of a Gloria Estephan medley. And it's not long before we too are caught up in the party mood right along with the rest of the good ole boys.

Hanging near the bar and feeling no pain, I abruptly notice — what feels like — a foot lodged in my crotch.

I look down and discover a perfectly pedicured bare foot, attached to a slender bronzed shin, that belongs to a gorgeous young cross-legged lady who has swiveled her barstool to face in my direction. With greater dexterity than my aesthetician's fingers, this girl uses her foot to inscribe a few flirty S-curves, followed by a couple of taunting figure-eights — she continues her pattern *ad nauseam*.

Before long, I notice the hottie sitting next to my babe, who is offering Alistair the same foot treatment I'm getting. Alistair is standing at attention — in more ways than one — but I'm not.

I stare at the foot in my crotch. Too bad this girl doesn't know what she's up against.

The last time I had a boner in the presence of a woman, I was on summer break between High School and College; making out with this foxy Italian girl on her parents' living room sofa. I couldn't believe my plumbing was working the way it should. But when it came time for us to move things up to her room, she literally started to move things. She walked over, unplugged the television set and picked it up right off the console. And this was not a streamlined portable TV. This was an old Zenith box set. The thing was huge — with simulated-woodgrain side panels. My friend mentioned wanting to take it with her up to her bedroom, so I offered to help. But after she glanced down at the modest bulge in my chinos, she declined my offer and just stood there — holding the TV in front of her chest. Awkwardly, she waddled toward the staircase, motioned me toward the front door and bid me goodnight. I remember losing my hard-on as she carried the gigantic TV upstairs on her own and I stepped outside. At the time, I hoped she'd become barren due to the electromagnetic exposure from the warm television. But now, all these years later, I can happily report that she and her partner Gail are doing just fine — raising two kids in Muncie.

Well, my sexy friend here on the barstool must have developed a Charlie-horse — since she just stopped massaging my limp dick. She is looking at me with a peeved expression, and strapping on her silvery stiletto. And with her shoe securely fastened, she gets up, and drags her friend away from the bar. So Alistair and I move onto the two vacant stools and order two more drinks.

While we wait for our next round to arrive, I think I should apologize for driving the women away. Alistair is disappointed — but then again, his face always looks this way so it's hard to decipher the truth.

Several drinks later, after having inhaled enough secondhand smoke to warrant buying a pack of Nicorette gum for tomorrow morning, we decide to get out of this bar. We accelerate toward the front door as the businessmen sing along to *Y.M.C.A.* Now *that's* where I draw the line.

Once outside, reeking of smoke and liquor, Alistair takes off with a peppy spring in his step. "Let's go!" he shouts, all cheery drunk.

"Where to," I ask, rehearsing my English accent.

"Anywhere but here," he scoffs.

When we arrive at the six-lane highway near the main square, Alistair shrugs at the traffic and heads toward the crosswalk. Hum. Maybe his judgment improves after a few drinks? And after we cross the street with the other civilized pedestrians, we soon find ourselves back at the row of bikes where we parked the scooter. I hope we're not headed home. The attendant locates Alistair's bike, wipes the seat clean, and we're back in the saddle for more unprotected, high speed, weaving and dodging — only this time we're intoxicated.

Luckily, it's not long before we arrive at our next watering hole. We park the bike and maneuver our way up the stairs into a grand stone entranceway of a nightclub—illuminated by two giant flaming torches and flanked by a pair of impressive bouncers. The guards check our passports, demand *six hundred dirham apiece*, and then give us a solid, hands-on, full-body pat down. Shit. I think I just spent fifty bucks. But I guess the aggressive grope-job makes it worth the cover charge.

Once inside, we make our way through a grandiose open-air passageway lined with more of the enormous torches—a cliché set design for *Tales of the Arabian Knights*—and we soon enter a giant foyer, confronted by one massive staircase leading up, and another spiraling down.

"Downstairs," Alistair shouts over the throbbing music and heads down, "we'll have more fun downstairs." He continues yelling over his shoulder, but I can't understand everything he's saying—something about upstairs being reserved for rich Saudis. "It's a real bore up there."

"I'm fine wherever."

After we hit ground level, Alistair bellies up to the bar with the two drink passes that were included in our costly admission, and retrieves a complimentary pink concoction for each of us. The stingingly sweet drink goes down in one gulp, and the next thing I know we're flailing about on the dance floor. The lights are flickering, the beat is tribal-techno, and Alistair's moves remind me of the first time I saw my dad dance when I was a kid.

Dad tore up the floor at my cousin's wedding, jamming to Elton John's newly-released *The Bitch is Back*. Looking back now, I realize he moved with a '60s swim/hitch-hiker/pony, fused with a '50s twist. He had on a brown leisure suit to complement his white-man-afro hairstyle. His bushy brown mustache, and his gold chains dangling beneath the half-buttoned western-painted silk dress shirt, made him the latest fashion trend. When he really got going, he'd expose his top teeth, bite down on his lower lip, and bop his head to the beat. Extra cool. Alistair is probably a little stiffer than dad was—but he's close.

The club music suddenly morphs into a pounding rendition of *Into The Groove*, without the Madonna lyrics—and I make eye contact with the hottest Moroccan guy in the place. He's on the opposite side of the room, staring directly at me. I stare into his huge dark brown eyes—and start through the crowd in his direction. I dance across the floor as if I'm auditioning for a '90s boy band. I'm on. The dancing, the eye contact, the lighting, the Madonna mix—the whole thing—is a moment of staggering synchronicity. And the guy is perfect: tall, with light brown skin; dark brown hair, tightly clipped; and a lean hairless physique. Nice. So I guess it's *farewell* to any anxiety I had concerning Muslim men—this guy is too damn good to pass up.

I continue closer to my target with more dazzling moves than David Copperfield. And I'm almost there, when my man whips out a long-stemmed peacock feather. He holds the feather in front of one eye and trembles it hypnotically. Then, he performs a few snaps with the authority of a dominatrix wielding her flogging device. I might be in love. Next, he uses it as a feather duster, exploring every crevasse of his taut body. He taunts me like a lion tamer, then pricks me on the shoulder with the stem end of his prop. We've made contact.

Before I know it, his feather disappears into his back pocket and he wraps his arms around my waist. My heart pounds faster than the beat of the music as we straddle each other's thighs and execute a few compulsory lambada moves. He's unbelievable. My fucking knee better not go out from all the writhing. We continue dancing in silky contrast to the heavy bass line of the never-ending song, and we're amazing to watch—at least I *think* we are.

We haven't been embraced for long, when a mammoth bouncer walks over and separates us. He gives us a stern look as we continue dancing solo, like two young Catholic boys who have just been scolded by Sister Mary Diesel. I leave the dance floor, totally embarrassed. I forgot. I'm on Muslim soil. Homosexual acts are criminal. Shit. Our overt public display was not only unacceptable, it was unlawful.

My buddy follows me to an alcove near the bar, where we sit and exchange standard hook up conversation — his in broken English and mine in elementary French. His teeth are stunning, and his eyes light up when he speaks. He's going on about something that seems important to him. And although I can't understand more than every third word, I sit back and enjoy watching the movements of his perfectly sexy mouth.

A few minutes later, Alistair walks over with some random woman in tow, and the two of them strike up conversation with my man as if they're all old friends. Alistair is super drunk and wants to leave with this woman, and I'm super drunk and want to go home with this man. So when my guy confesses that he lives right down the block and can accommodate everyone in two separate rooms, the four of us stumble up the stairs and exit out of the club through the torchlit tunnel.

One block from the disco, we arrive outside a plain two-story apartment building. And the moment he opens the door, I see a living room full of various laundry items hanging from a tangled network of clotheslines. The clothes stretch back and forth in every direction, from one side of the room to the other. And the scent of fresh detergent in the air helps further enhance the ambience of this surrealistic interior décor.

I watch Alistair and his lady dash through the field of laundry and disappear into a back bedroom — like a pair of heat-seeking missiles. My man laughs at them as he leads me by the hand, over to the futon/sofa that occupies most of one wall. I sit down, look up at the laundry lines, and contemplate his assortment of sexy underwear. I suddenly wonder what, if anything, my date is wearing underneath his skin-tight jeans. Without saying a word, he stands over me, places his hand behind my head, and gently presses his groin up against my cheek. His package feels much better than that pesky big toe at the Quaker Oats bar. But I hope he's not one of those guys who likes to shove the back of my head the whole time I'm going down on him. That is *so* irritating.

I soon hear muffled grunts and groans coming from Alistair's room, and figure we'd better get busy before my ride decides to leave. And just then, he leans down and kisses me.

From here, things unravel quickly. Both of our shirts come off and belts fly to the floor. He's into playing rough and enjoys wrestling around. It appears that the wrestling match is an excuse for our clothes to be accidentally stripped away. I think we're getting naked by chance, rather than by choice.

As we proceed with lots of fast-paced rubbing, hugging, and intense squeezing, we're on and off the futon multiple times; several pieces of clothing have already fallen off the lines. Every so often, I attempt to slow him down. But he keeps going, whipping me around like a rag doll. I realize it's best to just play along with the charade and see where it goes, rather than resist. So I do. He's fun. And by the time we're both naked, he stands me up, grabs my arms, holds them behind my back, shoves me against the nearest wall, and starts fucking me between the thighs.

Legs perfectly straight, I cross my ankles to offer him a snug fit as he continues to pump uncontrollably. I pant with artificial pleasure, which seems to turn him on even more, but this position isn't actually comfortable for me—or my balls.

Racing toward the finish line, he tosses me onto the futon and thrusts his dick between my imaginary tits. I sink my ribcage in hopes of gaining cleavage and let out a feminine whimper. He moans.

"Yes...Yes...Yes," I shout, which seems to drive him right to the edge. I think I might be the woman of his dreams.

From time to time, I hear Alistair's girl screaming, "Oui... oui...oui," as if she's playing the same game I'm playing. Her high-pitched squeals make me laugh to myself. But I keep my game face on, and try not to distract my grinding comrade. Ouch.

He plants another rough kiss on my mouth, and follows it with a row of suctioned kisses traveling down my torso. And just when he reaches my navel, his phone rings. Fuck. I hope he ignores it. Even though I'm chafed from all this friction, it feels damn good to be getting laid.

I pretend not to hear the phone. But by the time the second ring happens, my man is gone. He bolts away and grabs up the receiver as if he too were on standby for Madame.

Flat on the futon, I stare up at the clotheslines and overhear him speaking Arabic. It sounds like he's upset. But what do I know of his language? I've picked up a total of three words so far: *inshallah* translates to *God willing*; *suckura*, or something close, means *sugar*; and *shohcran* means *thank you*. That's it. And those three might not even be accurate.

He hangs up the phone, returns to the sofa, and gives me a devastated hug. "Je dois partir."

"What happened?" I ask as we both search for our clothes. "Can I come with you?"

I find my underwear while he pulls on his jeans.

"No. I go alone. My mother…" he pauses, turns to me, and takes my face in his hands, "my mother…she is dead."

"What?"

He stares at me. "My mother…she is dead," he repeats, devoid of emotion.

I freeze.

No longer worried about locating my socks, I actually connect with him for the first time since we met. "Oh, no. I'm so sorry," I say, stunned to be caught up in such an intimate moment with a total stranger. "I mean, je suis désolé."

His face glazes over. "I go now," he says in monotone and turns to remove a fresh shirt from the nearest line.

Fully dressed, we take hands and walk toward the front door. But before he opens it, I pull him in for a hug. "Maybe we'll meet again someday." I realize it's unlikely.

"Also, me." His tears begin to flow.

As our embrace strengthens, I look down past his shoulder and see a ceramic vase on the end table with his prop peacock feather resting inside. Hell. Tonight started out so well. I never imagined it would finish like this.

We're still hugging near the front door, when Alistair and his girl come charging out of their room. The girl, wearing only a bra and panties, escorts Alistair outside and immediately reenters the apartment. My man lets go of me to tell her what has happened. So, as he brings her up to speed, I slip out the front door. There's not much more I can do.

The moment I shut the door, Alistair rolls his eyes at me. "For Christ's sake," he says and walks away, "not every goodbye is sentimental...but I hope you had yourself a good shag...I sure as hell did."

I don't respond to him as we walk back to the scooter — and I don't think he even notices. But one thing's for sure. I've already decided it's best not to talk about that guy or his mother. Otherwise, it'll become the topic of tomorrow night's dinner conversation. And I don't think that's fair. Up until now, I've considered all the staff gossip and jabbing to be harmless fun, but it doesn't seem right to me, to turn that guy's loss it into another house story.

After we fetch the bike from the few that remain, we start our drive home in the frosty early morning air. There is hardly any traffic as we speed away from town toward the house. And the whole evening seems like a blur. I hold my arms around Alistair's waist, duck my head down to block the cold breeze, and reconsider my decision to leave that apartment. On one hand, I could have stayed to comfort him, but on the other, I've got to go back to Madame's — or face scrutiny later. If Barbara ever found out about how I walked out on a grieving one-night stand, my interrogation would be severe. I can't deal with her ridicule. My man will be okay since his friend is with him, right?

Damn. I can't believe we didn't exchange info.

I don't even know his name.

6

Christmas came and went last week—as did New Year's a few days ago. Not long ago, I told Alistair we should do something special. "You know, a little holiday party," I'd said. "Go ahead, sounds brilliant, knock yourself out," he answered, as if he could give a shit.

But I couldn't gain any momentum with the staff, so I lost interest. Alistair never called me on it, and everyone worked through the holidays like any other day. No big deal. I mean, I didn't expect to have a traditional Christmas—in Morocco—but failing to acknowledge New Year's seemed totally strange. Guess I'll have to double up next year.

And to make matters worse, Madame is still not home. Supposedly, she and René decided to take a vacation after she checked out of the clinic—but no one actually knows when they will return. On the upside, Barbara is with them, so that shifts the dynamic amongst the staff. A much softer mood guides the house—and that's nice. Although I do have to admit, it's tough being obsolete.

I'm running out of new ideas for the show. And solo yoga in my room is getting stale fast. Really, how is Broadway going to buy a show in which nothing happens? In fact, it's been so boring recently, I think I might become the first personal trainer to ever develop bedsores while on the job. Maybe I should close Act One by baring my blisters—the big reveal!

Well, regardless of how I intend to shock the audience before sending them out to the lobby, everything around here is getting on my nerves. I can't believe that even something as special as having a laundress at my disposal could become irritating. But it has. No joke. The minute the clothes come off my back, little elves remove them from my room. Then, later the same day, the clothing is magically returned to my armoire—pressed, pleated, folded, and starched. Seems great. Except it's uncomfortable to know that my co-workers handle my underwear more than I am. Weird. And first thing this morning, I found myself compulsively adjusting the angle of the soap dispenser in my bathroom. When I looked down at the counter and realized that I had aligned my cosmetic products from left to right in the exact order I planned to use them, I worried that my brain had been shifted to autopilot. In the reflection of the bathroom mirror, I noticed how I'd prepared a freshly creased triangle of toilet paper on top of the roll. What's happening to me? This is my private bathroom. Have the housemaids infiltrated my mind in some subversive act of domestic abduction?

But here I sit—trying to get online at the staff computer in the kitchen—while everyone else goes about morning business as usual. The Internet signal is still shaky and almost every time I'm lucky enough to get on, I soon get bumped off with a message that reads:

> We are sorry to inform you that you have been temporarily blocked from this website. Your IP Address—or perhaps someone from the same geographical area as you—has been requesting large amounts of content in a short amount of time. This has caused your IP Address to be flagged as spyware or some other malware. In general, we do not allow bots, spiders, or crawlers to access our website.

Yeah. I wish I could have a hand in something this exciting and deceptive, to serve at the helm of this bot/spider business, to participate in international cyber-sabotage. But the truth is, I'm not savvy enough for that line of work—or driven enough to care.

Success—here we go—an email from mom:

Hi Matt, Merry Christmas! Hope you're having a great day.
Did Santa make the rounds in Morocco?
Sorry I missed your call the other night,
I was out with the girls at a daiquiri shindig.
Thinking of you. Talk soon. Love, Mom

Great—even mom is out partying, while I'm here, shackled in paradise. Oh, and I love how she mentioned the daiquiri party, but failed to give its full name—*Dildos & Daiquiris*. That's right, my swinging mother is obsessed with these twenty-first century parties—à la Tupperware—where women get drunk and order sex-toys from a catalogue. The last time we talked about it, I was too embarrassed to hear the details. But mom quickly justified the parties on three levels: one, they always assign a designated driver; two, the hostess makes a good commission on stuff the girls are going to sneak off and buy anyway; and three, ten percent of the proceeds from each party goes toward research and development of new earth-friendly/non-toxic toys.

Bump.

Shit. That damn spider message again—and some pop-up ad about cellulite.

Thoroughly distracted by this stupid advertisement for diet pills, I become paranoid about developing a paunch to go with my bedsores. And before I know it, I dart out of the kitchen, run back to my room, and plot out my own prison cell workout.

I've got to change things up; no more boring Yoga.

I take a few minutes to choreograph a half-assed step-routine to do on the low ottoman, and set up a hopscotch course using the throw pillows as landmarks. I put on some music and dive into my first real aerobic workout since I got here. Based on my raunchy moves at the disco, I think my knee can handle it.

About twenty minutes later, right in the middle of doing pushups—feet up on the bed, hands on the floor—the telephone rings.

"Allô, Matt," I pant over a blaring Whitney Huston track.

"Are you all right?" Barbara asks.

I peek at the clock. Shit. Ten forty-five. Are they back?

"Sure. What's up?"

"Madame has returned. Report to the terrace at once."

Click.

I shut off the music and get a glimpse of my sweaty, blotchy, red face in the mirror. Fuck. I look like a nuclear plant worker who has just been hosed down after radioactive exposure. I can't go to Madame like this.

After a quick cold shower, I take another look in the mirror—Pillsbury-doughboy having a hot flash. Hell.

The phone rings again.

I answer and act calm.

Barbara is perplexed as to why I haven't left yet.

"Oh, I was just out the door when I heard the phone ring," I ramble, fumbling to get dressed. "So I came back, to see what's up. So...what's up?"

"Madame is waiting," she hangs up.

Damn. I fly out the door.

Minutes later, I round the corner of the house and sprint toward the service stairs to Madame's room. I charge up the spiral staircase, mindful of my knee with every step. And the moment I step out of the darkened stairwell onto the sunny rooftop garden, I spot Barbara on the far side near the trellised workout area. She's annoyed.

I walk across the large patio area in her direction, trying to appear cool, but I'm not sure I can play this off.

"Matthew, I cannot understand how a five-minute walk should take seven. There is no excuse for such behavior."

With no explanation for my tardiness, I stay quiet.

"Well. Today, it does not matter. Madame has changed her mind."

"Seriously?" I look toward the workout area and see that Madame's seat is empty. I glance at my watch. It's a hair past eleven. "Go tell her we can still do it."

"Madame will see you tomorrow at eleven sharp. Not *eleven-o-one*."

Fuck. Did Madame actually cancel because I was late, or is this another one of Barbara's games? I smirk. "Whatever." I turn to leave, and swallow my impulse to let Barbara have it.

"Matthew!"

"Yeah?" I turn around, as if concealing brass knuckles.

"You understand...what it means to be *at the ready*?"

Duh. "Yeah. I get it." Bitch. "See ya tomorrow at eleven."

Totally disappointed, I head toward the service stairs.

The air is still; not a dog bark to be heard.

And even when Barbara reenters the house behind me— still—no dogs. Dead calm. This isn't normal.

After I climb down and exit the stairwell, Alistair appears on the walkway in front of me. He's walking toward the gazebo, carrying two gravy boats in his white-gloved hands. I wave as if he might not see me. "Hey, what's up?"

He gives me his understated/unconcerned look and keeps going. "I could ask the same of you."

I cross the lawn to meet him inside the gazebo. The lunch table is only set for two. Darn. "Oh. I just went upstairs to work with Madame, but it fizzled."

He places the empty gravy boats on his side-station and lifts an eyebrow. "Madame and René are in town at the moment." He moves to the table. "Of course she's not having a session."

"How do you know?"

Alistair starts into his tinkering routine. "They returned from holiday late last night, but Madame arose early and decided to stop in on a sick friend before lunch."

"Then why'd Barbara call me upstairs for a workout?"

"Obviously, she takes you for a fool."

My face heats.

"Why don't you go upstairs and give her a piece of your mind?"

"Uh, yeah. I probably should." My neck tightens—reminded of being put in the middle of my parents' divorce when I was a kid.

"Go ahead. March up those stairs and tell her to *piss off*." Alistair exits the gazebo toward the house.

I follow him a few steps down the walkway. "Yeah. I think I will."

"Face it, if you let her get away with this one," he stops and looks at me, "things will get worse. Trust me."

I freeze as Alistair continues toward the house.

But before I know it, I'm already upstairs—bolting across the terrace toward Madame's bedroom. What the hell am I thinking? Barbara could fire me. But Alistair's right, I have to assert myself.

As I approach the corner of the house, ready to enter the workout area, I hear music playing. It's not the call to prayer this time, it's some random '80s rock tune, coming from a transistor radio or an old cassette player.

Depeche Mode? The Clash?

I pause near the French doors that lead into Madame's office, and spy through to the other side. Fuck. It's Barbara—she's reclining on a chaise lounge; her uniform unbuttoned and rolled off her shoulders. Her stockings are peeled down to her ankles and I think she's wearing Madame's sunglasses. She's holding a cold drink, leafing through the pages of a magazine, and turning the pages fast enough to fan her sweaty chest. Is this her way of practicing early retirement?

Watching her, I imagine how I'd inflate this moment for the show. I could choreograph an elaborate struggle with Barbara and make this into a scene in which I duke it out against myself on the upstairs balcony—*mano-a-mano*—like some Errol Flynn movie. But I'm not living an old swashbuckler. This is for real. I have to confront her; tell her to bug off.

The longer I watch, the more my temper dissipates.

She's lonely.

This is her entire world.

And *so what* if she wants to play games to control the minions around her. I don't have to buy into her bullshit. I can rise above it. Case closed. Issue resolved.

But as I shift to leave, the song ends and Barbara spots me through the French doors. Crap.

She lowers her magazine and glares in my direction.

I hold steady and stare her down with the intensity of a bull threatening its matador—my nostrils might actually be flaring. This feels fantastic; I refuse to break.

Even as the next Mode/Clash song begins, Barbara holds my gaze and doesn't move a muscle.

Neither do I.

Another beat passes before she randomly gives in. Her shoulders drop, she shoots me a wicked smile, and flips to the next page of her magazine.

And even though a huge sense of victory washes over me, I refuse to budge. I hold my sneer for one more moment, just to let her know I mean business.

Then, as she sips of her drink, I walk away—justified. I've leveled the playing field. Yeah, bitch. Take that.

7

The following morning, before I get out the door for coffee, my phone rings. "Good morning, Mathieu!" René sings out like Debbie Reynolds. "I am calling to let you know that we are departing Paradis this afternoon, en route to Burgflucht."

"Cool," I blurt, excited for a change, "where's that?"

"Austria, my dear boy, our Alpine retreat. And it might be downright cold...but not to worry," he continues, "dearest Olivia will be with us on the mountain, there to make things pleasant... you two have met already, yes?"

"No, no, not face to face, only through," I hesitate, thinking he might find the word *email* mundane, "correspondence."

"Well, then, as you are well aware, she is positively charming." He sets the phone down—without hanging up.

I hold the line and say nothing. Nut-job. He's the one who called me.

I can hear him frantically typing, banging away on his keyboard, and mumbling to himself. So is there more to the story about meeting Olivia—what the hell does he want? I continue to hold; if I hang up first, I'll be busted for sure.

I finally gather the nerve to speak. "René...will there be anything else?"

"Oh, Mathieu, is it you?" He picks up the receiver. "How thrilling you called...did you hear that we will be moving to the mountain today?"

I decide to go for it. "Earth-shattering!"

"Ta-ta, Mathieu…see you on board." René places the phone down on his desk and continues typing.

I let things linger for a minute, then hang up, and dodge out of my room. He must be losing it.

When I get to the kitchen—first to arrive for staff coffee—I find Alistair setting the table, clanging cups and saucers. From the look of frustration on his veiny forehead, I know better than to interject. Just let him ride this mood out. As I sit down, he smacks a wooden trivet in the center of the table, and exits into the butler's pantry.

Next, Barbara enters from the side door, carrying three empty wine bottles. She crosses over to the distant recycling bin.

Alistair reenters with a tray of coffee and milk and sits down at the table with me.

Barbara acts too busy to notice—reorganizing dishes in a nearby cupboard—but she sees us.

Barbara's presence soon becomes so annoying, that Alistair gets up with an audible huff and walks back out to the pantry.

And the moment he leaves, Barbara comes over to the table to pour herself a cup of coffee. I wonder if she wants to talk about yesterday on the terrace? She stands over me with one hand on her hip, purposely banging the teaspoon inside the cup as she stirs in a spot of milk. Then, she snaps the spoon down onto her saucer with such authority that I jump. She takes a sip but refuses to make eye contact with me.

I'm not apologizing to her, if that's what she expects.

The instant Alistair returns with bread and jam, Barbara leaves again—abandoning her coffee.

Alistair sits down once more, and we share some random silent pouring, reaching, jamming, buttering, sugaring, stirring, and sipping.

"Matthew, did you hear…we're moving to Austria this afternoon?"

"Yeah. René called me."

"Lord, help us...wait until you see him on board the plane." Alistair takes a sip of coffee. "That man will behave worse than a child on Christmas morning."

"To be honest, I'm surprised I'm going with you guys."

"What are you talking about?"

"Well, it's been a long time since I worked with her, and I—"

"Calm down, boy. Madame will start anew once we are settled at Burgflucht."

Barbara walks back in, carrying three more wine bottles, and Alistair gives me a look to imply she's crazy. It's as if she is going off stage, downing the bottles like some wino, and then reentering with the empties. I sip my coffee and try not to laugh— but her drinking problem is definitely being written into the show.

As she crosses to the recycling area, Alistair watches. "That cow," he says under his breath with a vindictive tone, "she's a bundle of nerves today because she'll have to deal with me on the flight later. The only staff traveling on the jet today will be you and I..." he pauses as Barbara leaves again. "And that cow."

I reach for a slice of toast, realizing we've never discussed his past relationship with Barbara. "Oh, I thought she was ticked off with me about yesterday."

"Did you stick it to her good?"

"For sure. She knows she can't mess with me now." I smile and slather on more jam.

"Good for you, Matthew." Alistair dunks his dry bread into his coffee. "Just watch, how she behaves on the flight. She'll pretend to be sick and need to sleep the entire time." He plugs his mouth with the wet bread and stands up. Chewing away, he swigs down the rest of his coffee and begins to walk out of the kitchen. "Not that there's anything worth discussing when it comes to that cow."

By the time he's gone, I realize I've lost my appetite. I'd better get packed.

So here it is, only eleven a.m., and Bahir is driving us to the airport in Marrakech—so much for leaving this afternoon. For the past half hour, I've been stuffed into the middle seat of the minivan, with Alistair and Barbara on either side, and the house dogs piled up on our laps. There is luggage up front and in back; dog hair and tension flying. Apparently, the dogs have to clear customs with us—poor Charlotta hasn't stopped shaking since we left the house. And Antoinette and Celeste are anxious too, but at least they're getting it out of their system—one yap at a time.

Once we arrive at the airport, Bahir unloads the baggage and passes it off to a security guard, while Alistair and I corral the dogs toward the entrance. Barbara hurries inside to the restroom—acting like she doesn't know us—and Bahir jumps back in the driver's seat, toots goodbye and leaves.

The plan is for us to get through security with the dogs and board the fifteen-passenger jet, before Madame and René—both with international passport clearance—get chauffeured onto the runway. I'm having flashbacks of my horrendous arrival in Marrakech and can't imagine how this plan is going to work. But after we step inside the—private departures only—terminal, I realize that today is going to be different. Completely civilized.

And sure enough, within minutes, we are cleared through to the other side, boarded into a van, and driven out onto the runway to meet the plane.

The moment we come to a stop, the doors release automatically and the dogs scamper out of the van. The animals move like a single, thunderous ball of fur as they bound up the stairs into the plane. I laugh. Even tiny Charlotta scrambles fast enough to avoid burning her little paws on the hot tarmac. These creatures have done this before.

After bypassing the crew, Alistair climbs the stairs and leads the way toward the rear. I follow close behind and feel completely spoiled as I greet the pilot and enter this aircraft. First off, I see a nice bar area up front, followed by a few groupings of roomy bucket seats throughout the center of the cabin. The place reeks of new car smell, and fresh flower arrangements are everywhere. I love how the flooring offers a nice cushiony rebound with each step.

I follow Alistair toward the back. He walks with his chin tucked down, almost skimming the back of his head along the ceiling—reminiscent of The Headless Horseman. But by the time he and I reach the staff seating, the dogs have already occupied the two inward facing banquettes that line the rear of the plane.

When Alistair steps into the restroom and closes the door, I look behind me, only to find that Barbara is still outside talking with the crew. So here I am, alone with these dogs; nowhere to sit. The dogs are sprawled out in such a way as to make it impossible to snuggle in without disturbing them. If I move them to the floor I might be brought up on charges—but if I don't, it's going to be a very long flight from here to Austria.

I hear Alistair flush the toilet and see him open the bathroom door. Yuck. He didn't wash his hands.

Then, without blinking, Alistair walks over and clears both banquettes in a single swipe. "Get down!" he scolds, as the pooches catch their bearings. "And stay down!"

"Thanks," I say, as he plops down and a small cloud of dog hair floats into the air. "I wasn't sure how to deal with them."

"A swift kick in the liver is the only remedy." He grabs a newspaper near his seat.

I sit down facing him, and just when I do, the buttery leather upholstery nearly sends me sliding onto the floor. Luckily, Alistair is already caught up with a front-page story and fails to notice my mishap.

Soon, a fancy black car pulls up outside the plane.

The house dogs bark wildly and rush to the front of the plane—it must be Madame. I watch out the window, as Madame and René approach the stairs. Madame seems fine. René is his usual self.

And it's not long before the dogs calm down and obediently follow Barbara toward the back. Once she arrives, she pauses as if deciding where to sit. "Matthew, I am a bit under the weather," she mentions, "may I curl up in this corner next to you?"

I politely accept Barbara's request and Alistair peers over his paper as if to say *I told you so*. Then, as soon as Madame and René are loaded up front, the pilot announces that our flight has been cleared for departure. Apparently there's no delay, here in the kingdom of the elite.

As we taxi onto the runway, René impatiently moves from one seat to the next, adjusting the lighting and checking the recline-ability at each spot. He's acting like a neurotic Goldilocks, in search of her perfect chair, but no one seems to care. Madame sits all the way up front, reading a book in a forward-facing seat — ignoring René. I love how calm she remains, regardless of what is going on around her.

And soon after we're airborne, the three flight attendants begin offering the five-star treatment to Madame and René — hot towels, cozy slippers, sleeping masks. Jeez. How far are we going? My stomach lets out an embarrassing rumble as the crew starts bringing out platters of goodies — all of which Madame turns down. I wonder if I should've brought my own snack?

Luckily, the attendants eventually come to the back of the plane and offer us the same degree of service.

Barbara orders hot tea. Alistair requests sparkling water.

"Ginger ale sounds good," I add.

Alistair looks at me. "Order what you wish," he demands, "these girls will do as we please."

Once the flight attendants return from the galley with our drinks in hand, Barbara mentions she would like some honey, *please*, and Alistair matches her with a request for a few drops of bitters, *if you would be so kind*. Next, Barbara wants lemon, and then changes her mind to milk and lastly cream. Soon after, Alistair demands a squeeze of lime and then decides he needs more ice on the side. And by the time the ice arrives, he needs a pair of tongs to remove some of the ice from his glass — now it's too cold.

Wow. These two are relentless. It's hard to believe, but they are now calling for adjustments in cabin temperature, requesting obscure reading materials, and insisting upon new travel slippers with better padding. As Alistair and Barbara go on with their long list of demands, I figure it's some kind of a round-robin challenge. Maybe they are competing to see which one can exhaust the wait staff first?

Barbara finally settles down, takes a few sips of tea and retires on an empty stomach—while Alistair and I start gorging. We munch on salmon, caviar, miniature quiche, little unknown tarts, and other fancy cocktail-party food. The crew keeps bringing out the snacks while Barbara snores softly in the corner. I think the flight attendants are cramming everything on us at once, in order to avoid any more special requests. I want to apologize to the women for Alistair and Barbara's behavior, but instead of speaking up, I just sit here and pig out.

"To be honest," Alistair begins, his mouth full of lobster salad, "I rather enjoy the mountains in winter. Of course, the Austrians are a ghastly bunch." He kicks a dog away from his feet. "But you will find the landscape to be stunning."

"I can't wait. I've never seen the Alps."

"You know, this is where I first encountered Madame, many years ago." He dips a small grilled chicken wing into a side of hot sauce. "I was serving at a café in her little hamlet."

I nod to let him know I'm still listening, but it's hard to look at his messy mouth.

"Madame and her friend were enjoying tea at my station one day." He blinks in slow motion and reaches for another chicken wing, then handles a few on the platter before deciding on a drumstick. "And although I could tell they'd been acquainted for years...I knew they'd never once confided a genuine story from the heart." He pauses to dip and chew. "During ski season, these two would meet for tea...on a bimonthly, weather-permitting basis—simply because they shared a similar orbit within the stratosphere of extreme wealth. You know the type."

I don't.

Before he continues, Alistair takes a big forkful of the mixed seafood salad—that I'm afraid to try. "Rest assured, Matthew, taking tea is more than a social obligation for these ladies. *Tea* is what interrupts the idleness of the afternoon."

As Alistair finishes his thought, the flight attendants arrive with more miniature desserts. I discreetly inhale a cream tart while Alistair grabs for something lemony. "So how did you and Madame actually meet?" I ask, as he swallows and finally wipes his mouth.

"Well, there they were…Madame and her friend, delicately picking at the tiers of sandwiches, scones, cookies, and cakes… and midway through their meal, I offered to refill the teapot. But, these ladies were so caught up in conversation, they offered no response…so I replenished the hot water and unobtrusively disappeared."

Alistair goes on to explain that when he presented the check that day, Madame's friend disagreed with the total and started to debate with him as to why he had imposed a sharing charge when the restaurant was currently half empty. Alistair's witty retort, describing how he saw the restaurant as being half full, didn't go over well. Without pause, the café manager arrived at the table and hastily adjusted the bill to reflect one tea service—for two patrons—and confirmed that the additional hot water would be *gratis*. Unfortunately, due to this incident, Alistair was dismissed on the spot and escorted off the premises.

"Incensed, I departed the café while Madame and her friend bid farewell kisses near the cloak room." He pauses to rinse the chocolate from his teeth, swishing his water as if it were mouthwash. "Minutes after I stormed out, furious…not sure what I would do to support my children, Madame saw me sitting at the bus stop. She sent her driver over to speak with me and he explained that Madame was most sorry to see me without a job. The driver jotted down my name and number, along with a few references…and he mentioned the possibility of a position opening soon. Luckily—out of the kindness of Madame's heart—I was invited into her house, less than three weeks later."

Great story, I think to myself and munch another treat. I'll beef it up for the show.

But before I finish my umpteenth snack, Barbara lets out an oversized yawn to warn of her awakening. I watch Alistair close his eyes and pretend to be asleep. So predictable.

Barbara sits up, scans the floor—littered with Alistair's canapé wrappers—and lets out a sigh; she reaches for a finger sandwich. "That will undoubtedly linger on my breath for the next two days," she complains, now chewing on warm tuna fish. "Matthew, perhaps we should see if Madame would care for an in-flight stretch class?"

"No, no. That's okay."

"I thought you *wanted* to train her," she sneers, stands up, and straightens her uniform as if preparing to speak with Madame.

"Well, yeah, I do. But I don't wanna impose."

"I shall go see."

I watch Barbara leave, assuming this is another stunt. But nonetheless, I rinse my mouth with water and get myself together. I glance at Alistair, who seems to be out cold, and then look up front.

Barbara is with René, caught up in some nonsense about how to refold his newspaper. She takes his paper, reworks it, and hands it back to him—one fold shy of a pilgrim hat—and walks back in my direction. "Madame is resting. There will be no workout."

Whew. "Oh. Okay. Maybe later." I let out a conceited smile.

"Here, take this." Barbara hands me an envelope from inside her uniform pocket. "Each staff member receives a New Year's bonus." She sits down. "This year it is some starter euros."

"Cool." I glance inside at the stack of colorful bills. "This is great."

"Well, one does not know if the euro is great or not, this

idea of a shared currency may not serve everyone equally. You understand…the euro has just gone into circulation, so time will tell—and by the way, remember not to hold your extra dirham, those you must spend."

"Why's that?"

"No bank outside of Morocco is willing to exchange that currency."

"For real?"

"Yes, they are worthless elsewhere."

"Well, thanks for the bonus."

Why am I thanking Barbara instead of Madame?

Maybe I'll bring it up the next time we train.

"Matthew, I was reading an article recently…one that listed Madame's neighborhood in Austria, as the sixth most-desirable skiing location in the world." Barbara sounds irritated it didn't make top five.

"Hey, that's cool…what else was on the list?"

"Oh, you know…the usual places—"

The pilot interrupts, over the loud speaker, with news of our initial descent.

I look out the window.

Blue sky has turned into sheer rock face. We're at low altitude, nestled between two mountain ridges. I turn to Barbara hoping she will distract me from the fact that it looks like we are about to clip a wing. "Usual places like where?" I ask as we hear an emergency beeping sound.

The pilot returns with another announcement, telling us to please ignore the automated proximity warning. He assures we have plenty of clearance between the mountains—and this alarming sound is a common occurrence.

Great. Blame computer error.

I can already hear the pitch for the evening news: *Heiress, dead in plane crash, story at eleven*. Then—sixty seconds later, at the end of the piece—the news anchor says: *several lapdogs and three staff members also perished*. No names, no recognition—

merely a mention that we *perished*. And of course, just like in showbiz, the dogs get top billing.

Still lost in my imaginary telecast, I feel the plane touch down. Damn. Rough landing. But at least we're down.

The dogs go wild—bouncing, barking, and jumping for joy. And René adds to the commotion, right up until the lead flight attendant releases the cabin door.

By the time we three worker-bees move from the rear of the plane, Madame, René, and the dogs are already into their car on the way home.

Being last to exit, I pause at the top of the stairs and take in a deep breath of the refreshingly clean, cold mountain air. The wintry Alpine landscape looks as fake as a postcard, and the red-clay world of Marrakech now feels like *eons* ago. When I look down to the foot of stairs and see the shivering crew waiting for me to deplane, I notice a fancy black car standing by—like the one Madame drove up in earlier—ready to whisk us away.

Not bad, I think to myself.

I could get used to this life.

Later, when our car pulls into the driveway of a quaint, snow-covered chalet, I'm disappointed. This can't be the place—it's only a modest, two-story, A-frame cottage, tucked into the steep hillside surrounded by pine trees. And at the foot of the main door is a descent-sized wooden landing, but not much else in terms of curbside appeal. Not very *Madame*.

As we come to a stop, our driver, Kan, mentions that he will take care of the household luggage for us. "Go inside...I can manage, no problem." He speaks with a lilt that reminds me of my Bangladeshi neighbor in Brooklyn. But I don't know anything about Kan's background.

"Thank you, Kan," Barbara says, before she jumps out, grabs her bag from the trunk, and climbs up an exterior staircase to the left of the house.

The moment I step into the driveway, two wolf-type dogs

lope in my direction. "Keep calm," Alistair warns. "Siberian Huskies can smell fear. Carry on, they're harmless."

The two dogs—each with an intriguing pair of mismatched eyes—sniff me up and down. I hold steady as one licks my hand, scenting the mishmash of items I had for lunch; the other one sniffs around my feet as if preparing to take a piss. Suddenly, tails are wagging and they both dart off in Barbara's direction, charging up the stairs behind her. Damn. That was lucky. I guess my acting training is paying off.

Alistair grabs my suitcase from the trunk and motions me toward the house. "After you, sir."

"I can take something," I mention, hoping to sound like a team player.

"We have it under control, now march!"

I hurry onto the wooden landing, and read the small wooden sign next to the glowing doorbell: *Burgflucht*. I love all this nonsense of naming houses. Maybe I'll name my place when I get home. Why not? I could call it: *Château Whyteman*.

I think I might freeze to death while Alistair continues to fidget with the lock. "Maybe it's frozen shut?"

"Ah, come off it, boy," he mumbles, huffing on a key that almost fits. "Madame and René just passed this way moments ago...damn stubborn thing."

Once we manage to break in, Alistair holds the door open with his foot, and allows me to go first. And the moment I step inside, I can't help but let out a low whistle. Alistair smirks, but I don't care. I'm beyond impressed. Back at mom's place in Indiana, we'd be stepping into the mudroom—a little place to drop our boots and hang winter coats—but here, it's much more than hooks. Madame's giant square-shaped foyer looks more like a ski shop than someone's entranceway. It has built-in wooden benches on all four sides and is stocked with tons of expensive-looking winter sports' gear. It's so large, I bet it could host a dozen houseguests for hot toddies. Hey, maybe I'll learn to ski while I'm up here?

"Onward!" Alistair wheels my suitcase through the foyer toward the start of a hallway that reminds me of an upscale mining shaft. "Into the hillside," he says, as if entering uncharted territory. "Don't be fooled by the intimate foyer, Matthew." He pauses a moment, allowing me to catch up. "The home is obscured by the mountain...you will find the upper levels to be quite spacious."

I follow him into the start of the passageway. There are no more benches at this point, just a windowless, rectangular tunnel—dimly lit and painted steel grey—with purposely rough, textured walls.

Within the first few steps, a spotlight automatically turns on to illuminate an abstract modern painting hanging on the wall to my left. Cool. I wish I had motion-activated lighting in my apartment. Then, as we continue forward, there are more spotlights and even more awesome paintings. Holy shit. We're triggering one light after the next—almost every three steps now. And the paintings keep coming.

Alistair mentions Rothko and Pollock. "Early O'Keeffe here...late Snodgrass there." He steps forward and the next light kicks on. He pauses again. "This one's middle Horthmanhoff."

Having no idea who Horthmanhoff is—and feeling claustrophobic in this never-ending hallway—I glance back to see if Kan might be following, but no one's around.

I stare toward the front door and watch the first section of lights go dark. Okay. I definitely want this lighting effect for my show.

But when I turn back toward Alistair, he's already gone ahead. And by the time I catch up to him, we've hit dead-end at an open elevator. The artwork next to the elevator looks like an Andy Warhol, but I figure I don't need to bother Alistair with any questions right now.

So I'm just going to pretend it *is* a Warhol.

"Let's go up." He wheels my suitcase inside and holds the door for me. "*U* is for you." He selects the *U* button on the panel. "Your room is on *U*."

"That's easy enough."

He points to the panel. "*E* is for egress, *C* is for central, *M* is for Madame, and *X* is for emergency."

Alistair reminds me of Nat King Cole: *L, is for the way you look at me*. But before I can carry on with the song in my head, the elevator door clangs open and we step out on *U*. We make a quick turn to the right and come to an abrupt halt in the wide doorframe of a sparsely furnished interior space.

"Welcome to Galleria." Alistair ducks down, overreacting to the fairly low wooden ceiling.

"How beautiful," I gasp, spying several large drawings on yellowish paper in big fancy frames—ink or charcoal, I can't tell. But if this area is known as the gallery, what the hell do they call the entrance hall—*pre-show*?

"Here we've got Picasso, Picasso, Picasso," he hurries forward, still speaking in monotone, "Matisse is thrown in there somewhere." Alistair unexpectedly presses his shoulder up against a wall-panel.

Cool. It's a camouflaged door that leads us into a small corridor, up a few stairs, and into my room. Oh, goody, this place is going to be fun. Maybe I'll get lucky and discover a hidden room behind a rotating bookcase.

I pause in the doorway.

My charming bedroom feels immediately welcoming—unlike my room in Morocco. This room is decorated in several tasteful shades of blue, and has one small—barred—window that looks out onto the snowy yard.

"A sophisticated ton-sur-ton décor," Alistair explains while placing my bag on top of the light-blue canvas luggage rack at the foot of my dark-blue twin bed.

"Thanks for bringing my bag in," I say, by the time he's already halfway out the door.

"My pleasure, sir." He disappears around the corner.

I pan the room and consider how I'll rehearse my new scenes. But when I peek inside the closet, I totally lose focus. I fixate on the neat rows of hangers just waiting to be filled. Goose-bumps. There's enough closet space here to hold more than my entire wardrobe from back home. But this is outrageous. Even my laundry elves won't know what to do with all these hangers.

The moment I shut the closet door, Barbara yells for me.

"Matthew," she repeats, "come now...I will show you around the house."

Knowing I have no other choice, I answer as if I'm *at the ready*. "On my way."

But as I turn to leave, Barbara appears in the open door-way. She points out that the door to René's office area is directly outside my door and his living quarters are connected to his office. She whispers that I will most likely be able to hear his business, which means he can also hear mine. "Take heed," she says, as if I've now been fully initiated into the ranks of the nosy staff, "mind your Ps and Qs."

Not long into the tour, I realize that my curbside impression of this place was totally wrong. As Alistair promised, it's huge in here. The main living areas have stunning mountain views and many rooms open out onto large wooden decks, positioned to avoid seeing any neighbors. Who knows, maybe Madame owns the entire mountain?

As we continue around the house, I recognize artwork by Soutine, Klimt, Klee, and Lichtenstein—okay, so I recognize them after Barbara mentions the artists by name.

"Matthew, each painting is connected to an alarm...please do not disturb—it means more work for everyone...to deal with the security company."

"Good to know." I give her a complacent smile.

But after her third reference to the alarm system, I roll my eyes, and shoot her a big raspberry tongue behind her back. What? Does she really think I'm going to forget about the alarms and accidentally lift a painting off the wall?

Barbara moves us along and keep things interesting. She's not just showing me the billiard room, the smoking room, the study, the spa, and the cinema; she is giving me the heads-up about how to get around the house without ever being seen in the main living areas. I accept that this knowledge will ensure any unwanted collisions with visiting diplomats.

"This passageway was constructed to transport the escorts of Monsieur." Barbara opens a door on the rear wall of the cinema. "Monsieur preferred his companions…always French…to enter the house bare-chested, therefore, this tunnel is heated. It connects the main house to the garage…and from the garage, there is another tunnel leading to the guesthouse. This way everyone can be happy, *non*?"

"Absolument!" I say, giving her my best René impression and thinking about how this Underground Railroad for Hookers could be big hit on Capitol Hill.

She laughs. "Matthew, you must never be caught using this passageway." She seals the door shut. "Unless of course you are topless—and wearing a beret."

I smile. "Got it!" I say, now wondering why she can't be chilled out and casual like this all the time.

After the cinema, Barbara rushes past the door to the music room door, and hurries upstairs to the kitchen. Here, I'm introduced to an Austrian chef and his French sous-chef. And after we exit the kitchen, Barbara whispers to me that this is a rare occurrence—to meet a Frenchman who admits to playing second-fiddle. I laugh, not sure I get that one.

In the pantry area, we meet up again with Kan, who turns out to be from Sri Lanka—not Bangladesh. And he's the head butler in this house—not a driver. As I listen to Kan speak, I realize it's going to take some serious rehearsal time to capture his particular dialect—otherwise, I'll sound cartoonish. And seconds before Barbara leads us away, Kan explains that he and three housemaids live here year-round, in order to maintain this property and the guesthouse across the street.

Duh. How naïve am I?

Extremely, I think to myself.

I never once considered that a new location would also mean new personnel. Talk about slow on the uptake.

Unannounced, René peeks his head through the door to the ironing room, where he must have overheard Barbara informing me about the ins-and-outs of paper bag recycling.

"Mathieu...my turn now!" he exclaims, in his usual melodramatic urgency. "We must take our driving tour in town before sundown, I insist."

And before I can say goodbye, or thank you—René takes me by the arm, pulls me out into the hallway, and leads me into elevator.

"*E, E, E*," he whispers, obsessively pressing the exit button.

Doesn't *E* stand for emergency?

As we ride down, I ask René if I should stop in my room to get my winter coat. He laughs at what I think is a pretty simple question.

"No, no, no, Mathieu...a coat will certainly not be necessary." He steps out of the elevator, spins to face me, and my Warhol brightens up. "We will simply take our driving tour, cruise the town square, and be back up the hill in no time." He spins to take off toward the front door, and the lights pop on as he goes. "Besides...every car seat is heated!"

As René scampers forward, a light at the far end of the tunnel blinks on. Someone must be walking toward us.

"Is that you?" A smooth female voice echoes from the darkness up ahead.

"Yes, it is I!" René hammers back. "Is that you?"

Blink.

Another light comes on, reducing the darkness between the woman and René.

"Yes...it is me," the liquid voice replies, closer now.

Blink. Blink.

And within seconds, the final shadowed painting lights up—the Pollock—and a beautiful, bronzed, dark-haired woman appears in front of us.

"Oh, my dear, dear...dear!" René gives her a big hug. "What news do we have from along the Riviera? Do tell."

As I watch them embrace, the haphazard spatters of paint on the Pollock canvas remind me of René's brainwaves—going every which way at once.

"What can I say?" She separates from his hug. "Life could be worse."

"Indeed." René chuckles.

She turns toward me with a warm smile. "You must be Matthew."

"Yes, hi." I accept her hand.

"I am Olivia."

"Hey, glad to finally meet you," I say and forget to let go.

"Likewise...and Happy New Year to you both." Olivia releases my hand and shifts to René. "Is it not difficult to believe, that Matthew has already been with us since the first days of November?"

"It most certainly is," René adds, adding nothing new.

"Madame is most pleased," Olivia says, to both of us. "And that is what matters—yes?"

"For sure," René answers, and shifts his feet a few steps in the direction of the front door. "Well, Olivia darling, do pardon our rush...we must catch up soon!" He speeds off.

"Yes, of course." Olivia starts toward the elevator. "Enjoy yourselves."

"Bye." I hurry down the hall to find René.

Back when I was exchanging emails with Olivia about the contract with Madame, I could tell we'd hit it off. But I never imagined Olivia to be so attractive. Relating to her as Madame's personal secretary, I—for some reason—assumed she'd be dowdy. But boy was I wrong. Her almond-shaped eyes have an alluring hint of Egyptian goddess, and her olive-toned skin gives her a healthy glow. She is around my age, thirty-five at the oldest, and appears to be the most rested staff member—for sure.

Just now, her dark shoulder-length ponytail was slicked back from her flawless face and her uniform was simple. She was wearing a smart-looking black cashmere turtleneck sweater, a pair of black slacks, and black penny-loafers. I love how she accessorized her black outfit with a copper and cream, paisley-print scarf—very tasteful.

"Olivia has just returned from Côte d'Azur...if you are lucky, Mathieu, we will visit this spring. Côte d'Azur is Madame's oldest property, the mother ship if you will." René pauses as we step outside onto the landing. "Do remind me to ask her about the whereabouts of that boat," he continues, now leading us into the driveway toward a narrow snowplowed lane, "look, smoke rings...I'm blowing smoke rings." René applauds himself as he watches the warm air exit his mouth in the shape of an almost circle. "Watch...I know how to French inhale as well." He pauses to snort.

After a fairly short walk down the lane, we step into a huge, well-heated, and clean garage. René peruses the collection of vintage automobiles as if he's playing a game of eeny-meeny-miny-moe. He whispers in nursery rhyme rhythm as he gazes into the space and uses a loose-wrist gesture to refer to each car. "Alfa, Bentley, Maybach, Benz....Aston, Audi, Jacquie, Lamb." He continues with his game until he settles on a glossy bright-yellow one, then motions for me to hurry over and join him on the passenger side.

The instant René opens his car door, I notice a ruggedly handsome white man with sandy-blonde hair, walking up from the rear of the garage. This muscular, fifty-something guy, is wearing a black suit, white dress-shirt, a thin black tie and hurriedly putting on a chauffeur's hat. "René...will you be needing assistance today?" The man's masculine voice matches his tough-guy exterior. Hot.

"No thank you, Niko." René replies in a tone that is about an octave lower than his normal voice. "Mathieu and I will be just fine on our own."

I nod toward Niko while he closes René's door, but know better than to start a staff-on-staff conversation in front of René.

Okay. So Niko is the driver, Kan is the butler, and Inoke, Ulani, and Tida are the three new housemaids. I'm pretty sure that's right. Shit. I shouldn't agonize over it. All these name will have to be changed for the show anyway.

I have no idea what type of fancy car this is, but its color reminds me of the onset of my father's mid-life crisis; the day he drove home in a brand new, 1979 canary yellow Firebird—complete with spoiler sprouting off the trunk. I think my parents' divorce took place within a week after dad rolled into the drive-way in his new chick-magnet, but it might have been longer. After their separation, mom spent her share of the money redoing our basement. She chose to cover the basement floor and walls with psychedelic orange and yellow shag carpeting. She also installed avocado green lighting fixtures—on remote dimmer switches— and a swanky wet-bar area with smoky mirror tiles. Very mod.

Our Indiana basement, once my studio for recreating the Bobby-and-Sissy dance numbers from *The Lawrence Welk Show*—I danced the role of Sissy and used a broom to play Bobby—had now been transformed into her den of debauchery. Mom's new hangout became a place for her and the other neigh-borhood divorcées to play cards, drink stiff gin martinis, and listen to records by Herb Alpert and The Tijuana Brass. On alternate Fridays, the group would gather for art appreciation and do string art, paint by number, paper-maché or macramé—and sometimes hook rugs from a box—while listening to Neil Diamond.

In order to avoid the whole basement scene, I spent my summers dancing outside on the back patio, and moved inside our single-car garage during winter. And because those formative years were spent on cement slabs, and poured concrete, I believe I developed enough scar tissue to render me free from shin splints for the duration of my professional career. But come to think of it, that method of early training could have also contributed to my current knee injury. Damn. I guess that makes that old Firebird a bright yellow, home-wrecking, career-ending sports car.

René drives—this Porsche, for all I know—like a bat out of hell, racing his way down the icy hillside as if we're on a toboggan run. It's like he, Alistair, and Bahir all went to the same bogus driving school.

"Mathieu, look yonder...you will see the house where Luke Richey first lived in hiding." He points toward a dense cluster of pine trees. "You must know of him...he is American."

I nod, feigning vague recognition, knowing that René will continue with his story whether I admit to knowing this Luke guy or not.

"In 1983, Richey was indicted for evading fifty-million dollars in U.S. taxes—but he fled! He first hid in that house with a distant cousin...but later moved over the border on the other side of those hills." He takes one hand off the wheel to gesture behind him. "To this very day, our clever man lives scot-free in Switzerland...eating all the fondue one could fathom."

Blown away by the majesty of the Alps, I'm half-listening as René elaborates about more rich folks who have beat the odds. The view from up here, looking down into the frozen valley, is jaw-dropping—especially with the late afternoon sun. And as I take in this landscape, I consciously add this moment to my sense-memory bank. Maybe someday I'll be cast as an Alpine explorer in a made-for-TV movie and need to recall this image.

"What a shame." René motions toward an injured skier being airlifted into a helicopter. "That puts him out for the rest of the season...nice chopper though." Then, as we speed past a roadside café, the scent of Barbara's favorite tea—Parisian Earl Grey—streams in through the car vent. "Delicious!" René exclaims as he accelerates toward an intersection.

The moment we come to a stop at the traffic light, I get an intense craving for hot chocolate and stare out the window at a group of privileged schoolchildren who have just coasted down the bunny slope into the arms of their nannies. This place is awesome.

I've never seen anything like it before. My only winter-mountain gig was a brief stint, fresh out of college, at some two-bit resort in the Poconos. In hopes of earning my Equity card, I said *yes* to lots of ridiculous stuff, including the absurd Christmas review—*A Very Merry, Mary and Joseph*. I was hired as the sole understudy for all three of the singing/dancing Magi. But no one ever got sick or missed a show, so I never performed. I remember riding the bus back to the city—crushed—no closer to my union card. But to this day, I'm relieved I didn't go onstage and have to face the conservative audiences who complained nightly, about how the show was blasphemous and full of historical inaccuracies. I guess I dodged a bullet with that one.

A few traffic lights later, we arrive in town, greeted by a vibrant scene of people strolling the streets in fashionable ski attire. Exclusive designer shops line the town square and impressive window displays advertise the world's finest crystal and the galaxy's softest cashmere. Everyone is out shopping and dining. But many seem to be doing nothing but posturing for the onlooker like me.

René pushes random buttons on the dashboard as he whizzes through town, one hand on the wheel and one hand on the CD player; no regard for signals, street signs or pedestrians.

"At this spot, Mathieu," René points toward a standing-room-only bar/restaurant, "one finds sexy ski professionals, mingling amongst adoring fans. Last season, I—"

But instead of finishing his thought, he rolls down his window, turns the car stereo on, selects CD number one/track ten, cranks the volume up full blast, and starts singing at the top of his lungs—*The Lonely Goatherd* from *The Sound of Music*.

I sink down in my seat. People are staring. Hell. I'm all for a good show tune, but this is totally uncool.

As René yodels out the window with Julie Andrews, my butt breaks into a sweat. My moment of sensory joy has ended and I've snapped back into reality—or back into what I've come to accept as *reality*. I've got to shut off this damn seat-warmer.

"But honestly, Mathieu," he yells over the music, "one might speculate *what* Austria would proclaim, if not for the birth of Freud and Hitler...and for providing the filmic backdrop to the greatest movie of all time?"

Mozart, I think and laugh to myself, as I click the button to cool my buns.

René grinds the car into high gear and proceeds out of town. "Mathieu," he shouts before lowering the volume on the CD, "we must check the weather for this evening...as you know... things change rapidly here on the mountain."

"Oh, okay."

"I always use iheartweather.com for my Internet weather report...do you think it best, Mathieu?"

"Always," I say, as he cranks the volume up again and restarts the track from the top.

With the yodeling at a deafening pitch, we coast into the driveway and come to a stop in front of the garage. Niko arrives in the driveway in time to open René's door. I jump out and un-stick my sweaty pants, trying not to appear obvious.

"Thank you, Niko," René says—using his Niko voice, "that will be all." He drops the car keys into Niko's gloved hand and walks away.

René leads us back along the plowed lane toward the house, and soon steps inside—leaving me outside on the landing. He holds the door open just a crack, and looks at me as if I'm here to sell him a box of Girl Scout cookies. "All right, Mathieu, enjoy your dinner this evening and perhaps we shall resume our workouts as of tomorrow morning."

"Sure thing," I answer with a smile and squelch my impulse to push inside.

Then, in classic René style, he shuts the door and locks me out of the house—no coat on.

Too embarrassed to bother Niko in the garage, I decide to wait just long enough to allow René to make it into the elevator and start upstairs, before I ring the buzzer.

Thirty, Mississippi—I press the glowing doorbell.

"Who is it, please?" A static-filled voice answers through the intercom.

"Hey, it's me. Matt!" I think I'm speaking to Alistair.

"Wave to the camera," he laughs and buzzes me in. "I should make you stay out there all night. However...if it wasn't for you, I would never have snogged that babe in Marrakech—thanks, mate."

Clearly, Barbara is nearby and Alistair wants to make damn sure she knows about his recent escapade. "No prob." I hurry inside, close the door, and shiver my way into the mining shaft.

As I start toward the elevator, I decide to have a little fun with the automatic lights. I strike a different pose each time the next one clicks on—an abstract shape in response to each painting. Then it hits me. I could get the same special effect for the show by using the *as seen on TV* clap on/clap off light. This way, I'd save money in the budget to put toward replicas of these paintings. Smart.

By the time I pass though the hidden door panel in Galleria, the phone in my room rings. I rush over to my bedside table and answer, only to be greeted by a dial tone. Crap. Barbara must have timed my walk from the front door to my room. Fuck her. I was not late in answering that damn phone, and I refuse to check the switchboard for a message. She can go to hell for all I care. I slam down the receiver and the phone rings again.

I grab it up, totally peeved. "Allô, this is Matt."

"Oh, Matthew, it is Olivia. So this is your extension, yes?"

"Oh, hi, sorry. I mean—"

"I tried you once, but thought perhaps I had misdialed."

"No, no, you're right." I soften. "At least I think I'm in the right room?"

Olivia laughs. "Of course you are," she pauses. "Would you care to come upstairs for a visit?"

"Sure—I'd love to...just tell me where."

"Return to the elevator and press *M*," she pauses again as if she's busy, "I will meet you there, on the landing."

"Cool. I'll be right up."

Once inside the elevator, I realize I'm doing something forbidden by going up to Madame's private area. Then again, maybe it's okay since I've been invited.

Earlier, during the house tour with Barbara, we didn't walk through the top floor of the house. Barbara just pointed skyward, as if referring to heaven, each time she mentioned Madame. But she never offered to show me around.

I close my eyes to center myself.

"Matthew, are you all right?" I hear Olivia ask.

I open my eyes. The elevator has opened onto a plushly carpeted hallway. "Yeah. I'm fine, just resting my eyes a minute." I step forward, feeling stupid for riding an elevator as if it's a roller coaster.

"Welcome to Burgflucht." She gives me a big hug.

"Thanks for getting me over here."

"It was my pleasure...come this way—I have work to do, but we can get caught up at the same time."

Olivia leads the way along a corridor that overlooks the main staircase. This is a nice change of pace. Unlike chasing behind Alistair and Barbara or being battered by René's driving, she walks at a normal pace. At last, someone around this house strikes me as regular—except for her extraordinary looks.

"Look up," she whispers, being careful not to disturb the dogs. "Is it not fantastic?"

The hard-to-miss ceiling is vaulted with big heavy wood supports, and most everything is painted white/off-white. I guess white is Madame's thing.

"Fierce." I answer as Olivia turns the corner.

We walk into a large dressing area with mirrored closets and built-in cabinets. It feels like we've just entered in a private fitting area in some exclusive bridal shop.

"You can sit over there." Olivia points toward a cushy

white chair. "Make yourself comfortable."

"Sure it's okay?" I ask, thinking I might leave a mark.

"Of course...no reason to be bashful."

As I sit down, Olivia turns her back to me and slides open a wide door that reveals an illuminated walk-in closet, lined with shelves and stocked full of clutch purses. Each bag is resting in its place as if on display in a showroom. Some sparkle, others shine, but each looks as beautiful as the next.

"That's a lot of purses," I blurt, "a drag queen could go wild in there."

"I know." She laughs. "And these are only the ones she keeps here in Austria." Olivia looks at me. "I wish you could see those she has given away...not to mention thrown away." She pauses and turns to remove one small section of purses. She then carries them into the dressing area and places her armful into a lined laundry hamper in the same order as they were on the shelf. "All of these are from the 1950s as you can tell." She walks back toward the closet.

"They're so pretty. Is there a dress to match each one?"

"Yes...or there was at one time anyway." Olivia moves a soft white dust cloth across the empty shelving. "Some survive... but others only live on in photographs."

"For real?"

"After an outfit had been photographed, it was never worn again."

"Kind of like Hollywood?"

"I suppose."

"So where'd they go?"

"Well, the publicized dresses," Olivia begins, now returning the hamper of purses to the closet shelf in their precise order, "those Madame considered disgraced by the press...would be sent out with the garbage before morning."

"Chucked out—just like that?" What a waste. I shake my head in disbelief.

Olivia notices my bewildered expression. "I know. And

sometimes Madame will go through phases where she would like to dispose of everything."

"Really? Why'd she wanna do that?"

"It is her prerogative. When she tires of it...she wants rid of it." Olivia returns to the dressing area with her next stack of purses. "Once, back in the '80s, Madame decided to stop wearing skins and tossed out a truckload. René had to convince her to keep one fur coat for her travels to Russia."

"Only one, eh?" I hope she'll catch my sarcasm.

"Yes." She smiles and leaves with dust cloth in hand. "And so Madame kept one...but the remainder went directly into the dumpster."

"Gee. Couldn't she give 'em to charity?"

"No. The items she refused to donate...I believe she felt most ashamed of ever having owned them in the first place. She simply wanted them gone."

"Do you guys ever have a problem with trash pickers?"

"You mean, *scavenging*?"

I suppose her word choice does sound better than mine. "Yeah, it happens all the time in New York."

"Oh, that is funny...however, this concept has never been a problem for us...since our neighbors have their own garbage to comb through—if they are so inclined." Olivia returns her current stack to the closet and gathers another.

"So how long have you been with Madame?" I hope she's willing to open up.

"My entire life," she answers without missing a beat, eyes trained on her work. "Well, almost my entire life...from the time I was seven."

I chuckle. "Don't you guys have child-labor laws over here?"

"It is not that." She laughs and continues dusting. "I came here to live with my Aunt Lucetta, who was then executive secretary for Monsieur. My mother knew that I would have a better life in this house."

"Oh, I see. So where were you born?"

"I was born in Italy, but I grew up around the world... traveling with Madame and Monsieur. They treated me as if I were a granddaughter."

"That's cool...moving around like an army brat?"

"*Army brat*? I am not sure of this expression."

"It just means you were always the new kid in school."

"No, no...for me, Aunt Lucetta was my teacher, I had no actual classroom."

"Well, in that case, we'd say *home-schooled*."

"Then it is more this way...she taught me everything... French, English, Spanish, German."

"Awesome...you speak four languages?"

"Five, counting Italian."

"Wow, that's sweet. I'm totally jealous. I wish I could count Indiana-French as a second language."

She laughs again. "We can practice, whenever you have the time. It simply takes practice."

"I don't know about that. I've already learned so many catchy song lyrics and cheesy dance steps, my mind's a jumble when I try to start something new...are you fluent in all of them?"

"I could claim *fluent*, in three out of five. Although I have plenty of phrases in the others—mostly obscene." She gives me a impish look.

"Well, in that case...maybe we *should* practice." I pause as Olivia reenters the closet to replace her newest section of bags. It looks like we've journeyed from the '50s to the '60s, and now we're venturing into the '70s. "So where's your aunt now?"

"Zia Lucetta?" she asks, glancing in my direction and sounding totally Italian. "She died when I was only twenty-two... Madame and Monsieur loved her very much and they entrusted me with her responsibilities."

"Oh, I'm sorry." I say, thinking about her aunt, not realizing that it could sound like I'm taking pity on her for having to work this job. "I mean, I'm sorry to hear she passed away."

"Thank you. Zia Lucetta was a remarkable woman…I had tremendous respect for her."

"And what about your mom?"

"Is this one gorgeous or what?" Olivia asks from the back of the closet, as she holds up a little disco-inspired neon-colored sequined clutch.

"Amazing!" I yell, and wonder if she consciously decided to change the subject. Maybe she just didn't hear my question about her mother? "I guess *one of a kind* doesn't have to mean *classy*, right?"

"My favorite of them all." Olivia laughs, places the disco bag back on the shelf, clicks the light off, walks out from the closet, and slides the door closed. "Utterly useless, that silly clutch—the paparazzi would have loved that one." She walks to the opposite side of the dressing area and slides open another closet door. This door reveals a series of wide, yet shallow, white-lacquer drawers. "Tell me, how are things going for you?"

Maybe it's a giant jewelry box? "I'm doin' okay…just wish I were busier."

"She loves having you around." Olivia pulls the bottom drawer open.

"Who…Madame?" I say, curiosity peaked.

"Yes." Olivia answers while I obsess over the drawer. I stare at the single rows of winter-white cashmere gloves resting side-by-side; each pair carefully spaced and each glove arranged palm-side down.

"Madame tells me that you are wonderful!"

"That's good," I say as Olivia lifts up the first pair of gloves, gently shakes it in midair, and replaces it into the drawer—now palm-side up, but still in the same spot. "But I feel like I've hardly even worked with her. I mean, our workouts…when they were happening were so short. I think I've learned more about the dogs than I have about Madame."

Olivia laughs to herself. "Well, Madame is most pleased… pleased because René is happy with you, and Barbara has yet to say a negative word." By the time she has completed her sentence, she's already flipped and freshened the fourth white pair.

"But if you don't mind me asking, why does Madame have a trainer around if she's not interested in exercising each day?"

"You are here because you are part of her staff. And people," she pauses as if searching for the right word, "of her circumstances…live by specific requirements." She lifts up another white pair. "For as long as I can remember, there has always been a trainer on the grounds." Shake. Flip. Replace. Retrieve.

"So why not ask a local trainer to be on call?"

"It is impossible…there would be too much town gossip, you understand? She has always used an American trainer. And to be honest, I believe Madame likes the idea that you do not seem impressed with her. You Americans seldom are." She finishes with the final pair and closes the first drawer.

"So in my case…ignorance *is* bliss!"

She looks at me with a serious expression. "You have a special position, Matthew. As trainer, you are the only staff member who may give instruction to Madame…the rest of us are here to receive orders," she delineates.

"That's cool. I'd never really thought about it like that."

"It is true." She returns to her task.

"So does Madame ever change up the ranks, you know, the way she used to do with her wardrobe?"

Olivia opens the next drawer and begins the same process again. More gloves—all winter-white.

"The only time I ever witnessed an abrupt change in personnel, was on the very day Monsieur passed away. Madame had his three bodyguards dismissed and insisted that all weapons be removed."

"I guess that's what scares me," I hesitate, not sure what I'm thinking, "I'm afraid of becoming useless."

"Trust me. You have nothing to worry about…my fiancé, Danté, the dog walker in Mykonos…he remains on the roster—

even though the Greek dogs have long since passed."

"Fiancé, huh? Have you guys set a date?"

"Not yet...long engagement," she continues without looking up. "Madame is not interested in restructuring the payroll at this time."

Dare I ask Olivia about what happened in Mykonos? "That seems so generous of her, to keep staff around, especially when there's no work for them."

"Well, what some consider generous, others might deem senile. But the point is...it is her money and she will do as she pleases."

"So, does Madame ever talk about the money?" I venture, almost sure I know the answer.

"Never." Olivia slides the second drawer closed—the poor gloves facing skyward as if screaming to get out. "It is simply there, but never discussed."

"Sounds like debt to me." I smile—but my joke falls flat when I realize that Olivia doesn't know what it's like to max out a credit card.

As Olivia opens the third drawer, I hope for pink.

Nope. More white.

I give Olivia a moment to get started with the gloves, before deciding to poke a bit further. "So, where'd the money come from? Were Madame and Monsieur both born into money?"

"Yes. She had her share, and he his."

"Must be nice."

"But take note...old money only affords new money, when one plays the proper cards." Olivia sighs as if she's had enough and slides the drawer shut. "I shall have to pick up with these later."

Oh, no. Does this mean I'll never know the color of the gloves in the next drawer?

"Apologies, it is already quite late and you need a moment to relax before dinner." She heads toward the elevator. "Please forgive me for keeping you."

I follow her out. "No, not at all, it was great." I say, begging to hear more stories. I want to find out more about the family fortune, more about Danté — Mykonos. "Thanks. That was fun." I step inside the elevator.

"See you at dinner." She waves as the door closes.

Okay, she's the best. Not so freakin' weird like everybody else. Hell. I've gone for months without an ordinary conversation and that just seemed so normal. Nice change.

When I arrive outside my bedroom door, I hear René on his office telephone — another one of his weather conversations. I enter my room, close the door like a sneaky teenager, and glance toward the phone. How many violations could I have racked up?

Suddenly dizzy and overstimulated, I kick off my shoes and drop onto the bed. The altitude must be getting to me.

Lying here, I can still hear the distant sound of René speaking with someone at the airport. He has called to confirm the weather report for tonight. He's now explaining that after cross-referencing several websites, he's unable to believe any of the online predictions — so he's double-triple-checking with local authorities.

I'm ready to conk, but it strikes me as funny that someone could call the airport and speak to an actual human. Yet another aspect of privilege I'd never considered.

8

The next day, I startle awake, starving, still in my clothes from last night. Shit. It's five a.m. I slept through dinner.

After a quick shower, I decide to head upstairs to raid the kitchen, before the staff shows up for seven o'clock coffee. But I have to be careful, off-hour eating counts as two demerits.

When I exit my room, the corridor is pitch black, so I run my hand along the wall. No light switch. I make my way down the few stairs to the mystery door that opens into Galleria. The door swings wide, into complete darkness; still no switch.

As I slide my hand along the smooth wall and pray for divine intervention to help me avoid a picture frame—Barbara would be so proud if I set off security—I soon feel a raised panel and take my chances. Press. Whew.

The lights of Galleria come up to an ambient level, and the only noise is a sleepy hum, coming from the several small humidifiers that are sitting on the floor—one beneath each picture.

I walk over to the far wall to check out the giant Matisse, and stand in awe of the huge charcoal study that depicts a woman stretched out beside a reclining bull. The simplistic broad black lines on off-white paper divulge the artist's process. Certain sections are undone, but my eye fills in where the lines fade. Spectacular. It captures a specific day in the studio, perhaps one fleeting moment of inspiration. Maybe it's a sketch for another work—or a study that hit the cutting room floor and got swept up for millions after the fact? Regardless, this piece is much more fascinating than seeing a completed work. I love it. I can't remember the last time I appreciated something so immediately.

Above the hum of the humidifiers, a little voice echoes in my head—one that sounds exactly like Barbara's—reminding me not to linger or block the pathway. Reluctantly, I pull myself away from the artwork and move through the concealed door that leads upstairs to the kitchen. Then, halfway up the stairs, I return to shut off the lights in Galleria. Another two demerits spared.

Relieved to be alone in the kitchen, I make coffee and scrambled eggs. I shove down toast with jam, and practice my French while reading one of the newspapers from Barbara's recycling bin. I should get up at five o'clock every day—this is not a bad deal. But the moment I'm finished eating, terrified of being discovered, I tidy up the kitchen, and use my best photographic memory to return each utensil to its exact position. Shit. This is much more stressful than re-shelving my Uncle's porn magazines when I was a teen.

"Bon matin, Monsieur Van Winkle," Olivia's warm voice interrupts from somewhere behind me, "you slept well."

I close the cabinet door. "Oh, hi, yeah...actually, I did." I turn around—happy to see her. "But I woke up starving."

"Well, we missed you at dinner last night, that is for sure." She looks stunning in a replica of her black slacks and black turtleneck sweater from yesterday. "Thought it might be best to let you sleep." She reaches for the teakettle.

"I guess I really needed it," I say, distracted by the thought of forgetting to check for eye-boogers this morning.

"Not to worry, my friend, it is most often the case—the first night on the mountain."

"Did I miss much at dinner?"

"Not much...however, Barbara took on one of her moods." She fills the kettle with water.

"Oh, really...what happened?"

"Madame's newly assigned nurse, Tatyana, arrived at the

start of our meal. And Barbara was insulted by her timing…as if it might have been intentional."

Nurse? Is Madame okay? "Oh, that's too bad," I say, noticing that today Olivia has on a blue-and-white rectangular-patterned scarf, instead of her copper-and-cream paisley one.

"When I stood up from the dinner table to welcome Tatyana into the staff housing area," she pauses to light the stove, "Barbara started cleaning up the serving dishes as if everyone had finished."

"Had you?"

"No—we had just taken our first bites." Olivia leaves the teapot to boil and moves into Kan's pantry.

I follow.

"Later, Tatyana and I managed to grab a plate from the refrigerator," she continues, "in peace and quiet, I might add."

"Well, I'm glad it worked out for you guys…so how do you know Tatyana?"

"Oh, we do not. She arrives from the service that Madame has used on various occasions. She seems to be fine."

"Is Madame so ill she needs a full-time nurse?"

"A mere precaution, Matthew, nothing to be concerned about."

"I hope so. I mean, I can't wait to get back to work with her. We had a good thing going in Morocco…until we stalled out."

By now, Olivia has poured a shot-glass of apple juice and prepared a little snack. Her breakfast is perfectly styled with two pieces of Melba toast, three fresh raspberries, and garnished with a mint leaf.

I look up from her plate. "Is that it for you?" I ask, trying not to sound judgmental.

"Along with the tea, this is plenty." Olivia looks down at her portion as if the third berry might be one too many. "Listen," she says, now backing out through the pantry door and turning toward the staff dining area. "The moment they open the pass, I will be leaving. But you may call my mobile anytime."

My heart sinks. The only *normal* person is leaving.

"O. Visciolata," she continues, "my number is there on the bulletin board." She nods with her chin in the direction of the staff computer and starts to sit down at the table. "Once Madame gets settled here on the mountain…I am sure she will begin to exercise again."

I exhale and sit down facing Olivia.

She pauses a moment, places a napkin on her lap, appreciates her plate, and enjoys a tiny swallow of juice. What does she mean about *opening the pass*?

"So what news are you hearing from the city these days?" She looks at me with a somber expression. "I meant to ask you last night, but I did not want to intrude."

"About New York?" I deflect.

"Yes, have you any updates? I suppose everyone has been bothering you about it? But it is only because we are concerned." Olivia lifts one of the berries onto the dry cracker and takes a bite that would even seem small for a bird.

"Well, I haven't heard much recently."

She tilts her head in disbelief.

"I mean…when friends email, it's almost like they don't want to talk about it." I pause again.

Olivia gives me a look, implying she knows I'm stalling around her question but doesn't interject.

"My friend David told me that cars are honking horns again and said people have started pushing in the subway."

Her eyes soften. "Perhaps, this means things are returning to normal."

"Yeah." I nod, realizing I've suppressed my feelings about David for months. "I guess so."

"So tell me more about David." She smiles. "He is just a friend?"

My heart pounds. "We're more than friends, I guess—but no longer boyfriends." How did I ever think I'd be able to avoid him for a year just by coming here?

Olivia shows concern. "Why? What happened?"

"No major blow up." I take a deep breath. "We just couldn't make it work."

"So where do you stand now?"

"Good question...I'm not really sure."

She gives another encouraging look.

"I think we're officially exes...but I hope we'll patch things up while I'm here." God that sounds like a stupid plan.

"Oh. I see." Olivia pauses as the teapot whistles in the kitchen.

"I'll get it."

"No, Matthew, I can go."

"Really, it's no problem." I hurry toward the kitchen, happy to avoid both traumas—David and 9/11.

By the time I return with the hot water, Olivia has arranged two teacups on saucers, and placed a white china teapot in the center of the table. "Do you favor hibiscus?" She pops open a canister.

"I've never tried it...sounds good."

Olivia scoops some tealeaves into the pot, adds the boiling water and closes the lid.

"May I?" I act all proper and start to pour.

"Not just yet, it should steep for a moment," she mentions without dwelling on my *faux pas*,"so, were you and David in the city that day?"

"Yeah, we were at my place." I take another deep breath, accepting my role as witness to the tragedy.

"It must have been horrendous." She snags the final berry from her plate. "It was sickening, even for those of us here on the other side of the Atlantic...but how terrifying to have such an attack in your own backyard."

"I know. It's still hard to believe it's real...and almost impossible to describe the sense of emptiness that followed. Weird thing...both towers had already collapsed, by the time David and I woke up that morning...so we just stayed under the covers and watched it on TV...almost like it was happening somewhere else."

Olivia glances at the teapot and places a small metal strainer over each cup. "It is probably okay now." Her tone is as soothing as the smell of the tea. "Here in the house, we maintained our schedule that terrible Tuesday, but everyone was most concerned."

"I have to say," I pause and pour her tea through the strainer, trying not to spill, "it was incredible to see New Yorkers come together afterwards, everyone wanted to help out...that part was amazing."

Olivia smiles as we set the strainers aside and pretend to clink teacups.

"Damn. It feels strange, though." I sip. "I haven't allowed myself to think about any of this since I got over here...is that wrong?"

"Not necessarily. That is how many of us choose to cope. We carry on."

"Yeah. But this time, I've buried my head in the sand."

"You are not alone. It is quite easy to forget about life elsewhere...especially when we are here, busy with Madame." She pauses. "Do you like it, the tea?"

"Yeah, it's great."

"Well, not to change the subject...but before I forget." Olivia glances at her watch. "I wanted to remind you, if you have any questions about Madame or her program, please feel free to discuss those issues with Tatyana. She will serve as your liaison."

"Oh. Okay. But what about you, where're you gonna be?"

"Paris. I must check in on Madame's apartment...but will return in no time."

Something tells me, when Olivia says *apartment*, it's not quite the same as my studio.

"Sounds nice. Wish I could come with," I say, only half-kidding.

Without warning, Barbara pounds into the room with a bucket full of newspapers. "Could someone please explain how these ended up in the garbage!" She charges toward the kitchen.

"Good morning, Barbara." Olivia reveals a hint of sarcasm. "Did you sleep well?"

"Why?" Barbara storms past us. "When the recycling is there in plain sight."

"She is actually not so bad," Olivia whispers, looking in the direction of Barbara's jet stream. "One just needs to give her space."

"Oh, I know, we did fine in Morocco...but that doesn't mean I'd want to be stranded on a deserted island with her."

Olivia chuckles and finishes her apple juice.

Uncomfortable about continuing with Olivia while Barbara hovers in the kitchen, I decide to get going. "Well, I'd better get back downstairs...in case René is looking for me."

"All right, be well," she smiles, "and I will see you upon my return."

"Bon voyage!"

"Merci, monsieur." She laughs. "Look...you see, we are already practicing."

"Cool."

"Ciao, ciao."

By the time I get downstairs, I hear René stirring in his room. I shut my door just as he starts screaming through the wall. "Mathieu! Are you awake?"

I don't respond.

"Mathieu!" He yells with greater urgency.

I say nothing. Hey, if he plans to call me like a dog, he's got another thing coming. He can pick up his phone and dial my extension.

My phone rings.

"Goodness, Mathieu, I was worried sick. I have just now been calling and calling but there was no answer. I thought you were perhaps buried alive in the snowfall. After all, Mathieu, this is indeed the largest reported snowfall in an eight-hour period since the recording of weather. The airport is closed, the roadways are blocked, and we are now officially *snowbound*! Can you believe it? At first I didn't either, but after I phoned the airport to confirm whether or not the Internet predictions were in fact true — and they said *yes* — I knew it was serious. Three sources said it was going to snow like this overnight and continue throughout the day today — and it did...and it still is!"

As he comes up for air, I go for it. "How phenomenal," I sneak in, with upward inflection.

"Now tell me, what do you think...since it is clearly inclement...shall we try our hand at some indoor exercise?"

"That sounds like a great idea." I match his enthusiasm.

"I should think so, Mathieu. I shall meet you in cinema."

Without offering any further details, René hangs up. So I head over to the cinema, and move the furniture aside to prepare for his workout.

Yesterday, Barbara explained how one room can double as two spaces, the screening room and the gym. "At these prices," she said, "we must make use of the space — the best way we know how."

And even though I realize that René didn't say *when* he would meet me in the cinema, all I can do is get organized and be ready for him to enter.

So now I am. Ready and waiting.

Thirty minutes later, René saunters in, wearing a new training ensemble and carrying a mug of coffee. He steps into the center of the room and strikes a pose. He has on red Lycra leggings with shocking knee-high yellow knit leg warmers, white jazz shoes, and an asymmetrical red, yellow, and blue Spandex tank top. To complete his outfit, he has several black accessories including an unnecessarily wide elasticized waistband and two cotton-terry wrist warmers — both on the same wrist. A black silk headband across his forehead brings contrast to his signature round white sunglasses.

"Mathieu, do you love it, or what?"

I'm shocked speechless, but try not to show it on my face.

I take a beat. "You look marvelous!"

"I know," he shrugs, "now watch this."

René places his mug on an end table and proceeds to fasten two black suspenders to his thick elastic waistband and pulls one over each shoulder. He then takes a third shorter black elastic and attaches it to the two vertical lines to create one horizontal line just below his collarbones. "My Mondrian-inspired grid," he says. "Avant-garde color-blocking, n'est pas?"

"For sure—so cool." I sound majorly impressed.

René skips over to the control panel for the projector, fumbles around with the sound system, pops in a videocassette, and returns to the center of the room. He then stands frozen before the huge movie screen, watching his homemade recording of a fashion show—skinny boys modeling bathing suits, clopping down the runway to a tinny beat only they can hear.

Doing my damnedest to gather his attention—and my own—I walk over, stand facing him, and begin the workout session. The light from the overhead projector flickers into my eyes with enough intensity to trigger a seizure, but I don't let on. From René's perspective, it must look like I'm being run over by the hordes of gorgeous male models. But I just pretend that this happens all the time.

Multiple measures later, René returns to the control panel and mutes the sound, but leaves the picture playing. "Mathieu, can we practice the dance now?" He adjusts his suspenders, tugs his padded thong underwear, inserts a CD into the machine, and takes on a big grin. "This is the music I have selected for this year's composition."

"Oh...the dance...sure." I don't have a clue.

As we wait for the music, the male fashion show continues in the background like a Chaplin film. And the moment the music comes on, René taps his feet and thrusts his hips to the beat.

"Mathieu, it is called *Little Red Corvette*—recorded by the artist previously and currently known as Prince...do you know of it?"

"Sure." I don't add that Prince's music reminds me of being an insecure prom date.

"Last time around, we used a different Prince song, one by the name of *Raspberry Beret*." He does a tight spin in place— actually, a perfect pencil turn. "But I think corvette will be much better."

Kevin never told me about this. "I'm sure it'll be great."

As René continues to bop, I consider what other surprises he might have up his sleeve. I look at the door on the wall behind him—the one that opens to the hooker tunnel—and wonder if I should make a run for it?

9

Much to René's disappointment, our snowbound status didn't last long. Most of the roads were plowed open within hours of first hearing *Little Red Corvette*, and Olivia took off for Paris later that same day. I was disappointed too.

For the past several days, there has been no mention of Madame wanting to resume her workout, so I've been keeping busy rehearsing René's dance routine every morning. Surrounded by his video-runway boys and costumed like a giant parrot, René has started referring to the dance as his cardio-blast. And he's obsessed with working on it.

"No!" I shout at him the moment he finishes each run through. "It's not strong enough—do it again, from the top...*six, seven, eight!*"

No matter how many times we rehearse, René loves the role-play and thrives on being scolded for flubbing his kick-ball-change steps. It's hilarious to watch him obey. And for me, playing the part of bitchy choreographer has become a great way to vent my frustration.

"Did you find it to be substandard, Mathieu," he pleads, begging to be reprimanded.

"Yes. Completely unacceptable!" I shout with imposed confidence.

He gives me his shy-dog look, before we start the whole routine over again.

Today, René is thrilled that we have just completed setting the choreography—with less than a week of rehearsal. And it pains me to admit: he actually looks pretty good, good enough to be mistaken for a retired show-boy. Will I end up like this in thirty years time? Damn. I've got to get my show on the road soon.

"Mathieu, the steps are in the can!" Sweat glistens on his forehead. "Now the real work begins."

"Are you ready for what lies ahead?" I tease.

He wipes his glasses on his wristbands. "You bet I am! Do you agree that we should set a performance date?"

Performance date, what? Does he think Madame wants to sit through this? "What if we get a few more days under our belt, and take it from there?" I'm terrified at the thought of getting a bad review in *The Blue Blood Times*.

"Very good idea, Mathieu!" He sashays out the door.

After restoring the cinema seating, I head back to my room. And within a minute or so, my phone rings. I answer, hoping Madame has decided to see me again.

"Hello, Matthew. I am nurse Tatyana calling," a hoarse-sounding voice says, in a thick Russian accent.

"Oh, hi, Tatyana, how's it going?"

"Very well, thank you. Are you available, for to make meeting with me?"

"Sure...does Madame want to workout?"

"Soon she will be ready. Yet before her time with you... we must speak."

"Sounds good to me. Where should we meet?"

"Please come third floor elevator and I find you there."

"Ok—now?"

"If you please, Matthew."

Hoping to make a professional first impression on Tatyana, I reach for my— basically empty—notebook for Madame's workout notes. I also grab one of the fancy house pens and René's medical file. As I dash out my door, I realize I've hardly scanned René's notes since the first day in Morocco. But I bet Tatyana can shed some light on his complicated history—oh, I should probably tell her about the uncontrollable bleeding in the garden.

Once inside the elevator, I realize I don't really know what Tatyana's like. Ever since she arrived last week, she's been taking her meals upstairs to stay close to Madame, so I've hardly even seen her. Rumor has it, she's shy.

The moment the elevator door opens, Tatyana offers a handshake and walks away. I barely get a snapshot of her petite frame, grayish eyes, mousy brown hair, and her dorky library-lady glasses.

"Follow me, Matthew." She continues along the railing toward Madame's dressing area. "We speak in private." Her soft demeanor evaporates the instant she opens her mouth. So much for *shy*.

I follow Tatyana into Madame's wardrobe area and glance at the closet of lacquered drawers, concerned about how those cashmere gloves are surviving without any air circulating. Then, after crossing the room, Tatyana slides a door open, and leads us into a narrow hallway. Neat. When I was up here with Olivia, I figured this door was just another closet.

We pass through a vanity area, turn to the right, and arrive into what looks like a 1950s infirmary. The carpeted section of the dressing area comes to an end and white tiles take over the floor—scaling halfway up the walls. A dull green cot rests along the far side of the room with a pair of pale gray curio cabinets opposite. The faint smell of disinfectant lingers in the air. Rows of glass canisters with metal lids display cotton balls, tongue depressors, and long-stemmed cotton swabs. A collection of old surgical saws adorns one wall. These decorative pieces look more like artwork than actual tools. And Tatyana—in her starchy white nurses uniform, sheer white stockings, and bright white clogs—looks picture-perfect in this space.

"Matthew, I show it to you the record of Madame." Tatyana takes a seat on a padded stool and wheels over to a white enameled tray table.

"Okay." I sit down on what could be the only stationary chair in the room.

"Inside here," she motions to a huge stack of files on the counter next to her, "we see notation of Madame's entire history medical."

"Boy...that's a ton of notes. Have you read all that stuff?" "Of course, Matthew...my job is to know everything possible," she says, without sounding snooty. "Perhaps we look at facts together?"

As Tatyana lifts a file from the stack and begins to translate Madame's chart aloud, I finally get a better look at my new co-worker. Her button nose and innocent-looking face is stippled with faint brown freckles—accented with wispy brown bangs. She's about twenty-five, but vibes older. With an even closer look, I notice how her blue/gray eyes tend to fluctuate like the murky shades of a mood ring; her pale skin tone reminds me of why Alistair has nicknamed her *the anemic one*.

"You understand," Tatyana looks up from the documents, "here we find no medical notation for Madame to be ill...her problem is one of lazy woman."

"Really? So it's not actually life-threatening—nothing serious?"

"Laziness can be serious problem." She suddenly sounds like a young Barbara. "Madame is past two-year anniversary for death of Monsieur...and yet she remain depressed."

"So she needs more exercise, right?"

"Yes." Tatyana slides her stool toward a low filing cabinet. On the wall above the cabinet are three vertical paintings—hinged together to make one piece. They are brightly colored, probably oil. The first panel looks like a distorted skull with only bits of flesh remaining. The center one depicts the soles of the feet all covered in blisters. And the third section looks like an impression of severely arthritic hands. Aggressive style. But I love it.

"It is triptych," Tatyana says, noticing my interest. She pulls a file from the drawer. "It is by the name, *Modern Science...*

phrenology, reflexology, palmistry." Tatyana rolls back over to her table. "Gripping, yes?"

"Very cool," I say—wondering what the hell *phrenology* is. "So do you think Madame believes in all this stuff?" I walk over to take a closer look at the painting.

"No, Matthew. I think Madame believes in artist who created painting."

I laugh at her comment and inspect the heaviness of the paint on the canvas.

"Look inside paint layer...you find words written from artist pen. These words are to describe emotional, spiritual, and physical regions of the skull, the feet, and the hands. It is up to you...if you choose to believe this geography...these connections."

"It's awesome." I head back to my chair, blow away by the fact that Tatyana went from nurse to docent in the blink of an eye. I momentarily visualize her leading museum tours in those clunky white clogs.

"I like it here in my workroom." She looks down at her file. "Madame's oxygen levels remain low. Her constitution... it take extra time to acclimate for high altitude. At this moment, Matthew, I make some marching in place for her—but that is all."

I scribble some miscellaneous notes in my Madame book, acting official about it. "So...can you let me know when she'll be ready for more?"

"Soon we make regular program for her."

"In the mean time," I say tentatively, "would you mind if I ask you a question about René?"

"He is not for me patient...however, I listen."

I hand her René's portfolio. "I couldn't make sense out of all these medications he's on."

Tatyana shuffles through the first few pages and shakes her head in disbelief. "Is it accurate?"

"I don't see why not."

She sighs. "If Monsieur René is taking all this...he is

upon severe problem with drug interaction."

"Really?"

"Yes." She sounds like she's trying to prove her innocence to the jury.

"But can't you tell if they're old...maybe outdated prescriptions?"

"According to this papers, everything it is current. Monsieur René has many doctors, in many different countries to make prescription."

"Aren't they supposed to keep track of that stuff...the different doctors?"

"Is not forever the case, Matthew...many times, from one country to the next...the patient, he can pay cash money to receive what he want...when he want...no question."

I guess that's no big surprise. "So based on this information, can you tell what René's major problem is?"

"Drugs."

"No, I mean his illness...if you see any."

"No illness, Matthew...just the drugs. This man, he is addicted to pills."

"Crap. I thought he might have early Alzheimer's, you know, something like that. He told me his mom—"

"Of course he could have the Alzheimer," she interrupts, "he could have many things." She pauses to collate his pages. "But this combination of drugs is to kill him...long before he makes crazy."

"So, do think I can help him?"

"Matthew, we are here to serve Madame...she is our first concern. Do not waste time with Monsieur René."

"I guess you're right...but I was just thinking—"

Tatyana cuts me off with a laugh as if she's heard enough. "It is no guess. I *am* right." She stands. "You and I...we accept station in house of Madame." She hands René's portfolio to me. "Not in house of Monsieur René."

I stack Madame's notebook on top of René's portfolio and

grab the house pen. "Well, thanks Tatyana." I head toward the door. "I hope there's good news about Madame soon."

"I let you know," she says, and stays put as I leave.

The following morning, after I finish with René, Tatyana calls my room. "Madame is ready for to work."

"Really?" My inner-skeptic comes out. "When?"

"Now." Tatyana speaks as if our line could be tapped.

I hesitate. "For how long?"

"Madame is to make decision."

I laugh. "No pressure," I say and the line goes quiet again. "Tatyana?"

"We meet in music room." She whispers. "I come for to assess situation."

"Oh, okay, cool." I hope Tatyana doesn't plan to interject her ideas during the workout. That would be awkward. "See you there." Click.

As I rush through Galleria, I get the jitters as if it's my first day again. Barbara had pointed toward the music room during the house tour, but we didn't venture inside. I wonder what it's like, and I wonder if I've lost my touch with Madame? Back in Morocco, Madame was intrigued with me. I was her shiny new toy. But nowadays, I'm no better off than the rest of this staff—just another tarnished fixture.

The moment I open the music room door, I'm bowled over by its majesty, and damn near lose my mind. Have I entered a whole new wing? Impressive. This room looks more like a ballroom than a music room—large enough to host a chamber orchestra and a select number of lucky patrons. Hell. The grandeur of this room surpasses the main living room, and the floor-to-ceiling windows, facing the Alps, offer a breathtaking view—not to mention, the floor is to die for, so danceable. No doubt, this is where René dreams of doing his cardio-blast performance.

Off to one side is a grand piano—and a harp, of course. I spy groupings of framed sheet music, and shelves loaded with leather-bound books, probably catalogues of music. And there are just the right number of flowers clustered around the room — begonia? Any more pots would make it look like a funeral parlor.

Holy bejeezus.

How could I still be in awe of this lifestyle?

It's just another room full of more rich-people stuff.

Focus.

Before long, I've arranged a couple chairs in the center of the room, to serve as a workout area — not too close to the windows in case there's a draft.

Shit. Tatyana needs a place to sit too.

So, after moving Tatyana's chair to three different spots, I decide she should sit slightly behind Madame — out of sight, but within arms reach in case we need her.

Damn. Do I need a seat for Barbara too? What if she makes a cameo? Well, she can stand. I'm not going to accommodate her too.

So what the hell is going on? It's been fifteen minutes since I rushed over here. Where are they?

I move to the door and glance into Galleria.

No activity to speak of. Typical. More hurry up and wait.

As I head back toward the workout area, I randomly hum the first few measures of *Some Enchanted Evening*, my first audition song. It seems weird to be doing *South Pacific* with snow covered mountains in the background. But it could happen. I could be rehearsing an experimental production — one in which Bali Ha'i has merged with Antarctica, a statement on global warming.

I walk over to the piano, pluck out a couple notes to find pitch, and sing a few bars. Shoot. Either my ear is way off, or this piano stinks.

I finish the first verse and start to laugh, reminded of how David used to say, that if the singer of this song happened to be a twin, he could substitute the emotion of seeing his sibling in utero, and change the lyric from *across a crowded room* to *across a crowded womb*. Hell. I miss his stupid antics.

But he's a jerk. Seriously. I'm glad we're taking a break.

He's hardly even tried to contact me since I got here. And when he does, it's usually a super short email—so short I can't tell what's going on with our relationship. He's always sidetracked with silly stuff, like joking about a hot stable boy on staff, or asking if Madame likes to have Edith Piaf recordings pumped out of the manicured bushes. When David and I were on tour together, I loved all that silly stuff. That was our bond—one-upping each other. But now it's irritating. But now that we're apart, I wish he'd give me more clear-cut support. I wish he'd ask me if I'm really doing okay—coping with not dancing. He should tell me he cares about the fact that I got fired from my first Broadway production ever. And even though I don't want to talk to anybody about my injury, it's callous of him not to ask. Fuck. I don't get it. I don't understand how one careless instant could alter the rest of my life. After all the bullshit I put up with—paying my dues—doing theme parks, riverboats, and regional crap. At long last, I had a shot at first company and I blew it. I blew it all with one stupid-ass landing.

I look down at the piano, strike another key, and skip to the end of the song and sing out. I look out the window at the mountain peaks, and decide to go full voice for the powerful ending. I open wide: *ne-ver let her go!"*

"Am I interrupting?" Madame asks from behind me.

I turn around. Holy shit buckets. She and Tatyana are arm-in-arm in the doorway. They heard me for sure. "Oh, hi!" I squelch my impulse to apologize. That high note felt too fucking good. "Come on in." Duh. Like she needs my invitation. It's her house.

They walk forward a few steps, before Madame releases Tatyana's arm—proving she's fine on her own. "You have a beautiful voice, Matthew."

"Oh. Thanks." I clear my throat, and watch Madame head toward the chairs. She's unsteady. "I'm a little out of practice right now."

Tatyana heads toward her seat, no interest in small talk.

Madame pauses, almost at the workout area. "To my ear, you sound much better than someone who merely carries a tune."

I gesture to her seat, surprised that Madame recalls a detail from our lunch conversation way back when. "Sorry for getting carried away." Damn. I can't believe that slipped out.

Madame steps up to her chair. "No need to apologize, Matthew, you are most welcome to use the piano—anytime." She motions toward the open space in the center of the room. "And for that matter, you may practice your dancing as well." Madame begins to sit. "It would make for a nice change...to bring some life into these rooms."

A lump fills my throat. Will I ever—really—dance again? "Thanks so much." I sit down facing Madame.

Tatyana takes her seat and gives me a look: *what about the workout?*

Madame sits up straight and places her hands on her lap. "Shall we begin?"

"Yeah. Let's do this." I smile and start the warm up, like we've just met yesterday. I begin with the same gentle exercises we'd been doing in Morocco. And although Madame is out of practice, she always seems to enjoy our time together—regardless of what we're doing—so I'm not too worried.

Madame watches as my arms go over my head. "I am quite a fan of Oscar Hammerstein," she says, now holding her arms out to the side.

"Me too." I lower my arms to match hers. "Just do a few small circles here."

"Matthew, have you ever had the opportunity to perform *South Pacific*?"

"Now bring both arms forward." I chuckle. "Actually, I did...back in Junior High. I was cast in the role of Emile, the French plantation owner."

Madame looks star-struck as she lowers her arms down to her side. "Is that so?" She pauses from the workout.

I laugh again. "It's kind of ridiculous though, since the whole cast was a bunch of kids."

"I am sure it made for a nice learning experience." She sits up again, ready to start anew. "And who can tell, Matthew, you might very well mature into the role of Emile in time for the next West End revival."

I lead her into some leg extensions, impressed that she's up to date with the current London theater scene. "Anything's possible, right?"

"Indeed. I believe the songbook to be over there somewhere." Madame gestures to her left. "The complete Rodgers and Hammerstein."

I peek over at the wall of caged bookcases. The mesh doors remind me of a high-end chicken coop. "Looks like a great collection."

"Many bits of old Broadway, not to mention, the obligatory classical pieces." She laughs. "As one might expect."

"Neat."

"Are you a fan of Cole Porter?" Madame pauses from the workout once more.

"For sure. *Anything Goes* is the best, don't you think?"

"Indeed, my favorite." She grins and starts into her ankle exercises, demonstrating that she remembers our whole program. "Mr. Porter was quite the clever man."

"Totally."

Tatyana stands up and removes a blood pressure sleeve from her uniform pocket. "I take pressure now."

Madame stops doing the footwork series. "Very well."

Tatyana steps over and looks at me as if talking musicals is compromising Madame's speedy recovery. "Arm please."

As I watch Tatyana wrap Madame's arm, I wonder what it must be like to have lots of staff constantly around, people always coming and going. Then, as Tatyana pumps away, I notice a display case of violins behind Madame. Wow. How'd I miss those? Her violins rival my dad's shotgun collection.

"Do you play, Matthew?" Madame has picked up on my obvious interest.

"Strings?"

"Or any musical instrument."

"No. Not much. I mean, I know enough piano chords to prepare for an audition, but that's about it. What about you?"

"Not one note." Madame laughs to herself. "I had little interest…to participate in music lessons. My parents," she continues, now gazing out the window, "would have preferred piano or flute." She pauses and looks at me, her green eyes beaming from the reflection of fresh snow. "But I wanted to sing."

"Opera?" I ask, assuming that's what an old-money family would expect.

"No, no." Madame laughs again and glances at her arm as if Tatyana's taking too long. "Not unlike you, Matthew…show tunes."

"Oh." I smile. "Cool."

"Unfortunately, in my day, female performers were considered floozies–with the exception of legitimate sopranos."

Tatyana's task ends with a hiss and a release of Velcro. "Is normal," she mentions under her breath and returns to her seat.

I smile at Madame and start our next set of movements — wrist and fingers. "Well, your violin collection is spectacular."

Madame glances down at her stiff hands. "Thank you." She looks at me. "The Stradivari belonged to the family of my late husband, so I maintain the collection out of expectation."

Jeez. Our family heirloom was great grandma's secret recipe for rhubarb pie — completely useless outside of fair season. "Four more like that."

Madame tilts her head, seemingly distracted. "Do you see how the catgut gathers dust?"

"Oh, uh, yeah," I pause, completely out of my league when it comes to the topic of antique dust.

"Francesca!" René bounds in through the door behind Madame. He has on a white terrycloth robe and puffy house slippers. "Pardon the interruption." He glides forward a few strides and slides to a halt.

I try to keep a straight face.

"I am with Matthew at the moment." Madame speaks authoritatively, without turning to look at him. "Whatever it is will have to wait."

"Very well then," René smiles, as if happy Madame has the strength to resist him. "Lunch will proceed as planned." He turns to leave. "Without the ambassador."

Madame's face looks unconcerned, so I keep going with the workout.

Tatyana shifts forward in her seat and taps at her bare wrist: *time's up.*

I pause. "Madame, shall we move on to the cool down?" I ask, still feeling weird about *shall.*

"What a fine idea," she answers with an eager stare.

"Okay. So come on up to standing and we'll finish with a calf stretch."

Madame stands and gives a look of determination. She walks around to the back of her chair, holds on for balance, and stretches one leg back in a shallow lunge. "Oh, how I love the ballet barre."

I smile, realizing that she does actually enjoy exercise, when she does it. "That's it. Just breathe into it." I let her stretch a moment. "Good. Now switch to the other side and you're all done."

"Most enjoyable, Matthew." Madame changes position.

"Good job today. I think you're doing great."

"We shall meet again soon."

By the time Madame finishes her stretch, Tatyana steps forward to take her by the arm. As they prepare to leave, little Charlotta races in through the open door. She barks once, speeds forward, and skitters around several times in the same spot, hot on René's slipper scent.

"Ah, ma petit bébé," Madame sings out to Charlotta,

"qu'est-ce que tu fais ici...qu'est-ce que tu fais?" Charlotta wags furiously at Madame's feet and hurries away, as if she's showing Madame the way back upstairs. Madame and Tatyana follow close behind.

Damn. I wish our sessions weren't so brief.

Training Madame reminds me that I am needed around this place. But who knows when I'll see her again.

Once the last chair is returned to its place, I walk back to the piano and stare at the keyboard. I'd love to practice some tunes for the show, but something tells me I've just touched this piano for the last time. Come on. I turn to leave. No servant would ever use the house as their own, even after being granted Madame's permission.

I hit the lights and walk out.

It's just not done.

10

Another week has passed. Olivia is still away, René is off gallivanting in the snow, and both Tatyana and Madame are MIA—I haven't seen either of them since we met in the music room.

At the moment, I'm acting busy. I'm cleaning my room, in anticipation of one of Barbara's spot-checks. She loves to swing by unannounced, as if to share an update on Madame. But what she actually wants is to catch me off-guard, burrowing in my pigsty. During our brief interaction, she will find an inconspicuous moment to observe the tidiness of my closet. I imagine how she might run her finger across the desktop—in search of dust—while talking about her passion for early cartographers. Then, right before she leaves, she'll glance down at the corner of my mattress— hoping to spy a homemade shank. And if I could get my hands on a plastic knife and some duct tape, I'd gladly fulfill her fantasy.

A few minutes later, as I return the vacuum cleaner to the storage closet at the far end of Galleria, I notice a small can of air freshener on the shelf. Ah, this should please Barbara—some fragrance to add the finishing touch to my cleaning job.

So I take the can back to my room, shut the door, pull out the little pin near the top, and—SHIT—it explodes everywhere! The can erupts with a thick cloud of bug spray that engulfs my room. In a panic, I impulsively throw the can out the window and watch the cloud of smoke rise up from the snow-covered lawn. How could such a small can carry this much power?

I take a gulp of fresh air, hold my breath, and blindly cross through the smoke in my room, to go open the bedroom door. And after rushing back to the window, I pant through the security bars, wipe my forehead, and take a moment to reenact Shelly Winters' heroic swim scene from *The Poseidon Adventure*. I think about the fact that Ms. Winters had an under-appreciated career, and ponder whether or not her brother, John, ever helped her financially. Was Jonathan Winters related to Shelly Winters?

The can on the lawn finally stops smoldering and — thanks to my open door — a cross breeze is clearing the smoke from the bedroom. But as the fog exits, I notice it's not slowing down. Fuck. I must have left the Galleria door open when I came back from the broom closet.

Chasing the rolling cloud of smoke, I hurry out of my room into the vestibule, and choke my way into Galleria. However, by the time I close the door behind me, I realize I'm too late. A thick haze has already infiltrated the space. And to make matters worse, I just heard the elevator clang open.

So here I stand, trying to appear calm, amidst the toxic cloud and the priceless paintings.

Footsteps. Please don't let them be Barbara's.

The next thing I see is Alistair — my shoulders drop. He's wheeling a pushcart full of wine crates and wearing a huge smile. Something must be wrong for him to be this happy. A clumsy smile crosses my face. "Hey, what's up?"

"Hello, stranger." He pinches a sneeze, squints at the haze and then looks me square in the eyes.

I meet his stare. Fuck. He's on to me.

"Barbara needs you in the kitchen." He sniffs and pushes the cart onward beneath the cloud.

"Oh, okay." I dodge toward the service stairs. "Thanks."

Before leaving Galleria, I check back to see how bad it really is, and notice that the humidifiers are helping the cloud disperse. Cool. Maybe that's what they're here for? Then, as I start up the stairs, Alistair sneezes again and blames his dust allergy.

"Useless housemaids," he scolds, "can't seem to get anything right around here."

The instant I enter the staff dining area, I pause in my tracks—broken dishes are all over the floor. Porcelain plates have been smashed; silverware has been strewn everywhere. Next, I see Niko and Barbara sitting quietly at the staff table, but they don't know I'm here.

She is slumped over with her head down in her hands, and he is leaning back against the wall with arms crossed, sunglasses on. I can't believe Alistair set me up for this. I can just hear him saying *gotcha*. Little fucker.

"I should have known better," Barbara says under her breath, her face still buried. "What was I thinking? How could I have been this stupid?"

I pivot to leave and Niko sees me. Crap.

He shifts in his seat. "Hey, Matthew," he calls out, "come join us, will you?"

Barbara slowly lifts her head and looks at me, too spent to speak.

I fake an apologetic smile and reluctantly move toward the table—navigating a path through the debris—and brush off a spot to sit down. "Hey...what's goin' on?" I ask casually.

Niko stands up, pats me on the shoulder, and looks at Barbara. "Talk things over with Matthew." He starts to leave. "He will explain."

Lord, help me.

"Why," Barbara's eyes wander aimlessly, "because, he too is a man like you?" She lowers her head again.

Niko peers over his sunglasses at me. "Thanks, man."

God he's hot.

Niko leaves in the direction of the elevator. "I will be in the garage if you need me," he says, and gives me one more look.

I nod at Niko, as if we're bound by a universal pact, as if there's an innate understanding of women shared between all men—gay, straight or otherwise.

Once Niko is gone, Barbara looks over at me. "Why do I trust men," she utters, "why on earth do men insist upon hurting women? And what do you think is going on in a man's brain when he acts like a dog?"

When Barbara says *dog*, I imagine a stage manager cueing the sound effect of a dog bark. *Woof. Woof.*

"Why, Matthew?"

I clear my throat to cover my pause. "I don't know," I pause, "that's rough, I mean, uh…that's a tough one."

Ignoring my fumbling response, Barbara surveys the floor. "When I first met Niko, he was the most handsome man I had ever seen." A slight smile waxes then wanes. "He looked like a young James Dean, and had the body of a young James Bond."

Okay. So, Niko's good looking and all, but this double James' comparison, seems a little over the top.

"Smitten, from the moment I saw him…all those years ago. There was just something about his deep-set eyes and the way he looked at me."

Oh God. Please don't let her get into the first time they had sex. "He seems like a nice guy."

"Well, he is not!" She brushes the remains of a dinner plate onto the floor. "He is a pig—a genuine couchon—and I should have known it from the start!" Barbara pauses, and picks up the one unbroken drinking glass from off the table, as if planning to crush it with her bare hands. "Matthew, would you believe that Niko has been fucking that mousy little bitch Tatyana?" She strangles the helpless glass. "What could he possibly desire with her?"

Don't respond yet, just chill.

Wait and see where she goes next.

"Ever since Tatyana arrived in casa," she quiets down, "this place has gone to hell…and you know of that cheap perfume she wears?" Barbara looks at me at places the glass back down to the table in front of her.

"Yeah."

143   Awaiting Madame

"Ooff. Well, Niko walked into my room this morning—her rancid odor all over him. I slapped his face, and he played innocent." She stares into the bottom of the empty glass like she's reading tealeaves. "Oh, but he knew why...and I ask you...how can anyone trust that little wench Tatyana? If we are not careful, that imposter of a nurse is going to kill Madame—immediately in front of our eyes."

After a long pause, Barbara slowly moves toward a storage closet. "Of course, this is none of your worry." She reverts to her usual professional tone, reaches into the closet, and pulls out a dustpan and broom. "But, Matthew, I do believe you should be made aware of what is happening upstairs." Barbara sweeps the floor calmly. "I will finish tidying here. You are free to go."

"Okay," I say and stand up, clueless as to how I'm going to finish my thought, "see you at dinner tonight."

Barbara offers me her hand, and guides me gently over her pile of broken dishes. "Watch your step...and thank you for listening...you have been most helpful."

"No prob." I exhale, and make a beeline out of the dining area toward the kitchen.

Assuming I'm in the clear, I hear Barbara dump her dustpan full of glass into the garbage. I consider grabbing some tea and cookies from the kitchen. But before I do, Kan springs out from his pantry station. *Surprise.*

"Come here. Come quick, boy. I have very important message for you."

His eager beaver routine just scared the shit out of me. "Oh, hi, Kan, what's up?"

"Everything is good. But Olivia...she is looking for you."

"Really," I say, hardly able to conceal my excitement, "is everything all right?"

"I cannot say...but you can phone her from here." He hands me the kitchen landline—with a mess of cord that looks long enough to reach all the way upstairs to Madame's bedroom. "Just press...star, six, two, three, and Olivia, she will answer."

As I dial the phone, Kan tugs at his vest and leans up against the wall as if he has nothing better to do than listen in on our conversation. After one ring, I peek around the corner into the kitchen. I see the chef and the sous-chef unloading wooden flats of fresh produce, and they too seem curious about listening to my phone call with Olivia.

I hear the second ring. "Maybe I should just go downstairs and call from my room," I mention.

"No, no, you should call from here," Kan insists, the moment Olivia answers.

"Olivia!" I yell with a pubescent crack. "Hi, it's me."

"Matthew!"

"Yeah. Where are you?"

"Look up," she says, as if stating the obvious. "Inside the dumb waiter."

I glance at Kan and mouth the words *dumb waiter*.

Not the least bit offended, Kan leads me across the kitchen to the huge marble-slab workspace in the corner. I glance at the long phone cord dragging on the floor behind me and hope Barbara doesn't walk in and trip over it.

As soon as Kan unlatches a steel door in the wall and points for me to look inside the compartment, I shove my head into the box. I see a flashlight flicker coming from up above.

"You're back," I yell into the phone and echo into the shaft.

"Only moments ago. Do you have time for a visit?"

"Sure...which way is best?"

"Take the elevator...but we must be quiet."

"I'll be right up." I rush to return the phone to its original spot, gathering the cord as I go. "Thanks, Kan."

His face takes on a proud-papa expression. "She is most beautiful woman. You are lucky man."

As Kan congratulates me, I see the chef give the sous-chef an elbow to the ribs. "Okay. Well, thanks again." I smile and split. "See you guys later."

The moment the elevator door opens upstairs, Olivia gives me a warm hug. "Things are still going well, yes?"

"Great." I lie—wishing I had called her every day since she left.

"When I did not hear from you, I figured everything was fine." Olivia starts down the hall, this time heading away from Madame's dressing area.

"Yeah, yeah. All good." I whisper, mindful of Madame and the dogs.

Olivia leads us into a den/library, where the interior design switches from Madame's typical white/off-white scheme, to earth tones, rich greens and browns. Very manly.

Paused in the doorway—as if to wipe my feet—I stare across at the stone hearth fireplace. I imagine this room is where Monsieur might have retired with the gentlemen after dinner, while Madame and the ladies would most likely assemble in the living room for Parcheesi. How civilized.

"News flash of the day," Olivia moves toward the far side of the room, "Niko and Tatyana are now an item, and Barbara is surprised to learn that her lover is cheating with another?"

"Yep. That's basically it." I traverse the open floor space where a big bearskin rug ought to be. "Barbara wasn't doing so great just now. It looked like she and Niko had a huge fight."

"This is what happens amongst the staff, Matthew. In fact, by now, there are no doubt rumors circulating about you and I as well."

"Us?" I laugh, positive I've never been the subject of a *straight* rumor.

Olivia giggles and walks behind a large slanted drafting table stacked high with printouts of digital photos. The low hanging triangular-shaped lamp above the table illuminates her face with theatrical intensity. She is wearing her usual black-on-black outfit, and her scarf today is a charcoal grey accented with bold white polka dots. Her exaggerated check bones appear even more pronounced and her eyelashes seem to thicken from the shadow.

"Well, nearly every member of the staff has slept with Niko at one time or another," she says, as if it's no big deal. "I believe, he and Alistair even had it off a few times."

"Really?" I sound nonchalant. But I'd sure as hell choose Niko too. "So, what's the deal with these guys...are they all *bi*?"

Olivia grins and opens up a decorative box. She begins removing art supplies—colored pencils, markers, a glue stick. "Are you kidding? They are simply bored—bored stiff." She lets out another small chuckle and takes an X-Acto blade to a sheet of paper and makes a cutout. "These men would penetrate a hole in the wall...as long as the hole had enough insulation."

I laugh as she motions for me to come around the table to stand beside her. "So how was your trip?" I ask.

"Formidable," she responds in French. "Can you imagine...it took me nearly two weeks to finish with Paris? And I leave tomorrow to begin on the Moscow residence.

Darn. I can't believe it.

She glances up. "We are going out tonight to celebrate."

"Where to? To celebrate what?"

"To celebrate ourselves." She gets back to work. "To have an evening outside the house, that is all...I wish to show you my favorite casino in town—I think you will enjoy it. I always do."

"That's sounds like fun. I've never really gambled, but I'm willing to try—do I have to dress up?"

"No, just be presentable." She lifts up a big stack of color prints. "But I cannot go out until I finish this entire project. These are the most recent inventory pictures."

"Do you need help?"

"No. No." She dismisses my offer, as if it would take too long to train me.

"So what are you working on?"

"I must first chronicle every item in each room in Paris, then I have the London townhouse to do, it's scattered over there somewhere. I am so far behind."

"Cool. Can I take a look?" I eyeball the stacks, thinking

I wouldn't mind a little side-trip to Paris, Moscow or London. But then again, what difference would it make? Barbara wouldn't grant me the freedom to venture out to a café or pub anyway.

"Go on, but try not to lose the order."

By the time I see a few pics of expensive knickknacks, Olivia starts shuffling three-ring binders and juggling a sterling hole-puncher. "Thank goodness for the digital age," she says and reaches for a manual pencil sharpener. "These days, all I need do, is make a photo and update descriptions later."

"All of this for one apartment?" I look at the reams of paper and wonder why it's not in a computer database by now.

Olivia sharpens one of the colored pencils. "Yes. Each house has its own book that lives in a separate residence. You understand...in case anything were to happen, the archive would still be safe."

"Is it tedious, keeping track of everything."

"Well, not so much nowadays. But years ago—yes. When Madame would walk though a living space and decide to move an ashtray from one end table to another, the book would have to be updated. I had to account for Madame's every design impulse... even if she later returned the ashtray to its original spot—which she usually would." Olivia continues cutting, pasting, and hole punching with the greatest of ease.

"Sounds exhausting." I notice a corner cupboard stocked full of similar binders. "So are all of those for inventory too?" I point at the shelving.

"From here over," Olivia answers, and cuts the cupboard in half with a strong vertical arm gesture. "These others are press scrapbooks."

"And what don't you do?" I ask jokingly.

"Well, the press aspect of my job is also waning. I used to have daily tear sheets to contend with...articles, photos, any public mention of the family would be filed away. That part was fun...especially before we relied on the Internet—I used to love playing detective."

"That sounds neat."

"Yes, it was great, truly. And although Madame rarely paid attention to the media, every once in a while I would share some scandalous tidbit with her. She could not help but to be flattered by the attention...both good and bad."

The desk phone rings.

Olivia snaps it up. "Allô, Olivia...oui, Madame. Mathieu? Non, Madame, non, il n'est pas ici...Je ne peux pas dire...okay... très bonne...oui, oui, je suis entrée...merci, Madame." Olivia hangs up and looks at me excitedly. "That was Madame."

"Yeah. I got that much." I laugh. "What'd she want?"

"She was looking for you."

"Shit. Did Tatyana call my room?"

"Not that I know of. Madame simply asked if you were available."

"And what'd ya tell her?"

"I told her the truth: *I cannot say*."

"Oh, no...do you think I'm in trouble?"

"Not at all. But I do think she wants to work again."

"That'd be awesome. I hope she does."

"Head downstairs, and I will let you know." Olivia rushes us out of the den. "If you do not hear from me, then I am certain Tatyana will call to confirm." She motions me down the hall.

I hurry toward the elevator. "See ya later."

Thirty minutes later, still waiting by the phone in my room and gradually adjusting to the scent of my bug-repellant bedspread, I decide to call Olivia for an update. I check her extension on the house directory and mentally replay Kan's dialing instructions. I carefully press star, six, two, three.

Three rings—no answer—four rings.

And just when I'm ready to bail, someone picks up. "Allô?"

I think that's Madame's voice. I hesitate.

"Oui," the woman says.

Damn. It's definitely Madame. If I hang up, she'll trace

the call to my room. I'd better say something. "Madame?"

"Oui?"

"Oh, hi, uh, this is, uh, Mathieu." I put on my fake French accent.

"Mathieu?" She's clearly puzzled.

"Oui, Madame...Mathieu...from America." I now realize I've probably totally confused her by mentioning America, when I'm actually phoning from downstairs.

"Oh, Matthew, what a pleasant surprise." She speaks in better English than my French.

"So sorry, Madame, for disturbing you," I blab.

"No disturbance at all," she continues graciously, "it is a pleasure to hear from you."

"Olivia mentioned that perhaps you would care to exercise today?" Why the hell do I get so formal with her—*perhaps you would care*, that sounds ridiculous.

"Oh, no, Matthew, merci...not today. I am the slightest bit under the weather."

"Well, perhaps tomorrow then?"

"Peut-être, Matthew...peut-être."

"Okay," I pause and search for a proper way to get out of this conversation, "see you tomorrow then." Ah, shit. Now that sounded like I didn't understand that she just said *perhaps*.

"Merci beaucoup, Matthew, merci." She hangs up.

Crap. I can't believe I just crank-called Madame. Now it's confirmed. I'm a nut.

I put down the phone.

What should I do?

Should I try Olivia again, or just drop it?

Fuck. Just drop it.

Five hours later, Olivia and I are entering a casino somewhere downtown. "Matthew, you made quite an impression on Madame this afternoon," she says, as we walk toward the reception desk.

"What d'you mean?"

"Madame said so herself." Olivia pauses to hand her passport to the clerk, then looks at me. "The instant she hung up the telephone in her study."

Following Olivia's lead, I hand my passport to the clerk and prepare my best naïve response. "For real?"

"Madame thought it was terrific you took the initiative to call her," she gives me a big grin.

Olivia receives the tags for both our coats and places her passport back inside her sparkly clutch—maybe her purse is on loan from Madame's collection?

"Hell. I was so embarrassed, I didn't wanna tell you...but I guess it's cool if it worked in my favor."

"Yes. I do believe it did," Olivia says as we pass through a large gaming area. "I believe that today was the first time anyone has ever directly confronted Madame for avoiding her exercise."

"Well, I sure didn't mean it that way."

"I understand, you took a chance with her," she veers off into a smaller adjoining room, "and it did not backfire. However, even Barbara knows better than to make demands of Madame. Do tread lightly."

"Got it." I nod to Olivia as we step up to a caged window where we each purchase a plastic casino card loaded with two hundred euros, from a woman that looks like she has held this job since before I was born.

"Matthew, do you believe Madame will ever be able to regain her strength? Truthfully, tell me your honest opinion."

"I cannot say!" I shout loud enough to be heard over the clanging slot machines.

Olivia rolls her eyes and lets out a hearty laugh when she hears that I've resorted to using the staff-favorite refrain.

"Very funny," she smirks as we move away from the cashier's window, "but do keep in mind...if Madame is still going strong when your current contract expires, you will have the right to renew for next year."

A rush of anxiety washes over me, as Olivia climbs onto a padded stool in front of a big red mega-slot. I pause and look around the room, hoping to distract myself from the thought of being seduced into this job for another year. The casino décor looks *Eastern Bloc*—whatever that means. The ceiling vents are filthy and these well-worn chairs need to be replaced. But why shouldn't I continue with Madame, I think to myself as I take a seat on the stool next to Olivia. The money is good, the food is outstanding, and the kooky characters for my show keep coming my way. "Thanks for reminding me about the contract," I finally say, now noticing that Olivia has already inserted her plastic card into the machine and is repeatedly pressing the spin button. I insert my card, then look at her to see if she is listening. "But I really don't know how I feel about that."

Olivia doesn't look up, so I cautiously take my first spin.

"You know, when we were emailing before I came over?" I look at her again, hoping to jar her memory.

"Yes." She answers without looking my way.

"You explained how I'd have plenty of time to rest my knee."

"Yes," she says flatly, "I am listening."

"Well, I have." I return to my game, losing points faster than I can push the button. "But I also thought this job would be a good gap year. I figured I'd have some time to evaluate my life in New York—from a distance—to help me decide what else I'd like to pursue."

"A year of introspection."

"Yeah. I mean I never really knew if David and I were meant to stay together—"

"And..." she jumps in, suddenly enthused.

"Well, let's put it this way...it's given a whole new meaning to the word *gap*. So far I'm just coming up blocked and confused."

She looks over and smacks me on the arm playfully. "Come on, has it truly been that bad?"

"Well, to tell you the truth, I feel underused. And I wish I knew I could return to New York and be successful at something other than acting, singing, or dancing."

As I finish rambling, a cocktail waitress walks over and offers us two muddy-looking drinks. Olivia presses her spin button once more and we each take a glass. "Cheers, Matthew, here's to you, to life, and to you and David working everything out!"

"To us," I say as we toast. Whiskey sour—emphasis on the sour. "Hey, I never asked you if Madame and Monsieur had any children?"

"Well, now...that came out of nowhere," she shouts over the ringing sounds of another's winning machine.

"Oh, sorry. You're right. I think I do that—change the subject—when I feel uncomfortable."

She presses her spin button and looks over at me. "So what does he look like?"

"Who, David?"

Olivia rolls her eyes as if I'm being ridiculous. She then reaches over to my machine, presses my spin button—proving that the machine only works if I tell it to work.

"He's hot—"

"I knew it," she stops and stares at me.

"But I'd never tell him that." I laugh and press my spin again.

She turns to face her machine and rubs her hands together vigorously, as if friction might summon luck. "Go on, tell me more." She presses her spin button and grabs for her cocktail.

"Well, he's a little taller than me...more built... more talented...and all-around better looking." I frown, letting her know I'm being intentionally self-deprecating.

She glances at me and laughs. "You are both in show business?"

I can tell she's begging for some juicy details. "Yeah. He's the hunky, leading man type...I get stuck with the innocent side-kick roles—best friend, boring neighbor. But enough about David, tell me more about your boy Danté."

"Oh, he is fantastic…quite the playboy though. At first, he was a bit too suave for my taste," she pauses to press her button again, "but over time, his charm grew on me."

Ding! Ding! Ding! Olivia's machine signals a big win. She sits back, and sips her drink as her numbers go sailing up. And with more than triple on her card, she immediately ejects it. "If you want more gossip, we must go someplace quiet."

"For sure." I eject my dwindling card and look at her. "But now look who's changing the subject."

She playfully punches me again. "Follow me, goofball." She takes off.

As we barrel through the crowd of hopeful gamblers, I think about how I'll need to hire a really good sound designer to recreate this casino environment. But it can be done. Then, as we pass a cocktail waitress, Olivia trades her empty drink for a fresh one. She motions for me to do the same and we keep walking. And after we pass the third roulette table, she leads us through a door into a separate lounge area where everything quiets down and the lighting becomes much softer.

"We can relax in here for a moment, Matthew." The aggravating sound of slot machines fade away and ambient lounge music takes hold. "It is VIP-only in here, but they all know me."

"This is sweet." Great sound cue—nice lighting and set change too.

The moment we sit down in our low bucket seats, Olivia swivels to face me and becomes serious. "So you want more about Madame and Monsieur?"

"Yeah, tell me everything."

She takes a breath and another sip. "Well, they only had one son. His name was Hubert. He died years ago, in a horrible accident. It was the worst day ever." Olivia closes her eyes and lets out a genuine sigh.

"I bet."

She looks at me as if speaking confidentially. "Hubert and

his wife were killed in a helicopter crash. While their only son, Étienne...fifteen at the time of the accident—was safe at boarding school. Ever since Hubert died, Madame has looked to Étienne to fill her void."

"I'm so sorry." I impulsively reach for some peanuts from the snack bowl on a table between our two seats. Olivia looks at me, indicating that the communal bowl is not to be trusted. My hand recoils. "God. That must've been awful, to watch Madame go through that."

"Unspeakable." She shakes her head a little. "On the day Madame learned that Hubert was gone...Zia Lucetta explained to me how she had never witnessed such sorrow. I remember as if it were yesterday." She pauses. "You see...family fortune might provide a level of physical comfort, but nothing in the world can guarantee one's emotional security."

"I never really thought about it like that. I guess I just figured life was hunky-dory when there's a ton of money around." I hesitate long enough to register my ignorance. "So, Madame and Monsieur never had any more kids?"

"No...well, not together anyway. Monsieur, he fathered two additional children with two other women."

"Oh...does Madame—" I stop, realizing I might be crossing a line.

"Yes...she knows. And the offspring are provided for financially...but neither child is permitted to publicly admit any connection to the family...or they relinquish their monthly stipend."

"So this means that the grandson—Étienne—will inherit the whole kit and caboodle?" I think I've followed her story.

"Basically. But with Herr Vollstrecken orchestrating her legacy...frankly, anything could happen." She takes another sip of her drink. "For all we know, René and the half-siblings might walk away with everything."

"Who's voll-sTRECk-hen...did I say that right?"

"Yes. Perfect pronunciation...fantastic German sound."

"Thanks." I grin, convinced I can pull off an authentic Barbara.

"Herr Vollstrecken is an egocentric businessman…one of Monsieur's long-term friends…you will meet him soon enough." She swigs the rest of her drink and stands up. "But enough with this serious chatter, let us continue our evening of debauchery."

"Ah, come off it, tell me more." I half-stand and chug my drink. "I wanna hear more about Mykonos."

Olivia starts toward the door. "Another time, Matthew. Mykonos is, how you say…a real downer."

Like a tragic helicopter crash isn't? "Promise you'll tell me sometime?"

"I promise. But not tonight…tonight I want to have fun."

Once we exit the VIP lounge, she gestures left, as if she has a plan. "Guess who taught me to gamble?" She glances at me.

I shake my head. "Who?"

"René," she blurts.

"Come on, are you serious?" I give her a suspicious once-over. "I thought for sure you were gonna say Niko."

Olivia puts her right hand up as if swearing the truth. "Yes, he did," she laughs as we continue across the main gaming area. "Now, I would not consider slot machines, roulette, and craps gambling…but when it comes to cards, René taught me nearly everything I know."

"That must've been interesting," I say, as we approach the blackjack table, "to see René sit still long enough to play a hand of crazy-eights."

"I know." She retrains her laughter and we take our seats. "And surprisingly enough, he is quite good at cards." Olivia pulls her seat up closer to the table and proceeds to buy some chips from the dealer—enough for both of us. "During the first week after Hubert's death," she whispers, as the dealer begins to deal. "Madame stayed in her room the entire time. René brought me out to the casino every night that week…I was barely old enough to gamble."

I tally my first two cards—nine plus four.

"Honestly, I do not believe Madame would have made it through Hubert's death without René to comfort her." She looks at her first hit from the dealer. "Monsieur went away on business and Madame was left to grieve on her own."

"How strange is that," I whisper, silently tabulating my third card—nine, plus four, plus jack—shit. "You make it sound like Madame and Monsieur were living separate lives?"

Olivia pauses and decides to *stay*. "Not always." She turns over twenty-one and collects a nice stack of chips. "But sometimes I suppose they were."

"Did Monsieur ever got jealous of René?"

"Not exactly," she answers with a distant look in her eyes, "Monsieur, you see, had his own companions...and I believe he was happy for Madame to have René."

Just as Olivia finishes her thought, the casino dealers start to rotate positions in the room. Our initial dealer, an emaciated woman with penciled eyebrows, relinquishes her spot to a hefty bald mustached man.

Midway into the next hand, my cards still stink. "So, what do you think'll become of René, once Madame's gone?" I *bust*, as she turns over another twenty-one. Crap.

Olivia gathers her new pile of chips. "Now that is quite a difficult question," she answers, so the dealer won't hear, "it is not easy to grasp the concept of René being able to function without Madame. But I am sure he will manage somehow."

After a few more rounds of blackjack, Olivia is ready to try her luck at poker and wants me to play too. "Oh, I don't know," I mention, discouraged about my losing streak. "I think I'll just grab a taxi and go on back." I snatch another shitty—but free—whiskey sour from a passing tray.

"Are you sure, Matthew...why not ride up to the house with me later?"

"I'm beat. But you should stay and have fun."

"Well, suit yourself...thanks for joining me tonight."

"It was great, really. Let's do it again—soon."

"Remember, I leave for Moscow in the morning." She hands me the ticket for my coat. "Not sure when I will return."

Bummer. "Not too long, I hope."

"Me too." She gives me a cheek-to-cheek kiss and walks away—leaving a long line of men gawking in her wake.

As I down my last drink, I watch Olivia take a seat at the high-stakes poker table. And the minute she sits down, she seems to have total control over the other players. Within seconds, I can tell she knows how to bluff like a champ and works the table like a pro. She is definitely René's protégé.

11

Today, smack in the middle of René's fifth consecutive run of *Little Red Corvette*, an elderly white man, with thick silver hair, walks into the cinema and lets out a piercing whistle. René and I both freeze and look toward the door as the man hails a salute.

The tall man is wearing loose fitting, greenish/yellow workout pants, and a matching sweater—chartreuse? His face is full of deeply contoured wrinkles and his grin bares a set of crooked teeth. "Bonjour chérie!" He yells from across the room, as if he is chewing a mouthful of grapes.

"Ah, mon dieu, Herr Vollstrecken!" René shouts and runs over to greet him.

René hugs the man with such boundless enthusiasm, I wonder if his legs might leave the floor and end up around the old man's waist. Oh, so this is the businessman Olivia mentioned in the casino last week.

"Tout okay, mon amore?" The old man garbles, still embracing René.

"Ah, oui, oui…how fantastic to see you again, Dagen. It has been quite some time."

As the music begins to fade, the old man turns his attention to me. He scans me up and down, just like René did on the first day in Morocco, but this time it feels totally creepy—even from a distance.

"Dagen," René says, now leading the man in my direction.

"May I present… trainer extraordinaire…Mathieu Whyteman."

The old man extends his gnarled hands and a shiver runs up my back. They are damn near gangrene. He leers at me, then latches onto my forearms with enough force to crack a walnut. I'm speechless.

René looks at Vollstrecken. "Mathieu will take fine care of you." His lazy wink lands somewhere between the three of us.

"Nice to meet you sir," I lie, repulsed by this man's nasty vibe and mothball smell.

"Mathieu," René begins, as Vollstrecken finally lets go of my arms, "Herr Vollstrecken is Madame's dearest comrade. His wish will be your command. No questions asked."

Vollstrecken half grins.

René gives Vollstrecken a peck on the cheek. Then grabs his glasses from the end table and scampers toward the door.

I shudder. Please don't leave me alone with him.

Vollstrecken chuckles as we watch René leave.

Oh God. Please stay.

And the moment René disappears, Vollstrecken turns toward me and fixes his eyes on my crotch.

My anxiety gives way to anger. I'll kick this jerk in the nuts if he tries anything.

The old man glances up at the movie screen. "Matty," he looks at me, "please turn off that horrible fashion show. We prefer to work without distraction," he slowly scans my body again, as if he might have missed something the last time around, "especially when we have such pleasures right here before us."

"Sure." I sprint over to the control panel, thrilled to put some distance between us. Breathe.

"Matty…we shall first have some light gymnastics…followed by a full-body massage with lots of cream." His eyes roll back.

Purposely stalling at the control panel, I explain to Vollstrecken that I'm the trainer, not the massage therapist—but he remains oblivious to the fact that I have a voice. So I cut off the projector, return to the center of the room, and begin the work-out without further discussion. I start with general stretching and eventually move into some slow-motion jazz-isolations; the jazz moves feel silly in silence and he looks ridiculous. Next, I teach him a couple basic yoga postures. But after the first few, he becomes more interested in watching me than participating.

"So flexible, Matty," he says with a suggestive grin. "Wherever did you learn such tricks?"

I ignore his remark and continue with the workout. But I can't wait for this to be over. Asshole.

Vollstrecken suddenly drops his arms to his side and feigns exhaustion. "Okay, Matty, that was stupendous…now we do the massage."

"Okay." I say under my breath and reluctantly head to the closet. Hell. Now I know why Barbara showed me the massage table during our house tour. Fuck. I don't want to touch this bastard.

While I prepare the table with sheets, Vollstrecken turns his back and drops his workout pants to floor. He stands—naked from the waist down—exposing the most hideous flattened wrinkly old-white-man ass I've ever seen. His buttock hangs, sags, and droops in soft loose folds that flap over the back of his upper legs. In fact, his legs are so incredibly thin I can see his dry, ashy scrotum dangling beneath his hairy, narrow butt crack. I feel sick.

"You see, Matty?" He cranks his head toward me, sounding like he is setting up some bullshit story. "I have this German doctor, who would like to hook electrodes to my ass, in hopes of rejuvenating these erstwhile gluteals."

As he glides his bony hand over his sagging ass—lifting up the loose folds of flesh—I look down at the massage table and act busy. I realize he is the executor of Madame's will, but fuck him, I won't be around long enough to qualify for anything anyway.

"Matty…I wonder if you would be so kind as to probe around this buttock and openly share with me your professional opinion?"

I glance at him. But before I can answer, Vollstrecken does a sharp about-face, exposing his large uncut penis and bulbous low-sagging balls. As he boldly presents his long, thick, semi-hard bratwurst before me—gray with pink under-marbling—I nearly dry heave.

"Tell me, Matty, what do you think?" He pauses, his workout pants still caught around his ankles.

My mind is racing. I want to leave this room right now. Fuckin' freak. And I also think calling me *Matty* is condescending. But I'm at a loss for words.

"Matty...is there any hope for me?" Vollstrecken grins, slips out of his t-shirt, steps out of his pants, and mounts the massage table—face-up.

I immediately cover his crotch with a towel and he looks up at me, eagerly anticipating my answer. So, after a brief pause, I diplomatically begin to describe some exercises I know that will help strengthen his butt muscles.

He soon interrupts. "Ooh, Matty...those sound ideal... when do we start?"

Noticing his enthusiasm, I realize I'd better clarify. "Well, these exercises are for you to practice on your own."

"Ah! What a bore, Matty." He frowns. "To do it alone... now that is no fun at all—is it Matty?" He sulks.

I smirk, but quickly return to neutral—I could lose my job if I'm not careful around him.

He points to his gym bag on the floor near the door. "Matty, would you be a doll and retrieve my special massage cream?" he asks with a dramatic sigh. "I borrowed it from my hotel suite in Milano."

Fuming, and wishing I could just walk out the door, I go get the cream and come back to the table. I force myself to slather some onto his upper body; I don't think I can take much more of him.

As I massage his neck and shoulders, Vollstrecken tells me that he is a very busy man, traveling constantly. He looks up at the ceiling as if stargazing. "A little rhyme, Matty." He clears his throat. "Ready?" He gives me another nasty smile. "Whether in Paris, Rome, Sardinia or Crete...reflexology gratis is an expected treat." He laughs and looks at me. "You see, Matty...you have moved me to poetry!"

Hating the fact that I'm caught in this situation, I continue the massage, avoid eye contact, and pray that René will come back in and save me.

A moment later, Vollstrecken mentions that my hands feel much better than Kevin's ever did. Apparently, Kevin had a stronger touch, but he wasn't nearly as *intuitive*. Vollstrecken stares at me, watching for the compliment to sink in. It doesn't.

Not sure what else to do, I once again relax my facial expression. And as time passes, I do my best to ignore his banter and the gross smell of his lotion—a rank combination of Old Spice, Hai Karate, and Pond's cold cream.

"Oh, Matty...you're divine, Matty...you have the hands of an octopus...that is just what I shall call you...*my little octopus*." His face takes on a shit-eating grin and he directs me to massage his upper thighs. "Those hip flexors have always been a problem area for me." He points toward his pelvis in case I misunderstood.

Ah, hell, no. Walk in now René!

"Ooh, Matty—I just love it." He moans with intense satisfaction. "You know...third-degree palpation is one of the few legal delights still available whilst traveling the Orient."

I don't know what the fuck he means, but I now have both hands and all my fingers shoving deep inside the front of his upper hip.

He writhes in a moment of pleasurable discomfort. "Ooh...yes, Matty...ooh—but not too strong now."

As he subtly adjusts his position on the table, I'm hit with a hefty waft of his stale-Camembert crotch odor, and have to suppress my gag reflex. Then, knowing that it hurts him, I dig my fingers in even harder. Take that, ass-wipe.

Still massaging his hip, I suddenly notice his hand has started to wrap around my upper leg. The old man is coiling my leg like a boa constrictor, and he's groping around for more than a thigh.

I hesitate, not sure how to deal with this.

But then, without planning to, I grab him firmly by the wrist and place his hand back onto the table. What's wrong with me, why can't I find the words to stop him?

He exhales through both nostrils, and stares up to the ceiling—his pouting-mask on.

Conspicuously dodging his next couple advances, I move down to his calves and feet. Once I get there, his feet turn out to be more hideous than his hands—but at least I'm now out of arms reach. What should I do now?

I need a plan to escape this room and his stink.

I glance up. Fuck. He's stroking himself under the bath towel. This is unacceptable. I have to speak up. "Sir—if you'd like to take care of other matters...I'm willing to leave."

"Ooh, Matty...please," he pleads, now blatantly jerking off. "Please do not take offense."

"You've got the rest of the day for that," I say, shocked that I no longer care if repelling his advances is what gets me fired.

"Yes...of course I could handle it later, Matty...but it only seems to work when I am with *you*," he zings. "Matty, *you* do not have to do it...*I* will do it."

Fearing I might punch this fucker, I reach for a hand towel and wipe the excess cream off his feet. "Okay...so that's it for today."

"Thank you, Matty—just wonderful." He continues stroking himself beneath the towel as I hurry toward the door. "You know, Matty, we will be leaving in the morning...but I am already looking forward to seeing you the next time I come to visit...now, come here and give me a little butterfly-kiss goodbye."

But instead of going back over or even saying goodbye, I slam the door and leave.

Outside in the hallway, I prop against the doorjamb and fight the urge to puke. Will I really have to deal with that sleaze-bag again? I would never have taken this gig if I knew he was part of the package. Douche bag. Should I file a complaint; mention his actions to Olivia? Really. How close could he be to this family? From what I saw in there, I can't believe Madame would enjoy his company. Is he actually her sole legal advisor or just some nasty mooch?

Halfway back to my room, I realize I'm probably not going to say anything. I can't risk getting into a battle that leads to my dismissal. Hell. I'd return to New York with one working leg, no promotable skills, and no income. Not smart. But I do know, I'm not going to put up with any more of that dirty old man's BS—no way/no how.

As I dart up the steps toward my room, relieved to see René's door is closed, I wonder how I'd feel about Vollstrecken's behavior if he were a more sophisticated-looking older man. Would I be this upset right now if he resembled Paul Newman, Cary Grant or an age-progressed President Kennedy?

I drop onto my bed. Damn. Probably not.

But if I do decide to file a complaint against Vollstrecken, it *would* be considered a case of sexual harassment, since I'm not attracted to him, right?

12

At breakfast this morning, there was good news and bad news: Vollstrecken would depart today as planned; Olivia would stay in Moscow longer than expected.

I couldn't more details out of Kan and Alistair, without sounding like I was confirming their rumor—Matthew and Olivia are sleeping together. After our night at the casino, the entire staff assumes we're going steady. And I couldn't care less if everyone thinks I swing both ways—they do.

In any case, here we are, another endless siesta, and I'm aching to get outside of this house. Madame and René are both asleep, and I refuse to wait by the phone for Tatyana, Barbara or anyone else. I'm outta here. My idea is to hike into town and buy an inexpensive, portable alarm clock—since mine broke. However, I'll have to be quick about it in case Madame does wake up inspired to workout.

After a peaceful walk down the hillside, happy my knee seems stronger each day, I wander the downtown shopping area and soon decide to enter the only jewelry store that doesn't have an armed guard working as the doorman—but I'm wrong.

Less than three feet into the store, a chiseled security guard steps forward and demands to see my passport. "How may I direct you, sir?" he asks nondescriptly.

"Alarm clocks, please," I answer.

"With or without cuckoo?"

"Without, please."

"My pleasure." He points to the rear of the store.

As I move toward the back, I pass cases of glimmering silver, gold, platinum, and diamonds. I see timepieces that probably cost more than college tuition, and jewelry that must be worth more than the mortgage on dad's house. And the shop girls—mostly blond, extremely fit—are standing by, ready to serve, in their conservative navy uniforms with golden buttons down the front. I try to look cool. But as I trudge deeper into the store, in search of a Kmart blue-light special, I accept that I'm in the wrong place.

Once I arrive at the final display case, I peer inside and find nothing that even remotely resembles my cheap travel alarm clock. Shit. Of course it's not here. Just breathe and appear fascinated by these silly penguin pendants.

With great hesitation, I look up from the case and glance at the woman behind the counter. Her engraved nameplate reads: *Hilda*. I hope she speaks English. "Pardon me, Frau Hilda...do you have any travel alarm clocks?"

"Yes, sir. Indeed we do." She dons a pair of white gloves.

I tremble as Hilda unfurls a royal-blue velvet display cloth, reaches beneath the counter into a hidden drawer, and removes an unmarked cardboard box. Upon opening this mysterious box, she presents to me—here on the cloth—one small flip-top plastic clock. Then, like a model on the shopping channel, Hilda begins to softly pet and stroke the clock while offering a complete overview of my fine selection. She explains that this item is battery powered. She details how to set the time by rotating the buttons on the back, and how to set the alarm by flipping a little side switch—cleverly marked with the words *on* and *off*. This unique timepiece also hinges open and closed, and it's made entirely of durable plastic. Hilda seals the deal by adding that this unit also comes complete with a one-year warranty.

I take a deep breath. This is exactly what I'm looking for.

I want this clock. It's perfect. But I quake at the thought of saying *yes* to Hilda without first asking the price. This moment feels
worse than being in an upscale restaurant where the waiter doesn't
confess the prices of the specials. But really, how much could they
possibly charge for a cup of corn chowder?

I look down at the royal-blue cloth and nod—just like I
saw Olivia do at the high-stakes poker table. Hilda successfully
translates my body language and begins to wrap my clock in a
tiny plastic baggie. With great care, she slips the plastic-covered
plastic clock into its anonymous cardboard box—direct from the
Chinese manufacturer. She drops the box into a soft cotton bag
and smiles as she tightens the gathered opening. Apparently, I can
use this handy black drawstring bag as a carrying case while traveling to-and-from my safe-deposit box.

Hilda looks at me. "Sir, may I help you find anything
else?"

I become René. "That will be all for today, thank you."

Hilda carries my precious item on a little tray and escorts
me toward the front of the store. And once we arrive, my sweaty
hands smudge the pristine display case as Hilda turns away to
calculate my purchase. How embarrassing to have to walk away
at this point, unable to afford the cheapest thing in the store.

Hilda returns. "Twenty-nine even, please," she says,
blandly.

If she means twenty-nine hundred—I calculate in euros—
that's more than three thousand dollars. But if she means twenty-nine thousand, my card will be denied and I'll be the laughing-
stock of this store.

Without flinching, I hand Hilda my debit card, acting as if
money is no object for me. And after she runs my card and presents
the charge slip, I'm greatly relieved to see a decimal point nestled
immediately after the nine on my receipt. Whew. My shoulders
drop. I sign the receipt and thank Hilda for her kind service.

"My pleasure, sir." She leads me to the front door.

As Hilda waves goodbye, the armed guard opens the door

for me and tips his hat. They both thank me for my business.

I smile and step outside. Now *that's* customer service.

The moment I hit the snowy sidewalk, I shove my sweaty hands into my itchy gloves and hold my head high—gently swinging my thirty-dollar bag with pride.

Within blocks of the jewelry store, I see Tatyana stepping out of a shop up ahead of me, carrying a white prescription bag. I think that's her.

I hurry along the sidewalk and by now she's only a few yards away. "Tatyana?" I call out and wave when she looks back—it is her. "Hey, how's it going?"

"Matthew...everything fine for me. And you?"

I catch up to her. "Great, great. Are you walking up the hill...wanna go back together?"

"No, no. Niko is here with car." She points to a black BMW with super-tinted windows.

"Oh." I wonder if she'll offer me a ride.

"You come with us, yes?"

"That'd be awesome, if it's okay with you guys?" Clearly, I'm interrupting their tryst.

"Of course." She continues toward the car. "We go now, with new medication for Madame."

Once we arrive at the car, Tatyana opens the passenger-side door and jumps in up front, so I hop in back.

Niko looks at me in the rearview mirror. "Hello, Matthew. What brings you into town today?"

"Just a little shopping, no biggie." I wish I could see his sexy eyes, but his glasses are too dark. "What about you guys, quick stop at the pharmacy?" Condoms, penicillin—I joke to myself.

"Well, um..." Tatyana stammers, "enough time for one errand and return to house."

Niko shifts the car into gear.

I lean up toward Tatyana. "So what's up with Madame?

Why hasn't she worked again since the music room?"

"Soon, Matthew." Tatyana answers as if putting me in my place. "Her oxygen is once more not good."

"Yeah, but, exercise will help." I sigh, frustrated that we've already been over all this.

"When time comes, I let you know," Tatyana says, lips pursed, "patience, Matthew."

Niko glances in the rearview again. "She was speaking about you yesterday," he says, aching to share good gossip.

"Who? Madame?"

"Yes. I was driving her and Herr Vollstrecken into town and overheard everything."

Fuck. My knee throbs at the mention of that SOB's name, or it could be because of the downhill walk.

I discreetly adjust my leg position; they don't notice my discomfort. "So what'd she say?" I ask, as if I couldn't care less.

"Herr Vollstrecken was telling Madame of your magnificent abilities." Niko grins at Tatyana and they bust out with an inside-joke laugh.

All the rage I experienced yesterday comes flooding back. But I purposely contain myself. "Oh…really?" I sit back and fish for a seatbelt.

Niko takes on a snide expression. "Whatever you did for him, Matthew," he hesitates as Tatyana turns around to look at me.

"Herr Vollstrecken was pleased with service," she says, evoking her standard professionalism, "and this news, it make for Madame happy."

Shit. That kills any thoughts of filing a complaint about him, since quitting isn't an option anyway. "Well, if Madame's happy…that's good, I guess."

Tatyana looks smug. "Her mood is most important." She turns to face forward again. "I hope for her to leave mountain soon—to make better condition for oxygen."

As Tatyana quiets down, Niko slides his hand across the back of the seat toward her neck. She holds her gaze to the front and subtly shifts her body away from his reach. Niko is so damn cocky he obviously doesn't care if I know about their fling. But Tatyana must still think she's got a secret. Funny.

I let things linger a moment and eventually decide to break in. "So when do you guys think we'll move to a different house?"

"I cannot say," they respond in perfect harmony.

My eyes roll.

I should've seen that answer coming. "Well, it's pretty up here and all…but if I can't train Madame on a regular basis, I'd rather go somewhere else."

Tatyana's back stiffens. "The decision is from Madame. Is not for us to decide."

Niko removes his arm from behind Tatyana, downshifts into the driveway, and stops the car in front of the house—engine running.

The moment the brake goes on, I jump out. "Well, thanks for the lift."

Tatyana stays buckled up in front.

Niko prepares to shift. "Later, Matthew."

I shut my door while Tatyana waves goodbye; she doesn't say anything.

As I watch them drive off, I'm hit with a pang of jealousy. And I'm not sure why.

I head toward the front door. I like Niko and all, but I don't think I *want* him.

Strange. Maybe I actually do miss David.

I step onto the wooden landing. Or maybe I just miss the idea of having someone to turn to?

Damn. Is this what *loneliness* actually feels like?

I enter the foyer and slowly take in the ski shop.

Well, I'm not sure I've ever experienced being lonely, but I know I'm not willing to recall this desolate emotional state— eight shows a week—just to make my character appear complex.

How draining.

I move toward the tunnel of art.

In acting class, I remember learning that it's impossible to feign vulnerability. A truly accomplished actor should remain susceptible to emotional attack at all times. But that's not me; I'm not that deep—or that brave.

The first spotlight in the tunnel pops on and jolts me out of my turmoil. Crap. Now, for the sake of the show, I'll have to change *my* name too.

13

The following evening, I'm happy to be outside the house again. However, this time, it's for official business. René and I are walking down the hillside, on a mission to drop off a pair of shoes at a house that was once rented by the exiled Shah of Iran.

René has already explained how *these* shoes were left behind in Madame's foyer, earlier today, after the book-club luncheon. And the forgetful lady who owns *these* shoes is friendly with the lady who resides in the house, once rented by the former Shah.

It's a mystery as to why I'm with him, but it beats staying in my room.

"Mathieu, the present-day owners are neither politically nor otherwise related to the ousted Shah," René clarifies as we continue down the snowy path, "our absentminded dear...who left *these* shoes at Madame's today...has plans to stop at the Shah's house tonight. She will arrive in her snow boots, change into *these* shoes for a sip of brandy near the grand fireplace, and then change out of *these* shoes—back into her snow boots—before heading home, with *these* shoes in hand." He pauses and glances down at the orange recycled Hermès shopping bag that I'm carrying, which contains the sacred shoes. "Mathieu, please be careful with that bag...we dare not lose *these* shoes again. Unspeakable calamity. Now here, take this...keep it around your neck. In the event of an avalanche we will still be able to locate *these* shoes." And by the time he has finished his sentence, René has placed a dog whistle necklace over my head and meticulously arranged it to rest upon my sternum. "There, Mathieu…we must not falter." He gently tugs on the whistle.

I accept the lanyard with the poise of an honored graduate and we continue walking.

"In return for our kind favor," René starts again, "the lady of the house will be lending us a few movies to watch at home in the cinema."

I smile, understanding exactly what he means by *us*.

"Mathieu, truly…our fair lady has one of the world's leading collection of foreign and domestic films," he touts, as we approach the former Shah's one-time driveway.

I think this reference to *foreign and domestic* is just his colorful way of saying she's got a lot of movies.

Now standing outside the huge front door of this enormous home, René presses the doorbell. It's push-button operated and needs some elbow grease to make it ring. But once it does, it sounds as though we've just pulled the ropes in the bell tower of a gigantic cathedral.

René's eyes widen. "What joy," he exclaims as a cloud of warm air exits his mouth, "and by the way, Herr Vollstrecken sends his regards."

"Really?" I say, hit by a wave of nausea—come on, not him again.

"Whatever you did the other day," René says, as the huge door begins to hinge open, "why, he can hardly wait to return."

Shit. "Did he say when?" I ask, hoping it's after I'm long gone.

René shakes his head *no*. "He might arrive again at any time…there is no telling with Dagen."

From behind the giant door, a tired-looking butler steps forward to greet us. The butler motions us inside, closes the door, and accepts the Hermès bag from René—which I have just handed over. Wow. This is the entranceway I expected at Madame's.

A beat later, the three of us cluster in the grand foyer area, as the lady of the house feebly stands up from her chair in the large living directly room across from us. Her small body is perfectly framed by the roaring fire in the towering fireplace. And with the awkwardness of a newborn fawn, she moves slowly toward us — aided by two metal braces, but hindered by a white plaster cast on her right ankle. Her elbows buckle with each step.

When the lady arrives, she gives a formal hello to René — they both ignore my presence — and he steps forward to escort her back into the living room, where he helps her into her seat near the fireplace. The moment they are both settled, an elderly housemaid enters. The housemaid pours two shots of liquor; the butler and I stand patiently in the foyer. Then, as the lady of the house tells René the story of her broken ankle, I notice how the acoustics make for perfect eavesdropping.

"Earlier this week," the lady continues, "I was airlifted off the slopes by a most unattractive synthetic harness...flat on my back in an ice-cold, stainless steel basket — lined with a merino blanket. I still feel the fibers on my skin," she adds as René confirms her distressing tale with a shiver of agreement. "And to make matters worse," she takes a sip from her glass, "can you imagine...I was to be refused a Cognac once we arrived at triage."

"Most difficult to believe what is happening these days," René pipes up. "Positively absurd...entirely unacceptable."

As I continue listening in on their conversation, I become intrigued with the housemaid who stands in distant profile — her pale face, warmly illuminated by the light of the fireplace. The maid is positioned behind the complaining twosome; her arms tightly folded around her waist. I love how she maintains an unfriendly stare at the butler who is still next to me at the door — his head submissively bowed. Jeez. It's like watching a reenactment of Barbara and Alistair.

While the lady and René continue discussing her accident and the latest in movies, I consider the fact that the Shah might have had even more attendants standing by in this drafty foyer.

Awaiting Madame

And aside from being enormous, this house is no place I'd want to live. It's creepy. Probably haunted. Feels like a place Edgar Allan Poe might rent, in order to avert writers' block.

An instant later, I notice a photograph hanging on the wall beside me—a picture of the Shah and his family. The people in this picture remind me of the first time I ever made eye contact with someone from Iran. It was 1979. I was in my middle school biology class, when this new girl, with gorgeous dark eyes and thick black hair, walked in and sat down next to me. She introduced herself and I asked if she could show me how to spell her name. R-a-s-a explained that she had just moved to Indiana from Iran. I asked her where Iran was and wondered why someone would come live in the middle of nowhere, when they already lived someplace that sounded so much more interesting.

Rasa grabbed a sheet of graph paper and drew a rough sketch of the Persian Gulf; she outlined the surrounding countries of her homeland. But by the time she was finished with her map and added a star over Tehran, I still couldn't identify where she was from. Then, later that same day, we met in the lunchroom and Rasa mentioned her Iranian Empress—Farah Pahlavi—so I told her about our American Goddess—Farrah Fawcett. And in that moment, we became friends.

My friendship with Rasa lasted several years, but during our junior year in high school, Rasa started dating my best friend Chad, and I was jealous—jealous of him choosing to be with her, instead of me. And oddly enough, my friendship with Rasa ended that year on a weird note. It was1984. I was with Chad and Rasa at a pep rally in our high school gymnasium. The assembly was organized to help re-elect Ronald Reagan, but we weren't even old enough to vote. So I guess the idea was to inspire us to make sure our families were voting for Reagan—some covert operation. Everyone was holding posters, stomping the bleachers, and rhythmically shouting: *Four More Years—Four More Years!*

Poster-less in my dancer blacks, I remember feeling out of place. So to avoid getting fag-bashed in the parking lot later, I chanted along with my friends and tried to fit in: *We Want More—So Give Us Four!*

Chad was standing next to me with his arm around Rasa, when he suddenly left us and ran up to the microphone in front of the entire school. Since Chad was a popular jock, it didn't seem like a surprise that he'd be giving a speech. And after he introduced himself, Chad announced that he'd prepared a piece of political commentary—thanks to the guidance of our English teacher, Mrs. Ima Belcher. Everyone laughed at the stupid made-up name and in turn, Chad recited a limerick—probably written by his older brother:

> Take a wee look at their sad little clique
> Out in left field there's not much to pick
> Old Lady Ferraro
> She looks like a sparrow
> And Mondale—he's worse than a spic!

By the time Chad finished, the principal yanked him away from the mic and the crowd erupted with cheers: *Hey, Hey! Ho, Ho! Walter Mondale Has Got To Go! Hey, Hey! Ho, Ho!*

Chad ran back over to us, bypassed Rasa, and gave me an aggressive hug—the type shared between two closeted athletes during a successful moment of the game. He quickly released his grip and pulled back to arms length. "Yo, Matt! Reagan's gonna be the fortieth…and the forty-first President of the United States. Dude, is that awesome—or what?"

Duh. I knew Chad was dumb as a doornail, but in that moment, I didn't care; I loved the way he was holding me in public. It was almost like he was no longer ashamed of his feelings for me. And I was sure he was ready to come out of the closet. If he comes out first then I can come out too, I thought to myself.

With Chad still holding me by the arms, Rasa looked at me with fire in her eyes. "You can have him!" She then looked at Chad. "Because no man gets to talk about Geraldine Ferraro like that!" Rasa stormed off and Chad chased after her.

Hum. But now I'm wondering what ever happened to my Farrah Fawcett swimsuit poster.

Once I snap out of my daydream, I notice the lady and René walking cautiously toward the foyer. I smile at them, but then tilt my head down, since the butler is keeping his head down. Then, as René and the lady pass—once again failing to acknowledge me—they head down the grand hallway on my right.

As they travel down this long corridor, I realize that our brief errand of dropping off *these* shoes is going to take some time. Watching them walk, I'm fascinated by how the lady's injured ankle swings heavily to the right. The weight of her cast disrupts the balance of her lithe frail body. And with each awkward step, she pulls more to the right. It looks like she's going to bump into the wall if she doesn't change course soon. But then, right on cue, René gracefully crosses behind the lady and offers to assist her—switching sides just in time to avoid collision. So suave.

The lady takes René by the arm, smiles warmly, then takes another step forward and pauses mid-stride. She remains in place, repeatedly pressing down on a noisy wooden floorboard—using her good foot to make it creak. "Delightfully sinister…is it not?"

René, of course, agrees.

The lady and René continue moving down the hallway. Now they veer so far to the right, it's as if they are purposely avoiding the treacherous art installation on the other side. Mounted along the entire left wall of this grand hallway, is an immense collection of armor with lots of jagged edges protruding from the rough stones. Various medieval fighting implements along with fragments of metal suits have been deconstructed and abstractly arranged on the wall, representing defeat on the battlefield. Some of the chest-plates are punctured and shin guards are dented—or nearly destroyed. Large spears, heavy swords, and frightful daggers have been flung to the ground in despair, while partially melted articles of protective chain mail signify a fiery event.

I'm intrigued with this crumbling installation—but also

saddened by its obvious lack of maintenance. Even from where I stand, I see that the hardware is rusted, and a few of the narrow spotlights have burnt out. The dismembered armor looks neglected and I wonder if it ever gets dusted. My left fingers begin to tingle. And it dawns on me that my hand has fallen asleep. So I wiggle my fingers a bit and try to stay alert.

Rubbing my hands together, I look over and see that the butler is standing with his eyes closed—probably more asleep than my fingers. Next, I glance into the living room, and notice the housemaid frozen in place by the fire—looking like a wax figure that might soon melt away. Then, I check the hallway once more, only to see René and the lady going into a side room. And as they disappear from view, it washes over me—it's not only my left hand that has fallen asleep, it's the entire left side of my personality. I've become complacent in this job. I'm slowly rusting away—just like this metal artwork. My old sense of drive is gone and my showbiz personality has damn near calcified.

I imagine how good it would feel to cause a scene in here. I'd love to rip up that creaky floorboard and use it to pound on that wall, turning the art installation into a giant drum set. I could refocus these spotlights—onto me—and sing *gotta dance* at the top of my lungs while doing Gene-Kelly-barrel-turns down this hallway. Or I could yank down a suit of armor and do my favorite Fred-and-Ginger number.

But I don't.

I don't do anything.

I just stand by and hold my place in the foyer next to the narcoleptic butler.

In the blink of an eye it comes to me, the understanding that lack of personal identity is primary to my job description. I'm doing exactly what is expected of me. And I'm not sure what will prove more taxing, overcoming my fear of Vollstrecken or accepting this level of inaction for the remainder of my contract.

About fifteen minutes later, René and the lady slowly return. I try to look alive. But it feels like I've been standing here—

knees locked—long enough to develop a blood clot. Hoping I'm still able to walk, I casually shift forward. Hell. My first step comes out like a stumble.

"Oopsy," René says, looking at me while he gently kisses the lady goodnight. "It looks as though someone has been into the liquor while we were in the other room."

I ignore his comment—implying I couldn't hear him—and the drowsy butler opens the door for René.

Once we step outside, I notice René is now carrying a re-cycled Prada shopping bag. "Truly, Mathieu…what a shame you did not care to join us in the screening room," he mentions coyly and waves the bag in front of my face. "Her movie library is sim-ply to die for."

Inside the bag are several DVDs, but he shakes it so quickly I don't get a chance to see which films he's borrowed. "My, that's wonderful," I say, knowing he loves that expression.

As the butler closes the door behind us, René points over to the guesthouse. "There…see over there, Mathieu," he continues as we make our way up the driveway, "that is where an army of athletic male staff was housed, during the summer the Shah was in residence."

"Really?" I glance over at the guesthouse. It's larger than any suburban McMansion and I wish I'd been around to witness that hot scene. "How interesting."

"Most interesting indeed, Mathieu. And the boys that summer…oh, they were truly spectacular. Regrettably only a memory now."

Damn. This guy really gets around.

On the approach to Madame's front door, René is already saying goodnight as he accelerates toward the landing, obviously planning to enter without me. I let him get ahead.

After all, I *am* the hired help.

"Goodnight, Mathieu." He nearly disappears inside. "See you à demain for Prince."

"À demain, René," I answer. *À demain*, I repeat to myself.

The very second René latches the door, I hear footsteps marching down the exterior wooden staircase. The footsteps become louder and more distinct with each passing step, until Alistair appears at the foot of the stairs. "What the hell are you doing out here?" He whispers, edgier than usual, clearly not wanting to be noticed.

"René and I just got back from our field trip to the Shah's house."

"And he once again locked you out in cold, did he?" He glances up above the front door toward the staff windows, paranoia written all over his face.

Before I can think of a good comeback, I notice a light coming from down the lane. It's randomly blinking on and off. "Looks like somebody should change that flickering bulb," I say, without much thought.

The light goes off.

"What bulb might that be?" Alistair responds—knowing exactly what I'm talking about.

The light comes on and blinks off again, then turns on once more.

"That one." I point. "The one sending out Morse code."

"Oh, come off it," Alistair scoffs and grabs me by the arm, "that's just Niko checking the fuses in the garage."

"Whatever," I say, now wondering why Alistair has taken to touching me.

"If you don't believe me…let's just walk down there and take a look, shall we?" Alistair tightens his grip and forcibly leads me down the lane toward the garage.

Within a few steps, the garage light goes dark again— leaving only the moonlight to illuminate the snowy pathway. He moves us along as if I'm resisting, but I'm not—I think this is great, he's saving me from the boredom of my bedroom.

Upon entering the garage, we find Niko and Kan sitting in lawn chairs—beside a three-foot long, light switch panel. And sitting in lawn chairs on either side of the boys, is a matched set of

Awaiting Madame

slender, long-legged, blonde-hair-blue-eyed, former model-type girls. They are probably early-forties and could be identical twins—but I'd have to do a total-body mole examination to be sure. Man. I bet these two were flawless back in the day.

"What do you know." Alistair acts surprised. "Looks like a party in here."

"It sure is," Niko replies and draws his lady closer to him with a warm sideways hug. The women giggle as if they are a deliriously mute pair and Niko looks at me. "Glad you decided to join us," he says, as though I forgot to RSVP.

Alistair glances at me before looking at Niko. "I thought Matthew might be interested in seeing the grotto this evening."

Kan squeezes his chick around the waist. "Why not. The more the merrier."

"Sure, sure, sure," Niko stands, "shall we depart?"

I watch the group move toward the back of the garage. Niko's got on a smoking jacket over his uniform trousers, and he guides his lady with the ease of Hugh Hefner escorting a playmate. Kan just has on his uniform, and he's not quite as confident—but his babe doesn't seem to mind. Both women are wearing black knit sweater dresses that conform to their every bony protrusion. And I think they're even thinner than most of my dancer friends. Impressive.

Before I know it, Alistair and I have hung our coats, and we're following a few yards behind the group. I feel hip, with my new dog whistle necklace hanging over my snowflake-patterned sweater, as Alistair guides me by the arm once again. He totally underestimates my extreme curiosity.

After Niko leads us into the mechanics area of the garage, Alistair picks up a box of tall white taper candles. The candles are resting on a workbench, beside what looks like a ten-thousand-piece socket wrench set. Very random.

Niko then unlocks a heavy wooden door, flips on the light, and starts climbing down an old cinder-block staircase. The two women follow close behind Niko, and they move down the stairs as if it's not their first time to travel this path. Kan glances back at me, steadying the second twin by the hips. *Good call*, I think to myself and shoot him a thumbs up.

Kan laughs and continues onward. "Proceed, ladies."

By the time I step through the doorway, Alistair's breathing down my neck. "Hurry up," he says, "I've got to get us locked inside, before Barbara smells trouble."

I wonder if Tatyana knows about Niko's gathering? "Chill. I'm going."

At the bottom of the staircase, the tunnel begins. Correction: the *hooker* tunnel begins. And as we continue, I can tell we're heading downhill away from the main house, so we have to be in the section that links to the guesthouse. This passageway looks like the perfect location for a B-list horror flick. Any second now, I expect a mutant creature in bad makeup to spring out of the dark shadows and scare the shit out of us.

A few minutes later, Niko stops in front of an arched doorway and we all gather in anticipation. He pulls out a big iron skeleton key from the pocket of his smoking jacket and turns the antique-style key in the rusty-looking lock. As the heavy door opens, I feel like Gretel arriving at the house of the wicked witch: doomed if I enter, yet too starved to turn back. I can't wait.

Niko goes in first, turns on the overhead light and brightens the cave-like alcove with a not-so-flattering yellowish beam. The pale twins rush in behind him and take on a sickly jaundiced glow. I pause in the doorway while Niko, Kan, and the women spill onto the far end of a circular sectional sofa—girls in the middle. The gang looks over to the doorway and motions for Alistair and me to join them.

As I start in, the group reminds me of a hungry vampire quartet, anticipating their next feeding. Alistair pauses to latch the door and I plop on the nearest cushion, stiff as a corpse. Why am I suddenly uptight?

Niko notices my unease. "Get comfortable, Matthew," he smiles at his girl, "we will be here awhile."

Once I sink back into the plush overstuffed sofa and prop my feet up on the ottoman, I feel like I'm doing something terribly wrong—something much worse than jumping on the sofa at grandma's house. I motion for Alistair to come sit next to me. But instead of taking a seat, he begins placing the long-stemmed candles throughout the space.

While Alistair continues lighting candles, I look across the room and notice several rows of wine racks, stacked up behind sliding glass doors that encompass one entire side of the space. I imagine this dusty old wine vault houses a slew of precious collectable bottles and now realize that we are, most likely, seated in an area of the house that would be considered *off-limits* for staff parties.

Alistair lights the final candle and flips off the overhead light. The candles create a perfectly romantic mood, and the twins sigh with profound relief.

"Much better like this." Kan snuggles up with his chick. "Alistair, you are the king!"

"Do tell," Niko shouts, before Alistair has a chance to sit, "what do we have on the menu this evening?"

Alistair walks behind the sofa toward the sliding door, removes a key from his vest pocket and unlocks the glass door. "As per usual," he pauses to slide the door open, "we shall work our way from light to dark, yes?"

"Absolutely," Niko calls out, as if proclaiming *Happy New Year*.

As Alistair slips behind the glass door, Niko turns to me. "Would you be so kind," he points to a shelf near the door, "could you press play on the CD player?"

"Sure, no problem," I say, already heading over.

When the CD begins, the room fills with the robust sound of Celine Dion. "Okay, okay, that is good," Niko yells, "but it is too damn loud—"

Smart me. I've already adjusted the volume before he can finish. "How's that?"

"Much better. Thanks." Niko slips out of his smoking jacket, then starts to take off his work shirt.

"I just love her—this Dion," Kan says, as I get distracted by Niko's body. He's down to a white tank t-shirt, and showing off his goth-inspired tattoo for the twins. So sexy. He's way more built than I expected. Maybe I *do* want him?

As the music plays in the background, Niko and Kan initiate some light petting with their girls. And even though I'm not sure what's in store, I don't mind watching—four guys with two girls, I guess it wouldn't be *terrible*.

Before long, Alistair enters with a white linen napkin draped over his forearm and carrying a serving tray with six wine glasses. After graciously offering each of us a glass, he places his glass on an end table and shows Niko the first bottle.

Niko approves the label. "Pour away!"

The twins writhe and grab their glasses, as Alistair opens the bottle and begins to serve. I can't believe I'm sitting here. This mysterious grotto would no doubt qualify as any sommelier's fantasy hangout. And here I am—the mid-western boy whose only exposure to wine involved stealing sips of Blue Nun from his parent's locked liquor cabinet—getting ready to participate in the tasting of a lifetime.

After serving the first round, Alistair joins us on the sofa and Niko offers up a toast. "To great success in life."

We all clink and take the first sip.

It's white.

Slightly chilled.

I like it.

But I wish I could think of something else to say—something more sophisticated.

Wine continues to flow while the Celine Dion CD repeats in a loop. And as promised, Alistair makes the perfect progression from light to dark, careful not to overwhelm our taste buds. Everyone—except me—is caught up in conversation about complexity, acidity, intensity, tannins, tentacles, and tendrils.

Then, after five or so wines, Alistair introduces a party game. He explains that the object of the game is to rename a wine we've already tasted, based on a famous serial killer. "For example," he pauses to pick up the third bottle we sampled. "Jack the Ripper Rosé," he says, and eveyone laughs.

Immediately getting into the fun, I hold up our current glass and name it *Charlie Manson Merlot*. I then point to the previous bottle and deem it *Jeffery Dahmer Cold Duck*—everybody cracks up again, and I toot my dog whistle just to be silly.

Niko agrees to go next, and explains that his native Greece is the oldest wine producer in the world.

"And the point is?" Alistair interrupts.

"Well, I only recall one Greek serial killer, but I cannot think of a good wine for him," Niko sips, "Antonis Daglis, he was commonly referred to as The Athens Ripper."

Alistair smirks. "Figures you'd steal the word *ripper*," he pauses to swig his wine. "Isn't it fascinating…how the Greeks claim to be grandfathers of everything…yet they are unable to conceive of anything original post Zeus?"

As the group laugh/moans, Niko lifts his glass toward Alistair. "Touché!"

The two men drink as if calling a cease-fire while the twins launch into a shared story about the infamous Austrian black widow, Elfriede Blauensteiner. Apparently, this notorious woman from their homeland did away with a few husbands and got lots of loot out of it. And just like Niko, the twins don't have a specific wine connection for her, but they simply wanted to confirm Austria's importance when it comes to noteworthy killers.

I love how everyone's national pride seems to hinge on this subject.

Alistair chuckles and turns to me. "I would name Elfriede's wine, *Blauensteiner Gewürztraminer*!" He clinks my glass as everyone laughs again and looks toward Kan. "And you, fine sir," Alistair demands, suddenly sounding cockney.

Kan stands up and tells us he doesn't know of any killers

from Sri Lanka. But then he mentions that one of the world's most prolific serial maniacs, Thug Behram, came from India. "This lunatic…he have more than nine hundred murders, all to himself."

Alistair looks at Kan. "So how do you label his bottle?"

Kan smiles and sits down. "With this kind of crazy man, I would call his wine anything he tells me to call it!"

While the room cackles over Kan's comment, one of the blondes looks over at me. She smiles, one brow lifted, and gives me a flirtatious wave. Just drunk enough to play along with her teasing, I make eye contact and wave back. But before the energy of my wave can successfully travel through the space to reach her, she blocks it from the air and swats it to the ground like a pesky insect. She loosely shakes her head *no,* and impatiently flicks her hair, before pointing toward Alistair—he's standing behind me. Humiliated, I jab Alistair with my elbow and hope he'll notice the woman who is in desperate need of a refill. How dumb, to assume she would be flirting with me. My face turns red—or better yet, *Ted Bundy Burgundy.*

Alistair serves the impatient twin, and starts to refill my glass. I stop him half pour. "I think I'm done." I tug at my necklace as I stand. "Thanks for everything you guys."

The blondes stretch their long limbs side-to-side in perfect unison and wave goodnight. But I don't wave back this time. I just smile and grab a final swig of wine.

"Alistair," Niko slurs, "remember to adjust the inventory to cover our tracks for this evening."

"Already completed, milord," Alistair jests.

As I make my way from the sofa to the door, the room starts spinning. "Thanks again," I yell to the gang, while Celine belts out *merci beaucoup* in the background.

"Any time, Matthew," Niko shouts out over the musical crescendo, "any time."

After I hurry through the tunnel and start up the stairs toward the garage, I recall the nicer twin poking her slender nose into a glass of *Charlie Manson Muscadet*. She likened the aroma to the foul smell of Roman Polanski making love to Sharon Tate. Funny. But I doubt I could get away with using that description at a wine tasting class in Manhattan. Too lowbrow.

Walking along the moonlit lane toward the main house, flurries hit my face and the sound of crunching snow echoes into the valley. My best panther-like steps are still unbelievably loud. If I wake Barbara, I'm dead.

Fortunately, as I step onto the landing, the staff windows stay dark. I use my key to enter the front door and secretly hope that a car might zoom by. Maybe someone will catch a glimpse of me walking into *my* home? But no such luck. The street is lifeless, the guard dogs don't stir—even the motion-activated lights seem mundane—and the elevator barely makes a sound as I ride up.

After changing out of my clothes and into a fresh pair of pressed boxers, I reach for a black Sharpie pen to inscribe an *X* over today's date in my calendar. Wow. Three-month anniversary. That's three down, nine to go. I think I can make it.

Before closing the pen, I sniff the marker tip: notes of burnt blueberries and bitter plums, macerating in kerosene. Nice. Clearly, my palate is improving.

14

Two weeks ago today, we moved from Austria to England. I remember how the phone call interrupted our staff breakfast. It was crazy. The instant Kan hung up and told us to get ready to leave, everyone switched into panic mode. Barbara and Alistair popped up from the table as if the place was on fire, the housemaids went running toward the ironing room and Kan disappeared into the kitchen. Even Niko removed his sunglasses in disbelief. Then, acting solely on peer pressure, I ditched my strudel and rushed away too—unsure if I'd be invited or not.

Once I got to my room, I could hear René in his office, whistling the Popeye cartoon theme song. His whistling grew louder, until it was coming from right outside my door. "Mathieu! Mathieu! It is I, René!"

"Hey." I opened the door with gusto, ready to play along.

"Wait until you see *Knightsbridge*," he yelled, as if the door was still closed. "Massive...most marvelous!"

I smiled and allowed him to continue.

"Madame adjoined three London row-houses into one fabulous space—if only I had thought of it."

"I know. Olivia showed me some pics."

"Monsieur inherited the center townhouse from his father, and later acquired the properties on either side. It is simply to die for."

"How exciting," I added, thinking how nice it must be to

have the funds to convince your neighbors to move.

"Exciting indeed!" René paused as if snagged in thought. "But not to worry about me, Mathieu. I will be staying off-site during our visit." He smiled and regained momentum. "I have arranged for a hotel suite overlooking Hyde Park...not more than a stone's throw from Madame. You and I shall do our training in the park...given you have time to escape."

I liked hearing him say *our* visit. That sounded promising.

"Ta-ta then. Tallyho." He whistled away.

And by the time I grabbed my suitcase from the closet, Tatyana had called to confirm that I *would* be going. She described how she had reminded Madame of my importance. "Matthew is expert in field of breathing," she told her.

Lucky for me, Madame had nodded in agreement.

Tatyana then mentioned that she and I would be the only staff traveling with Madame and René. "Are you sure?" I asked. "No Alistair or Barbara?"

"Not for this time visit," Tatyana said. "Two caretakers live in London house...is plenty for such short stay."

"Works for me." I pitched a stack of neatly ironed t-shirts into my case. "What about Olivia?"

"Olivia is not sure to come, perhaps is better for Madame without distraction."

"Oh." I played it cool, even though I was totally bummed. "Okay, so is there anything else I should know?"

Next, Tatyana described how the current upstairs excitement was about finding the proper hat for Madame to wear to the funeral. She explained that Madame was traveling to London to pay last respects to Princess Margaret. "Queen Elizabeth's sister," she clarified. "And the problem is... Madame, she dislikes hats," Tatyana continued. "She finds the hats better suited for people with short necks. But I think she make hat problem for in order not to go."

"So why do you think Madame *is* going?"

"Perhaps, she think of it as obligation...or perhaps a

chance to spend valuable time with friends and family."

"Is Madame related to the Royal Family?" I accelerated my packing.

"No, no... invitation, it come from family of Monsieur."

"Oh, so he was related?"

"Perhaps somehow. I cannot say."

"Well, it's a good sign that Madame has enough strength and energy to go...don't ya think?"

"Yes, of course, Matthew—it is most important. Now she must move on regular basis."

During our stay in London, Madame turned over a new leaf. Every day, except for the day of the Royal funeral, Madame exercised twice. Tatyana had insisted that the exercise sessions needed to be as regular as receiving the B-vitamin injections. So, like clockwork, Madame and I would meet every morning before lunch and every afternoon after tea to train in the orchid room. This awesome glass atrium space—full of rare orchid plants— was suspended high off the back of the property. And the room had such a calming affect that even Madame's dogs would simmer down at her feet to stare through the glass floor into the court-yard garden below. Without the dogs involved, our conversations became more intimate. Well maybe not exactly *intimate*, but we discussed more than the weather. At each session she would ask something new about my career, my family or the cultural scene in New York. Tatyana was always there, seated behind Madame, but she minded her own business and sometimes even got a little shut-eye. Madame was always enthusiastic and appeared thankful for our workouts together. So, little by little, I opened up to her. But I knew better than to confess the one-man show. I just didn't think Madame would comprehend my desire to play Barbara on Broadway.

As time passed, Tatyana and I both noticed substantial improvement in Madame's mood and physical strength. Even Mr. and Mrs. Blessington—the caretakers at Knightsbridge, who had been on staff since Monsieur was a bachelor, and were considered the happiest Irish couple to ever reside in England—admitted to being astonished by Madame's dedication to exercise. Frankly, so was I.

One afternoon, toward the end of our stay, Madame requested to train outside in the courtyard. It was an unseasonably nice day, for late February in London, and I was happy Madame took the initiative to change from her routine in the orchid room. On that day, the auxiliary staff—ten or so workers who didn't live in—happened to be on-site. Looking back now, I wonder if this was a coincidence, or if Madame intentionally planned a show of strength to be viewed by her staff?

As instructed, I met Madame and Tatyana in the ground floor living room. Then, when I walked over to Madame, she turned to Tatyana and dismissed her. "You may take your lunch," Madame stated simply and headed toward the back door of the house.

"But I come with you." Tatyana stepped forward to open the door leading outside into the English garden.

"No, no, Tatyana." Madame hooked her arm around my elbow. "Matthew and I will be fine on our own."

Tatyana split toward the kitchen with an inaudible huff, while Madame and I headed outside. I remember how Mrs. Blessington politely stepped forward to close the door, covering for Tatyana's quick exit. And I also remember feeling awkward about escorting Madame for the first time—anxious about standing side-by-side with her. According to René, I was supposed to remain two paces aback. But with Madame linked to my arm, that was impossible.

"Matthew, I owe you an apology…for time wasted on the mountain."

"Oh, that's all right, really. I mean your oxygen level wasn't good…so why push?"

"No. No. There is no excuse. I must do more."

I steadied her along the path, impressed by her improved

determination and strength. "Well, things are going good now...
don't you think?"

"One must admit," she paused, let go of my arm and
walked forward—crossing one foot over the next—as if balancing
on a tightrope, "I am doing better."

"Yeah, for sure." I hurried forward and offered an elbow.
"Now, let's try to keep it that way." We both laughed and she took
my arm again.

"I must come upon a bit of willpower," she stated as we
rounded the curve of the oval pathway. "Dessert is my downfall."

Me too, I thought to myself as we approached the next
bend. "Well, you know, just take it one meal at a time." I guided
her forward. "There're worse things in life than having too many
treats."

She laughed a little. "I simply must. What is the point of
having improved oxygen, if one has unconscionable sugar levels?" Madame stopped and looked at me before we headed into
the next curve. "My goodness, Matthew, we must resemble a slow
motion carrousel...traveling round the garden thus."

I laughed at her comment, then immediately wondered if
she meant to be funny.

She smiled, confirming that I got her joke. "Shall we take
a seat yonder?" She motioned to the nearest bench.

"Sure. As long as we keep breathing."

Madame chuckled at my tag line and we walked over to
sit down on the bench, facing the back of the house. By the time
we got settled, I noticed the entire staff—including Mr. and Mrs.
Blessington—observing from inside. Nearly every window had a
worker, polishing away at the glass or adjusting the drapery. Even
Tatyana was dusting the kitchen windowsill, trying to appear casual.

"Look at those curious faces," Madame said. "Unconditional love."

Confused, I glanced at Madame and she pointed up toward the orchid room. "My babies," she clarified.

When I looked where she was pointing, I saw what she meant. Her lapdogs were sprawled on the floor in a heap, silently staring down at us from inside the glass atrium space. To me, they looked like one giant pelt with lots of beady little eyes. "They're so cute." I said, reminded of how David and I used to argue about purebred dogs versus adoption. He loved these Madame-type dogs while I wanted to rescue a big mutt from the shelter. But since we were on tour so much, never home long enough to deal with an actual dog, our debate became the thing.

Madame shifted her focus to me. "So, how is your knee coming along?" She sounded genuinely sympathetic. "Do you suppose you shall dance again soon?"

I turned to her, stunned she knew about my injury and amazed that she cared enough to ask. I hesitated. "I don't know," I said under my breath.

Madame took on an air of staunch courage and straightened her back, but she didn't say a word.

And within a flicker of sweeping silence, as I stared into her riveting green eyes, she afforded me the space to register my feelings. "I'm scared," I let slip, before I glanced away. "Scared, because I don't know what's gonna happen next…I mean…I won't really know what's going on 'til I go back to technique class."

"Is there anything I might do to help?"

I shook my head *no*. "I don't think so."

"Perhaps we could arrange time outside the house…time off…for you to study each day at one of the studios in town?"

"Oh, no. That's very nice of you…but I couldn't accept that."

"And why not?" she asked, mildly perturbed.

"Because I'm here to train you," I hesitated, "not the other way around."

She looked toward the orchid room. "Perhaps, I shall insist you accept my offer." Her serene expression punctuated the statement.

I knew she wasn't expecting a response, so I just allowed

her comment to land. And by the time I looked toward the back of the house, the staff silhouettes had faded from view — as had my moment in the spotlight. Tatyana was the only audience member remaining, still framed in the kitchen window, now motioning for us to come inside. I shifted in my seat to give Madame the idea that we should probably call it quits. But she stayed put and prolonged her moment with the dogs.

I waited patiently. No tension, no drama, and no hidden agenda. I just sat there beside her, overwhelmed by her kindness, assuming our conversation wouldn't go any deeper. And in fact it didn't. It didn't go anywhere. She's my boss — not my friend. But nonetheless, her generous offer of flexible work hours hit me with greater impact than any envelope of euros ever could.

Once Madame decided to stand, I was happily offering her my arm before her legs had fully straightened. She wrapped her arm around mine and we started along the path toward the house. "Off we go, Matthew."

"My pleasure, Madame," I said, realizing René would shit his pants if he could see how well I was playing his role.

That same night, at dinner, Mrs. Blessington was totally wound up. And her pleasant Irish brogue was even thicker than usual. She'd spent most of our meal recapping the Royal funeral, and Mrs. B. seemed convinced that the death of Princess Margaret was a huge wakeup call for Madame. "There's nothing quite like seeing your friend's ashes come out the crematorium," she cackled. "Why it sure gets the old adrenaline pumping...now doesn't it?"

Tatyana cut in as if needing to prove herself. "Madame make fresh start in London, and I am happy for to see this."

"Me too," I said, realizing how confident I felt in the garden while everyone watched.

Mrs. B. cracked herself up once again. "Goodness, I'd say Madame looks downright spry if you asked me."

Mr. Blessington joined the conversation, after handing his plate to his wife and requesting another heaping spoonful of buttery turnips. "To tell you the truth, I think Madame has plans to outlive the Queen Mother."

"Well, now, that won't be tough will it," Mrs. B. piped up, taking the last soda biscuit for herself, "since Queen Mum's hanging by a thread at one hundred and one."

Tatyana became more somber than usual. "People assume excitement…to celebrate one-hundredth birthday. But it also make lonely life, for person who live more time than all the friends."

Mrs. B. smiled and continued buttering her biscuit. "Well, rest assured, lassie…if Madame decides to see one hundred *two*… you can bet she will."

At that point, Mr. Blessington abruptly changed the subject to brag about how he was able to make the world's best meat pies.

"Yeah, sure, you can make 'em," Mrs. B. teased, "but when was the last time ya did?"

Ignoring his wife's heckling, Mr. B. recited a few of his recipes anyway. He used the illustrated cuts of meat—printed on the kitchen wallpaper behind him—as a means of reinforcing his secret method. By the end of his fourth recipe, Mr. B. had shifted his chair to sit with his head propped up against the wall, so it looked like he was wearing a crown of sausages. Tatyana and I chuckled at his sight gag, but Mrs. B. smirked as if she'd seen his stunt many times before.

Mrs. B. reclaimed the room. "Now tell us what you young kids plan to do with all this money Madame's been givin' ya," she blurted out—getting her husband to stop with the recipes.

"Lordy Lady, it's none of your business there, now is it?" Mr. B. walked over to the fridge to refill his beer mug.

"Well, the Mister and I put our kids—and our grand-kids—through school on it," Mrs. B. bragged. "And there's still more left." She begged Mr. B. for a sip of his beer.

"For me," Tatyana started, still sounding serious, "I send income home to Moldova. The money of Madame is for to help family."

Mr. and Mrs. Blessington gave Tatyana a look of respect, so Tatyana went on. "My sister, she is sick…cancer…and salary of Madame, it provide needed medications."

Mrs. B. bowed her head toward Tatyana and paused before she replied. "Oh, my darling, you're doing the right thing… but of course we're oh so sorry to hear about your sister."

The moment Mrs. B. finished, she turned toward me and fixed me with a stare. "And what about you lad?"

I went blank.

"What's up your sleeve?"

I panicked. "I don't know." I answered — hating the words the minute they left my mouth. "Guess I haven't really made a plan yet." Damn. How lame to confess that I'm busy paying physical therapy bills and credit card debt. Shit, so much for the illusion of my successful Broadway career.

"What d'ya mean, no plan yet," Mrs. B. mocked as she stole her husband's mug away from him. "Matthew, you aren't gonna live forever now are ya?"

After Tatyana's heartfelt cancer story, how could I admit that I needed the money just to survive in New York? What if I can't get another gig right away? Then, it washed over me, the thought of donning a fat-suit and becoming Mr. and Mrs. Blessington eight shows a week. I smiled. "I'm sure I'll put it to good use."

Mr. B. snatched his beer back from his wife. "Honestly lady, these kids, they're still young. So why don't ya just lay off 'em?"

"Fair enough, Matthew…but then how old are ya anyway," Mrs. B. asked, unabashedly.

"I'm turning thirty-three this year—"

Mrs. B. let out a hearty laugh before I finished my tought. "Now that's not so young…thirty-three," she said. "After all…let us pause to remember how they hung Jesus from the cross…right around that very age." Mrs. B. chuckled again and rubbed her hand lovingly atop her husband's potbelly.

"Though in biblical times," Mr. B. said with a smile and looked at his wife, "folks aged faster...much faster than they do nowadays. Our friend Jesus was considered *old* when he died and came back to life." He laughed at Mrs. B. and then turned toward me again. "Not to worry son, you've still got plenty of time left," he said, and gave a comforting grin.

Thinking back on this, I regret not telling Mr. and Mrs. Blessington that thirty-three *is* old—too old to continue dancing chorus boy roles on the regional circuit. And that's exactly what I'll be facing once I start auditioning again. What Mr. and Mrs. B. don't understand, is how gossip of a knee injury will plague the rest of my performing career. Even after I'm healed, the uninjured guy—who looks exactly like me—will inevitably get the part. In the eyes of the producers, I'm now considered *damaged goods*.

Damn. I've got to stop daydreaming about London. It's a total waste of time. We've been back in Morocco for three days already. And aside from the rainy weather, the only thing new around this house is *déjà vu*. I'm hoping to start with Madame again, but from what I can tell it's not going to happen anytime soon. Since we got here, she's remained on the third floor and has been refusing to see anyone, including René. She won't even come downstairs for meals. Sorry to say, I'm not even a blip on her radar screen.

Alistair and Barbara have also returned to Marrakech, direct from their—concurrent yet separate—two-week vacations. They're acting every bit as short-fused as before, so I just stay out of their way and mind my own business. I've completely fallen out of touch with Olivia, and that makes Tatyana happy. She's decided we're best friends, since we spent so much quality time in London. But right now, I'm being held hostage on The Walk with René, racing through the garden in the midst of an intense rainstorm.

"Mathieu, I refuse to lose the stamina we gained on the mountain. A sprinkle of rain is not going to stop me!" René shouts as we slosh past a lattice of droopy periwinkles. "These past two rainy days without any exercise...now that was enough."

Apparently, he's oblivious to our two-week lapse in London since I never saw him at Knightsbridge. Maybe that's why he's gone blank about his training. I imagine Madame told him I was *otherwise engaged* so he never pestered me.

René has just finished explaining the physiological benefits of returning to sea level, and is discouraged about the possibility of eating lunch inside today. I couldn't be happier that his chatter is muffled by the rain and blocked by my oversized slicker—on loan from Alistair. "As you know, Mathieu...the gazebo is completely protected from the elements. The staff need only find a suitable way to enclose the thirty-meter walkway from the house, in order to serve today's lunch alfresco as planned. If you asked me, I would say the Moroccans are using this sprinkle as an excuse to complain."

Staring into the downpour, I remember overhearing the kitchen staff mention that two local children had died in a flash flood yesterday—swept away by torrents of red mud. But he thinks it's nothing.

"Mathieu, we must find a way to remedy this outdoor eating situation." René stops dead in his tracks and stares down at the marshy clay tennis court. "*A River Runs Through It!*" He sounds disappointed. "That is the one. That is the name of the Brad Pitt film I was hoping to borrow from our fair lady's movie collection last month."

Oh God. Here we go again. Every time he thinks of an old movie, his train of thought shifts to his cardio-blast performance—whether or not he is ready to go public with it. René has flip-flopped on this issue numerous times. But after doing extensive research, he most recently decided against paying exorbitant royalties to Prince for a three-minute piece. At one point, he considered saving money by using a karaoke version of the song, but chucked that idea after only one run through. The instrumental recording just didn't have the same *oomph*.

René starts walking again and speaks directly into the storm, as if dictating to his secretary. "Phone Austria this afternoon—demand Kan return those films today!"

Screw that. I'm not his Olivia. "Anything else?" I play along.

"That will be all." He goes quiet.

Whew. He didn't get into the cardio-blast saga after all. His meds must be working.

Nearing the end of our waterlogged walk, René asks if I would please turn and face him. So I do, assuming he wants to stop and tell me another story. But instead of stopping, he charges forward and actually increases his speed, forcing me into a fast jog backward. Hell. This could totally fuck my knee.

"Oh, Mathieu, much better—with you blocking the rain from my face. Now why did we not start with this sooner?"

I'm hauling out, running backward in Alistair's plus-size galoshes—doing my best to remain vertical. Luckily, I was the blue-ribbon champion of my elementary school backward run competition, three years in a row. Unable to sprint, dash or hurdle to save my life, I became king of running in reverse. Then, one year—thanks to Rusty Shockmeyer who suffered a life-altering spinal cord injury during my race—the school was forced to cancel the event and I never saw another blue ribbon.

"Mathieu!" René shouts as if he doesn't realize that I'm still tracking face-to-face with him. "I do believe the floor in my room feels a bit damp for our regular alignment work. Shall we postpone?"

"What about maintaining your stamina and technique?" I pant.

"But it is raining." He whines as if missing his mommy.

"Why don't we do a few minutes on the floor in your room and then get you straight into a nice warm bath." I hope for a compromise.

"Oh, Mathieu, you are probably right...but for only a few

minutes. I have an appointment with my spiritual advisor…before that dreadful indoor lunch is served."

Minutes later, we huddle in front of René's door and slip out of our muddy slickers. And once we get inside, I start the bath water while René strips down to his tighty-whities. He drops down on the exercise mat at the foot of his bed and starts stretching without me. I soon join him, and we stretch just long enough to allow the tub to fill.

"Ah, merci, Mathieu," he cheers and springs up from the mat. "Truly fantastique, I am most happy you insisted."

Humming to himself, René moves into the bathroom and I head toward the door. "Bye, bye," I say, not expecting a response.

Relieved to be finished with him, I step outside and start getting redressed in Alistair's gear. Maybe Madame will call for her session today?

"Matthew," Barbara yells, and I turn to see her shivering beneath the awning. "The house phones are down due to the storm." She keeps her distance. "Please remind René that the Duchess is scheduled to arrive in time for lunch today."

Then, before I can ask how Madame is doing, she's gone—so I knock on René's door.

"Entrée!"

I open the door just a crack. "René, Barbara wants you to know that the Duchess will arrive today, before lunch. And, uh, the phone lines are down."

"Today!" He croaks. "Before lunch—no phones?"

"Yeah."

"Oh, Mathieu, not her, anyone but her."

His disappointment fills a long pause. All I can hear are some soapy washing sounds, so I start to shut the door.

"You are still there, Mathieu," he calls abruptly.

"Yes, René, I'm here."

"Oh, do come in—will you?"

I slip out of the half-zipped slicker, step inside, and enter René's bathroom—only to find him reclining in a mound of frothy bubbles, posing like a 1940s pinup poster.

"Mathieu...how long will the old crow be staying?" he asks, gently transitioning into his next pose.

"Barbara didn't say."

"In any case...it is a real shame," he says, increasing the arch in his back. "First, the soggy weather and now this tragic news."

I stand and wait tub-side while René reaches for a long-handled loofah sponge.

"You know, Mathieu...the Duchess...she is a wretched beast. She is the one who stole the first man I ever really loved... the Duke." He pauses to gently exfoliate his back. "I will never forgive her for that one, Mathieu...ever."

Come on, what Duke?

Without warning, René drops the sponge, submerges his entire body, and resurfaces with a perfect halo of suds encircling his face—just in time to hear a loud knock at the door. "Mathieu, would you be kind enough as to get that for me...it is surely my appointment."

"Certainly," I say—happy to go.

Anxiously planning my getaway, I open René's door. And find myself standing face to face with my Moroccan one-night stand. "Bonjour," the boy says. "I am here for René," he clarifies with a tender stammer and a glimmer of recognition.

My hand gets stuck to the doorknob. I can't believe he's René's spiritual advisor.

"Bonjour." I let go of the door and give him a big hug. "Je suis désolé," I whisper and start to well up, "I'm so sorry I left you alone that night."

The boy barely hugs back and gently pulls away. "I am here for René," he repeats, sounding detached.

The moment we separate, René walks in from the bathroom, wearing a plush terrycloth robe. "Voilà...my master is here," he projects, arms wide open.

As they embrace, I step back and look at my man, once

again mesmerized by his handsomeness. He smiles at me with a forgiving stare and I quickly wipe my eyes dry. I can't let my guard down in front of René.

"Mathieu, please tell Barbara that I will host the Duchess for lunch." René smiles, excusing me from the room, as he leads the boy toward his bed.

"Yes, René." I divert my eyes and leave.

Once I step outside and see Alistair's crumpled slicker on the ground, it hits me. So this guy is actually a *rent boy*. And the night we met, he must have become distracted by his mom's death and forgot to ask me for money. Shit, worse yet, this means that René and I have now shared a common sex partner. Yuck.

I step into the slicker.

Oh, hell no—I zip up—when I put this moment on stage, I'm leaving out all that detail. In my version, the rent boy appears at the door, confesses his love for me, and we run off to Jersey to start a family together—or some shit like that. In the show, René will be abandoned in his room—alone/naked/crying.

Fade to black.

15

It's still raining. And even though we've had a solid week of overcast weather, nobody seems any more depressed than usual. I'm sitting in the kitchen, prolonging afternoon tea, while Alistair and Barbara are acting busy with nonsense chores. He is taking inventory in the storage closet, and she is sitting across the room at the chef's desk, calculating exactly how many dinner rolls have been discarded each month for the past six months. Everyone else is back to work elsewhere.

"Could someone please open the door?" Alistair shouts from inside the closet.

Barbara holds still, and gives me a look that says *stay*.

"Help," he pleads, "the door is stuck."

Barbara gets up with a sigh and slowly makes her way over. "And I thought you were already out of the closet," she says with a sneer as she releases the door. She then heads back toward her desk and glances at me with an uppity grin.

Alistair exits the pantry, carrying an oversized basket of mostly green apples. He ignores Barbara's dig and sets the basket on the island counter in the center of the kitchen. By all accounts, this is the first time in a decade that Barbara has spoken to Alistair about anything other than work. And I'm so excited to witness this moment, it takes me a few seconds to realize that my dunked biscotti has dissolved in my hand and drifted to the bottom of my cup. Crap.

Now seated at the desk, Barbara tips her chin down and glances over her reading glasses, inspecting Alistair's apple collection. "Have you combined the Granny Smith with the Yellow Delicious?" She scowls.

"You always did enjoy checking out my basket, didn't you, Barbara," he pauses and looks over at me as if hoping to form an alliance.

I shrug my shoulders, like I don't know what could've gotten into her.

Barbara slurps her tea. "She smells good on you, the young trollop."

"Unfortunately," he says, walking toward the storage closet, "her smell is only skin-deep."

I grab for another cookie as Alistair steps back inside the closet. What the hell was that supposed to mean?

With Alistair still out of sight, Barbara rushes over to the stove and retrieves a large box of salt. She grabs a bulk container of ground pepper and hurries back to her desk. She glances nervously in Alistair's direction then reaches into a low cabinet near her station. From here, she pulls out a bunch of empty salt-and-pepper shakers and soon locates a tiny funnel. I figure she's creating more busywork for herself, in hopes of buying time to gather more information.

"Do go on," Barbara encourages, the moment Alistair walks out with a second giant basket of apples—mostly red this time.

Alistair plops the red ones down on the counter beside the green ones. "You see?" He addresses both of us and holds up a large red apple. "Each apple in this basket has an adhesive label... marking its date of expiration. And so does she," he threatens, "as far as I'm concerned, Tatyana's expiration date is drawing near."

Barbara accidentally spills an open saltshaker on top of her paperwork and anxiously tosses a pinch over her shoulder. "Would you not find murder a fairly stiff penalty for Tatyana's incontinence?"

"*Incompetence*." Alistair corrects Barbara and takes an angry bite of apple.

"Frankly, you are speaking to me as if this were your idea…to dispose of Tatyana." Barbara responds without looking up from her task. "But I knew from the start…I knew there would be problems with that girl."

"Bollocks! Damn mealy mess…" Alistair half-swallows, "she refused my advances—that frigid little bitch." He pauses and spits the rest of his apple into the garbage can beneath the counter. "Even after I promised to use protection." He wipes his mouth with his sleeve.

Barbara laughs, screws the cap onto her completed salt-shaker, and glances up in his direction. "And I suppose that was your idea of foreplay?"

I can't get enough of this.

"Well, the point is," Alistair begins, "that insipid child needs to be sent home on the next flight to the Maldives."

"*Moldova*." Barbara corrects him with a snide look. "And, I happen to agree with you…Tatyana can get out…and she can take those fake reading glasses with her."

"How could you call her bloody glasses *fake*?" Alistair frowns. "They're as real as the nose on my face."

"Not quite." Barbara walks slowly toward Alistair. "Those lenses of hers are made of plastic—no prescription."

When the two of them meet up behind the center island, they each grab an apple and bite down in perfect unison. And as I watch them chew, I'm glad I'm on their good side—if I wasn't, they'd probably be conspiring to have me fired too.

"Too tart," Barbara says and spits her bite of green into the garbage can.

"Vulgar rubbish," Alistair mentions as he tosses the rest of his red.

"Truly rotten," Barbara proclaims, spits again, and throws her apple away.

"Disgusting," Alistair adds. "But I do love a challenge."

"However, this might not be simple." Barbara turns to rinse her hands in the sink. "It pains me to admit...that Tatyana is rather shrewd."

"We must get inside her first, in order to hatch our plan." He curls his upper lip at the taste of yet another bad apple. "We'll have make her life so miserable, she will decide to quit."

Barbara dries her hands. "I believe that is what got you into this trouble to begin with," she jokes, "trying to get inside her, yes?"

I conceal a laugh.

"Very funny," Alistair chews nervously.

"*I* thought so." She lets out a hearty laugh, and walks back toward her salt-and-pepper station, totally ignoring my presence. "We will come up with something."

This is the bomb. I love it.

I'm as insignificant as a fly on the wall.

Entirely fed up with both baskets of bad apples, Alistair goes to dump them into the garbage.

"Com-post!" She belts out. "Those must be transported to the compost pile in the northeast garden."

So Alistair empties both baskets into a bin and drags the heavy can toward the door. "Keep your eyes open for any sign of weakness." He looks at Barbara.

"This one should be fun," she says, and twists the cap of her next salt-and-pepper shaker. "Loads of fun."

As Alistair shuts the door behind him, Barbara's pager sounds, and she promptly dials the chef's phone. She says something in German and then hangs up and looks at me.

"The Duchess will see you now."

"For real?" I ask, having no clue what to do with this woman I've never met.

"Yes, *for real*," Barbara mocks my accent, "and she has requested the yoga...you will train upstairs in her room."

"Oh, uh...okay." I stand. "Any scoop on her?"

"Not much. She is of Madame's generation, in prime

physical condition. Just give it to her good." Barbara laughs and shoos me out of the kitchen. "Now, go. I will take care of your dishes."

Standing next to the partially open window of her second-floor guest room, the Duchess lights a cigarette and takes a generous drag. She is a subtly highlighted brunette, who is not in *prime physical condition* as Barbara put it—she's in killer shape, for any age. I assume she loves baby pink, since her entire workout ensemble is baby pink. And her whole look—the stacked wig, the flawless nails, her slightly pulled face, and surgically puckered lips—tells me she's much more high-maintenance than Madame. But somehow, none of it's overblown.

I remain on standby near the empty yoga mat at the foot of her bed, as she takes her next drag. Her non-smoking arm is wrapped around her narrow waist and her free hand makes a little supportive cup for the elbow of her smoking arm. She closes her eyes and steadily exhales, as if savoring her favorite ice cream; she's in no hurry to continue her workout.

She soon opens her eyes and looks at me from across the room. "Matt...there is an old joke about people who talk a lot," she says, in her standard European English and inhales again. "Have you heard it?" she manages to ask, while sending a cloud of smoke toward the ceiling, maintaining one eye on me.

"I don't think so."

The Duchess takes another quick puff. "What do you call the twelve-step program for people who talk too much?" She uses her exhale to purposely delay the punch line. "It's called: *On-and-On Anon*. Get it?"

I laugh at her joke, surprised by my genuine response, and watch her put out the cigarette in an overly crowded ashtray. "That's funny."

"Well, Matt...that is our René all right." She walks forward, passing through her second-hand smoke, and steps onto the yoga mat. "He just goes on and on, does he not? This past week alone at table with him has been more than I can bear. And by the way…it will certainly take more than *twelve* steps to cure that chap."

"Deep lunge forward…and stretch both arms up," I command—trying to assert some authority. But before I finish my instructions, the Duchess is off the mat again, this time coughing her way toward the bedside table in search of water. "Take your time," I say. "After all…there's not much else to do in this rain."

"Precisely, Matt," she barely gets out, as the water washes down her irritated throat. "One could hardly be outside walking the garden today…could one, Matt?"

"Absolutely not," I grin, thinking about René's outdoor walking obsession—come rain or come shine.

The Duchess returns to our workout with renewed conviction. Then, with legs perfectly straight, she bends over and walks out onto her hands—into a plank position. Her back muscles flex like those of a much younger woman. She's got to be eighty/eighty-five, but her body is phenomenal. I wonder what she'd be like at this point in her life without cigarettes?

"Matt, if I do not complete ten push-ups every morning, I will never be able to wear another strapless gown."

"Now that's motivation," I call out. "Let's count down together…ten…nine—"

But after only two reps, the Duchess pops up again and grabs her hand towel from off the bed. "Whom am I fooling?" She laughs to herself while patting her dry forehead dry, and returns to her smoking spot. "The strapless gowns, the soirées, the black-tie affairs…all history now."

Without hesitation, the Duchess lights up again, assumes her wrapped arm, cupped-elbow smoking stance, and enjoys the first puff of her fresh cigarette while looking out the window at the rain. "Francesca and I became friends many years ago, Matt," she inhales and sits down in the padded chair. "Thanks to our husbands…and their womanizing ways." She exhales half way and then sharply inhales the next hit. "And now look…" she stalls—

seemingly confused as to whether the smoke should be traveling in or out at this juncture. "She and I are still here...going strong... while those two philanderers are cold in their graves."

The Duchess hacks another deep cough and swallows back some reflux. She takes another soothing inhale from her cigarette as if to suppress the urge to cough. "Matt, how old do you think I look?" she asks, sounding like Ann Bancroft speaking to Dustin Hoffman in *The Graduate*.

I like the way she keeps using my name. I think she's calling me *Matt,* because it's easier for her to speak in fewer syllables. And each time she repeats my name it sounds more endearing. "Are you familiar with Jane Fonda?"

"Yes, of course, she is the one who just divorced what's-his-name...the American fellow?"

"Dare I say," I casually lob, "you look much better than she ever has."

"Oh, you dear boy." She smoothes the wrinkles from her pink cotton tights. "That is all I needed to hear in order to face René at dinner tonight."

The Duchess takes another puff and puts out her cigarette before reaching for her ebony compact. "You know, Matt...René has Francesca frozen in time. He still believes us to be as prominent as we once were—during the 1950s and '60s." She powders her nose with three quick taps. "René no doubt anticipates that we are jetting off to party at Andy's loft this weekend."

If she is referring to Andy Warhol, it means that *was* a Warhol by the elevator at Burgflucht. But if she's referencing mom's favorite crooner, Andy Williams, it means it wasn't.

The next thing I know, she has another cigarette going and she's sinking deeper into her chair. It's going to be awhile.

"Oh, you should have seen her in those days, Matt." She floats both arms out to her side into a dreamy pose of grandeur and poise. "Francesca was the belle of the ball."

"I can just imagine." I stifle a sneeze.

"And what a shame...to imagine her armory of haute couture, deteriorating in various armoires around the world. Matt... you realize...one could auction Madame's collection of custom designer dresses and fetch more than enough to feed a starving nation."

I laugh to myself. Not according to Olivia's garbage tales. "Sounds incredible," I say, realizing how I've used this response with René many times, but saying it to the Duchess feels refreshingly new.

The Duchess allows herself one more puff and then tamps out this cigarette as if saying it will be her last—forever, amen. A few buds finally escape the ashtray and roll unnoticed onto the side table.

"Francesca was the woman who could wear anything and she looked amazing in everything." She motions for her water glass from the nightstand. "Chanel, Dior, Givenchy," she reminisces, as I fill the glass and walk over to serve her. "You name it—she owned it—and she wore it all as if it were merely prêt-a-porter."

I present the water glass, and wait for her to lift it off the silver tray. But instead of taking the glass, she ignores me and lights up again. Damn. Now I wish Barbara were here for water duty, so I could pull rank in front of the Duchess.

"When Francesca entered the room, all eyes shifted in her direction. In the most unassuming manner she could command the space without saying a word. One would notice her simplicity... the perfect proportion of her thin body...those captivating emerald eyes." The Duchess reaches for the glass, as if it's suspended in thin air. "One would see the lady herself—not the clothing or her stunning adornments."

I replace the tray on the nightstand and return to my post.

"Matt..." she looks at me, never once considering that I was her momentary manservant, "thanks to me...Francesca learned to select items off the rack, not so easy at first."

While the Duchess continues detailing her shopping trips with Madame, I become fixated on the long funnel of ash forming on the end of her cigarette. *When* will she flick?

"Francesca would make such sophisticated selections," she pauses to sip her water, "I often wondered if she and I had been shopping in the same store."

The long gray ash finally takes a tumble onto her pink tights—whew—leaving a big smudge for the anonymous laundress to deal with later.

"But our lives were more than shopping sprees. She and I were chosen to make our men complete."

What the hell is she talking about—*chosen, complete*?

"Is true." She takes her longest drag yet. "Only those women who have survived such an agreement might understand our peril."

Translation, anyone?

"We were married off to our gents in the same year, amid similar situations—our unions made for perfect business. Francesca and I developed a friendship sealed by fate." She hesitates and places her water glass down on the table next to her.

I watch her smoking hand move back and forth from her mouth with kelp-like elegance, and wonder if this bit about being in an arranged marriage is true.

"Ah, thank you, Matt." The Duchess stands up, tamps out her cigarette, and heads toward the door. "Thank you so much for doing me this favor today…it is certainly nice to have a handsome guru standing over me while I take a bit of exercise."

I follow. "My pleasure," I say—understanding that *favor* equals *no tip*.

"The pleasure was all mine, Matt…what a delight." She opens the door. "Tell me, Matt, do you suppose we should be at all worried about Francesca spending so much time upstairs?"

I step into the hallway and compose a diplomatic response. "It seems as though Madame prefers the peace and quiet of the third floor." My answer sounds like the best ass-kisser alive.

"Yes…I believe you are right, Matt…perhaps it is best to let her rest."

After she closes the door behind me, her coughing and throat clearing is still audible—even by the time I arrive at the service staircase. But before heading downstairs, I pause to look at a portrait hanging on the wall of the second floor landing. And although the features of the beautiful female subject are dissimilar to the Duchess, the woman in this painting shares the same aristocratic air. The painting is labeled: *1721—Sarah Churchill, Duchess of Marlborough*.

With great satisfaction, I start down the stairs, knowing I've just found a terrific stage name for Madame's chain-smoking friend: *Duchess of Marlboro*.

After dinner tonight, René called my room, antsy as ever, to confirm that the house telephones were working again. "Mathieu," he said, "if that old crow is performing the yoga...then you and I shall also perform the yoga."

"Of course," I said—not the least bit surprised with his desire to keep up with the Joneses, "let's do it."

"Ever since the Duchess drove a wedge between myself and the Duke...I wish she would just disappear."

I held the line.

"Mathieu...you can see—the old crow is only coming around at this point because she wants to ensure herself a pittance from Madame's final testament. It is actually rather pathetic," he paused, "to see those who have resurfaced as they believe the time is drawing near. Madame's grandson Étienne is even showing signs of restlessness." He paused again. "And let us consider the staff...they too must prepare for this era to come to a close."

Reminded of my conversation with Barbara in the cactus pass, I wondered if René was including himself when he mentioned *the staff*. In that very moment, the rain tapered off and a quiet rumble of distant thunder echoed through the line.

"Oh my, Mathieu...look at the time," he hesitated long enough to peek out the window, "let us face it...there is nothing we can do about it now—we merely have to wait it out and see."

He hung up the phone without saying goodbye. And this time around, I wasn't insulted by his manner. It saddened me. I got to thinking about René spending his entire life in the shadow of Madame. And thought about the sacrifices of the staff, those who have dedicated so many years of service to her—this is their home too.

My phone rang again and startled me.

"Allô, Matt."

"Oh, Mathieu! What reassurance to hear your voice—to know that the house phones are indeed functioning properly. I was simply petrified...did you notice the rain has stopped? Well, frankly it comes as no surprise since our friends at iheartweather. com said it would."

Click.

16

Lying in bed this afternoon, too bored to sleep, I suddenly hear the guard dogs causing a commotion. The barking seems to be coming from the area near the dog kennel—but shouldn't the dogs be up near the front gate at this hour?

In hopes of an adventure, I hop out of bed, throw on some shoes, grab my dog whistle necklace, and head outside in the direction of the barking.

By the time I clear the frog pond, I spot Tatyana, fenced inside the kennel area with two German shepherd puppies jumping up on her in a playful frenzy. She's not happy.

"Matthew!" She frantically rattles the gate.

"What happened?" I hurry toward the pen. "Are you locked in?"

"Barbara...she latch gate from outside and leave me caged with wild animals."

I toot my dog whistle to distract the dogs. "That wasn't very nice." I carefully open the gate, trying to keep the dogs in. They're the cutest things I've ever seen.

Tatyana slips out and brushes her uniform clean. "Barbara, she tell me we come see new puppies, but next, she leave me inside like prisoner."

"Well, there must've been some mistake." I latch the gate and wave to the pups. "Maybe she got distracted because Madame paged her?"

"No, Matthew." Tatyana hurries toward the house. "If anyone go for Madame...I go!"

I chase after her, eager for details. "Well, at least you're okay."

"It is not first time for this behavior, Matthew. Barbara, she is bad woman."

"You just have to stand up to her. You know, fight back. When I first arrived—"

"I give Barbara chance...and she remain bad." Tatyana ups her walking pace. "First, she take my extra uniforms and she hide them...next, she take my notebook for medical and she hide it...and then...she tell it to Niko that I make sexual disease."

"Oh, I'm so sorry," I say, considering how my situation with Barbara could have escalated to this point if I hadn't confronted her on Madame's terrace.

"Not sorry for me, sorry for Barbara." Tatyana stops in a shady spot, to inspect how badly the puppies have snagged her stockings. She attempts to brush the red clay from her shoes, but her white clogs are a mess. Tatyana charges onward, holding back tears of frustration. "She is not important person like us, Matthew...we come here for to save life of Madame. But Barbara... she is here for to clean the toilet!"

Tatyana leads us inside the laundry house. At any other time of day, this expansive room would be bustling with activity, but in the heat of the afternoon it's completely empty. She snatches a dressing gown off one of the racks, slips it on over her uniform, and discreetly disrobes beneath. She then tosses her torn stockings into the garbage and places her uniform into the washing machine.

"Well, just try to ignore her," I say, as she turns on the machine. I watch her walk toward the corner of the room that is set up like a shoemaker's booth. "Don't let her upset you."

"I do not cry for Barbara, I cry for Madame."

"Has Madame mistreated you?" I ask, not sure I understand.

"Madame, she never mistreat me." Tatyana buffs her clogs with a thick brush. "Madame have respect to me and she make place for me in her heart."

"Oh, I see."

"And my connection to Madame, it make Barbara jealous woman...angry woman."

I think I'm following her train of thought, but rather than ask for clarification I just let her continue.

"For instance," she pauses and looks up at me, "today, it is make public...the book about life of Monsieur."

"You mean, somebody wrote his biography?"

"Yes...and today, when I enter chamber of Madame...I find her with book. She is reading book and crying." Tatyana returns to her shoes. "So Madame, she ask me if I please take book away from bedroom. She does not want to see it again...this life of Monsieur."

"So you had to throw the book away?"

"Yes."

"Was that a big deal?"

"Yes. For Barbara is cleaning in bathroom at this time, and she hear everything. She is jealous for Madame to ask me for help—Madame, she trust me with personal detail...not Barbara."

Smiling through her tears, Tatyana walks over and unlocks a nearby closet. She opens the door to reveal more laundry supplies than most people would use in a year. And from behind the rows of detergent, she pulls out a fresh pair of stockings and rips the stubborn package open with her teeth.

"And Mister Alistair," Tatyana begins as she turns away to pull on her pantyhose, "he is on side of Barbara."

"How'd you know?" I wonder what clever tricks he came up with. "Has he been unkind?"

"One night he come to my room while I sleep...and he place my fingers in bowl of warm water. Why?"

I laugh. "Oh, that's just an old slumber party gag—to get the person to wet the bed in their sleep." I remember my own childhood pranks—itching powder, fake spiders, and freezing my sisters' bras.

Tatyana's face goes blank. "To wet bed…why? I do not like this kind of surprise…it is not funny for me."

"Oh, yeah, I know. It's a terrible trick," I backpedal, realizing I should've never teased my sisters the way I did. "But, you can't let them get to you."

"Ooh, Alistair!" Tatyana faces the washing machine and presses onto the lid as if trying to make it finish sooner. "The reason he is not to like me…because I refuse sexual advance."

"Man. I don't know what to say…I wish I could help."

"It is not problem for you to worry. And I do not lose job with Madame because of Alistair and Barbara—no!" Tatyana pauses with her back to me and presses her pelvis up against the washer. "And I miss Niko too…he is nice man Niko. Why is he left behind in Austria?"

"Well, good luck with everything." I head for the door, accepting her hip press as my cue to leave. "I'll be around if you ever need to talk," I say, knowing I don't really mean it.

Before exiting the laundry house, I glance back, only to find Tatyana still leaning up against the washing machine, lost in her thoughts of Niko. She's nutty for sure. But that was satisfying. I'll probably end up humping the machine in the show.

Heading back toward my room—ready to get out of this heat—I notice Olivia, hurrying across the lawn. "You're back!" I shout at the top of my lungs.

"Ciao, ciao. Come quick…I am in a hurry."

"Do you need a hand?" I ask, looking at the cluster of small flower arrangements she is carrying.

"That would be great. Are you sure you have time?"

"Are you kidding," I joke. And almost before my words get out, Olivia has handed me two of her five arrangements. "Hey, we missed you in London," I say, as we continue across the lawn. "This is ridiculous, it's been like forever since I've seen you. What'd you have to do…inventory the Kremlin?"

Olivia cracks a smile but keeps walking. "Not exactly. When I finished in Moscow, I learned that Madame would travel to London. So I thought it best to stay away."

"Why's that?"

"I believed she might become distracted with other business and continue to avoid her exercise...I heard she did quite well with you."

"Yeah. She was so disciplined. But it would've been a heck of a lot more fun if you were around."

"I snuck off to Mykonos," Olivia says as we approach the flower hut, "happy to have time with Danté again. I told Madame I would keep an eye on things from over there."

"Nice. So, Madame granted you a conjugal visit?" I joke as we step inside.

"Basically." Olivia sighs, lets out a big smile, and places her arrangements onto a large slate workstation. "Long overdue."

"I'm so happy for you," I say, now putting my bowls on the table. "Did you and Danté finally set a date?"

Olivia turns to face me and stops dead. "Not yet," she glances down, "there is simply too much to accomplish without adding the burden of planning a wedding." She pauses and looks up at me. "But this is hardly fair...you have barely mentioned David since our night at the casino."

"There's not much to say." I try to laugh it off.

"I am serious—tell me what is happening." Olivia props up against the table and positions herself as if planning to remain fixed until I speak.

I almost start to tell her the rent boy story, but decide not to. "Well, me and David spoke the other night, it was our third-year anniversary."

"Oh, I like that. Danté and I are coming up on four."

"Well, we had a bad phone connection, and didn't have much to talk about...we both agreed to email soon. Boring. I think he's seeing other people."

"What?"

I nod. "No biggie though…I've been through this before." My throat tightens. "After my first year with David, I realized we weren't going to be monogamous…since we were both on the road with opposite schedules…I knew it was gonna be tough, but also thought I could deal."

Olivia glances down again. "I understand. Danté and I also struggle with schedule."

"Oh, I'm not saying you and Danté won't work out. But being apart just isn't a great situation for me and David."

Olivia looks up. "Why? What is the difference?"

"Probably cuz I'm the jealous type. I get crazy when I don't know where he's at…and that doesn't work so well long-distance."

She playfully crosses her eyes. "Well, lucky for me, my mind is fully occupied." She points to her head. "Not one *iota* of space up here is allocated for suspicion."

I laugh. "But of course, now that I'm oceans away, David has become interested in commitment." My shoulders drop. "I'll keep the door open."

Olivia smacks her hand on the table like she's playing a game of slapjack. "I knew it!" She turns her back and reaches for some empty containers. "When you first told me of David…that morning at Burgflucht…I could just tell. Your eyes light up every time you mention his name. I think you are still very much in love with him. Are you not?"

"Well, I think I am too," I blush, "and being over here is helping me gain perspective."

"So the gap is narrowing?" Olivia smiles and picks up a huge bucket of yellow flowers.

"Yep. I guess so." I exhale as she moves the new flowers onto the table. The next thing I know, Olivia pulls a big handful out of the bucket while I contemplate the existing arrangements. "These are beautiful," I mention, as if she'd just asked me for my opinion. "I love how they're packed so neat and tight."

"Good. Because we need five replacements—and fast."

"Why? What's wrong with them?"

"They are purple."

"And what's wrong with *purple*?"

"Nothing—except that today is a *yellow* day."

I let out a slight sigh, relieved I opened up about David. "So that explains why I'm feeling so sunny?"

"Focus, Matthew." She snips away at the new flowers and tosses some in my direction. "The groundskeepers have fallen behind in this past week, due to the rainstorm...it washed away nearly half the gravel in the driveway. Today, they have somehow forgotten to complete Madame's arrangements first, before continuing to rake the pebbles."

I'm trying to copy what she's doing, but actually I'm just fumbling around, stuffing flowers into my bowl. "Is Madame upset," I ask, realizing I suck at this.

"No, not yet." Olivia looks over at my haphazard arrangement and lets out a huge smile. "Matthew, are you positively sure you are gay?"

"Hey, gimme a break. I'm not done yet." I strike a pose in defense of my pathetic-looking creation. "But if you think this looks shoddy, you should see me do hair." I give up with a laugh, and decide to just watch her work. "Olivia, why don't you ask the gardeners to do this?"

She chuckles and reaches for an additional container, as if her only option is to start a new one from scratch. "Normally I would...but they are conducting salah at the moment. And these flowers need to be up in Madame's room before she rings for tea." She checks her watch. "Nearly an hour from now."

"*Salah?*"

"Prayer."

"Oh. So how in the world does the Muslim staff have enough time to travel back and forth to town five times a day?" I wonder if I can take my misfit bouquet back to my room?

"No, no, the staff remains here on the grounds...in the mosque."

"Really...where's that?"

"Have you not seen it?"

"No, I haven't even heard about it."

"It is just over there," she nods out the back window of the flower hut. "The stone building on the other side of the sage plot. Madame constructed a sacred space for the workers, here on the property...both to be respectful of their faith, but also to maintain an efficient workday. Go on and take a look if you like."

All this time, I thought that building was for storage— René never once mentioned a mosque. "Cool, I'll check it out and be right back."

"Very well. But do not be long." Olivia pauses to set my defective arrangement off to one side, unblocking her creative juices. "I will need help going upstairs with these."

As I leave through the back door of the flower hut, I see about ten men filing out of the prayer room. I recognize Bahir, and the elderly man from the front gate, and a few of the other gardeners—whose names I still don't know. Bahir's face looks flushed with joy as he gently bumps his fist to his heart and nods in my direction. I smile and wave to him. Then, by the time I arrive outside the mosque, the men have gathered on the ground under a big shade tree. I pause, feeling like a trespasser.

"Now they enjoy mint tea." Olivia is standing right behind me. "Tea first, chores second."

I turn around and laugh. "Are you following me?"

"Yes." She says dryly. "Now look inside so we can take the flowers upstairs."

"I've gotta say," I look toward the gardeners, "I love ritual—it's all so civilized, so comforting." I look at Olivia. "I mean, in New York, if you wanna meet somebody for coffee, it takes three week's advance planning."

Olivia laughs and kicks off her loafers, so I step out of my sneakers.

"And speaking of schedule," she pushes open the door to the prayer room, "are you going inside or not?"

"Wow, those mosaics are incredible." I stare down at the floor then slowly make my way up to the ceiling. This space reminds me of an old single-room schoolhouse, where the rows of desks have been replaced with colorful prayer rugs. There is a small water trough/washing area just inside the door and the rest of the room is an airy open space, perfect for invoking inspiration.

"Leave it to Madame," she motions forward, "I just adore that subtle transition from the midnight-blue tiles into the pale yellow-green."

"Ah—it's stunning." I walk in a little. "And the narrow widows cut into the stones...very cool."

"Madame selected the orange and brown tapis for contrast." Olivia remains at the entrance. "But any Moroccan rug would look great in here."

"For sure, I love 'em. Don't you wanna come in?"

"I am not allowed any further than the doorway."

"Seriously?" I laugh and tug at my dog whistle necklace. "Because you're a woman?"

She nods.

I smirk. "To be honest, I wasn't sure I'd be welcome in here either."

"What do you mean, *welcome*?"

"Let's see...Gay/Methodist/Non-believer...pick one."

"Oh, come on. It is no different from strolling through a Gothic cathedral in Europe...one need not be Roman Catholic to appreciate its beauty."

"Then come inside."

"I cannot," her voice lowers, "I respect their tradition, and in turn, we maintain a healthy work environment."

I walk back to meet her at the door. "Why is everything angled toward the corner like that?"

"To pray toward Makkah," she says, as we put on our shoes. "You say *Mecca*, yes?"

"Yeah. I mean, I guess we do."

"Supposedly, it is the proper direction—but Madame also

Awaiting Madame

thought this angle best suited the architecture."

"So, why do you think she hurried back to Morocco," I pause, as we step outside, "when she's got so many other cool properties to visit?"

"Madame goes where she feels comfortable, and right now, that is here at Paradis." Olivia closes the door to the mosque and looks at me. "Keep in mind, Matthew, regardless of how many places one owns, one may only inhabit one dwelling at a time."

"But why not change it up?" I laugh to myself as we start back toward the flower hut. "In Brooklyn, my big decision is bathroom or kitchen."

Olivia smiles. "But sometimes, having too many choices can be stressful."

I realize she's right. But I wouldn't mind having this type of stress in my life someday. "Hey, can I ask you something else about Madame?"

"Of course, you know you can ask me anything."

"Well, the other day, when I was training the Duchess... she said that she and Madame had both participated in arranged marriages. Is she for real?"

Olivia laughs and stops walking. "Somewhat accurate."

"Come on...either they were or they weren't." I hope she'll fess up.

Olivia turns toward me. "Madame and Monsieur were first introduced to each other for strategic reasons...as were the Duke and Duchess. But it was entirely Madame's decision to accept Monsieur's proposal. And over time, they grew to love each other very much." She looks ahead and starts walking again. "Do you feel better now?"

"I guess so. I've just never met someone in that situation."

"And now you have. Do you find it to be important?"

"I'm not sure. Maybe I always thought true love had to happen naturally, you know, not based on some agreement."

She laughs. "So, only those couples *without* a prenuptial agreement are destined to live happily ever after?" She points to the flower hut. "Come along. We must place the flowers before Madame awakens. I will tell you more upstairs."

"Hum. Now I'm not sure *what* I thought." I chuckle. "Let me circle back on that prenup question." I look across the yard at the gardeners who are still gathered on the ground under the shade tree. Bahir stands up and motions for us to come over.

Olivia stops. "Bahir is inviting you to tea."

Already shaking my head *no*, I look at her. "Should we?"

"I am not permitted to join, but you must accept." She places her hand on my shoulder. "It is impolite to refuse."

"Okay. But what about the flower arrangements?"

She pushes me toward Bahir. "I will take tea with the women and head upstairs afterwards. Meet me in the kitchen when you are finished."

After a few steps forward I look back to Olivia. "But what about Madame?"

"Stop stalling, it is still not her teatime…now go."

Olivia walks off toward the flower hut while I continue toward the giant shade tree. I notice that each man in the circle is holding a narrow glass—etched with intricate markings. And each glass is full of pale green tea with lots of muddled mint leaves floating inside. One empty glass remains on a large round metal serving tray, sitting on the ground atop a decorative mat. But how'd they know to expect me? Is there always one extra?

I walk up to the group.

"Salaam," Bahir initiates, echoed by the rest.

"Bonjour," I say with a slight bow, and begin to sit down. And as soon as I land, cross-legged beside Bahir, I realize this isn't a smart position for my knee. But I do it anyway, thinking it's best to conform to the group.

The gardeners resume conversation in Arabic, while the front gate attendant lifts the simple metal teapot high above the tray and begins to pour. The tea spills from the Aladdin-type spout and free-falls nearly three feet into the glass without spilling a drop. Bubbles turn into slight foam and the tea steams up the glass.

The man places the teapot aside and motions for me to take the glass; everyone quiets down as I take my first sip. The whole group looks at me. So I sip again and nod out of respect. It tastes great. Very minty and super sweet. I love it. "Merci!" I shout with a toothy grin.

The men bust into laughter, and Bahir turns to look at me. My face goes red. I can tell I've got mint slivers wedged between my teeth. And within seconds, I realize it's harder to extract than spinach.

Once the men return to their conversation, I chill out, kick back, and enjoy listening—no longer concerned with trying to decipher their stories. And before long, I become absorbed in the rhythm and musicality of this moment. It's sheer bliss to observe their faces and appreciate the subtlety of their gestures. The weather-beaten gardeners appear completely at ease with their station in life and the entire group seems to share admiration for the front gate attendant. I guess longevity warrants respect. I could fabricate some details about what these men are discussing, but there's no need. This tranquil scene reminds me of the very reason I love dancing. Dance transcends words.

Soon, the heat of the sun seems to have lessened, and a sense of calm washes over me. On September twelfth of last year, if someone had told me I'd be sitting here now—under a shade tree in Morocco, sharing mint tea with a group of Muslim men—I would've said they were fucking crazy. But this experience makes me realize, I refuse to close myself off from the opportunity to learn from other cultures—even if that includes accepting my next gig as the dancing bear in a musical review on a bus-and-truck tour of Alabama.

"Monsieur loved to go fast," Olivia mentions and places the last of her yellow arrangements on the corner of Madame's office desk. "Jet aircraft, speedboats, cars…you name it." She sits down in what should be Madame's seat, then gestures for me to take a seat opposite. "Monsieur was addicted to the thrill associated with highflying stunts and daredevil behavior. I often heard him mention how he someday hoped to manufacture that feeling in a bottle. 'But what fun would it be if one could buy it from the store?' he used to say." Olivia pauses to arrange a few shallow basket-organizers on the desktop in front of her.

"Maybe Monsieur got off on tempting death," I state, hoping it didn't sound crass.

Olivia smiles and reaches for stack of letters and some envelopes. "He certainly did. Consider…when one has enough money to purchase anything and everything…what does one do?"

"Start looking for things that money can't buy," I let slip—as if I know.

"Exactly." Olivia shifts sheets of paper from one basket to the next, preparing what must be a letter-stuffing assembly line. "One begins to fixate upon any number of unattainable goals."

"Like my desire to dance the role of Romeo at the Met Opera House," I mime a big fencing gesture.

She laughs. "Yes. That one qualifies."

While Olivia continues her paperwork, I scan the framed photos on the walls of the office—all black-and-white shots of a much younger Madame. Posed with lots of important people, she is as striking as any classic Hollywood movie star. I recognize Queen Elizabeth, Nelson Mandela, Mother Teresa, and the Dalai Lama—but many I'm not sure about, though I bet just as famous. Interesting. No shots of Monsieur from what I can tell.

Olivia picks up on my curiosity. "Madame moves in exalted circles; however, she still has dreams—desires."

"Like what?" I ask sincerely.

"Well, on one occasion, Madame confessed to me that she would like to once again experience the smell of Paris in the '50s." Olivia pauses to remove a crooked staple with a pair of silver pincers. She clicks the stapler. It works. "And although I believe she was sincere, we both laughed it off."

"What's one of yours?" I wonder out loud, channelling Barbara Walters.

"Oh, I am not quite sure, Matthew. I was never good at looking forward or back. I simply do what comes next." Olivia concentrates her tidy working area. "I mean, what is the point really...to daydream about what could have been...or to wonder what might be?"

At first, her answer sounds comforting and Zen-like. But as I continue to watch her file the papers, I'm not convinced.

"Well, the ironic truth is," Olivia starts, more upbeat now, "we lost Monsieur because of his deep-seated desire to pursue his next thrill."

"What do you mean?"

Olivia swivels her chair around and grabs a thick leather-bound photo album off the shelf behind her. "This is the last series of photographs ever taken of Monsieur."

As I pull my chair closer to the front of the desk, Olivia places the album on the desk facing me. She slowly opens the cover and returns to her project.

I turn through the first couple pages. Monsieur reminds me of Gregory Peck in *To Kill a Mockingbird*. Handsome man. Yep. But as suspected, he's *not* featured on the walls of this office. "Where are these from?"

"Those were taken during his millennium voyage. Monsieur had planned to travel around the world to celebrate the new millennium at the stroke of midnight, in every time zone."

"So how many new millennium/millennia did he see?"

"About eleven."

"Why *about*?"

"Well, by the time he and the crew had progressed from the International Date Line back here to Morocco, Monsieur decided to forgo his quest." Olivia pauses from her work. She looks at me and her face empties as if remembering the very moment. "He complained of indigestion and was discouraged about being seven hours behind schedule."

"Didn't he know it's impossible, to actually be on time at the new midnight, hour by hour, zone by zone. Even I know that."

"I know. Funny, is it not?" She gets back to work. "And months before the trip, Herr Vollstrecken suggested to Monsieur that he might achieve his time-zone fantasy, by wandering around Antarctica with a pair of ski poles. But Monsieur found that option much too timid. He meandered throughout the house for weeks quoting: 'This Pole will not be caught dead holding his pole at the pole at midnight.'" Olivia chuckles and reaches for a dish of paper clips.

"So Monsieur was Polish? I thought he and Madame were both French?"

"One-eighth, or one-sixteenth." Olivia stands up to re-trieve another stack of what appears to be Madame's handwritten letters. "He would only admit to his Polish ancestry when he felt it made for a good joke."

I smile at her comment and look down at the photo album, spying another picture of another champagne toast. "Looks like a blast."

"If you say so." Olivia groans and sits. "We were all sick the entire time...sea sick, air sick, just plain sick/sick...racing from one spot to the next...in choppy water and turbulent skies— breathing recycled air...much fun!"

"So you were on the trip too?" I turn the page as Olivia folds her first letter. She burnishes the crease with an ebony ruler and slips the note into a pre-addressed envelope.

"Of course I was...who do you suppose took all of these pictures?" She gently places the first unsealed letter into the center basket, reaches across the desk, turns the next page for me, and points to a small picture in the lower right corner. "Here is the staff photo...you see how delighted we look? At this point in the journey, I was barely upright, Alistair was downright green, and Barbara had terrible hives due to an allergic reaction from some sort of Indian spice intended to bring luck in the New Year."

"She does look a little *itchy* in this one."

Olivia giggles. "Our staff photo was pitiful...but Madame insisted we have a little keepsake of the journey." Olivia drops another letter in the basket. "Now of course, I am glad we do."

Still looking at the staff picture, I realize Olivia is the only one in the group who looks more or less okay, but she's still not herself. I laugh. "It *is* pretty bad."

Olivia grabs the album up from the desk and folds it shut. "And that is because we had every possible illness." She scolds playfully. "You name it—someone had it." Olivia returns the album to its spot on the shelf and immediately starts working again. "The next morning, Monsieur, was still not feeling well, suffering heart palpitations...but nonetheless, he decided to fly to Côte d'Azur."

I'm speechless, and wowed by the fact that she has stuffed nearly twenty envelopes within only a few minutes. She's on autopilot.

She looks at me as if she's my tutor. "That is in the south of France, Matthew."

"Yeah, I know...I was just thinking how speedy you are."

Olivia doesn't miss a beat and grabs for what looks like a big pair of pliers. Staple gun? "Everyone speculated that Monsieur must have actually aged himself in the process of chasing all those new years." She slides the envelope flap inside the mouth of the pliers.

Duh. Embossing tool. "So what actually happened?"

She marks the first envelope with a curlicue *F*. "His heart failed." She sighs. "He was pronounced dead upon arrival at the airport in Nice."

"Were you with him at the time?" I wonder how many times she's worked this assembly line.

Olivia embosses another envelope and holds it up to inspect her precision. The raised monogram looks perfect. "No, only his physician, two crew, and Alistair."

"What about Madame, was she on board the flight?"

"No. Most fortunately not...Madame was in Mykonos when Monsieur passed. She abandoned the road race long before he did."

OH! So *that's* why Madame doesn't like talking about Mykonos. I wait a beat. "Did you have to break the news to her?"

"No...she heard from Barbara." Olivia stops and looks at me. "However, I wish I had been the one to share the news with Madame." She hesitates. "The tragic news of Monsieur's passing...it damaged Madame's association with the property in Greece. And since that day, she has yet to return... I do not believe she ever will." Her eyes darken.

"So it's just sitting—" I stop as the two Pomeranians yip their way into the office.

"Tanya...is that you dear?" Madame's unmistakable voice interrupts from behind me.

Olivia looks at me.

I freeze.

"Tanya?" Madame calls out in full voice, sounding stronger than I'd expect.

"Bonjour, Madame," Olivia shouts toward the bedroom. "I am here, working in the office." She returns to embossing.

Based on the excitement of the dogs, I can tell Madame is approaching. I stand up, tuck my dog whistle necklace inside my shirt, step off to the side of the desk, and face the doorway.

"Olivia," Madame enunciates. "Where might I find my Tanya?"

"I cannot say." Olivia answers respectfully.

Madame enters the room. "Good day, Matthew." She smiles in my direction as Antoinette and Celeste sniff at my feet. "Do we have an appointment this afternoon?"

"Oh, hi." I say as if she's stopping by my room. "I don't think so." I pause. "Unless you'd like to?"

Madame raises an eyebrow; she's not easily coaxed. "No, thank you, Matthew. It is much too warm again today—perhaps tomorrow." Madame turns to Olivia. "Do you suppose Tanya is available?"

"May I ring downstairs?" Olivia asks matter-of-factly.

"What a good idea," Madame's childlike innocence fills

the room. "Could you, please?"

"I certainly will, Madame...and may I bring you anything in the meantime?"

"No, no." Madame turns to leave and both dogs dash away. "Just Tanya will be fine, thank you."

As Madame walks toward her bedroom, I notice she is considerably weaker than the last time we trained in London. It's hard to admit that she's lost all the strength she gained, but she has—and she looks even thinner. I wish I could convince her to start working out again.

By the time Madame clears the doorway, Olivia has already dialed the phone, stowed her embossing tool, and motioned me outside toward the service stairs. "Tatyana, s'il vous plait," she says into the receiver as I slip out the back way.

In a heartbeat, I'm halfway across the rooftop garden—where Olivia catches up to me. We squeeze into the spiral staircase and giggle hysterically, all the way down to the first floor.

After pausing to regain our composure, we exit the stairwell, hurry toward the gazebo, and soon reenter the house. As we rush toward the foyer, I hear rumbles of conversation coming from inside the guest bathroom.

Olivia dodges around the corner, flips a switch on the wall near an intercom speaker, and we both stop—I guess she heard it too. She quickly adjusts the volume on the speaker and we listen for a second. It's clear. The voices belong to Alistair and Barbara.

"I served her the spoiled seafood as planned," he says, "yet she was back on her feet within a day."

I look at Olivia. "Come on," I whisper, "do you thing they're seriously trying to poison Tatyana?"

Olivia places a finger over her mouth and leans her ear closer to the monitor.

"This is no time to praise her resilience," Barbara scolds. "We must get on with the plan. I want her out of here...and after that sob story involving her brother," Barbara continues, "I have heard enough."

"What *brother*?" Alistair sounds confused.

"The brother with cancer—her raison d'être," Barbara says. "But in spite of this difficulty, I want that wicked girl out."

"Charlatan," Alistair half-shouts, "she told me her *mother* had cancer."

I look at Olivia. "Oops," I whisper, "I heard Tatyana tell the Blessingtons it was her *sister*."

Olivia's eyes widen as Alistair and Barbara go quiet.

Shit. Maybe they know we're listening in?

I grab Olivia's wrist, implying we should go.

But instead of leaving, she glues her ear to the monitor and holds me in place.

"Enough," Barbara sounds totally fed up, "we move into phase two!" The bathroom door rattles open.

Olivia resets the privacy switch on the wall and shakes free from my grip—but we stay frozen in place as Barbara exits the bathroom.

In the near distance, Tatyana appears from around the corner, and proceeds down the hallway toward Barbara. Then, as Tatyana and Barbara get closer, Barbara sticks out a foot and trips Tatyana to the ground. Tatyana lands hard on the slick marble floor. And Barbara continues walking—as if nothing has happened.

The moment Tatyana goes thud, Alistair rushes out of the bathroom to help her. But before he can rescue her, Barbara turns around. She sneers at Alistair with such intensity that he redirects his path and heads toward the kitchen instead—leaving Tatyana sprawled on the floor.

I guess *phase two* meant physical abuse.

The moment Barbara and Alistair move out of sight, Olivia hurries over to Tatyana. "Are you all right?" She asks, and carefully helps Tatyana stand. Olivia then explains that Madame is waiting. "Shall I go upstairs and stall for a moment?"

"No. I go to Madame," Tatyana says and reclaims her stoic disposition. "Barbara can try to stop me...but she does not."

I watch the two women inch toward the elevator.

Olivia gives Tatyana a gentle pat on the back. "Are you positively sure you are able?"

"Yes. I am fine." Tatyana rubs her elbow. "I am fine," she mumbles as they step into the elevator.

Still tucked around the corner, I wait for the elevator door to close then slip off toward my room—acting casual. But I'm livid. I feel like I should walk into the kitchen right now and tell Barbara and Alistair to *fuck off*—but my body isn't listening. I'm heading toward the security of my room instead. Those two have really mistreated Tatyana. And here I am, more concerned about saving my ass than sticking up for what's right.

I'm a schmuck.

But I can't rock the boat right now.

I know if I can get Madame back into the habit of training, I can make a difference. I can help her. I've got to buck up and swallow this one—for Madame's sake.

A few hours later, in the midst of staff dinner, Tatyana enters the kitchen wearing one arm in a sling. I watch her ask the sous-chef to prepare a meal—but she is only willing to eat items found in a can.

While Tatyana hovers near the stove, Barbara turns to me at the table. "Madame is planning to move again," she confides, careful Tatyana won't overhear, "you must be ready to leave at a moment's notice."

"Where do you think we'll go this time?" I ask, watching Tatyana stir together a concoction of tuna, black olives, anchovies, and sardines.

"No one yet knows." Barbara pauses as Tatyana exits into the pantry. "But we are lucky."

"What do you mean?"

Barbara shifts her seat to get a little closer to me. "When Monsieur was alive, relocation happened without advance warning. If he wanted to move, we would move. Any member of the staff, who was not *at the ready* when requested to travel, would be left behind. If we missed Monsieur's departure, we were expected to find our own way—at our own expense."

"Really?"

"Is true…to this day, I believe there is one helpless house-maid still finding her way home from somewhere along the Nile." She slaps her thigh and shifts her chair away from me.

I laugh too—out of some weird sense of obligation—but I realize she might not be kidding. I bet she's plotting to leave Tatyana stranded here in Morocco. "Well, thanks for the heads-up."

Barbara picks up her fork and steadies a large piece of grilled fennel. "To be smart," she grabs her knife and effortlessly cuts through the dense bulb, "pack your suitcase tonight."

At the end of our meal, Barbara brings out Madame's favorite cookies—French macarons—as an additional dessert. She positions herself behind the island counter and tosses one to each of us, as if pitching a winning streak at Yankee Stadium.

"In honor of excellent service," she shouts as the colorful sandwich cookies light up the room like a tie-dyed meteor shower. And after serving everyone else, Barbara lofts one to Alistair with the affection of a trainer rewarding her seal pup. "Well played, sir," she cheers, "well played."

But as Alistair's cookie soars across the room, Tatyana unexpectedly reappears from around the corner.

Interception!

"Thank you, Barbara. So kind." Tatyana pops the cookie in one bite and the whole room goes quiet. "Scrumptious."

I let out a laugh and immediately bite my lip.

Tatyana then looks at Barbara without flinching. "Today, you win battle…but trust me…I win war." She flicks a crumb from her sling. "I do not quit job with Madame for you," she scans the staff table, "or anyone else."

Boom.

Mic drop. She's out.

The fallout of Tatyana's dramatic confrontation leaves Barbara speechless. And I'm so excited, I decide to break the awkward silence. "Night, night, everybody," I say sarcastically, and stand up, "sweet dreams." I saunter toward the pantry. "See you in the morning."

Just another dysfunctional dinner at Paradis, I think to myself as I hit the screen door—happy to get the fuck out of there.

17

"The helicopter is waiting," Barbara says through the staticky phone connection, as if this information is common knowledge. "Bring your belongings to the great lawn…you will find us there."

And within minutes, I'm out the door, excited to leave, but still not sure where we're traveling. Thank God, I packed last night when she told me to.

As I approach the great lawn and see the helicopter in the distance, I'm reminded of how vast this area actually is. I notice Barbara and a pilot loading some baggage, and the sous-chef standing off to one side holding a tray of sack lunches. So, as soon as I arrive, I leave my suitcase with the pilot, take a brown paper bag off the tray, and step up into the helicopter—as if this is an everyday occurrence.

Barbara follows me inside. "All the way over." She motions for me to sit on the backward-facing side of the two banquettes. "We have three and three today…Madame and René facing each other here, closest to the door, followed by Alistair and Olivia in the center, then you and I."

"What about Tatyana?" I intentionally poke.

Barbara frowns but doesn't answer.

"Are the dogs coming," I continue, knowing that'll get her to loosen up.

"Of course." Barbara sighs and plops down facing me. "They will manage on the floor…or in our laps."

"Chop. Chop." Alistair ducks into the cabin wearing a goofy grin and carrying a wicker picnic basket. "Off we go!" He sits down beside me and places the basket at his feet.

In a blink, Olivia walks in with three sack lunches. She sits down across from Alistair. "Hello, everyone." She passes a bag to Barbara. "In the event you change your mind."

Then, with barely enough time to exchange *hellos*—let alone ask where we're going—I see that Bahir has pulled the car onto the lawn and he's already unloading Madame and the house dogs. René pops out of the back of the car to help Madame as the dogs hightail it in to greet us. Where's Tatyana?

René climbs in, assists Madame into her seat, and sits down facing her. He then waves out the window—like he's heading off to boarding school—as Bahir and the sous-chef drive away.

When Bahir toots the horn farewell, I realize that Barbara could have intentionally misled Tatyana about our departure time in order to leave her behind. I glance at Alistair to see if he's in on it. Maybe these two aren't done with the feud? I look at Barbara. Neither one of them is letting on. There's no way Madame will forget Tatyana.

As I glance out the window once more, I finally see Tatyana in the distance, skipping across the lawn with her tiny travel bag, looking like Fräulein Maria en route to the house of Captain VonTrapp. I knew it! I knew Madame wouldn't take off without her. But now I'm worried that René's obsession with *The Sound of Music* has rubbed off on me. Yuck. And as Tatyana steps inside the cabin, Barbara's face goes glum. Well, more *glum* than usual.

Madame looks at Olivia. "All accounted for," Madame says as Tatyana uses her good arm to lower a jump seat and manages to angle her knees to fit between Madame and René.

Olivia smiles and passes Tatyana a sack lunch.

And before I know it, the pilot seals the main door, welcomes us on board, powers up the helicopter, and lifts us straight up over the trees.

"Alistair, do tell," René calls out over the buzzing engine, "what goodies might we have for our picnic today?"

"Oh, lots of treats," Alistair answers, "once we're up. Promise."

Having now shifted places a few times, the lapdogs are happily sprawled out on Olivia and Barbara—seemingly hypnotized by the sound of the propeller. I take a deep breath and watch Tatyana offer Madame a magazine, but no one else moves or says a word. So cozy.

Fifteen minutes later, Alistair slips into his white gloves and opens the picnic basket. René leans over to peek inside. Ignoring René's curiosity, Alistair unfolds a tray table and hands it to me. I don't think it's mine. He then unfolds another tray and lines each with a linen napkin and puts some silverware on top. Alistair soon places his tray over Madame and passes my tray to René, before he uncorks a bottle of house white—nicely chilled. Next, he takes out two wine glasses, places one on each tray, and waits for Madame to acknowledge him before pouring.

"À Côte d'Azur," René toasts and regally lifts his glass toward Madame.

Oh shit. Are we really taking this rickety helicopter all the way to the south of France? Am I expected to survive on this lousy sack lunch and no restroom?

Madame smiles at René, then she lifts her glass in slow motion. They sip.

Alistair digs into the bottom of the basket and presents two ready-made lunch plates. They each have an assortment of cured meats, some nice looking fruit, a few cheeses, crusty French bread, crackers, cantaloupe, and lemon wedges. Man. I can't get enough of this. It's like I'm staring into someone's shopping cart at the supermarket, hoping to be invited over for dinner.

A short while later, Alistair's still acting busy, pretending to serve Madame—but she hasn't touched a thing on her plate. And no one has opened their sack. Olivia and Barbara are resting their eyes, without looking like they're sleeping, while Tatyana stares into space as if reading a TelePrompTer. Poor woman. The one-armed girl is shoved between Madame and René in such a way, that there's no way she'll have a chance to eat. Hum. I wonder if I could sneak a look inside my bag without rustling the paper?

Sooner than expected, the pilot comes over the loud speaker. He announces that we should be landing in twenty minutes and warns the descent might be bumpy. My stomach lets out a growl as if I'm starving. But I act nonchalant and continue to resist the temptation to look inside my bag.

Madame and René hold tight to their wine glasses as Alistair removes their trays and begins to repack the picnic basket. I totally give up on the idea of eating anything, but can't figure out *how* we could already be in France—isn't Spain down there somewhere?

Not soon enough, the helicopter begins to hover. While the pilot lowers us straight down, I can't see anything except water and sky. I guess we're landing on an island. As we continue down, I still see only water—maybe it's a small island?

Then, out of nowhere, a section of king-sized yacht comes into view and we touch down without so much as a shake. Sweet! This moment will be awesome on stage. Really. Who doesn't like to see actors on bungee cords? On second thought, I wonder if putting a huge boat in the middle of my show will conjure up memories of *Titanic*, the musical. Hell. I can't believe that catastrophe is still on the road in Europe. What a joke. Hadn't those survivors already been through enough without having to live through that theatrical mess? But I also wonder how long it will take before *9/11 The Musical* gets a green light. For real. There is bound to be some jerk already working on it. Let's face it, nothing is off limits where there's potential profit. Well, truth be told, I bet I wouldn't be so jaded on this topic of disaster plays, if I'd booked the workshop rehearsals for *Hindenburg*. Oh, well. I'll just have to make Madame's boat unique—her ship will need to do something more spectacular than merely sink or stay afloat.

The moment the engine cuts off, the dogs stir, René applauds, and the pilot releases the cabin door. Madame stands up determined to leave. And just as with any other ordinary travel day, Madame, René, and the house dogs exit the aircraft first— Tatyana close behind.

I watch Madame step onto the deck, and spy a long line of crew, standing in a row, all wearing matching white sailing uniforms. The crew members welcome Madame and present her with silver trays full of tropical-looking cocktails and assorted hors d'oeuvres. Tatyana gently guides Madame past the receiving line without pausing, while René stops to accept a drink from the cutest boy on the team. Tatyana continues to lead Madame away from the helicopter, while the house dogs scurry along behind her. The dogs sniff at the feet of the crew, but don't dare beg for a treat or tinkle on deck. Alistair hops out of the helicopter followed by Olivia and Barbara.

And by the time I step out, Olivia is there with a smile. "Welcome to the Alboran Sea, Matthew."

I give her a blank look. "Where?"

"The westernmost section of the Mediterranean Sea."

I grin. "Oh, okay. That sounds better."

Olivia points off in the distance. "Look over there...the Rock of Gibraltar."

I shield my eyes from the glaring sun and squint across the glistening water. "Fierce," I gasp. The Prudential Insurance logo in real life.

"Matthew," Alistair says as Barbara vanishes behind the receiving line, "you are standing atop one of the most expensive charter ships in the entire world."

Charter? Isn't that just a classy term for *rental*? "Cool." But why are we renting a boat when René implied that Madame owned one of her own?

"And, Matthew," Olivia adds as the three of us move toward the crew, "Madame has agreed for you to stay in the VIP area on Bridge Deck."

"Sounds impressive, but what do you mean, why?" I

reach for a cocktail with lots of crushed ice in it.

Alistair grabs an appetizer. "It means that Madame and her grandson Étienne are in the Master Suites," he grabs another. "Only one flight above Bridge."

"Upper Deck," Olivia clarifies, handing Alistair a napkin. "While Barbara, Alistair, and I will be housed in the standard cabins beneath you."

"Main Deck," Alistair mumbles and takes another appetizer from a different tray.

I reach for a skewer of grilled seafood. Delicious. "Well, I don't mind being down on the Main Deck with you guys."

"You must be kidding, Matthew," Olivia laughs. "And miss out on this chance to sail Bridge Deck in absolute luxury?"

"Come along, honored guests," Alistair says sarcastically, "let us have a look around."

Alistair leads us down the ramp away from the helicopter, while the crew members follow like a flock of white birds, moving in formation. We walk over to have a look at the Jacuzzi—so the row of attendants also walks over to the hot tub area. It seems excessive, to have this much crew-on-crew attention, but as I reach for another tasty skewer, I remind myself it's their job to appear busy.

We pause against the railing with drinks in hand and look out across the sea. Alistair looks at me. "We have more than sixty crew on board," he brags. "Not counting us."

"Sounds like a lot," I say, now happy I didn't eat that sack lunch. "So where does the crew stay…on Main Deck with you guys?"

"Oh, no!" Alistair shouts with a wide grin. "The ship's crew resides two decks below us." He looks at Olivia. "Not a single porthole amongst them."

Olivia smiles at Alistair but then takes a sip of her drink as if trying not to gloat.

Alistair looks at me again. "I was onboard this baby years ago with Monsieur." He runs a hand along the fiberglass railing.

"Isn't she gorgeous?"

"Remarkable," I say, purposely trying to change up my responses, "I can't wait to see inside."

"Of course, we are at rest at the moment," Olivia adds, "you will have a much better sense of her once she goes."

The three of us stay upstairs by the hot tub for a while, and sample at least one of every hors d'oeuvre. And after we make it to a second round of drinks, I turn toward Olivia. "So what exactly did you mean...when you said Madame *agreed* for me to stay in the VIP section? And when you mentioned the room assignments, I noticed you purposely left out René and Tatyana."

"Oh, did I?" Olivia plays dumb. "No, no, I meant to say Tatyana has a small room upstairs next to Madame."

Something seems fishy. "So that leaves me and René alone on Bridge Deck?" I glance at both of them. "What's up with that?"

"Here, try this one," Olivia nervously force-feeds me some grilled eggplant, "the aubergine is to die for."

I look at Alistair and wonder what Olivia could be dodging. His annoying expression doesn't help; it just makes me more restless. "Come on you guys, what's really going on?"

"I am sorry to be the one to inform you," Olivia says as Alistair laughs and reaches for a fresh drink, "Herr Vollstrecken has arranged this cruise for Madame... and he requested that you stay on Bridge Deck...to be closer to him."

"Oh God, no! Please, tell me you're kidding."

"Not kidding," Olivia apologizes.

I turn to her. "So you guys already know how much he bothers me," I confide.

She nods. "Yes, he speaks constantly about how *terrific* you are."

"But listen," Alistair chimes in with a hearty laugh, gives me his fresh drink, and takes away my empty. "It is only temporary, we should be off this boat in three-days time. Now come on, drink up."

I cringe. "Three days!" I slug back the icy cocktail at the same moment the ship's horn blows.

As we set sail, I ask Alistair for another slushy drink. Gulp. I get nailed with brain freeze. Son of a bitch! I can't believe I'm locked onboard this ship with that jerk.

"Ohh, Matty..."

Fuck. His garbled voice comes from somewhere behind the assembly of crew.

"Do come inside, Matty..." he calls, even louder, "come inside before you take windburn across that precious face of yours."

I turn slowly, hoping to wake up from a bad dream. And just as the formation of waiters reshapes itself, there he is. Shit. It really is him. "Oh, um, hi—Herr Vollstrecken."

Alistair swaps out my glass for another fresh one, pats me on the back, and gives me a shove forward like he's my boxing coach sending me into the ring for the next round. I clear my throat and shift into game mode. "Hey, how are you?"

"Just grand, Matty...just grand. Most trilled to see you.

I try not to gag.

Vollstrecken gives Olivia a big smooch on the cheek. "Tonight over dinner, my dear, I will need you and your steno pad, ready to notate the conversation with Éteinne."

I don't think she likes it, but she's hard to read.

"I certainly will," Olivia answers flatly. "Already planning on it."

"Oh, thank you, dear," Vollstrecken pauses, looks at me, wraps an arm around my shoulders, and leads us a few steps away from the group. "Matty...come inside with me. I will show you to your suite."

My stomach churns as Vollstrecken guides me away from Olivia and Alistair. I glance behind, hoping for a save, but I know it's too late to change this situation. Christ. Alistair's surrounded by crew, lost in a platter of something delicious, and Olivia looks helpless as she waves goodbye and mouths *sorry*.

"Matty, I hope you will find your accommodations suitable." Vollstrecken motions for the crew to disperse. And they do.

I turn clammy.

He leads us inside the ship and down a flight of stairs. "Welcome to Upper Deck, my dear boy."

"How pretty," I say blandly, thinking it's actually pretty tacky.

As we stroll through the hallway, I damn near hyperventilate. Vollstrecken points to the doorways of the master suites. "Madame is in this one and Étienne is over there...most magnificent, these rooms."

I nod, but no longer feel obliged to actually respond.

We soon pass the spa, the cinema, and peek into the gym area—I pray there's no massage table. And eventually, we step outside again, arriving at a large sundeck on the back of the ship. "Matty, do you enjoy shuffleboard?" He looks down at the numbered triangles painted on the deck.

"Yeah. I guess so." I haven't played since I was a kid.

"Well, in that case...we will have to make a date of it."

Damn. I should have lied.

As we depart the sundeck, we spiral down an outside staircase, onto the infamous Bridge Deck, where we enter inside again, this time into a slick nightclub/lounge area. "Matty," he points to the small cabaret stage, "perhaps you will take to the boards for us one evening...and perform one of your favorite song and dance routines?"

I wish I could get his fucking bony arm off my neck. "Oh...I doubt that." I answer, thinking I could sneak in here and try out some new material—but not in front of this bastard.

As Vollstrecken shows me out of the lounge area, we pass through the library, and soon arrive at the special guest suites— one for me, one for René, and one for him. He opens the door to my room and gestures for me to go on inside.

I slip out from under his arm and step into the doorway. Whew. At least I don't have to share a room with him. "Thanks so much." I purposely block him from entering.

He hesitates. "Matty, my room is right over here," he whispers, pointing directly across the hall.

"Well, thanks again," I step back to let the door swing shut, "I'm sure we'll chat again soon." I look straight ahead, but envision my eyes rolling back.

He stops the door with one hand. "No. Thank *you*, Matty." And with that, he gives me his signature leer and gently pulls my door closed.

A shiver runs up my back.

Without thinking, I grab the nearest chair and wedge it up under the doorknob. I then peer through the peephole to watch him leave. What a fuck-face.

Once I turn around, I pause to catch my breath and take a good look at the room. Amazing. And even though this boat is the complete opposite of Madame's minimalist sensibility, it's still jaw-dropping. With a keen eye and a limitless budget, any set designer would have a blast creating this opulent nautical theme gone wild. And whether it's considered *chic* or not, I love my room. I've got a huge king-sized bed, a nice sitting area, a big marble-looking bathroom, and a totally awesome balcony. Damn. Vollstrecken must think I plan to put out for him. Nasty fucker.

My phone rings and I make a mad dash to the nightstand.

It's Olivia. "Are you okay?"

"Barely!" I respond with full drama-queen attitude.

"Not to worry," she speaks collectedly, "Herr Vollstrecken is sure to remain on his best behavior—since Madame plans to finalize her business with him...trust me, I will go directly to Madame if he tries anything. So, tell me, how is your room?"

"It's beautiful for sure. But I'm still freaked out...his room is right outside my door."

"I know."

"Listen, Olivia...I counted at least three empty cabins on Bridge Deck. Why don't you guys just move up here?"

"I wish we could," she says calmly, "but it would be improper for us to overstep boundaries. We cannot move without an invitation."

"I know…I get it," I say, sounding ungrateful, "I'm just so nervous around him."

"Matthew, put Herr Vollstrecken out of your mind, and enjoy the luxury of this moment…once we disembark, you will have a memory to last a lifetime. Oh! And remember, your dinner will be served at seven o'clock tonight, one flight below." She suddenly sounds distracted. "As you know, I will be at table with Madame."

"Okay, thanks. I won't keep you…miss you at dinner."

It's past eight o'clock now, and I'm outside on the rear of the Main Deck, dining with Barbara and Alistair—no Tatyana as usual. The sea is calm and I can't believe I'm sitting here under these heat lamps, having just watched the sunset from the deck of this whopping boat. The three of us are sharing a huge skillet of paella, accented with big chunks of seafood. For the past hour, we've been eating like there's no tomorrow and drinking like the world's already come to an end. I look at my dinner companions. Barbara is tipsy. Alistair is pretty far gone. And I'm downright drunk. It's a riot to look beyond our table and observe six waiters standing by just to serve us three. Ha. If we've got six, Madame must have ten attending her table in the formal dining room.

I sip my wine and watch Barbara reach for another helping of saffron rice from the bottom of the shallow serving pan, and try not to stare as she drags the rice onto her plate in an unusually sloppy manner. She then reaches back into the pan with her bare hand, grabs a piece of whitefish, and tosses it onto her plate. Next, she takes a big mouthful of bread and swallows some wine, while still chewing the bread. Hell. This isn't like her. It's like she's morphing into Alistair. Maybe she's having a bad flashback of Monsieur's millennium voyage?

A few minutes later, Barbara beckons one of the waiters to refill her wine glass. But instead of letting him complete his job, she steals the bottle, pours her own, and scolds him for lack of technique. As the waiter steps away, Alistair glances across the table at me, but soon returns to staring down at his plate.

"An indelible silence," Barbara says in a disconnected manner, before pausing to sip her wine. "Oh, what a silence it was...the night I lost my baby girl." Her eyes become mysterious, faraway. "I have not thought of it in ages."

What the hell? What is she talking about?

I grab my wine glass and slide down in my seat, dying to hear where she's going with this. Alistair isn't reacting, so I assume that means he's heard this one before. But I haven't.

Barbara takes another swallow of wine. "Not a single sound was transmitted through the baby monitor the night it happened...I heard nothing...and nothing was heard in the mother's room," she continues aimlessly. "From the grainy images captured on the black-and-white security camera, it simply looked as though I was standing over her bassinet, comforting my innocent baby girl." Barbara pauses, glances at Alistair, then sips from her glass. "And I was...I was merely helping her off to sleep."

Listening inquisitively, I casually lift my fork and push a few empty clamshells around my plate, before deciding to tackle another piece of chewy squid. Fuck. Did she smother some kid?

"Soon enough, the autopsy results were presented." Barbara swirls the small bit of wine now left in her glass. "And after the arduous court case came to a close, the loss of my baby girl went on record as yet another case of *Sudden Infant Death Syndrome*...SIDS," she clarifies. "It happens all the time."

I'm not sure if Barbara means that nannies are often suspected of killing babies or that crib death is fairly common. But either way, I'm in shock. Speechless. I can't believe Madame would have hired her if this were true. Maybe she's making it up? Maybe this is Barbara's version of a campfire ghost story?

I glance at Alistair for a clue, but he just half-rolls his eyes and lifts his wine glass in search of a refill. When I look over at Barbara again, she's enjoying more paella as if she plans to stay here all night. I can't tell if they're both putting on a show or not.

Minutes later, I'm still contemplating Barbara's tragic tale, when a group of new waiters barge onto the deck—singing *Happy Birthday* in German. The headwaiter is carrying a big fluffy white mound of cake with sparklers on top, while the rest of the servers parade behind him, waving more sparklers.

"Baked Alaska!" Alistair shouts as Barbara stands up at her seat.

Once the headwaiter arrives in front of our table, he presents the cake to Barbara. She curtsies, steps forward, gathers a sinister alcohol-induced grin, and watches the flames burn down—acting like she's involved in making a detailed wish.

I can hardly look at her. Her story left me queasy. I'd like to believe the whole thing was a sick joke. But was it? If so, she's one deceitful bitch—even more two-faced than I imagined. But if it was fabricated, I've got to hand it to her, she's ingenious.

During dessert, the staff not only gave us slice after slice of the baked Alaska, they offered many different treats, hand-passed on silver trays. Thankfully, the topic of conversation transitioned from *baby killings* to complaining about *how dry* or *too sweet* everything was. But the negative reviews didn't slow my appetite, they just fueled my curiosity about what we might taste next. Throughout our binge, I couldn't shake the idea that Barbara might actually be a guilty woman gone free. That explains a lot, I thought as I stumbled through the hallway toward my room—praying to get locked inside before Vollstrecken finished his meeting with Madame.

And the instant I got back to my cabin, I made a drink and got comfy outside on the balcony, under some blankets. So, here I sit, sipping a cocktail, sailing the Mediterranean in the lap of luxury—with a chair jammed under the doorknob—laughing about having just refilled that tiny vodka bottle with water, before restocking it in the minibar. Apparently, cheapskate-dancer-habits really do die hard.

18

Barely awake and hung over from last night, I hear my phone ring. "Mathieu, come quick!" René shouts into the receiver. "There is something you must absolutely see with your own eyes!"

My head throbs. "Be right there."

I hurry into my faux marble bathroom, splash my face with water, pull on my trainer outfit, and hurry two doors down the hall to his room. From outside his door, I hear a recording of applause, along with some hand clapping coming from inside the room. I knock. "René, may I come in?"

"Yes! Yes!" He responds impatiently as I begin to open the door. "Of course, Mathieu, there is no need to knock," he adds.

After I enter, I see that his suite is exactly like mine, except the floor plan is reversed. And I find René standing in the middle of his room, dressed in his cardio-blast outfit. He's bowing down in front of Vollstrecken, who is reclining on René's bed— wearing a half-open terry cloth robe with nothing underneath. I flinch.

"René, darling," Vollstrecken garbles through clenched teeth, adjusting his robe open to reveal more hideous flesh, "do it again from the top...for Matty."

René clicks his computer and soon starts his *Little Red Corvette* routine from the top. He's giving it his all, nailing every step, selling it like he's in front of the footlights at Radio City Music Hall. He looks great. And for some odd reason, I feel like a happy stage mom. We've worked so hard to get it to this point.

As he continues, I consciously implant the choreography into my memory bank. I'll I have to notate this exact sequence in the show journal—it's too good to alter a single step. No kidding. Camp like this doesn't come easily.

Vollstrecken beams as René approaches the end of his dance and the canned-applause track kicks on. René moves into a very deep squat—as if he's a prima ballerina kneeling on the apron of an opera house stage. Vollstrecken starts clapping and smiles in my direction—so I start clapping too. The audience recording cuts out and I look at René. "It's terrific," I nearly yell, "I think it's perfect."

"Thank you, thank you, thank you." René humbly recovers from the floor. "Now come over here, Mathieu. Come take a look at this." René motions me toward his desk, where he locates a new window on his computer. "Mathieu, take a look at this boy." He looks down at the screen. "Is he incredible, or what?"

René soon shows me a fade-in/fade-out slide show of racy photographs, featuring a hot naked brown-skinned man with a perfect body, big dick, and nice teeth. Shit. Is he going to ask me about my one-night stand with his spiritual advisor? These pictures aren't of him—but this guy is similar. "Handsome," I say matter-of-factly, "is he a friend of yours?"

"No, no—not yet," René grins, "someday soon, I hope." René abruptly pauses the slideshow and forcefully clicks to open another window on his screen. "Now watch this," René insists, while starting a homemade video of—what appears to be—the same boy playing a concert piano solo. The man in the video is shirtless in tight blue jeans and incredibly sexy, but it could be somebody else.

"It's Handel," René boasts. "And one must admit...it takes real smarts to achieve such prowess."

"Matty," Vollstrecken pipes up from the bed, "René is implying, that he has officially located the escort of his dreams."

"So it seems," I say sarcastically, as René swats me on the

shoulder like a bashful adolescent girl.

"That talented boy," Vollstrecken continues, crooked teeth exposed, "is a twenty-six year old Brazilian, currently living in Hamburg."

I look at Vollstrecken, ready to tell him to go screw himself. "Oh, okay."

"Matty...that boy is a good-looking concert pianist with the ability to auto-fellate."

Come on. That's a joke. How could there be a hot, self-sucking concert pianist?

"Can you imagine that, Matty," he says—as if setting up a punch line, "having the ability to *handle* oneself—while performing *Handel*?"

René bursts into laughter and drops back into the deep bow, while Vollstrecken sits up on the side of the bed and looks at me. "You and I, Matty, are going to fix René up with that boy... next month. Shall we?" He turns to René. "As a little gift for you, René?"

"No, no, no," René sings, "I shall treat myself to such pleasures when I am ready."

"Matty and I would like to see the video recording of *that*," Vollstrecken stands up and walks toward me, "wouldn't we, Matty?" Once Vollstrecken reaches me, he locks his arm around my neck and leads me toward the door. "Come, Matty. I must shower now and will need your help in the loo."

Shit. I don't know how to dodge this one. Fuck.

As Vollstrecken guides me into the hallway, René catches up to us. "Goodbye, boys," René calls cheerfully and closes his bedroom door—probably thrilled to have a moment alone with his Internet boy-toy.

"Matty," he begins within a few steps, "I have recently spent time in hospital and will need assistance bathing." He opens his door, leads me inside, and drops his robe. "I must wash this unruly hair today."

I grimace and get walloped by a hefty nose full of his

stale-cheese odor. I force myself to follow him into the bathroom and soon start rinsing his reptilian back with warm water. I do my best to control the temperature and pressure of this hand-held nozzle. But secretly, I wish I could turn it on high and blast him off his feet. I wish I could make the water hot enough to scald him back into the hospital—*burn unit* this time.

Vollstrecken leans forward to keep his gauze-covered chest wound dry. "Matty...they removed nearly a third of my right lung this time around."

I don't say anything.

I don't feel anything either.

I just stand here with the water hose while he washes his hair. Now hoping he gets enough shampoo in his eyes, to sting him into a heart attack. Dickwad.

After rinsing his hair, Vollstrecken asks if I will scrub his back with a washcloth. So, I do—reluctantly.

And before I finish, he turns around to face me, tugs at his semi-hard dick, and exhales. "Now we wash the cock-and-balls, Matty." His robust tone is frightening, but I don't fall for it.

Without missing a beat, I put some shower gel on a fresh washcloth and hand it to him. "Here you go." This mooch needs to hire himself a valet.

He pouts, takes the washcloth, and vigorously washes his low hangers. "Ohh, yes, perfect, Matty." He presses his crotch toward the nozzle and directs the spray up into his foreskin. "It's perfect, Matty...keep it right there."

I stay on the magic spot for a split second, but refuse to offer this jerk a water-jet happy ending. Fully recognizing his desire to linger in the shower, I shut off the water, click the nozzle into its place, and hand him a big towel. "All finished," I say, as if he's been a good doggie.

"Oh, Matty," he moans, snuggling the towel, "it is nice to feel clean for a change."

"I'm sure it does," I say—hoping he knows I'm referring to his filthy personality.

"Thank you for helping me, Matty...but of course...I do wish you could help me with other matters as well."

I walk away. "Have a good day," I say, almost at the door.

"Bye, Matty. I will meet you on deck after siesta for our game of shuffleboard."

"Okay," I answer, not fully registering that I'm accepting to play.

When I open his door to leave, I suddenly hear the sound of wet meat slapping on moist flesh. Then, as I step into the hallway and turn around to pull the door closed, I see him holding his towel up above his head with both hands. He's standing there, rapidly shaking his hips from side to side—playing his testicles like castanets against his damp thighs.

"Just drying off, Matty," he shouts as I shut the door, "just drying off."

Finally outside his room, too anxious to go back to mine, I charge down the hall toward the library. Maybe I'll find something good to read, something to get my mind off of everything. Then, after selecting a couple of—hopefully trashy—novels, I hurry back toward my room.

Within a few steps, I notice a handsome well-dressed businessman, standing in the distance, having a conversation in Vollstrecken's doorway. He's an Italian-looking guy, probably early thirties, and he doesn't seem to be a crew member.

Shit. It's Madame's grandson Étienne.

And there's no way to reroute myself.

Fuck. Now it's too late to change direction anyway. Vollstrecken's door just closed, and the man in the hallway is already looking at me. Breathe. Keep walking. Don't speak unless spoken to. And remember that most of the staff considers Étienne in line with nobility—so don't screw this up!

Only a half-step away from my door, Étienne graciously reaches out to shake my hand. I pause and make eye contact, ready to go in for a firm one. And when we shake, I give Étienne a big smile—but he doesn't say anything to me. Then, as I try to let go, he continues to hold on — still not saying anything.

I decide to break the uncomfortable silence. "Hi, I'm Matt, nice to meet you," I say, upbeat, realizing I probably smell of Vollstrecken.

Étienne stays quiet, but keeps my hand — and now I feel stupid for speaking first. With his eyes fixed on me, the high-plucked arch of his eyebrows suddenly reminds me of the actor Alec Baldwin. In fact, the intense look Étienne is giving me right now is exactly the same look I got from Alec, the day I randomly bumped into him a few years ago at a deli in New York.

The amazing Mr. Baldwin was standing in line in front of me, ordering a triple espresso from the girl at the register. In addition to his turbo-charged coffee, Alec was interested in a serving of fruit. "Do you have any fruit?" he asked.

"Nope," the girl said — sounding like any worn out New Yorker at the crack of dawn on Sunday.

"Maybe some assorted chopped fruit," he patiently tried again.

"Nope," she repeated with a sigh.

"Okay, that's fine then. I'll just have the coffee."

The moment the girl walked away to make his coffee, I looked into the refrigerated case beside us and saw a large bowl of chopped fresh fruit next to a vat of cream cheese. The sign in front of the bowl was clearly marked: *mixed fruit salad*.

I gently tapped Mr. Baldwin on the shoulder.

He turned around as if to greet an adoring fan and looked me deep in the eyes, just like Étienne is doing right now. "Yes?" Alec said as he lifted up through the crown of his head like a mighty bird.

"Is that what you wanted," I asked, casually tapping on the glass toward the bowl of fruit — failing to admit that I was, and still is, a huge fan.

"Why, yes. Yes it is." Alec sounded resolute. "That's exactly what I wanted."

"You just left off the *salad* part," I joked. "When the girl comes back...ask her for an order of mixed fruit *salad* and see what happens."

The girl returned with Alec's coffee. "Anything else?" she asked.

"Yes, please," Alec hesitated, "may I also have a side of mixed fruit salad to go?"

"You got it," she answered and took off to pack his fruit.

Alec turned to me once more and did the look. "Thanks, man." He placed his hand around my upper arm. "Thanks a lot."

"Sure," I said—purposely contracting my bicep. "No prob."

When the girl came back to the register she interrupted our little moment. "Is that it?" she asked, moderately confused.

Alec removed his hand from my arm. "That'll be all, thanks."

After Alec paid for his order and walked out of the deli, I caressed my arm, stepped up to the counter, and ordered my own triple espresso—with a side of mixed fruit salad.

"Étienne! Étienne!" René shouts from behind me. "Ah, I see you have met Mathieu!"

"Yes, René." Étienne finally lets go of my hand as René arrives.

"Is it true that you are leaving us?" René says to Étienne, while I attempt to vaporize on the spot.

"I stopped down to say goodbye to you and Dagen." Étienne glances at Vollstrecken's door. "Olivia and I are headed to Valencia. We shall rejoin at Côte d'Azur."

Without acknowledgement, I slip into my room and ease the door closed—now unable to hear their conversation. Damn.

But before I even have time to drop my books or lodge the chair under the doorknob, my phone rings. I rush over to answer, as if the ringing might disturb Étienne.

It's Olivia—she confirms she's leaving again.

"No. You can't." I plead, as if I deserve a say-so.

"Étienne and I will make a brief stop in Spain. I will see you on dry land in a matter of days."

Is Olivia cheating on Danté with Étienne, or are these two really just traveling together on business? "Okay—well have a good time, see you soon."

"Ciao, ciao, Matthew. I must run, Étienne is waiting." She hangs up.

Seriously. Could I blame her for fucking around with Étienne?

I hang up, drop my books beside the phone, and head to the door to lodge the chair.

I mean, really, which would I choose—the dog walker or the heir apparent?

Shit. Fuck. Damn. Piss. Hell. It's four thirty! And I just woke up—late for shuffleboard. So without so much as a glance in the mirror, I hurry upstairs to the rear of the Upper Deck only to find Vollstrecken with René—both clad in sailor whites and wearing matching captain's hats—in the midst of game.

"Just in time, Matty!" Vollstrecken shouts with his sickening grin. "I am nearly ready to finish him off…then I will start with you."

I wave to them both and try to appear enthusiastic. "Take your time."

"Matty, get settled yonder…in the cabana." He pokes an elbow in the general direction. "Enjoy a beverage in the meantime."

As I move across the deck in the direction of his faint gesture, I notice two side-by-side shelters; each draped in blue-and-white broad-striped canvas. But the first tent looks more upscale and is occupied by two sexy cabana-boys, while the second tent appears to be vacant. The first tent has chaises lounges with thicker cushions and fatter pillows and is set up with crystal glasses and silver platters—versus Lucite next door. Even the flower arrangements in the first tent are more dramatic, with long-stemmed flowers jutting out in perfect asymmetry.

I instinctually head toward the single-stem bud vases in cabana number two. And when I step inside, I find Barbara sitting in the shady corner—looking much better than she did last night at dinner.

"Thank goodness you made it," she says, as if I might be the one who is too hung over to function. "Cava?" she asks, already pouring.

"Sure, thanks."

"Matthew, we must develop a strategy." She hands me the bubbly. We clink.

"Are you gonna play too?" We sip.

"Of course. We are a team."

"Sorry to say...I haven't played shuffleboard since I was at church camp."

"*Shovelboard*, Matthew, say *shovel*...you will sound more knowledgeable of the sport. Now, how long ago was this church camp?"

I look at her and shake my head. "I dunno. I was a kid."

"Well, here is the plan...you understand the concept of the game, yes? You must use the long-handled cue to push the disk into the numbered areas on the deck. From the front of the pyramid leading back, you gain various points in those numbered compartments. However, you want to avoid the furthest panel, where it reads *ten-off*...minus ten points if the biscuit lands there, *in the kitchen* as we say."

"Okay."

"With each turn, simply aim to smash them into the kitchen...or knock them off deck." She snickers. "The disk, Matthew, not our opponents."

"Got it!"

"Oops, he is calling us over now." Barbara leads us onto the course to meet the guys. "And remember," she whispers, "our mission is to humiliate...without taking obvious pleasure."

The moment we arrive, Vollstrecken hands one of the long

sticks to Barbara. "Why…if is not the graceful tyrant herself," he gives me a teasing look, "and her honorable associate."

Barbara accepts the stick. "Thank you, Herr Vollstrecken," she nods and passes it to me. "To you, fine gentlemen," she receives the next stick, "to the reigning champions of the high seas tournament."

René smiles. "'tis true!"

"Thank you for those kind words, Barbara," Vollstrecken says, "but our last victory was many moons ago."

"Nonetheless," Barbara lets out a ridiculously wide smile, "still a victory."

René lifts his stick toward the sky. "Let the games begin!" He shouts as Vollstrecken lines up to push the first disk.

Nearly an hour later, Barbara and I are resting in our cabana, seven points ahead, and on the verge of winning the entire match.

I face Barbara. "Thank God, Vollstrecken decided to take a break." I reach for the icy champagne bucket. "My knee was really starting to ache." I place the whole bucket on my leg to ice it down. "Wasn't sure how much longer I'd last."

"Matthew, we have to make a choice now," Barbara whispers and hands me two aspirin from her uniform pocket. "We could decide to forfeit the game…or go back out there and allow them to tie it up." She slugs her cava and reaches into my bucket for a refill.

I pop the pills and grab for my drink—now warm and flat. "What do you mean *forfeit* or *tie*? I wanna win!"

"Of course we want to win, but we must not."

"Since when? What happened to all that talk about destroying them?"

"Matthew, I was coaxing you into the spirit of the game… of course you understand that staff is forbidden to win against their employers."

"Yeah. I get that part, but I don't think I'm willing to accept it. And PS: I don't work for René or Dagen."

"Matthew," Barbara whispers fearfully, and refills my glass, "his name is Herr Vollstrecken."

"Yeah. Him too." I swig my drink like a trucker.

Barbara gently returns the bottle to the bucket. "Therein lies the rub," she smirks. "We *do* work for them."

My stomach drops. "What?"

She looks me dead on and softens her usual squint. "Last night during dinner, Herr Vollstrecken was granted control over all personnel."

My face goes blank. "For real?"

"Yes." She drinks.

"Holy shit." I've been traded. "I thought Étienne was supposed to take over…not Vollstrecken."

Barbara's eyes widen. "We have been officially transferred to Herr Vollstrecken's employ. René is second-in-command. He will step in if Herr Vollstrecken becomes incapacitated. Meanwhile, Étienne is managing her properties and physical assets."

"This is bullshit," I blurt, wondering if she's up to another one of her tricks, "I never agreed to this."

She leans in. "We have all agreed, Matthew. Our contracts are strictly worded…we shall obey the wishes of Madame…or her assignee(s)."

I sink into my seat; my knee on the verge of frostbite. "This is crazy."

"Call it what you want," she crosses herself like a good Catholic girl, "but I speak the truth."

"Well, that's it then. I'm done." I return the ice bucket to the stand. "I'm not gonna work for him. I'd sooner push that freak overboard and work for René." I pause to limber my knee. "There's not enough money in the world to keep me here."

"Oh, Matty!" Vollstrecken's bellow penetrates the canvas separating the two tents. "Shall we continue?"

I look at Barbara. *Did he hear me?*

Barbara shakes her head *no*. "Ready when you are," she

yells to Vollstrecken with a diplomatic tone and stands up. "Let's go," she whispers to me, "game face."

Barbara walks out of the tent and I follow reluctantly. Then, halfway across the deck, she gives me a look, begging me to give in. I nod at her to imply that I'm willing to lose the match. And we did. We lost big time.

When it came to match point, Barbara and I were trailing by one. It was my turn to shoot and I knew I was supposed to slide my biscuit off to the side and surrender the game—but I wanted it to look convincing.

As soon as I stepped up to take my turn, I set up my disk and Vollstrecken turned away. He looked toward the water, gloating with René about their superior shuffleboard skills. Then, as I drew back my arm to push the disk, I imagined how satisfying it would be to ram that puck right up his bony ass. I figured I'd slam Vollstrecken in the ankle; play it off as an accident. I was preparing to launch into my best soap-opera apology, and had convinced myself that everyone, including Barbara, would feel sympathetic watching my scene.

But what actually happened after I drew back, I hit the disk much harder than anticipated. In fact, I hit it so hard that everything went into slow motion. I watched the disk glide across the deck toward Vollstrecken, traveling straight for his gnarly feet. Then, just my luck, the disk clipped another disk, chipped up off the deck, flipped on its side, and started to roll like a bowling ball.

Vollstrecken and René both turned around when they heard the smashing sound. They laughed uproariously as the disk sped toward the open railing. My disk was headed overboard—no way for me to stop it. Vollstrecken turned to face the water, quickly positioned his stick like a rifle, and gazed toward the horizon. "PULL!" He cried out.

Right on command, my disk flew off the deck and took a swan dive into the water.

I was mortified.

Vollstrecken let out a gunshot sound and mimed a huge kickback. He turned to René and burst into a belly laugh. "It seems as though Matty prefers shooting skeet!"

René threw his arms around Vollstrecken and screamed with joy. "Our undefeated title still unsurpassed!"

After the guys came over to console our loss and headed away to their tent, Barbara and I stayed on deck to re-stack the disks and hang the sticks. "So where's all that crew hiding now?" I said to Barbara as we tidied up.

"Shh…relax."

Hearing Barbara tell me to *relax* was something I never imagined could happen. But it did. And she was right.

I don't have to hang around here that much longer, so I'd better chill. If I lose my job while sailing international waters, it's going to be one *helluva* swim home to freedom.

19

We're now docked somewhere in the south of France. I can't see any celebrities from my balcony, so I assume we're not in Cannes. But wherever we are, it's beautiful. Last night, Barbara told me to stay in my suite today, until she phones to confirm that Madame, René, and Vollstrecken have disembarked. However, since a porter just stopped by to take my suitcase away, I know it's almost time to leave.

"Land ahoy!" René yells in the hallway.

I rush over to my door and spy through the peephole, just in time to see him banging on Vollstrecken's door. Next, I see Vollstrecken step into the hallway and the two men move out of sight. The moment they are gone, I pull the chair away from the doorknob and my phone rings. Barbara tells me to stall for three minutes before heading toward the exit of the ship. "Follow the signs to reception."

"Got it."

"And thanks for being so professional, Matthew."

"Oh, no problem." I lie, thinking about how I've avoided everyone by hiding in my room for the past two days. "It's not like I actually have a choice in the matter."

"I understand," Barbara laughs as if she's undergone a lobotomy, "it has been a difficult adjustment for everyone. But we have managed."

I'm not sure what to say, so I just hang a second. How can

she think this transition of power is acceptable?

"See you downstairs shortly, Matthew."

"Okay."

When I arrive on the Reception Deck, I begin thanking the long line of crew. While shaking hand after hand, it dawns on me that Barbara must adapt to change, or she'd go even more insane than she already is. This is her life, her world. And acceptance of any given circumstance is the only way to understand and maintain control of that world.

I soon notice Madame and Tatyana up at the front of the line, already preparing to walk down the off-ramp. Cool. It looks like Tatyana spent some time in the ship's spa. She's had a total makeover. Her fake glasses are gone and her hair has been dyed auburn — reshaped into a fun pixie-style cut. Maybe Madame helped her decide on which shade of red? I want to rush forward and explain to Madame that I refuse to work for Vollstrecken, but somehow that seems a little dramatic and inappropriate right now, so I continue shaking hands. Next, I see Barbara stepping up to the exit. So I pick up the pace, skip the rest of the hand shaking routine, and smile to the remaining crew as I rush toward the door. Was I supposed to have left a staff tip in the envelope in my room?

By the time I arrive at the top of the ramp, Madame has already made it to the bottom. And now I see Niko standing in the parking lot, beside a big black SUV with all four doors open. Niko? Then, as I start down the ramp, I watch Madame, René, Vollstrecken, Tatyana, and the dogs, pile into his vehicle and begin to leave. And as their car pulls away, I notice Alistair chatting with Kan, and motioning me over to another car — Barbara is getting in the back seat. What's Kan doing here?

At the end of the ramp, Kan greets me with a big hug. "Hello, buddy," he shakes me by the shoulders and leads me to his car, "is good to see you again."

"Hey, what's going on? So we're lucky enough to get you and Niko in France too?"

"You got it boss," he answers, as Alistair jumps in up

front and I get in back with Barbara.

"Welcome to Toulon," Kan continues, as we pull out of the parking lot, "Niko and I are here to serve…because we still have the strength to serve."

"I don't get it."

"Matthew," Barbara starts, "the staff at Côte d'Azur is so old, they make Mr. and Mrs. Blessington look like springtime chickens."

Kan laughs again and glances back over his shoulder. "Scab labor has been called in." He looks forward again. "And do not be alarmed by our detour…Madame has decided to take a walk today, before going up to the villa."

Barbara leans forward in her seat. "Kan, did she request our presence on this walk?"

"Yes. She mentioned having everyone come along…to clear the lungs after being confined on the yacht."

"Rest assured," Barbara shifts back in her seat, "this production of taking a walk shall not last too long…thanks to Madame's sea legs."

Within a minute or so, Kan has made a few quick turns, and we eventually veer onto a scenic two-lane highway. "Ho, ho…I did it!" A wide grin magnifies his jawline. "Look, I caught up to them…Niko is now directly in front of us."

Alistair looks toward Kan. "Perhaps Madame plans to take a stroll near the ossuary?"

"I believe it is possible," Kan answers.

Alistair then turns to look at me. "The family plot is up in this direction."

"We shall have to wait and see," Kan says. "But, Alistair…I have a feeling you could be right."

A little while later, Niko turns off the highway, so Kan follows. Niko leads us through a security gate, up a narrow driveway, through a fancy ironwork arch, and into a wooded area. The driveway winds through the woods and soon opens to a hilly lawn that looks like a cemetery. But rather than having lots of gravestones lying around, there are just several small, ancient-looking stone houses, dotting the subtly landscaped property.

"Alistair, you were right," Kan grins, "the ossuary."

"Coming up on our right…" Alistair plays tour guide, "we have the mausoleum of Monsieur and those of his ancestors."

But by the time Alistair finishes his sentence, Niko comes to a stop, and so do we. Kan barely has time to shut off the engine, before the entire entourage—including the dogs—spills onto the driveway and stands *at the ready*, awaiting Madame.

Niko steps around the front of the SUV to open Madame's door, while Tatyana pops open a white parasol. Before Madame stands up, Tatyana is there to shade her from the late afternoon sun. Tatyana holds the umbrella with a nearly straight arm, and doesn't dare acknowledge Niko's presence—even though he is obviously taking in her new hairstyle. I think he likes it.

The rest of us remain on standby, as Madame and Tatyana walk slowly toward a cobblestone path that leads from the driveway, across the lawn, to the nearest tomb. René and Vollstrecken fall in line behind the ladies, and stroll arm-in-arm—wearing khaki pants with complimentary cardigan sweaters loosely tied atop pink Oxford-cloth button-down shirts. The men laugh uncontrollably as they watch the house dogs take flight across the green grass. The dogs run with such exuberance, it's as if this might be the first time they've ever been allowed to take a shit without requesting permission.

Alistair, Kan, and I are clumped together by the front of our car, when Kan motions for me to join Madame on her walk. "You are her trainer," he explains, "you must go with her…in case she would like to make her walk into a jog."

Alistair chuckles at Kan's joke, as I glance down the driveway; Barbara has wandered off toward the woods, busy picking flowers. I look back at the guys. "Okay. I'm off," I whisper to them both. "Wish me luck."

I head toward the cobblestone path and dread being near Vollstrecken again. But at the same time, I'm excited to be joining Madame again. Our workouts in London were awesome, but everyone except Tatyana missed out on seeing that. So this is my chance to strut my stuff in front of the whole group. I'm ready. Just stay calm, and remember to follow Madame's lead.

Once I reach the group, I take a deep breath and stay at the rear as we proceed up the gently sloping pathway. René and Vollstrecken take turns stepping forward to bother Madame with snippets of nonsense gathered from today's newspapers. The two men tirelessly attempt to impress her, but their trivial facts seem to do nothing for Madame—except reconfirm her choice to spend her time in the privacy of her bedroom.

After a couple minutes, I check behind to see what the guys are up to. Kan and Alistair are leaning against the hood of our car, acting like cool kids, while Niko is propped against the SUV, enjoying a cigar. Niko notices that I've looked back and he jokingly grabs his balls. Kan and Alistair notice Niko razzing me. They laugh at him and I laugh too. But I soon refocus on Madame.

Steps later, I'm obsessed with Madame's weak ankles and consumed by the unevenness of this cobblestone surface. Then, as the house dogs rush into view and start playing dangerously close to Madame's feet—obviously foreshadowing a broken hip—I suddenly feel responsible for Madame's entire well-being. It's like I'm some secret service agent, who's been assigned to protecting her pelvic girdle. And as I continue observing Madame's slow, feeble steps, I envision how I might dive, kneel or squat to ensure her safety. Maybe that's why I'm here—to serve as her human crash pad?

Nearing the gate of the tomb, Madame pauses, closes her eyes, and bows her head down. The group becomes motionless and the dogs gather at Madame's feet. But within a few seconds, Madame lifts her head up and turns toward Tatyana. "That is quite all right." She gestures for the parasol to be put away. "Our next stop is yonder." Madame points toward another stone building and steps off the cobblestone walkway.

The dogs scamper away, while René glides forward to

Madame. He motions toward the gate. "This is Monsieur's spot," René says tenderly. "Would you care to step inside?"

"No, no." Madame turns to walk away, obviously determined. "We move onward."

Tatyana tucks the folded umbrella under one arm, and takes Madame with the other.

I immediately realize Madame is having a tough time walking on the grass, so I decide to move forward to help Tatyana. When I make my move from the rear, René swoops in and beats me to the punch. Crap. Then, as René takes Madame's free arm, Vollstrecken gives me a nasty look, implying that I'm out of line, but I continue ahead of him anyway. I don't care what he thinks. Go ahead—fire me. Fuck-face.

I discreetly step up to Tatyana and slip the umbrella away from her without saying a word. The parasol passes between us as seamlessly as a baton in a relay race. Tatyana smiles but doesn't look at me. Next, I step off to the side, pause to allow Vollstrecken to pass, and then pivot into my spot behind him. What a prick.

When we arrive in front of the next mausoleum, Madame stops outside the gate and the dogs return to her feet. She lets go of Tatyana and reaches forward as if to open the latch, but René opens it for her. René then escorts Madame through the gate and up a few rocky steps, before Vollstrecken moves inside the enclosure to join them.

"Et voilà," Madame hesitates, "mon jeune fils—Hubert."

The two men stand on either side of Madame, physically supporting her, as she begins to read aloud from the French inscription etched into the side of the building. Madame articulates the solemn passage with dignity and resolve, but the pain and despair of losing her only child resonates in her voice.

I understand enough of her words to piece together that her son was considered to be an inspiration to others—and he would have made a greater impact on the world, had he not died at such a young age.

Once Madame finishes, she bows her head down for a

moment of silence. She then looks up toward the dates on the mausoleum — *1945-1985* — and soon turns away, ready to leave.

Before Madame takes her first step, Barbara unexpectedly walks up beside me, carrying a ragged bunch of wildflowers. She steps over to the open gate and places the flowers on top of the fence post.

Madame starts down the stairs — aided by René and Vollstrecken — and once outside the fence, she pauses near the flowers and smiles at Barbara. "Merci," Madame says under her breath and walks in the direction of the driveway.

As Madame passes me, I feel like I'm invading her private moment, so I avoid any opportunity for eye contact and allow her to pass. But I can't really tell if she knows I'm here or not.

Barbara casually follows Madame and glances over at me, probably wondering why I'm carrying a white umbrella.

Whatever. I roll my eyes after she passes.

Tatyana then cuts into place behind Madame, René, and Vollstrecken — but ahead of Barbara. And I submit to my place at the rear. Pecking order complete.

As the entourage continues across the lawn — house dogs leading the way — I look over at Niko and Kan who are still beside the cars and I realize that Madame's staff completes her. We are, in a sense, her family. And by some stretch, I've learned to fit in. Somehow I've managed to cope with this mixed-up bunch, so I guess that's makes me as nutty as the rest of them.

20

Ever since we arrived at Côte d'Azur, I can't get over the fact that Kan fibbed. When Kan was driving us away from the yacht, and he said that Madame wanted to take a walk before going up to the villa, he forgot to mention one important detail. It's not a villa. It's villas, plural. This terraced property along the coastline, with five homes looking out to the sea, is beyond comprehension. Barbara describes the estate as typical Mediterranean. But if this is *typical*, sign me up.

Madame, Étienne, Olivia, Tatyana, and Barbara are staying in the Main House, which is built out on a ridge, up high enough to afford unobstructed views of the water from nearly every window. René, Vollstrecken, and I are housed next door, slightly lower, and we suffer through with merely a standard view. Alistair, Niko, Kan, and the so-called *geriatric* staff, are in the smallest dwelling, two tiers down the driveway—even their view is incredibly picturesque.

Under normal circumstances, the two remaining guest-houses would be occupied in rotation. But recently, Madame's private physician, Dr. Duchamp, has moved into one of them full time. It happened on the morning of our third day here, when Étienne and Olivia returned from Spain and he decided his grandmother looked gaunt. Olivia immediately contacted Dr. Duchamp and arranged for him to remain on-site. Then, a day or two later, Tatyana confided to me that Madame was going downhill fast. She said, that as of a few weeks ago in Morocco, Madame had stopped eating everything except dessert. And by the time we were on the boat, Madame was down to *tea and consommé*. Apparently there's no specific diagnosis for her condition; however, everyone agrees, Madame has not been herself lately.

Over the past ten days now, Madame has refused to see anyone and the only person she wants to be around is Étienne. And based on recent conversations with Olivia, it's true — Vollstrecken has taken control and my job is in jeopardy — he wants to save money wherever he can. Frankly, that's just fine with me. I think I've gotten more out of this gig than I ever expected to get, and there's no hell way I'm staying over here to work for him — screw that.

"Mathieu, come quick!" René shouts from outside my bedroom door.

I peek out into the hallway — just in time to see the long train of a white silk robe, dragging along the hardwood floor and disappearing down the hallway. So of course, I follow.

"Are you there, Mathieu?" he asks, now making a turn into the living room. "Come quick — it is time, it is time."

The moment I exit the hallway, I get the complete picture of René in his shiny gown. So glamorous. And for some reason, the living room is decorated with several long strands of multicolored paper lanterns — hanging lengthwise across the space. I then see Vollstrecken reclining on the sofa — drinking a bottle of beer — and wearing the same silk robe as René, but his is in red.

"C'est magnifique," he says as René twirls in place with arms held high, showing off the action of his garment. "Bravo, darling…but what do we have for Matty to put on?"

René hurries over to a nearby closet and pulls out a long black silk robe and holds it out in my direction. "This one, this one," René stammers, as if trying to figure out whether he's thinking to himself or actually speaking out loud. "Mathieu shall don this fine piece."

"Why," I pause and soften my tone, "why, thank you."

"Oh, Matty…stupendous," Vollstrecken says, while I put the robe on, over my trainer outfit. "Honestly, Matty…take a look at that fabric and just imagine how many silkworms must have been forced into retirement because of it." Vollstrecken pauses and snaps his fingers abruptly. "Two more, Niko!" He hollers toward the kitchen.

Niko enters, wearing a black silk robe, just like mine, and he's holding a tray with two bottles of beer—Tsingtao.
René takes one. "Thank you, Niko," he gathers the train of his gown, then sweeps through the living room to join Vollstrecken on the sofa.

I can't figure out why Niko is serving, but nonetheless, I accept the remaining bottle from the tray and stand in place, wondering where and *if* I should sit down.

By the time Niko disappears into the kitchen, René and Vollstrecken invite me to join them in the sitting area. René then explains that today marks the thirtieth anniversary of Dagen's first journey to Beijing—hence the Chinese theme.

"Back in those days, Mathieu, making such a voyage was no easy feat," René clinks bottles with Vollstrecken. "Even on the coattails of President Nixon."

They pause to drink, so I do too.

"Now, gentlemen," René begins again, exuding black-tie formal, "before our meal, I have prepared a video program showcasing the artistry of Chinese jump rope. Then, after lunch, we will retire to a game of Chinese checkers and make time for building chopstick structures if that sounds intriguing."

"Listen, Matty," Vollstrecken looks at me, "when René brings out the mahjong tiles…that will be our signal to vamoose."

I crack a slight smile at his comment. And although I still detest this man, I'm no longer afraid of him. Maybe I feel safe because René is here—or because Vollstrecken knows the jig is up? He won't win with me.

"What on earth!" René shouts, jumps up from the sofa, and rushes over to a narrow table near the front door. "I nearly forgot...these are for us as well." He carefully opens a wooden cigar box before he walks back over to present Vollstrecken with a pair of green gemstone earrings. He then hands me a pair—clip on. René snaps his in place and explains how jade stones have the power to prevent fatigue and can delay decomposition of the body. "These will certainly help create a peaceful transition into the next realm," he says calmly. "So today...we wear these jewels in honor of Francesca and her imminent journey."

My stomach sinks. *Imminent journey*?

As I put on my earrings, I wonder if we should phone Madame and offer her a pair. I bet Dr. Duchamp wouldn't mind—especially if René explained about the healing powers.

"Matty, if Francesca ever found out that these rocks had been removed from the vault," Vollstrecken pauses to look at René, "why, she would undoubtedly rise up from her bed and kill us both!"

Asshole. I knew he was nothing but a mooch.

Vollstrecken takes a moment to clip his earrings onto the collar of his robe, and René clarifies that the jewels are merely on loan to complement our costumes. They are not a party favor. But I wonder if—technically speaking—we're stealing. Shit. None of this seems right.

A few minutes later, René and Vollstrecken are nestled up on the sofa in front of the muted television, watching the jump rope video and reciting a non-chronological history of China. While I sit off to one side and pretend to be engaged in their stories, the two men randomly account for everything they can think of—everything from The Ming Dynasty, to the 1989 student protests at Tiananmen Square. Then, in the midst of their hard-to-follow conversation, Niko walks in with another round of beers.

Suddenly anxious, I wonder why the hell we're just sitting here drinking if Madame is actually on her deathbed. Shouldn't we attempt to do something to help her? I can't believe how callous these two men are acting. Her dearest friends, are hanging around talking about trivial shit instead of being with her. It doesn't make sense. Maybe they know Madame's going through another brief episode and she'll bounce back like she always does. Or maybe they know it's too late for any extreme measures? Fuck.

René and Vollstrecken each grab a fresh drink and begin to debate how the construction of the Great Wall may—or may not—have permanently altered the Earth's rotation on its axis, while I reach for my bottle and consider chugging it. This is worse than the usual crazy.

It's not too long before Niko walks in again, this time carrying a dinner gong. Niko strikes the gong and invites us to lunch.

"It is certainly nice to have Niko serving at table today," René motions for us to exit the living room. "Alistair has become insufferable...both he and Kan. I will not have anything to do with it—I am simply not interested in being sad at the moment."

"Of course, it *is* sad," Vollstrecken pipes up as we pass through the dining room and proceed outside onto the terrace. "But we have no choice in the matter...and I for one am not willing to starve myself like that Gandhi fellow."

"Precisely," René agrees, as we gather at a large round table, set for three. René then holds up his beer bottle, looks out at the clear blue sea and clears his throat. "Today, we straddle the fissure between yin and yang," he projects, "we exist upon the hairline division between heaven and the netherworld. And we accept that our path, here with Francesca...here, in this dimension... will soon come to an end. We lift our glasses in celebration of a life well lived, and to acknowledge that we shall, each one of us, be reunited with Francesca, sometime in the future. Reunited in a realm beyond this one."

"Santé!" Vollstrecken affirms robustly.

As we sip our beers in honor of Madame, my upper lip begins to tremble with sadness. I tighten my jaw and hold my breath, hoping to tamp down my impulse to cry. Shit. It's hard to believe I've only known her a few months, and I'm the one who is overwhelmed right now—while these guys who have been with her a lifetime seem fine. I'm also not sure how I feel about being reincarnated as a personal trainer. Is that what René meant? Damn. Don't tell me I might have to relive all this again.

We finish the toast and I walk around the table to sit facing away from the water. As I catch my breath, I flash back to my welcome lunch with Madame in Morocco. I choke up again. I remember sitting with her in the garden gazebo, so optimistic about our year ahead. And now I wish we'd had more time together—not for the sake of my show, but just to really get to know her better. I wish I knew how she actually felt about living—what I used to consider—a life of *privilege*. I'd love to ask her if the untold riches were actually worth the trade-off?

By the time I sit, Niko approaches from the kitchen, carrying a huge platter. "Lunch is served," he announces and places the platter in the center of the table.

"Peking duck!" René calls out, claps his hands like a giddy schoolgirl, and motions for Niko to carve. "We have our little pancakes here, along with some scallions, cucumber, and carrot sticks…and the essential sweet bean sauce on the side."

Niko has barely made a dent in the duck by the time René finishes his description, but that doesn't concern Vollstrecken. He reaches for the nearest edible leg and drops it on his plate.

"Oh, how divine." The bastard licks his fingers and turns to me. "Matty…Confucius say…Peking duck is more delectable than chicken à l'orange. Would you agree?"

"Yes." I answer plainly—clueless about the difference.

As I continue watching Niko carve, I realize I'm pissed! This situation is one of the most uncomfortable moments I've experienced since I came over here—second, only, to having Vollstrecken on the massage table. And I can't believe they don't care. Is this *denial* or what?

René abruptly sets his empty dinner plate off to the side. "Looky, looky," he begins, "before we soil the table, please take a moment to locate your animal on the chart—based upon the year of your birth."

Vollstrecken and I follow René's lead. We look underneath our plates and find paper placemats, illustrated with the twelve signs of the Chinese Zodiac.

"See here, Mathieu…you are the Rooster," he laughs. "Roosters make fine dancers and actors."

"That's me all right," I say, trying to perk up.

"Just look for the year," René whispers to Vollstrecken, who appears to be studying for an exam. "There is no need to read the entire menu."

Vollstrecken looks up at René. "I was busy reading yours, dear — the Rat."

"I know," René says. "Rats are spontaneous, zestful and spirited individuals," he recites from memory. "Well liked by others."

"Mostly true," Vollstrecken cough/laughs and looks down at his placemat. "Ah. Here we go…1929 — my year…year of the Snake."

Holy shit. I almost spit in my beer. That's perfect.

"The Snake," René pauses while adjusting an earring. "The Snake is an excellent seducer, and a lover of material possessions.

What a riot. I figure the person who authored this placemat deserves a medal for psychic achievement. That's damn good for someone who has never met Vollstrecken.

"True," Vollstrecken reaches for a thin pancake and smears it with sauce, "all true."

Fifteen minutes later, the three of us have devoured the entire duck — leaving only the carcass for the help to pick at in the kitchen later — and René is anxiously anticipating dessert. "Whenever you are ready, Niko."

Upon clearing our dinner plates, Niko presents each of us with a small dish of lychee fruit ice cream, garnished with a fortune cookie. René stands up at his seat. "Fortunes first," he demands and cracks his cookie in half, just as the telephone on the terrace lets out a startling ring.

René drops his cookie halves and nearly trips over his

gown as he rushes away from the table to answer it. And within seconds of picking up the receiver, his face goes gray. He listens for another moment and slowly hangs up.

"René, darling," Vollstrecken says, "what is it?"

"It is time…" René moves toward the dining room door as if he's in a trance, "Dr. Duchamp has contacted the coroner."

Vollstrecken stands up, removes the earrings from his robe, tosses them into one hand, drapes the gown over the back of his chair, and follows René inside.

I take off my earrings but suddenly feel stuck to my seat. Confused.

Could Madame really be gone—just like that?

Niko walks over with a pot of tea. "Do you want some tea or another beer?" He speaks as if he's still on the time clock. "I can bring you anything you care for."

"That's okay, I'm good." I slowly stand and take off my robe. "Are you gonna need help cleaning up?"

"No, I plan to take my time over here, to avoid the confusion next door…and when they need me to drive…I will drive."

"You sure?"

"No worry."

"Okay, well, thanks, Niko." I head inside. "See you later."

After returning my earrings to the cigar box near the front door, I walk toward my bedroom. There is not a sound to be heard and I've gone numb. The house is freezing cold and the smooth hardwood floor feels like sliding across an air hockey table—icy, with thousands of tiny vents hissing at my feet. I shiver. I can't believe she is actually gone.

I calmly enter my room and, without thinking, begin packing my stuff. I'm haunted by René's voice echoing in my mind—*it is time*. Then it dawns on me, my job has officially ended. Should I call Olivia for confirmation or should I just keep packing? I don't know. If my boss is dead, do I need permission to leave? Is there some clause in my contract that states I have to stay and be exploited by Vollstrecken? Fuck him.

About ten minutes later, René calls to ask if I'll come to his room. "Mathieu, I simply cannot be alone right now," he says, with genuine despair in his voice.

And as I agree to stop by, I wonder if I should tell him I'm already packed for New York. But I don't. "Be right there, René."

When I enter his bedroom, I find him idle at his desk. René eventually prepares an Evian-bicarbonate cocktail and checks his blood pressure. His pulse is racing as he downs his drink and he tells me he is full of mixed emotions. He then recites the Kubler-Ross model of the five stages of grief—totally dazed. "Where does one begin?" he asks rhetorically. "What should one feel like…and what might one wear?"

I listen in hopes of giving him space to process. But my mind is also racing. I never truly loved this job—but I know I will miss Madame. I doubt I'll ever come across another person quite like her.

"Mathieu, we must go to Francesca." René stands up, a blank stare in his eyes. "We must go to her now." And with that, he drifts out the bedroom door, still wearing his white silk gown.

René leads us away from his room, outside to the service-only walkway, and proceeds toward the Main House. As we walk along the cliffy edge of the narrow pathway, I glance through the trees and see Dr. Duchamp speaking with Barbara and Alistair in the driveway. The house dogs are also outside, frolicking madly, and no one seems to notice that we're headed up to the house.

I follow René into a passageway that soon delivers us inside to the grand staircase. As we hesitate at the foot of the stairs, it feels like a vacuum is sucking the life right out of the house. Nearly every door stands slightly ajar and there's not a single staff member to be seen. A nervous tingle shoots up my spine. I don't want to go up these stairs. But soon enough, René steadies himself on the banister and we cautiously begin to climb.

Less than halfway up, we both pause as Vollstrecken exits Madame's room. He hurries down in our direction. "She is there," he says as he passes, "I must meet with Étienne."

Vollstrecken walks past, without so much as a glance, and a huge sense of relief washes over me. I'll never have to see that creep again.

"Just breathe," René whispers to himself as we finally arrive at the top of the stairs. Then, the moment he swings the bedroom door open, he lets out a fizzy-water burp and looks inside the room. Madame's white four-poster bed, almost identical to her bed in Morocco, is framed before a huge window overlooking the sea. René's back stiffens when he sees the outline of Madame's body, lying beneath a crisp white sheet. He walks tentatively to her bedside and lifts up the sheet—just high enough to look at her face. "Mathieu, she has on the jade earrings."

I'm scared to go look.

And before I can even step forward out of the doorway, Tatyana walks in from the back of the bedroom. She's wearing an oversized, steel gray, beaded evening gown with big shoulder pads hanging down toward her elbows. "Ah! Pardon, monsieur," she shrieks. "I did not hear you come in." She turns to walk away.

"Young lady!" René calls out. "What in the world are you wearing?"

Tatyana stops and turns around to face him. "Yves Saint Laurent."

"Let us not be insulting, my dear," he pauses to fold the sheet down around Madame's collarbones. "The question is...*why* are you wearing a dress that obviously does not belong to you?"

I glance at Madame's face. My stomach jumps—she's colorless.

I look over at Tatyana. Her new red hair looks amazing against this dress.

"Forgive me, monsieur." Tatyana stands up tall, admiring herself in front of a full-length mirror. "But it is mine."

"My dear child," he says, suddenly using his Niko voice. "Have you entirely lost your senses?"

"No, monsieur...Madame, she offer dress to me—as gift of service." Tatyana reaches inside her dress and pulls out her nurses' log. "See, monsieur," she persists and points at her open book, "Madame signed agreement before she passed."

"But the point is...even if she did, my dear...that dress is horrendous on you."

Tatyana drops her head. "Forgive me, monsieur, but I love it." She looks at Madame with respect. "And I plan to wear dress one day...for special occasion."

René looks at Madame, takes a deep breath, and sits down on the bed. "The night she wore that dress, she was ravishing, beautiful beyond reproach." His voice cracks. "1985...the State Dinner in America, hosted by President Reagan and First Lady Nancy. It was Francesca's first public function after Hubert's death." Tears stream down his face. He chuckles at Tatyana and turns toward me. "Though I do believe Francesca was glad she attended, because she met that American actor," he looks out the window. "Uh...what is his name, the dancer?"

"Patrick Swayze?" Tatyana perks up.

"No!" René wipes his eyes and looks at me again. "The *trained* dancer."

"I'm not sure," I mumble to René as Tatyana closes her notebook.

"Travolta...yes, *John* Travolta." René smooths the sheets over Madame's chest, and tucks her into bed. "Oh, how she loved that man."

Tatyana and I exchange a glance, but neither of us moves a muscle. There's not a tailor in the world that could make that dress fit Tatyana properly.

"Now, go on girl, go!" René shoos Tatyana out of the room. "Go change out that ridiculous costume." He watches her leave. "Your job here is finished!"

As I watch René sit motionless beside Madame, I wonder what's going through his mind. In a heartbeat, he has become obsolete—and I know he knows it. What will become of him without her? Despite the fact that René initially sought out Madame as a sponsor, I know he truly cared for her—and she him. I suppose he'll receive a hefty settlement and no doubt live out the rest of his life in luxury. But things will never be quite the same.

Faster than any quick-change artist, Tatyana reenters the bedroom—now wearing her uniform and carrying the dress with her. "Monsieur," Tatyana enunciates, "I leave now—and take dress with me."

Apparently baffled by her stubborn attitude, René looks at me, then looks at Tatyana—but he can't seem to find the words to address her.

"I come inside house to serve Madame," Tatyana continues, "and I accept dress as token of service."

René stands ready to duel, but he remains stuck in place as Tatyana proceeds out of the room.

Ignoring the possibly of hearing René's reply, Tatyana nods in my direction and fades out of sight. As she heads down the staircase—the dress draped over her better arm—René speeds off to catch her. The moment he passes me, a cool breeze from the rush of his silk robe sends me into a pissy-shake and blocks any impulse to say goodbye.

I'm relieved they're both gone, but feel out of place—alone with Madame's body—so I move toward the staircase, hoping to make it back to my room unnoticed.

But before I hit the doorway, I suddenly hear Olivia whispering my name. "Matthew," she repeats.

"Olivia?" I turn around. "Shit. You scared me to death." I watch her approach from the back of the room.

She glances at Madame and continues toward me.

I walk to meet her; her scarf of the day is black. "How are you holding up?" I whisper as if Madame might overhear.

"All right, I suppose." Olivia answers and we share a hug. "But I feel strange," she says, heartbroken but trying to keep it together. "Of course we all knew this moment was coming...but it is still most difficult."

As we separate from our hug, I look at Olivia and realize I'm never quite sure what sounds good at a funeral. I look over at

Madame and back to Olivia. "I was just getting to know her."

"I am crushed." She pauses, now on the brink of losing it. "I believe I am most overwhelmed, from notifying all the newspapers." She slowly leads us away from the bedroom into Madame's dressing area—an area almost exactly like the one in Austria, where all the clutch purses and cashmere gloves are stored away. "It felt as though I was reliving Madame's death with each and every phone call."

"I'm so sorry….that must've been awful."

"Utterly tiresome. Madame's obituary was already on file with most publications and Internet sites." She slides the closet open. "Yet I had to give final approval for it to go to print. Here take one." She hands me a long garment bag, as if she is still on a schedule.

"So, it's already been posted online?" I watch Olivia for my next cue.

"Yes…it happened in cyberspace, a few hours before she was actually gone…just start bagging." Olivia pauses to encase a magnificent turquoise evening gown. "Madame agreed that her passing should be announced on the Internet…in spite of the fact that she despised computer technology."

"Damn. I'd hate to find out online…you know, that I was dead, before I died." I shimmy my first bag over a stunning violet dress.

"Madame did not learn of the preemptive announcement…so I suppose it was acceptable." Olivia finishes her next dress and hesitates as if seeking my approval.

"You know we don't have to deal with these dresses right now." I say cautiously. "Maybe you should go rest up?"
Olivia doesn't answer right away. She just stands frozen in front of the closet, staring at Madame's incredible collection. I don't think she knows what else to do. Frankly, I don't either.

She eventually breaks the silence. "Perhaps I shall bag… and you could follow behind to deal with these stubborn zippers?"

"Okay," I utter, accepting she needs to do *something*.

Minutes pass, and she's not slowing down.

"So, what's next for you?" I ask without pushing.

"Probably the jewelry," she says matter-of-factly.

"Come on—you know what I meant." I raise an eyebrow. "In life."

"I cannot say…there is so much to be done first…I will not have time to consider options for quite a long while."

"Will you have to oversee the packing at every location?"

She stops bagging, looks at me, and finally starts to cry. "That is what I have been doing…ever since you arrived. I have been closing up the homes…organizing everything for auction, donation or dumpster. It was Madame's command."

I take her by the hand and lead her over to a seat in the corner, thinking I should have figured this out sooner. "Are you saying Madame decided to dissolve everything?" I ask as we both sit down.

She grabs for a tissue and pauses to blow her nose. "Not exactly. But Étienne would like to make a fresh start. In honor of his grandmother, Madame's name will be etched in stone everywhere…hospital wings, libraries…museum cornerstones."

"Sounds better than having only one measly headstone," I blurt, then choke on a nervous laugh as my tears start to flow.

Olivia tosses me the tissue box and tries to compose herself. "You are right, it is *much* better." She nearly smiles.

I reach for a tissue. "So, are we just gonna sit here and take turns crying?" I pause to blow my nose.

She shifts forward in her seat and smacks me on the knee, encouraging me to buck up. "Étienne will be every bit as generous as his grandmother was. The primary difference…he will do it publicly…whereas Madame always went about things anonymously." She stands up as if she is suddenly okay. "Do you want to look online and see? The entire charity plan is outlined in the press release." She drops her head and lets out a sigh. "I mean, in the obituary."

I stand and give her another hug. "I'll look it up at home."

"I don't want you to go…but of course you should." She pulls back to look at me. "David will be surprised to see you home so soon. I hope the gap continues to narrow for you guys."

I start to well up again. "I'm sorry I never met Danté… maybe at your wedding?"

Olivia sniffles and snaps her head toward the bedroom, as the house dogs start barking wildly. We separate.

"Shh." She puts a finger over her mouth.

Between barks, we hear Barbara and Alistair speaking in Madame's bedroom.

Olivia turns toward me. "They must be with the coroner."

"I should probably go," I whisper.

"All right," she takes on her serious business stance, "and by the way, I will convince Herr Vollstrecken to have you paid out for the remainder of your contract."

"For real? That'd be awesome!"

"Shh." She laughs without making a sound. "It is the very least that sleazy-ass-scum-bag can do for you." She punches me on the shoulder. "Now go…get out of here. But *do* stay in touch."

I laugh. "Promise."

Hearing Olivia cuss makes me realize, we never practiced swearing in each of her five languages. That would have been fun. "Take it easy," I say and tiptoe off in an exaggerated pantomime, implying I don't want Barbara or the dogs to catch me.

Olivia sniffles again, tosses one arm up—and playfully shoos me away.

But before I exit down the back staircase, I pause and look back. I watch as she picks up another garment bag. A beat later, as she calmly zips the next bag closed, I head toward the service stairs. She will be fine—as long as she has her list of things to do.

21

Timing my escape from Côte d'Azur was tricky, but I managed. I sat tight, watched the driveway from my bedroom window and prayed for a lull in activity, until it seemed safe enough to make a break for it. And with no interest in asking for help or phoning a taxi, I barged outside and rolled my suitcase down the driveway.

The sunset was spectacular; the sky was full of navy blue stalactites floating atop pink cotton candy clouds. And for some reason, I thought I could just wheel my way down the hillside and find the train station, or maybe hitch a ride to the airport—supposed to be easy in Europe, right?

But my plan came to an abrupt halt, the moment I arrived at the security gate—I was locked inside. There was no guard to be found and I didn't know the exit code. Shit.

After poking around the panel and dialing in a bunch of random numbers, Kan drove up behind me. "Matthew, what are you doing?" he asked as the gate swung open and nearly knocked me over.

"Oh, just heading out, going home to New York."

"Long walk." Kan laughed like a fool. "Well, come on, get inside." He unlocked the doors. "I will give you a lift to the airport at Nice."

"Are you sure? I don't want to cause any problems."

"No problem. I have to collect Étienne's wife...now come on," he demanded again and I jumped in.

Along the way, Kan explained that Étienne's wife is not nearly as beautiful as Olivia, and he also informed me that long-distance relationships are difficult. I started to tell Kan that Olivia and I were just friends, but then figured it didn't matter. Kan also told me that I should not be shy about submitting an invoice to Vollstrecken for the new airplane ticket. "He will be happy to pay, just ask him."

I nodded in agreement but knew I wouldn't ask, since I don't want any future contact with that freak—even if Madame's estate *should* reimburse the change fee.

When I asked Kan what was next for him, he said everything was going to work out fine. "I will serve Étienne...along with Barbara, Alistair, and Niko," he continued, "we will have many happy years together in his household."

"What about everybody else?" I asked as we approached the terminal. "What about René?"

"I cannot say," he said with a snort, and stopped at the curb. "But I have heard rumor, of René placing a bid on an estate in Ibiza—I think he will like it there...the beautiful beaches, the nightlife." He paused to catch his breath as I opened the car door. "Can you imagine, Matthew, all the pool boys standing around... attending René?"

"Sounds good to me!" I laughed, quickly thanked Kan for the ride, said goodbye, grabbed my bag, and slammed the door— thrilled to finally be free.

During the flight home, the airplane entertainment system conked out within the first hour. And even on the final day of this absurd gig, I found myself with nothing to do but wait. I was waiting to get home; waiting to sort my mail; and waiting to see how I'd feel when David and I reunite. But mostly, I was excited about really digging in on my solo project.

After finishing every bite of the bad airplane food and leafing through a bunch of magazines, I pulled out my show journal and started looking over sketches from these past five months.

Soon, the woman seated next to me peered over my shoulder and started reading along. I first noticed what she was doing when she let out a slight laugh and then acted as if she was clearing her throat. As I continued perusing my notes, I realized that I didn't mind her reading over my shoulder because I figured I'd never see her again. I considered explaining to her that I'd created these scenes as a means of survival. I wanted to tell her that I was in a place where nothing was happening. I went into my own little world—like Sally Field did, when she played Sybil and she was chained to the piano after her evil mommy had given her an enema. But instead of explaining myself, I just skimmed through the pages and made mental notes of what she liked, and what she didn't. She became my one-person focus group.

Once René entered the story—flouncing his way through the house tour in Morocco—the lady was totally hooked. And when I got to the part about my mother and her obsession with shag carpeting in the '70s, she nearly refused to let me get past her to go use the restroom.

As I was climbing out of my seat, the flight attendant made an announcement about rebooting the entertainment system. The woman looked up at me with panic in her eyes—will he forgo reading his scribbles in order to watch some cheesy movie?

Walking toward the rear of the plane, I admitted to myself that this woman is bored out of her mind, and that's the only reason she's interested in my material. But she did seem genuinely intrigued with this world where time stands still—where people go insane trying to please those around them.

Standing in line for the fully occupied restrooms, I briefly reconsidered the nature of my lighthearted one-man show. For a fleeting moment, I imagined self-producing a more poignant site-specific reading instead. I fantasized about standing at the Fresh Kills Landfill on Staten Island—literally atop a soap box—and shouting my stories into a megaphone as a means of protesting the giant carbon footprints generated by the world's wealthiest few. I'd get super angry and declare injustice. And even though

I've never considered political theater my forte, this piece would be my vehicle. I could make a difference—a large-scale difference.

But by the time I stepped into the airplane bathroom and latched the door, I'd already accepted that my friends wouldn't want to trek out to Staten Island and realized I'd be better off sticking to the lighter side of theater. Then I confirmed to myself, that regardless of what form the show takes, *it will happen*.

Early this morning—high on caffeine and ecstatic to be home alone at *Château Whyteman*—I was feverishly storyboarding the end of Act One, when I received an email from a not-so-close dancer-friend. She wrote to congratulate me on my decision to spend a year overseas as a volunteer in the Peace Corps. She admitted being envious; confessed that she too had always wanted to take time off from performing to do the same thing. But she didn't think she was brave enough.

So, while ignoring the racket of recycling trucks outside the window, I jotted back—without clarifying her misconception. I told her I was nearly finished with my commitment and explained that I'd never felt better about reaching out to serve my fellow man. And with that, I tooted my dog whistle necklace, clicked *send*, and plunged into Act Two.

ABOUT THE AUTHOR

Former professional dancer, current Pilates instructor, and every-so-often choreographer, Dan Weltner is a SAG-AFTRA member in good standing. Tall enough to waltz with Nicole Kidman in flats, yet short enough to play gay-best-friend opposite Kristin Chenoweth, his residual income from previous film projects afforded the time to write this bio. To inquire about readings, upcoming projects or wedding dance choreography, please contact danielweltner@gmail.com.

ACKNOWLEDGMENTS

E. M. Rees, mentor extraordinaire: thanks for sharing your thoughtful insight and for knowing how to pose the right questions to help navigate this journey.

To my entire family, especially Mom and Don: thank you for the constant encouragement and for wading through multiple drafts without over-lending opinions.

Ricardo and the boys: thanks for propping me up during the early stages, not to mention the continued reality checks along the way.

Lisa and Jackie: kudos to your incredible eyes for detail.

Lizzie, Kim V, and Pat: thanks for influencing various aspects of my life that allowed this project to evolve.

And to Leslie M: Thanks for the *push*, in the best possible sense of the word. I appreciate your boundless support, the not-so-subtle nudges, and your fabulous perspective.

Made in the USA
Lexington, KY
20 July 2015